Happy Reading from Dan
Best Wishes -
Peter

BEARING DRIFT

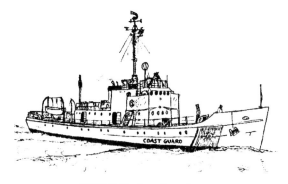

USCG Cutter Cuyahoga
1927-1978

PETER SLOAN EIDENT

———∞———

PIRATE PRESS

———∞———

PIRATE PRESS

Drawings by William Eident, Elizabeth Eident,
Kelly Eident and Paul Eident.
Cover design: John Jezierny for CSB Design, Woodbridge, CT
Text design: Elizabeth Eident

ISBN 978-1-4507-6532-9
1. Shipwrecks-collisions
2. Coast Guard
3. Woods Hole
4. Falmouth
5. Cape Cod
6. Cuyahoga
7. Blackthorn

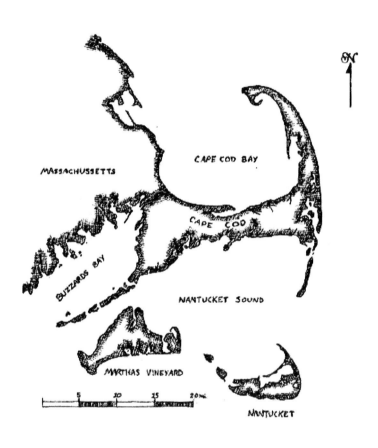

MASSACHUSSETTS

CAPE COD BAY

CAPE COD

BUZZARDS BAY

NANTUCKET SOUND

MARTHAS VINEYARD

5 10 15 20 mi.

NANTUCKET

PIRATE PRESS

In memory of the Guardians
who gave their lives to their country:
USCGC Cuyahoga
20 October 1978

SA Michael A. Atkinson
SS1 Ernestino A. Balina
YN1 William M. Carter
OC James W. Clark
OC John P. Heistand
FA James L. Hellyer
MKCS David B. Makin
SA David S. McDowell
OC Edward J. Thomason
OC Bruce E. Wood
LI Wiyono Sumalyo, Indonesian Navy

In memory of the Guardians
who gave their lives to their country:
USCGC Blackthorn
28 January 1980

SS1 Subrino Avila.
SNGM Randolph B. Barnaby.
MK2 Richard D. Boone.
SA Warren R. Brewer.
QM2 Gary W. Crumly.
DC2 Daniel M. Estrada.
EM2 Thomas R. Faulkner.
SA Willilam R. Flores.
SS3 Donald R. Frank.
DC3 Lawrence D. Frye.
QM3 Richard W. Gauld.
SA Glen E. Harrison.
SA Charles D. Hall.
MK1 Bruce Lafond.
FA Michael K. Leke.
MK1 Danny R. Maxcy.
SA John E. Prosko.
ET1 Jerome F. Ressler.
CWO Jack J. Roberts.
SA George Rovolis, Jr
ENS Frank J. Sama.
EM3 Edward F. Sindelar.
MKC Luther O. Stidham.

Prologue

———∞———

"The fault, dear Brutus,
is not in our stars, but in ourselves,
that we are underlings."
-Julius Caesar,
William Shakespeare

Courage is a word I rarely use. I can look back upon most of my fifty-four years as unremarkable, devoid of hardship, danger, and sacrifice. But one night, the random walk of life took me down into the place where courage was the only light, where heroes arose, and where other heroes died. A place where random chance separated life from death. For twenty-nine years, that memory was locked in a back room of my mind; the door was closed and a "do not disturb" sign hung from the knob. For reasons not completely clear to me, I needed to open that door. I needed to understand why eleven of my shipmates died. I needed to start searching for answers, and I started where that night began.

As I drove past the black iron gates and majestic brick buildings of the U.S. Coast Guard Academy, I wondered whether anybody remembered or still cared. I was headed to the Officers' Candidate School, OCS, on my way to the memorial for the Cuyahoga. The damp breeze chilled me to the bone, reminding me of my brother's childhood observation: dampness makes cold colder. Just as the Eskimos have more names for snow than you can count on your frozen fingers and toes, Cape Codders have almost endless descriptive terms for "damp." The wind blew off the Thames River in New London, Connecticut, and I could smell the salt air mixed with diesel, a smell I'll never forgot.

When I opened the door of Chase Hall, I saw the bright shining brass of wheelhouse equipment recovered from the bridge of the Cuyahoga. I was instantly back on deck as the shock and terror of the Cuyahoga's last seven minutes on the water replayed in my mind, as it had a thousand times before. The screams, moans, and calls for help over the roar of rushing water made my knees shake. Yet one more time, I could see the ship on her side with every man fighting for his life, but this time the solid presence of her shining brass brought the sinking into even more vivid recollection. One thing about the Cuyahoga, the brass was always polished.

I wiped at a small tear rolling down my cheek as I was dragged back to the moment by the military cadence of an officer candidate (OC) walking briskly toward me. He gave me the greeting of the day, "Good afternoon, Sir." Then, instead of turning left out the passageway, he turned toward the memorial. He seemed to be joining me in my reflective thoughts. I thought he was just being nice as he stood at attention for about five seconds, then performed a perfect about-face and marched out the passageway. Then another OC, with his hat on and probably on watch, greeted me. He also turned and saluted, stood for a few seconds, and performed the about-face and went on his way.

"Suddenly, I realized that every *officer candidate was honoring my shipmates.*" They hadn't forgotten the Cuyahoga. Indeed, after twenty-nine years, my shipmates are still honored every day by every officer candidate in the Coast Guard. I hadn't been remembering that night all alone.

∞

I had no appointment. I didn't even have a plan. I just walked down the hall to the staff offices hoping to find someone who knew something about the Cuyahoga. I found the commander of OCS, Commander John C. O'Connor III, Ed.D, between appointments. Commander O'Connor was tall and fit and only his graying hair and rank would give away that he was middle-aged.

I introduced myself, "I'm Peter Eident, and I was in OCS Class of six tack 78." I watched the blood redden his Irish face. "I was aboard the Cuyahoga when it went down."

He told me that the memory of the Cuyahoga is a valuable part of the OCS curriculum and that all OCs must acknowledge the memorial on the OCS Quarterdeck as they pass; that they must reflect on the OCs who lost their lives that day for a few moments. He said the Cuyahoga wheelhouse brass is polished on the midnight watch every night.

He said quietly, and I could hear the emotion in his voice, "We have to learn from this tragedy so that our men who made the ultimate sacrifice didn't die in vain."

He told me that while he was completing his OCS training aboard the Coast Guard Academy tall ship, the Eagle, nearly twenty years ago, he found himself following the same route as the ill-fated Cuyahoga: turning up the Chesapeake into the Potomac River. Although training to be an officer, he was also a seasoned Coast Guard Senior Chief Quartermaster (QMCS) with many years of experience at sea. As he observed the training regimen for the new sailors on that cruise, it was obvious that not much had improved in the way officer candidates were being prepared for sea duty.

Some time after that cruise he took a bold step and wrote a letter to his superiors asking whether the Coast Guard had learned anything from the Cuyahoga. This would generally not be a good career move for a junior officer, but instead of tying him to the ship's mast or keel-hauling him, they sent him to Harvard for a doctorate in education and put him in charge of the OCS program.

The commander asked me whether I would consider speaking at the Officer Candidate School's 30th Cuyahoga Memorial Service, to give them a personal account of the Cuyahoga Collision --something that would make it more real to them.

I felt totally inadequate, I wondered to myself, "What would I say to these officer Candidates?" So, I asked the commander, "After all this time, what did we learn from the Cuyahoga? If I could say there were lessons learned, it could give some kind of purpose to what we lost. I just don't know where to look."

He said, "Look at the situation and find the error chain. Then find out how to break it."

"Where do I find that error chain?"

"Start at the beginning," The commander said.

The Error Chain

Accidents involving ships or planes are rarely the result of one cataclysmic event. Almost always a combination of factors leads to the deadly result —one thing leads to another. In hazardous conditions, mistakes are often made that lead to more hazardous conditions, and those conditions lead to more mistakes. Often, if any one of those mistakes could have been avoided, the hazardous conditions ameliorated instead of added to, there would have been no catastrophe. To avoid the mistakes and diminish the hazards, you need to recognize what's happening and break the chain.

∞ Captain Kidd Bar, Woods Hole, MA ∞

1.

"Once upon a time, there was a tavern,
Where we used to raise a glass or two
Remember how we laughed away the hours,
Think of all the great things we would do."
-*"Those Were the Days,"*
Gene Raskin, Mary Hopkin

It was late August 1978, 2:15 a.m., and I was sitting in the dark on the back porch of the bar while they kicked the last of the regulars out. We had to be down to the staff and selected inner circle before my going-away party could start. While waiting, I started to think about the next day. I would be taking a flight from Providence, Rhode Island, to Virginia, starting a whole new life in the U.S. Coast Guard. I thought about how often you pick up hints, see signs, and receive subtle messages that tell you when to make the big decisions.

I remembered my father saying, "What the hell's wrong with you? Are you gonna work in a bar your whole life?" Not so subtle perhaps, but certainly a sign.

My reminiscence of Dad's words of wisdom was interrupted when an eighteen-year-old celebrating his birthday decided he could join in the nightly after-hours party, staggering to the dark porch after bouncing off both door jambs of the four-foot-wide door. Backlit by the bar lights, the six-foot five bouncer, Bill Wixon, looked disturbingly like Frankenstein, even without the neck bolts. He was in hot pursuit of yesterday's minor celebrating his induction into the drinking majority. Bill told the young man, "Come on, the night's history. You don't have to go home, but you can't stay here."

When order was restored, my mind wandered to the amazing day when I was a senior in high school and they lowered the drinking age to eighteen. I'm not sure of the logic behind the change in the law, but it went something like this: with the Vietnam War winding down, not enough eighteen-to-twenty-one-year-olds were dying, which was depressing the mortuary industry, so our lawmakers figured they could augment war fatalities with DUI deaths. By all statistical measures, their plan worked surprising well.

In response to the increased market, entrepreneurs started to buy old bars, nightclubs, and pubs. Two guys from Boston, Michael Shers and Bill Crowley, bought the Captain Kidd in Woods Hole, Massachusetts. The first selectman, the New England equivalent of a town mayor, told them that, when the drinking age was twenty-one, nineteen-year-olds were drinking and now that the age limit had been lowered he didn't want to see any seventeen-year-olds drinking. If the establishment got caught serving the under-aged, the bar would immediately lose its license. One night, when I was in the bar, they offered me a job as doorman because they figured that, as a high school senior, I knew approximately how old everybody was —my job was to keep the minors out. I remember once carding my high school English teacher just for the hell of it.

I had two other things going for me: I was a 240-pound defensive lineman, and my Uncle Arthur Robichaud was night captain of the Falmouth Police Department. In a pinch, a few connections wouldn't hurt.

Before Sher and Crowley bought the bar, it was frequented by sailors, fishermen, Coast Guardsmen, and bikers. These entrepreneurs wanted to turn it into a preppy bar. The transition was bumpy.

The Captain Kidd Bar was named after the famous pirate, Captain William Kidd, who derived most of his notoriety from his protocol for dealing with classified information. Legend has it that, after he accumulated his bounty and buried it somewhere along the East Coast, he killed all his diggers under the concept that "dead men tell no tales." He was a highly literate sea captain who was a privateer in the employ of both King William III, a.k.a. King William the Turd as he was generally known by his subjects, and the colonial governor of New York. In fact, Captain Kidd, not unlike the pirates working there today, frequented Wall Street.

∞

The Captain Kidd was graced by a full-sized wall mural of the burying of the treasure, painted by Captain Joe, a very popular bartender and personality at the Casino Bar and Nightclub in Falmouth Heights. When I was six, Captain Joe once gave me a quarter after church. I always liked him after that. The bar's front door opened on Water Street, the main street of Woods Hole, and the bar was a long, narrow room, behind which was a screened-in porch standing on pilings over Eel Pond. The bar itself —ornate with brass and marble and dark mahogany, a marble bar-rail, a beautiful mirror, and ornate finials —Rumor had it came from a 1930s speak-easy in Baltimore. The tables and chairs were far less valuable. The seats were old barrels covered with carpet, and the tables were just bigger barrels covered with varnished wood.

The dining room was along the street, and people wondered why they hadn't built it facing the harbor. The original owner explained that his patrons were all fisherman and sailors and most of them were sick of a water view. They wanted to look at land and cars, but mostly they wanted to watch girls walking down the street.

The jukebox selection was eclectic: some BB King and Hank Williams for the rustic clientele, and for the preppies that came to watch the rustics, Springsteen, Gordon Lightfoot, James Taylor, and Jimmy Buffett. For the late-stage hippies we featured Dylan, Cat Stevens, and for irony, Loudon Wainwright III. Thank God, no Barry Manilow in this man's bar, except… of course… "Weekend In New England." Recognizing that they were becoming the main attraction, many of local rough characters started going down the street to the Leeside.

∞

My six closest Kidd colleagues finally joined me out on the screened porch to commemorate the evening of my matriculation into the real world. Smelling the familiar mix of salt air and stale beer, I got a sick feeling in the pit of my stomach and thought, "What the hell am I doing? I'm starting to feel seasick already."

Being the youngest of five kids, no matter how dire the situation and no matter what the odds, I'd learned to always fight back, which was the only thing my brothers respected enough to quit torturing me and let me live. I reminded myself that I was signed into the military, and there was no backing out in my family. I had to go.

We started to tell our old stories again. Even though we knew them by heart, they still made us laugh until we cried. The bar crew had earned the nickname "Captain Kidd Rescue Squad." Once, a sailor had a little too much to drink and took a sharp right on the gangplank leading to his ship and fell between the ship and the wharf. His companion went for help. Bill Wixon and Terry Smith, fellow bartenders/bouncers, heard the call and raced to the dock. They climbed down the dock ladder and were able to retrieve the unconscious former patron. Pulling a 200-pound person up a ninety-degree ladder that's covered with slippery algae was no mean feat, and they had issues with his head getting stuck between the ladder rungs on the way up. Terry, who was a trained EMT, was able to revive him on the dock and bring him back to life. Terry Smith was Falmouth's star hockey goalie and later played for Boston College, but this was perhaps his greatest save. The merchant mariner came out of it with no more than a bad hangover and a confusing series of bruises on his chin and forehead.

Steve Dodigan, another bouncer, was driving home at 2:00 in the morning when he saw smoke pouring out of a shed attached to a house on Woods Hole Road. He stopped his car and started peering through the window to see if anyone was in the house and saw a woman sleeping. He banged on the door and started yelling to wake the lady. She was so terrified of a huge guy banging on door she hid and wouldn't come out. We enjoyed telling Steve that his looks could keep woman from coming out of a burning house. Steve insisted that she yet to smell smoke. Steve reverted to plan B and then dashed off to the fire station and banged on their door. They quickly got out to the house and convinced her to leave and put out the fire. Rescues are never easy.

∞

And then the conversation on the screened porch turned to Bill Wixon's less auspicious rescue, one I could eloquently recite due to my excellent vantage point from the shoreline. He had spotted another one of our former patrons struggling in the water behind the Kidd and jumped in to pull him out, but the guy started fighting with him. Bill ended up pulling off his arm, which it turns out was prosthetic, a fact that Bill remembered one second after having the shit scared out of him. It was fun to hear a former professional football player scream like a little girl. He was probably strong enough to actually rip an arm off, and for a moment there he clearly thought he had. He and the patron were still flailing around in the water when Bill realized they could just stand up. So he pulled the guy onto his feet and walked back to shore with the guy cursing him all the way. Not everyone wants to be rescued.

∞

Not everyone liked the Captain Kidd Rescue Squad. Once, after a particularly vicious fight resulting in an unceremonious patron-bounce into the gutter, the bouncers and bartenders had locked the door and settled down for a calm nightcap when they saw a pickup truck pull up in front of the Kidd. Just as somebody said, "Hey, doesn't that truck belong to…," they heard the sound of a two-stroke engine starting up and wondered what it was. As sawdust suddenly shot across the floor, followed by a chainsaw blade emerging through the locked front door, all employees were headed for the unmarked emergency rear exit, the windows overlooking Eel Pond. Four huge grown men perched themselves on the windowsills like giant pigeons, ready for a desperate escape leap into the pond. They figured a chainsaw wouldn't work under water. The assailant simply carved a large X in the door and went home to sleep it off. He was probably going for the mark of Zorro, but a person should never drink before spelling with large power tools. The assailant, a carpenter/fisherman but not the peaceful kind, was barred from the Captain Kidd for a month, and he had to pay for the door. The manager even let him install it himself to keep the price down.

The Captain Kidd Rescue Squad didn't have as rich a history of saving lives as the U.S. Coast Guard did, but the intent was there and their hearts were in the right place. Everyone wants to be a hero. I particularly wanted to be able to save someone. I'd lost my mother that year.

This should have been a good year, graduating from college and getting engaged, but my mother wasn't there to see my graduation and she wouldn't be there to help plan the wedding. None of us had a chance to save her, but it would have changed everything if we could have. My mother was always the idealist in the family. Her favorite quote was President John F. Kennedy's "Ask not what your country can do for you; ask what you can do for your country." My being a Coast Guard officer would have made her proud.

I shouldn't be hesitating to take this step, I told myself as the others continued to tell stories. It's time to go and take that shot at saving lives, in respect to her memory.

When each of my brothers had come of age, I remember that Mom recited from the Bible: When I was a child, I spoke as a child, I understood as a child, I thought as a child; but when I became a man, I put away childish ways. While not an exact quote, it got the message across. I had been working for five summers. I was a repeat offender, a person who took an extra summer before joining the real world.

∞

Normally, there would have been a lot more people at my party, but they had thrown my big going-away party the previous summer. I did not attend. It was going to be a surprise party, and the person assigned to take me there failed at his duty, felled by too much ice tea, Long Island-style. In the bar business, all parties start at 2:00 a.m., and my friend who was supposed to take me to the surprise venue had passed out at about midnight. I had gone home, a little disappointed that nobody threw me a party, but perhaps it was good that I missed the party. I avoided about thirty cream pies, the would-be hurlers, paid assassins —I mean pie assassins —lying in wait for me.

The truth is I deserved the pie treatment. The prior summer, I was paid to protect the judges at a "gong show" talent contest at a local bar. The judges got wind that they were going to be hit by pies, so they hired me to guard them. Before the show, the pie-throwing act approached me and told me the only talent they had was in ambushing people with pies, and if they didn't get the judges, the show would be a flop and nobody would laugh. So, for the sake of show business, I allowed the pie assassins to attack the talent judges, as long as I had two of my own to throw.

On the occasion of my first going-away party, the pie assassins finally gave up waiting for me and the whole event turned into a pie-flinging orgy. The judges, who were from Boston, were hungry for revenge, but the next morning I went away to college for the fall football season. I was saved by the mistake of someone with diminished capacity. Maybe I was just saved by pure serendipity.

In the beginning of the season at Brown University, one of my teammates asked if I would switch numbers with him. His high school number was the same as mine and he wanted to maintain it. I was willing to switch, so he proudly wore our shared high school number and I became Brown Bruin #71.

Toward the end of the season, as I ran through the tunnel at Harvard Stadium, I saw a big commotion behind me. Some Boston ticket-holders were getting kicked out of the stadium and my teammate was covered in cream pie, almost obscuring our venerable #70.

I'd innocently escaped another assassination attempt, dodged the Boston cream bullet, but I was living on borrowed time. The pie wars got out of hand and went from good-natured cream up the nose to the potential for broken noses from excessive delivery force. The word "arrest" was starting to be tossed about, and so the pies stopped flying. The Cape Cod bars figured that, if the Viet Cong and the Americans could call a truce, we could, too. Thus, I successfully avoided getting hurt in two major conflicts.

As I sat out on the Captain Kidd deck with my friends, overlooking the water and telling sea stories, I realized that I was starting to sound like Richard Dreyfuss in his role as the marine biologist trying to compete with Robert Shaw's character, Quint, in the movie Jaws. While they sat there chumming and waiting for Jaws to attack, Quint retold the story of the greatest shark attack in human history: the USS Indianapolis had just completed the top secret mission of transporting key components of the nuclear bomb when she was torpedoed by a Japanese submarine. The cruiser lost 300 men in the attack, and 880 men entered the water without lifeboats. Because it was a top-secret mission, and because of the incompetence of the commanders who received the mayday, no one responded to their cry for help. Four long days went by, and more than 500 men died from being ripped apart by white-tip sharks or from dehydration. When Quint finished his shark tale, he crushed his beer can. When Richard Dreyfuss told his much tamer story, he crushed his paper coffee cup for emphasis. I wondered whether I would ever have a story that would justify crushing a beer can after the telling, or even a story worthy of crushing a paper cup.

There had been another going-away party the night before the storytelling session, where I said goodbye to my fiancée and my family. Tonight's party was just my Kidd colleagues, who happened to include my sister Bethanie, a part-time waitress and full-time scientist. Bethanie chimed in that her fiancé was under contract with the Marine Biological Laboratories, so he was out in the middle of the night chumming for sharks to see what attracted them.

I said, "I know what attracts sharks: blood in the water or swimming at night; at least that's what I always imagined when I was in the ocean and couldn't see what was heading my way"

Bethanie replied "That's what people think, but blood attracts them from far away…it's electric current that attracts them up close and makes them attack. The Navy is spending millions trying to figure out exactly which currents sharks react to so that they can stop them from attacking their underwater remote sensing buoys."

Bethanie's day job was draining blood from horseshoe crabs. She missed her big shot at fame one night at the Kidd when a guy ordered a drink while he was waiting for the Martha's Vineyard Ferry. He asked my pretty blonde sister, "How would you like to get eaten by a shark?" She instantly replied, "How would you like to get slapped by a waitress?" As it turned out, the dude was part of the advance team from California for the movie Jaws, which was filmed on the Vineyard. She still claims that was the worst pickup line ever, although I kind of liked it.

My sister had moved back home to help when my mother died, and she was working two jobs while trying to keep Dad company. She probably would have thrown over the waitressing job for the movie spot in a heartbeat. With four brothers, she was always good at playing the victim, and she would have been a perfect fit because there was a history of show business in our family. She must have watched the movie version of Benchley's Jaws with a profound sense of regret mixed in between the moments of theater terror.

The highlight of my family's show-business background was Dad's stint as a professional wrestler before World War II. During the day, my father was a butcher at the A&P in Nantucket, but he spent his nights in the Nantucket makeshift open-air wrestling arena. His stage name was Blondie Ryan. While blonde, he definitely wasn't Irish.

This was not Greco-Roman wrestling. This is the kind of wrestling where the bad-guy wrestlers spit into the crowd and only eye-gouge when the referee is not looking and the crowd is. Keeping in character, Dad preferred the role of villain. There were nights when the Nantucket fog was so thick in the open arena that the crowds could barely see the wrestlers. It was a great place to drink fresh homemade beer, meet new people, engage in lively conversation, and then end the perfect evening with a small brawl. Often, because they really thought my father was evil, he would have to fight his way out of the arena.

∞

We were still drinking and sitting on the porch as the sky started to lighten, and we all realized that my nights at the Kidd were over for a while. It was time to leave, and all my old friends, these people I had grown up with, were now giving me slightly boozy advice.

"Don't volunteer for anything."

"No more knocking people down. They take that seriously in the real world."

"Be safe."

"Do what you're told and nobody gets hurt."

"All good dogs are black." This was from my brother's best friend, Steve Dodigan, the other Kidd bartender/bouncer. He was referring to his dog, Jet. He and Jet grew up in my house as much as in his own, so I had to agree. In fact, in Falmouth and Woods Hole and Martha's Vineyard, nearly all mutts were black, a fact memorialized by the Black Dog Tavern and hundreds of thousands of Black Dog T-shirts worn as far away as Abu Dhabi. Being black is a real advantage for a dog that is in the cold water a lot because it can warm up quickly through solar energy. But it's not such an advantage in the Arizona desert or for a roaming dog when he encounters his number one predator, the car, at night. Only the most vigilant black dogs survive.

My brother Bill had already given his advice before he went out to sea: "Keep your head down and don't stick out. Then you'll be fine." As I was leaving, all my friends wished me luck and told me to be careful, but I wasn't worried.

The night before, my brother Chris had given me the advice that stuck with me the most. Chris, a safety expert who worked for the U.S. Navy in New London, Connecticut, said, "Even though you're in the military, if you don't smoke, you don't drink and drive, and you wear your seatbelt, you'll probably be safer on average than most people in the United States."

So we all staggered to our cars and drove home.

The Error Chain

The truth is, we really don't understand the probability and the negative impact of hazards, also known as risk. If we are what economists call rational humans, we generally prefer to avoid risk —especially when death or grave bodily harm might be the result if we don't avoid it. However, we are instinctively driven to take risks for fun, for personal gain, for the sake of others, or for duty. My dad used to tell my brothers and me, "Don't take stupid chances."

Good advice, but at the moment when one must make a choice, it's hard to distinguish a stupid chance from a regular chance. The difference is only, and always, brutally clear in retrospect. While mistakes were tolerated in my family, repeating mistakes was not.

However, most of us will take chances to rescue another human being, even if that person took a stupid chance to end up in danger. Bill Wixon did rescue the amputee, so it wasn't a true error chain incident, but Bill's save was actually harder than the other two —it just wouldn't make a good newspaper article.

It's hard to rescue the unwilling or the panicked, let alone someone who qualifies as both, even in shallow water. In fact, almost two-thirds of all drowning deaths occur in water that is not over the victim's head. Most of these happen in one of the most dangerous places in the world —the bathroom. These victims are people who can't stand up: the baby, the invalid, and the drunk. The most unfortunate individuals in this statistical group didn't drown in the bathtub. An unlucky segment of this population drowned in the toilet. What are the odds you could drown in toilet? Not bad, when you consider that most people who hug the toilet, taking the porcelain bus for a spin, are really drunk and on the verge of passing out.

Unknown or unfamiliar conditions certainly play a role in most major accidents, but so does alcohol, which plays a role in almost 45 percent of all accidental deaths. Statistics tell us it's not good odds to be a drunk invalid alone in the bathroom. My Uncle Frank pointed to another perspective on this statistic: "Since most people drink, it's those darn teetotallers who cause the majority of accidents."

All the people who were saved by the Captain Kidd Rescue Squad were drunk, saved by the not-so-sober. Who else is up at 2:00 a.m. to save anybody? Diminished capacity rules the night.

2.

*"… the flag of piracy flew from my mast,
my sails were set wing to wing"*
- *"Growin' Up"*
Bruce Springsteen

I stared out the window as the bus pulled out of the Norfolk Municipal Airport. "What the hell am I doing?" popped back into my brain. I was on the first leg of a journey that would bring me to the seventeen-week officer candidate training program, where I would learn what I needed to know to become a Coast Guard officer. In 1978, the Coast Guard's Officer Candidate School was in Yorktown, Virginia. Unlike the Army, Navy, and Marines, the Coast Guard doesn't have an ROTC program, so they take kids right out of college and a few select enlisted Coasties with credit equivalent to college experience (as in they got drunk a lot, I guess) and turn them into 90-day wonders, though we actually were in for 119 —but who's counting.

I remember talking to my Uncle Frank, whose son Franny had joined the Marines, about joining the Coast Guard. He said it made sense for me because I was tall and if the boat sank I could wade back to shore. Compared to the Marines, the Coast Guard had a reputation for being a relaxed branch of the armed forces. However, the Guard brass had recently decided to take discipline more seriously, beginning with inductee training by experienced Army and Marine drill sergeants. This information was only revealed to me about one month after I signed up for OCS. The importance of timely intelligence was immediately clear to me. The Coast Guard personnel comprise less than 2 percent of the total U.S. military in uniform. The Coast Guard is greatly overshadowed by the Navy, which is twenty times larger. Now that I was signing up, I was about to agree to the proposition that was the unofficial motto of the U.S. Coast Guard: "You have to go out; you don't have to come back."

I had studied the map from our atlas and knew that the Coast Guard Training Center at Yorktown was located next to a key battleground of both the Revolutionary and the Civil Wars, and not far from Jamestown. I thought to myself, while Massachusetts touts the significance of the Plimoth Plantation, it was established thirteen years after Jamestown. We came in second, but it was the most celebrated second-place finish in the history of the world.

Then I saw the ramparts and redoubts of the Yorktown Battlefield. While the American Revolution might have started in Massachusetts, it certainly ended here at Yorktown. Because of their superior numbers, the success of the French and American armies' siege was inevitable —but the overall outcome certainly wasn't. It took a 200-year occurrence, the only major defeat of the invincible Royal Navy in either the seventeenth or the eighteenth century, to seal off a potential retreat for Cornwallis's troops. It wasn't John Paul Jones or any part of the Continental Navy that contributed to the victory: it was the French Navy under Rear Admiral François Joseph Paul Comte de Grasse who engaged the British and drove them to scuttle their mission to evacuate Cornwallis, forcing them, instead, to retreat from Chesapeake Bay to the safety of the high seas. Ironically, a year later this French fleet was entirely destroyed by this same British fleet in the Battle of the Saintes in the Caribbean.

When Cornwallis surrendered his position in Yorktown, he was too mortified to attend the official ceremony. His troops, astonished at the outcome against what had been viewed as an almost comical ragtag fighting force, played "The World Turned Upside Down." The victorious rebels played "Yankee Doodle" that day, a song previously used by the British to mock Americans when we fought by their side in the French Indian War. The Brits' taunt was that the Yankees thought they could stick a feather in their coonskin caps and look like as good as any British dandy with their fancy military decorations (macaroni). And the British claim that Americans don't have a sense of irony.

Major General McClellan's experience at Yorktown, during the Peninsular Campaign of 1862, was pretty much the opposite of the Revolutionary War outcome. McClellan launched a D-Day landing of 100,000 soldiers in order to attack Richmond from the south and put a quick end to the war. McClellan, considered the inventor of "analysis paralysis," was delayed for a month by 11,000 soldiers at Yorktown because he badly overestimated Confederate strength. Unlike the Redcoats, the Confederates were able to escape and retreat from Yorktown, fighting a drawn-out battle that kept the Union out of Richmond and ended up prolonging the Civil War.

John Paul Jones is considered the father of the American Navy, and his statue stands over the midshipmen of the Naval Academy in Annapolis, Maryland. John Paul, best known for his famous bellicose statement —"I have not yet begun to fight!" —had already done some fighting on a personal basis. He was wanted for murder in two different jurisdictions prior to his appointment by the Continental Congress. The tardy fighter added Jones to his name to circumvent his extradition to the ports where he was under indictment.

Like many of the masters before him, John Paul Jones's greatest success was in attacking lightly armed merchant vessels and sharing a third of their bounty with his sailors. J.P. Jones took the war all the way to the shores of the British Isles and surprised the English. His strategy was a big morale builder for the Colonies and an enormous giant scare to the British merchants. This loyal American patriot later became an admiral in the Russian Navy.

These sailors were not only swashbucklers and privateers, but they were renaissance men of their era. They mastered geometry, mathematics, astronomy, meteorology, oceanography, geography, hygiene, emergency medicine, business, and the art of dispensing justice to circumvent the ever-present threat of mutiny. The myth that sailors in Columbus's day actually thought that the world was flat was created by junior high textbook editors. No sailor who witnessed a ship mast fade below the horizon would ever have thought that.

I was about to become one of them: a puddle pirate, a shallow-water sailor in the Hooligan Navy, the Wavy Navy, the Brown Water Navy, Broomstick Navy, part of the U.S.C.G., aka Uncle Sam's Confused Group (all nicknames courtesy of the "deep water" Navy).

In fact, there is a little truth to the Coast Guard being a little wavy. The Coast Guard took on three major civil services: The Life-Saving Service, The Lighthouse Service, and the Bureau of Marine Inspection and Navigation. Imagine, here are these civil service employees minding their own business, and suddenly they have to start wearing a uniform, marching, and saluting. While some opted to remain in the civil service, most saw the career advantages of going with the flow and integrated into the military way of life, albeit reluctantly.

Most of these militarily merged employees became petty officers, and some of their managers became commissioned officers. These officers often lacked the military decorum of their seasoned Coast Guard brethren —let alone the military attitude of members of the Army, Navy, or Marines. Additionally, the newly merged civil services had discordant duties, and those missions were to be carried out by isolated civil servants scattered across the country's shorelines, lakes, and rivers. These factors contributed to their lack of uniformity and discipline.

The Lighthouse Service was dealt a particularly insulting blow in 1939 when they were annexed just before the 150th anniversary celebration of the government's Lighthouse Establishment. Picture the lonely lighthouse keeper picking up his weekly mail delivery and discovering that he's been transformed into a petty officer at two-thirds his current salary. Happy anniversary.

∞

I knew what that lighthouse keeper went through. My new salary would be about half what I had been making at the Captain Kidd as a bouncer/bartender, but as the bus pulled past the gatehouse of the U.S. Coast Guard Reserve Training Center, I was thinking of my brother's good advice: "Go with the flow, keep your head down, don't stick out."

Little did I know how much help I was about to get in my effort to blend in among my new brethren. The first stop was the barbershop that doubled as a brutal photography studio. Good looking men were walking in and mutant victims were emerging. But they all blended together effectively. I had cut my hair very short just the day before, shorter than it had been since I was six, hopeful that they would consider it close enough. No dice. It came off. They don't just cut it off. They cut it off one side first, or give a temporary Mohawk, take a picture, and everybody laughs at you. I got a dome on the top of my head since it wasn't very long to begin with. It didn't generate the laughs the other creative haircuts got. I felt inadequate.

The haircut ritual goes to a basic instinct of grooming. Humans are the only animals with continuously growing hair that must be cut. Humans groom their hair to attract mates and to advertise that they have superior genes because they have that extra time to groom. Pirates took pride in their long, flowing hair. The more flamboyant, the more successful —and perhaps the more dangerous. Pirates displayed pride in having survived a shipwreck by wearing a pierced earring. Personally, I didn't care about the haircut, long or short —grooming was just a chore to me —but I wanted no part of earning an earring.

After the haircut, we had our eye exam and were given two pairs of government-issued eyeglasses that were considered fashionable by Buddy Holly —and only by Buddy Holly. They were nicknamed BCGs (birth control glasses) because the fashion look would repel members of the opposite sex. Wearing the BCGs, combined with my shaved head, I was looking "bad" —not in a good way.

The Error Chain

By definition, war is a hazardous condition. Mistakes while serving in war can be minor, causing an inconvenience like a demerit, or they can be major and change the course of history.

In 1776, the British feared that if the American colonies pulled away the other colonies would fall like dominoes. They were also overconfident: they thought they could easily march in, win a few battles, and then turn the fighting over to loyal British citizens who happened to live in America. Their plan was to Americanize the war.

The war against America was not particularly popular among the common folk in Britain who normally volunteered to fight, so the British decided to hire brutal Prussian mercenaries to supplement their troops. The hiring of paid thugs proved to be their biggest mistake. The use of mercenaries didn't win the hearts and minds of Americans.

The war simmered on without a resolution and became more and more expensive. With lukewarm backing from the home front, the British couldn't raise taxes for this unpopular war. They were forced to borrow what they could and cut back on funding for their military. Without the proper resources, it was only a matter of time before military effectiveness suffered. The French sensed the British didn't have the necessary commitment and that they could finally score a win.

This error chain caused a humiliating defeat of the strongest military force in the world at that time. The world turned upside down. While the outcome of that war didn't cause an immediate domino effect for Great Britain, any more than the Vietnam War caused the domino effect feared in a later era both losses certainly made the world tilt for a moment.

3.

"Now a life of leisure and pirate's treasure
Don't make much for tragedy..."
-"Better Days"
Bruce Springsteen

After we checked into the administration office, three of us were sent to the barracks to stow our gear and face our next crew of tormentors. The entrance was a twenty-by-forty-foot room with hallways going off in two directions and a small desk on one side. This room was called the OCS Quarterdeck, but it looked like a lobby to me. I should have suspected an ambush, but I was probably still recovering from my head-polishing session.

When we were walking diagonally across the room toward the desk, an officer suddenly appeared from the side office and started yelling, "What the hell are you guys doing!?" Apparently we had committed a very serious infraction; we walked across a rug that occupied 90 percent of the space in the room. How could I have known that this particular rug could not withstand my shoes?

I kept silent, but one of the guys in our little trio voiced my very thoughts, "How were we supposed to know you couldn't walk on the rug?" We were then shown a small sign about one foot off the floor near the door we had entered: "OCs ARE PROHIBITED FROM WALKING ON THE RUG." The officer asked if we could read, or did we think the rules were not for us. Then he said, "I know you can read, 'cause you took a test to get into this outfit. You think you're above the rules, don't you?" This was our introduction to Lieutenant Emory, company officer. His Southern drawl was cranked up to its maximum intensity, and I was sure his next question was going to be whether we were queers or steers.

All three of us were shocked speechless, and before we could even muster a reply to the officer, he said, "I'm giving you a break this time, but it's the last time I'm going to be nice to you." I thought to myself that this guy had a strange concept of nice. He ended by saying, "Get your stuff put away and get out of my sight." Then he walked away, muttering underneath his breath loud enough so we could hear. "It's going to be a long seventeen weeks." That was the only part of the conversation I agreed with.

I thought, "Nobody had ever treated me that badly before (except for close relatives, of course)."

The OC at the desk was grinning ear to ear as he processed our paperwork and handed out supplies and the keys to our assigned barracks. Class (04-78) had just graduated, and the next OC class in attendance had completed ten weeks —now they were looking forward to being the senior OCs. The guy behind the desk was a member of this class. We were given a spiral-bound manual that was to be our bible and told to read it from stem to stern. It included a section that we had to memorize called "The Spindrift." According to the guy at the desk, this document would answer all our questions and give us the knowledge to get through the next seventeen weeks. We were to put on our uniforms, and if there were any questions regarding how to put on the uniform, we could refer to the manual. Within a few minutes I was down the hall trying to open the door to my new room when I heard another group getting reamed, apparently upon entering the Quarterdeck: "You guys think you're above the rules?" Let the head games begin.

∞

After we changed into our uniforms, one of the senior OCs was dispatched to give us instructions on what to do if an officer was in the hall. The first OC who saw an officer was supposed call out, "Officer on deck!" and then we were to "brace." Brace, in boot camp, means to throw one's self flat up against the bulkhead (wall) in the attention position. We were shown how to salute but told not to salute if we were not covered (hat off), and we should never be covered indoors unless we had duty or were dressed for colors.

As we were talking with the senior OC, an officer came down the hall, and someone yelled, "Brace! Officer on the deck!" And we did. Well, it turns out we were one of the worst groups ever at bracing, or at least that is what the officer explained to us, thoroughly and in no uncertain terms. He then told us to go read our manuals and try to somehow improve upon our first pathetic attempt at military acumen.

Recognizing that I was in over my head, I returned to my room and dived into the manual, which started with a brief history of the Coast Guard. The Coast Guard is the oldest continuous seagoing service in the US. After the American Revolution, the military services were disbanded because President Washington was dead-set against having a standing army or navy, which he thought would encourage foreign entanglements. The first treasury secretary, Alexander Hamilton, needed to get money to run the government and pay off war debts, so he tried to collect money through tariffs on imports. No one was paying, so the government needed a collection enforcement agency. Thus the Revenue Marine (which was later the Revenue Cutter Service and finally the Coast Guard) was born.

Hamilton also knew that he had to justify the taxes collected by showing captains and other businessmen that the federal government could contribute to commerce by building infrastructure that would allow maritime business to be more efficient, safe, and secure. He started building lighthouses and life stations that would never have been funded by a free market. The United States fought its first war as a sovereign nation over the security of its merchant fleet. The War of 1812 was fought to stop the British from seizing our ships and sailors. For many years the Coast Guard reported to the Treasury Department during peacetime. In times of war, it was handed over to the U.S. Navy. Not wanting the competition, the Navy tried to permanently take over the Coast Guard a number of times, but each time the Treasury Department resisted and was able to hold on to it. When you sign the checks, you carry a lot of clout. The concept behind having two separate seagoing services was that the US Navy's main business was war, or preparing for war when not actually in one, and the Coast Guard's main business was commerce (and later humanitarian service). While the Navy can help out during a humanitarian crisis and the Coast Guard can join the fighting during a war, both services need to get back to their core business when the crisis is over.

In 1967, the Coast Guard was shifted to the Department of Transportation, and in 2003 it was placed under the control of the Department of Homeland Security. In short, the Coast Guard was a foster child that never really understood its changing parents, and the parents never understood their problem child. Consequently, the Coast Guard's mission has shifted on occasion, the service picking up responsibilities and sometimes losing them.

The Revenue Marine's first commissioned officer was Hopley Yeaton. His name might not be as familiar to most Americans as, say, John Paul Jones, but in truth the Coast Guard has always tried to keep up with the Navy regarding service history and traditions, and Hopley Yeaton is, in some ways, the Coast Guard's J.P. Jones.

A few years before I entered OCS, I read that the Coast Guard Barque Eagle moved the remains of Hopley Yeaton from a cemetery in Maine to New London, Connecticut. The move was reminiscent of the USS Brooklyn carrying the body of John Paul Jones from France to the U.S. Naval Academy in 1906.

Yeaton's remains were laid to final rest in a crypt near the Academy chapel, which looks down over Yeaton Hall. When strange things happen or a student miraculously pulls off an unexpectedly good grade, it's often attributed to the ghost of Hopley Yeaton.

The first ships used by the Revenue Marine were rigged as cutters, which are defined as single-mast sailing vessels with a mainsail and at least two headsails: a forestaysail and a jib. Today, even though they are motorized, nearly all Coast Guard vessels are called cutters. The bow of every Coast Guard vessel is decorated with the Coast Guard racing stripe, which was designed in 1964. If you want to remember what year, use a protractor to calculate the angle of the stripe. The racing stripe was first used in 1966, and because of a combination of good design and strong branding, many other nations adopted the same sixty-four-degree stripe (or variations to include their national colors) for their coast guards, a real tribute to U.S. Coast Guard leadership in marine safety. Almost anywhere in the world, if you see that stripe you know you're either in safe hands or about to be busted, depending on the side of the law you have chosen.

∞

My reading was interrupted when my roommate, Arne Denny, entered. He was about five foot ten, a strong, wiry guy with brown hair and an intensity that I was not used to. He wore his hair short and favored crisp light blue shirts and dark blue pants with shiny black shoes.

He was an AT2, a second class aviation technician in the Coast Guard, and he had applied from within the service. He had been through boot camp before, and he knew what he was up against. While some people kind of like the challenge, he was just ready to put up with it. He was wary and looking forward to trying to get through this with as little discomfort as possible. Arne told me that I better skip the history and get right to the immediate requirements.

He started to read the manual and summarize the lowlights of what we were going to have to do. I was just blown away. He read, "We are not to speak unless spoken to; but when we do talk to an officer, we have to start with sir and end with sir."

I asked Arne, "Doesn't that seem a bit redundant?"

He also said that, when we encounter someone and we are not marching, we have to give them the greeting of the day.

"What is that, a secret password like 'the hungry gull flies to the dump?'"

Almost completely exasperated, Arne looked up and said, "It's good morning, good afternoon, or good evening."

He resumed reading shaking his head. "We are to march nearly everywhere, and if we are by ourselves or in small groups, we are to double-time everywhere we go. We are to start with square meals, and by square meals, I don't mean three well-rounded, healthy meals. We are required to sit on the front three inches of our chairs, back and head straight, and eyes looking straight forward. We are to bring our forks straight up until they are parallel-to-mouth, then straight-into-mouth, executing a perfect right angle."

I asked him, "Does this mean the familiar and practical path of the hypotenuse is no longer available?"

He just kept reading. We could never talk in line, smoke, or even chew gum. I asked Arne to scan the manual and see if we were allowed to have pets, specifically ferrets —I always wanted a ferret. Arne continued to ignore my comments, even after I told him to check the index under ferrets.

Then Arne said, "At least we don't have to do 'nuts to butts.' At boot camp we had to line up close to each other —real close. I mean REAL close, pushing bodies into each other until our nuts were pushing the guy's butt in front. While this may be appealing to the Village People, I found it disturbing."

I then told Arne, "I hope they season the food with saltpeter, because I could foresee some potentially very embarrassing situations, especially if a guy 'kind of liked' the guy in front of him." Arne did mention that one guy in his platoon was a little too enthusiastic about the spooning in the lunch line and eventually washed out.

Arne and I went back and forth like this for a couple of hours, he reading to me and me being insufferable, until it was time for our first meal. Some of the better informed OCs had gotten to Yorktown the night before and were waiting at the guard post at 8:00 a.m. to process in and start their prep as soon as they could. We met up with all the OCs for the first time at the afternoon meeting before chow. We all looked alike. I couldn't even tell which one was me. At least I was blending in successfully.

∞

The proceedings started with motivational speakers, all of whom told us that, having looked over our group, so far they were very disappointed in us. They needed every OC, but it looked like a lot of us were going to wash out. My first thought was, "How did they figure me out so fast?" This was probably everyone else's first thought too, but I was not aware of this at the time. I assumed they had me pegged. Wasn't I sticking in? After some less intimidating announcements we were ready for our first meal.

We all lined up in silence and waited to make our selections. OCS was just one command among many, and we shared the dining hall with the other schools' students and staff members. The other Coast Guard trainees, not subject to our discipline regimen, gawked and laughed about our shaved heads and the discipline we displayed in the line. I picked the clam chowder as my starter, spaghetti as my main course, and an ice cream bar to round it out.

I sat down and started in on my chowder. In the process of negotiating the right angle to my mouth, I started to lose a large portion of the contents of my spoon. After a few spoonfuls, the mess was getting larger and I was getting hungrier, and I wondered if it would be all right to take the entire bowl and do the right angle thing with that. Looking around by shifting only my eyes, I noticed that not only was no one else doing that, but no one else had chosen the soup. I gave up on the soup and started in on the long strands of pasta. Because I couldn't look down, I found that I couldn't properly wrap the strands around the fork. Frankly, I didn't know what was going on down there between my fork and the mess of pasta, but it appeared to be a struggle in which the spaghetti —which was trying to remain on the plate —was winning. Soon a few eyes were gazing in my direction with total disbelief. Someone brought his napkin to his clean chin and started to wipe in the hope that I would realize that my chin looked like it had been through a knife fight. Not being a total idiot, I wiped my chin and could see the napkin soaked up a significant amount of sauce and a nice chunk of pasta that should have made it into my digestive tract. I considered licking it off the napkin.

Before I was even a third of the way into my meal, a bell went off. It appeared that everyone in our group had a place to go, and I figured I should probably follow them. As I was placing my tray on the conveyer, I took a last longing and mournful look at my uneaten ice cream bar and thought, "How the hell was I going eat that with a knife and fork?"

I was used to consuming about 4,000 calories a day but was lucky to get 150 out of that meal. I recalled five years earlier when my mother was serving an incredible antipasto and lasagna dinner to a West Point football recruiter. After the strawberry shortcake, the West Point coach blurted out, "Oh, by the way, we're not starving the cadets anymore." That badly worded comment certainly got our attention. He quickly recognized that his casual statement caused concern for this family who obviously enjoyed good food. He then said, "I thought you might have seen the article about the investigation into the cadets who were suffering from malnutrition." Well, it turns out that, as the freshmen (plebes) sat at the dining tables, the upperclassmen were grilling them on all the things that they needed to memorize. The freshman cadets only had a few minutes to eat, and they couldn't eat while reciting the Uniform Code of Military Justice, so they ended up going hungry day after day.

My thought was, "I like to eat. I'm good at it, and I consider it my key core competency. I'm not going to like that."

After the evening meal, we had a short meeting and started to get our rooms ready for inspection. Having witnessed the spaghetti incident, I think Arne realized he had been severely handicapped by having me assigned as a roommate. Of course, he never told me that.

I followed his lead and started to clean the room stem to stern. We also had to work together to clean the common areas. We made the floors shine to the point you needed sunglasses. We scraped off excess wax from the moldings and wiped down all surfaces. We studied the instruction manual on how to put our uniforms and gear away. Each article of clothing had specific folds and specific placement in our lockers, ostensibly in preparation for our packing of lockers aboard Coast Guard cutters. Some items had to go athwart ships and some had to go fore and aft. Arne had to explain to me that athwart ships just meant sideways. When pulling in lobster traps with my dad, we didn't tend to use many official nautical terms, but we did use bow and stern, and I at least knew fore was forward and aft was in the back.

After all that work, I then focused on belt buckles. The two brass belt buckles came with varnish that kept them from tarnishing. Using military logic, we had to remove that coating from both and then polish them until they shined again. Then we had to be careful not to touch them because without the protective coating a fingerprint would look absolutely grotesque and might cause a ship to sink. The shoes, too, had to be polished, including the spare pair. I polished them until I could see my reflection. I showed them to Arne for a pre-inspection review, and he pointed out that they were very sloppy around the lace holes, there was some excess wax in the stitching between the sole and top of the shoe, and the side of the heel was not completely polished.

"Come on! They can't be that picky!"

He just shook his head in disbelief.

Arne asked me how many rolls of masking tape I brought, and I told him none. He said I could borrow one of his.

"For what? If we're going to be putting up black light posters, I'd rather use tacks." He then explained the last thing we would do before inspection was de-linting, getting every piece of lint off our uniforms using masking tape. This I had to see and I did, many, many times.

∞

As I lay in bed, I tried to remember why I decided to go to OCS. I joined the Coast Guard because I thought it would be an adventure, but also because I thought I should serve my country. After college, my fellow alumni were going off to law or medical school or taking jobs at Morgan Stanley, but I was going to serve my country, even if it killed me. I was starting to think that it might.

Since age twelve, I had planned to go to either West Point or Annapolis, and I had worked hard in athletics and academics to fulfill that dream. I was the youngest of five kids: four boys and one terrorized girl. My dad was the meat manager at Falmouth's A&P, a part-time major in the National Guard, a part-time landscaper, and a commercial shell fisherman. He grew up during the Great Depression, and if there was work available and there was time in the day, he didn't turn it down. He would say, "Make hay while the sun shines because it doesn't always shine." My mother was a housewife. I thought that I wouldn't be able to afford a first-class education without attending one of the free academies.

My family had been a happy nuclear group of six, but just when my parents thought it was safe to have unprotected sex, I came along and ruined everything. At least, this is how my brother explained my existence to me. While my oldest brother, Paul, had a new Buffalo Bob suit that included the six-shooter and holster and a professional photo session at every birthday, I was left with a broken gun, one cowboy boot, and one badly focused picture. That picture is the solitary evidence that I was ever a child. I was what people referred to as "a trailer" or, as my brother would put it, just a horrible mistake.

Some fathers wanted their children to follow in their footsteps, but not my dad. As soon as my brothers and I reached fifteen, my father got us jobs working in the A&P storeroom. My dad could have gotten us jobs bundling in the fresh air or as cashiers, but he wanted us in the storeroom. The A&P storeroom was located in the cellar underneath the meat cooler. On the Cape we use the term cellar, not basement, but there is a bigger difference. A basement is a place where you play ping-pong and that often has wall-to-wall carpeting, but a cellar has roots growing through the stone foundation walls and a wall-to-wall dirt floor.

The storeroom supervisor was Anthony, a deaf mute, but no one would have said it that way then. Even when he was sixty years old, he would still be called "that deaf and dumb boy" loud enough so even the stone deaf could hear. He wasn't dumb in the intelligence sense —we were told his IQ was much higher than normal —but his communication skills were, at best, sub-par. So he was relegated to the storeroom.

Anthony was my brother's boss, and I remember, when I was six, going with my mother to pick up my brother Paul and Dad at work. We got there twenty minutes early so she could shop, and I went down in the cellar to watch my brother work. I would hear Anthony say in a very high pitched voice, "Grahh, grahh, grahh."

And my brother would say, "Anthony, was that a case of regular canned corn or creamed canned corn."

Not having a clue what Paul said, Anthony would reply, "Grahh, grahh, grahh."

So my brother, reading body language, tone, and inflection, would use his intuitive abilities to figure out what Anthony was saying, and about 90 percent of the time he would be wrong.

Years later I would hear from training specialists that the spoken word represents only 20 percent of the message. Even forty-plus years later, however, I still can't identify a request for creamed corn from regular corn through body language.

The cellar ceilings were just less than six feet and had a constant flow of condensation from the coolers through the floorboards, melted ice from the chests, and fish and meat juices that weren't picked up by the sawdust. Cellars are supposed to be damp, but this cellar had dampness on steroids. The room also had two dim light bulbs that were evidently so wild they had to be kept in cages.

Creamed corn is apparently only eaten by four old ladies worldwide, and so it wasn't a fast mover and was on the bottom shelf in the corner of the cellar where they kept the spider webs. The cellar was so overcrowded that getting anything was like playing those games with the little tiles that have one missing and you have to rearrange them to make a picture. The vintage cream corn case had been marinating in ooze for quite some time and, of course, when the case was picked up, the cans would rain down on the floor near my brother's feet and on my feet, and worst of all they were mixed in with wet cardboard.

On the Cape, wet cardboard meant one thing: earwigs. Earwigs (Dermaptera) are brown skinny bugs with pinchers on their butts that make cockroaches seem sexy. They make you believe that Mother Nature was actually evil. My brother Bill told me they were called earwigs because they would get into your ears and eat their way through your brains to escape out the other ear. The welcome relief of their exit was short-lived, however, when their eggs hatched.

Whenever my mother told us to study so we would be able to go to college, Dad would always chime in and say, "These boys don't need to go to college because Anthony is always gonna need an assistant." We got the message.

I had plenty of time to reminisce about the A&P while doing mindless tasks like cleaning the wax out of my shoe eyelets. I had time to wonder whether Anthony was still there and if he needed an assistant.

The Error Chain

Sometimes you don't know what you're getting yourself into and lose your point of reference, why you thought you were there in the first place. Of course, that was the point of some of the OCS's arbitrary rules. I was ill prepared for the dynamics of a square meal and made a bad menu choice, but I ignored other warnings too. In fact, I ignored every legitimate early warning and then pretended nothing was wrong, perhaps the biggest mistake of all.

4.

"You have to go out,
But you don't have to come back"
-U.S. Life-Saving Service Motto
Unofficial Motto of the U.S. Coast Guard

Our day started dark and early: 0445. We were out forming up to take a two-and-a-half-mile run. I remember hearing a commercial about the Army that said, "We do more things before nine in the morning than most people do all day." I could never see how that was a selling point for people under twenty-five. If they said, "We sleep 'til twelve, play with guns, and screw off all day," they'd be fighting off the recruits.

On alternate days we swam for forty-five minutes, and I was surprised that some of my classmates didn't know how to swim. I thought it would have been a prerequisite for joining the Coast Guard, but then, maybe Uncle Frank was right about the wading to shore

After the run, we prepared for room inspection. On the first inspection, I got four demerits. My spare hat was askew in the drawer. I guess I opened the drawer too quickly and the hat moved slightly. There was also a wax splatter on the leg of my rack; I should have seen that.

Morning uniform inspection on the parade ground went OK, only two demerits for a "bad reef." The tuck on my shirt wasn't tight enough. That had always been a problem because I am a bit top-heavy, and when I move my arms my shirt pulls up.

We then went to breakfast and did the square meal. I now had a solid demerit lead. Wait, this is like golf, I thought. It's the low score that wins. Then, back on the parade ground for more drilling. I had to do twenty sets of push-ups, twice for one infraction: being out of step. The officer couldn't hear me counting the first set. "Sir, nineteen, Sir. Sir, twenty, Sir. Permission to recover, Sir."

"Are sure you did twenty? Give me twenty more!"

"Sir, yes, Sir. Sir, one, Sir..."

∞

Luckily, I wasn't the worst at drilling and marching, an honor that went to OC John P. Heistand, a college kid whose family had a long Coast Guard tradition. His brother was a lieutenant commander in the Coast Guard Reserve, a fact that probably haunted John as he stumbled his way across the parade ground. OC Heistand was light skinned, tall, and had a little baby fat. He wore his hair short and favored crisp light blue shirts and dark blue pants with shiny black shoes. Back in college, I had to memorize the names of my fraternity brothers during rush week, and I used a system: one guy was fat (Tiny),

∞ John P. Heistand ∞

another was going prematurely bald (Dad), another owned nothing but Red Sox shirts (Yaz), but here there were, uniformly (no pun intended), no clues. But Heistand was impossible to forget all the same.

Heistand was in love with the Coast Guard, and no matter how much they yelled at us, he always maintained a determined smile —not the kind they tell you to wipe off but the kind that says, "It's OK to yell at me. I'll try to do better." From a young age he had read everything he could get his hands on about the Guard, and he was our resident expert on Coast Guard history and trivia. His enthusiasm was contagious; he was impossible to dislike. But when it came to drilling, he seemed to take his cue from Gomer Pyle. One officer quipped, "He is the only man who could march alone and still be out of step."

One morning, we lined up for morning colors, and the company officer, Lieutenant Emory, barked "parade rest." This order required us each to push our weapon out "smartly" while holding on to its muzzle. Heistand lost his grip and the weapon "smartly" somersaulted towards Emory. This was the third time he had dropped his weapon, a practice generally frowned upon but especially unappreciated when conducting precision drilling. Emory had warned Heistand that if he dropped his weapon again he had a big surprise for him. He hinted that it was a new, innovative way to use a training aid and that it had never been tried at OCS before.

Emory immediately dispatched Heistand to the gunnery to exchange his weapon for "Big Mutha." Heistand immediately doubletimed to the gunnery. We were at attention and looking straight ahead, wondering what a Big Mutha could possibly be. In less than a minute we saw a group of officers doubling over with laughter. Then out of the corner of our eyes we saw Heistand double-timing back with Big Mutha, short for Big Mother-F*****, a training aid used to teach students how to clean a gun. It was a replica of an M-1 but nearly twice as long and three times heavier. Then we could see other commands lining up for colors also starting to laugh, and it is true, the sight of Heistand's baby face, shaved head, and this disproportionate sized gun might have been the funniest thing I ever saw. He looked like a toddler carrying his daddy's rifle.

Then Lieutenant Emory looked away, but you could see him starting to break up. And we all laughed, including Heistand. Heistand was granted permission to join the ranks and the students quickly composed themselves.

The base commander, Captain Blaha, and the OCS head, Commander Loy, were last out to colors. By that time, everyone was relatively composed. At first, the officers didn't notice, but as they stood at attention, they almost simultaneously started to smile, then to laugh a composed laugh and shake their heads. They were expecting innovative training methods from Emory, and they were getting them.

I would have been mad if it had been me who was ordered to carry Big Mutha, but Heistand kept his determined smile and laughed with us. He took it with grace, but he had, if not a newfound desire for not screwing up, a more profound desire to get it right.

To a hammer, the whole world looks like a nail, and in boot camp, the solution to all problems is simple: humiliation. It works surprisingly well. From that point on, neither Heistand nor anyone else ever dropped a rifle at OCS.

I never really saw the benefit of precision drilling. It seemed like a lot of manpower wasting its time. I kept thinking to myself, "Shouldn't we be learning how to pilot a boat or tie a knot or something?" However, I do have to admit that, on the second day, as we marched to dinner singing the Coast Guard Hymn Semper Paratus, my hair stood up on the back of my neck.

∞

On the second night, as I lay in bed, I heard it start to rain and thought to myself, "Maybe there won't be any marching tomorrow." Boy was I stupid. Bad weather doesn't slow down the Coast Guard, so we certainly would march in the rain many times.

As the visibility decreased, I started to hear a cacophony of foghorns. That sound reminded me of being tucked into bed by my mother on wet, foggy, or snowy nights. She would tell me the story of the Andrea Doria and the miracle child, and I could imagine myself as the miracle child. There was always something scary about fog, but also something comforting like a great fuzzy blanket as distant horns called out to each other, "I'm here," "I'm here," and the lighthouse called back its elongated, "Here's home."

In the sailing days, horns and bells could be heard by ships in the deep fog, but now horns are often muffled by high-powered diesel engines drowning out their message.

Once Dad, my two brothers, and my long-suffering sister and I were out on Vineyard Sound in our tiny skiff. A deep fog set in before we could get back to shore. Without the aid of a compass, we were immediately disoriented and at the mercy of listening for the foghorn for direction. My dad asked what direction we thought the horn was blowing from. We all immediately pointed in different directions.

We could have made good headway but didn't know in which direction our destination laid, so we turned off the engine and drifted. When we heard the sound of a boat approaching, Dad told us to yell and scream as loud as we could, acting as a makeshift foghorn because we didn't have the mandatory foghorn or fog bell on board. Having spent most of my eight years being told to be quiet, I thought it was incredibly fun yelling and screaming with full license. My sister didn't need any encouragement and was really screaming. In fact, she didn't seem to be having any fun at all. We bought a foghorn after that trip, and my brother made good use of it, sneaking up behind my sister on subsequent cruises with or without fog.

The waters off Nantucket are the mixing area for the Labrador and Gulf Streams. The warm Gulf Stream waters heat the air above it, and when the warm moist air travels over the cold Labrador eddies, the result is "pea soup," every sailor's fear. On July 25, 1956, the confluence of these currents created the setting for the Andrea Doria and the MS Stockholm collision.

The Andrea Doria was the pride of the Italian commercial fleet. She was built in 1951 and was considered one of the safest ocean liners in the world. The 697-foot ship had a double hull and was divided into eleven water-tight compartments. Any two could be filled without endangering the ship's safety. Unlike the Titanic, the Andrea Doria carried enough lifeboats to accommodate all passengers and crew, and she was equipped with the latest radar. The Andrea Doria was on the ninth and last night of its transatlantic crossing from Genoa.

The MS Stockholm was a smaller passenger ship of the Swedish-American line that had just departed New York that afternoon. With a combined speed of forty knots, the two ships were approaching each other on the heavily traveled ocean highway corridor off dangerous Nantucket. The Stockholm went from clear skies into a fog bank, and the Andrea Doria was already in this fog bank and had only slowed slightly. The Andrea Doria identified an oncoming ship on the radar but never actually calculated the closest point of approach on the radarscope or on a maneuvering board. The Andrea Doria also never made radio contact to ascertain the other ship's course.

For reasons still not apparent, the crew of the Andrea Doria did not correctly identify the speed and direction of the Stockholm, and didn't identify the feared phenomenon of constant bearing and decreasing range. The Andrea Doria had activated the wailing whistle of the ship's foghorn and closed all watertight doors. The Stockholm had yet to prepare for reduced-visibility navigation. The Stockholm never heard the Andrea Doria's foghorn over the ship's own engines.

Recalling the story while lying in bed listening to the rain, my mind jumped to one of my required memorizations from the "Spindrift" section of the OCS manual, which was supposed to be the key to all nautical knowledge: What is a head-on situation? When two power-driven vessels are meeting on reciprocal or nearly reciprocal courses so as to involve the risk of collision, each shall alter her course to starboard so that each shall pass on the port side of the other.

Under the rules of the road, while ships are supposed to turn right in extremis or dangerous situations, they tend not to turn right because, if they do, they may leave the channel, which often results in running aground and all the ensuing damage, paperwork, and embarrassment. When the Andrea Doria did identify the contact, she turned left, exposing the starboard beam to the fast-moving Stockholm. The Stockholm rammed the Andrea Doria at nearly a ninety-degree angle, or as my father the butcher would say, it T-boned her. The collision immediately crushed more than forty people who were asleep in their cabins, and the Stockholm penetrated two of the watertight compartments. Because the ship's fuel tanks were nearly empty from the long voyage, the Andrea Doria's lack of ballast made it list severely, eighteen degrees to port. The written procedural requirement from the shipbuilder would be for the Andrea Doria to pump in seawater to the empty tanks for ballast, but that would require pumping it back out into a filtering system, and that cost money. To save money, the common practice was to only pump in water if they were going to encounter heavy seas.

The Stockholm immediately assessed its damage and conducted a head count: they had lost five crew members and gained one passenger. This was always the high point of my mother's bedtime story, the "miracle girl," a fourteen-year-old girl who was thrown from her bunk onto the crushed bow of the Stockholm and suffered no major injuries. Her half-sister and stepfather were killed, but her mother, although badly hurt, survived.

The girl's father was a news reporter on ABC radio in New York. He broadcast a professional account of the collision, not telling anyone that his daughter had been a passenger on the Andrea Doria and was feared dead. The next morning, this broadcaster, Edward P. Morgan, was told of his daughter's miraculous survival, and he made an emotional broadcast that was just as dramatically recounted to me by my actress-mother on foggy nights throughout my childhood.

Despite the fact that there were enough lifeboats on the Andrea Doria, the ship's list to starboard made it impossible to launch the lifeboats on the port side. The lifeboats on the starboard side were launched empty. The usual process of lowering the boats and the passengers entering them through the lower windows had to be abandoned because the lower decks were now underwater.

Many of the Andrea Doria's crew, recognizing the seriousness of their situation, forgot about the usual protocol of women and children first and jumped the queue. They were the first ones in the few usable lifeboats. When the survivors in the first three lifeboats climbed aboard the Stockholm, the Swedish crew discovered they were all crew and not a single passenger. The Swedes became incensed that the Italian crew abandoned their passengers and fist fights broke out, which did not contribute to the effort to save the passengers of the Andrea Doria.

The Captain of the Stockholm didn't show outstanding altruism. He was reluctant to use his lifeboats in fear that his ship might sink and there wouldn't be room for his crew and passengers.

Without most of the trained crew remaining on board, the passengers on the Andrea Doria started to panic. Parents were throwing their children over the side into the lifeboats. Many children were hurt and two were killed in the fall.

Luckily, cowardice did not rule the day. Unlike the situation during the sinking of the Titanic, most ships within range altered their courses to offer assistance. Baron Raoul de Beaudean, the captain of the eastbound liner SS Ile de France, which had passed the westbound Andrea Doria, turned his ship around and saved the day. The baron dispatched his crew in lifeboats and, using Jacob's ladders, nets, and other lines, picked up most of the survivors. On board the Ile de France, passengers gave up their staterooms to the cold and injured survivors. Coast Guard rescue helicopters picked up the badly injured from the deck of the Ile de France and carried them to Boston for medical treatment.

In all, more than 1,700 people were rescued that day before the Andrea Doria found its final resting spot in the bottom of the Atlantic: 40 degrees, 29 minutes, 30 seconds north; and 69 degrees, 51 minutes, 0 seconds west. She remains there today, a popular dive site, and she continues to take lives in deep water diving accidents: 15 divers to date. She's considered the Mt. Everest of the SCUBA world.

The Andrea Doria is only one of 3,000 shipwrecks in the underwater landscape off the Cape. This whole area has always been treacherous for sailors and a hotbed of activity for rescuers. While Cape Cod was formed by glaciers, the glacial moraine eventually eroded away, creating mountains of sand that are in continuous motion. This

shifting sand, while apparent on the dunes of the Cape, is also shifting under the water, forming shoals and creating rips. These shoals
extend more than forty miles south of the Cape, and while responsible
for warm waters during the summer, often reaching 73 degrees, they
are also responsible for over 3,000 shipwrecks. By some accounts,
over 25% of all wrecks in the North Atlantic occur off Cape Cod, a far
greater propensity for demise then the Bermuda Triangle myth. The
legend of these dangerous shoals kept the captain of the Mayflower
from sailing south to the Pilgrims intended destination: the mouth
of the Hudson River. Instead, they sailed around the Cape to a much
harsher climate, less fertile land, but to the land of the Wampanoag
tribe who were looking for allies with fire sticks.

For over two hundred years, on average two ships go aground every
month off the Cape Cod. It was not until the late thirties, when the
Cape Cod Canal was widened, essentially making Cape Cod an island
that the onslaught of shipwrecks stopped for the costal-bound traffic.

Every year my dad took us all to Truro to visit Cape Cod National
Seashore, which his National Guard company helped build some of
the infrastructure. The seashore has a heritage center that celebrates
the heroism of the Lifesavers.

In 1797, the Massachusetts Humane Society started putting up huts
along the beaches of Wellfleet and Truro. The huts were used by sailors
who were able to make it to shore and offered protection so that they
wouldn't freeze to death through the night.

Almost a hundred years later, in 1872, a lifesaving service was put
into operation along the Cape beaches. Stations were erected every
five miles on the beach, and six or seven surf men and a keeper lived
in each station and kept a continuous lookout. Their assignment was
simple: if they spotted a wreck, they had to go out and save the sailors.
Their motto was: "You have to go out. But you don't have to come
back." That motto and its expectation of courage was one of the strongest elements drawing me into the Coast Guard. I was about to join
the tradition of these men and women who were ready and willing to
put their lives on the line in the most hazardous of conditions to save
their fellow mariners.

Lightships were used when terra firma locations were too far from
the sea lanes. Perhaps the most famous lightship was the Nantucket,

which held the first beacon a transatlantic ship would see when coming to the great port of New York. Steamships would focus their radio beacon on the Nantucket lightship and knew they were on the right course to avoid the Nantucket shoals. On more than a few occasions, however, beacon navigation ran them straight into this and other lightships.

Lightship 117 at Nantucket was sideswiped by the SS Washington in early 1934, and four months later, on May 15, 1934, she was rammed and sunk by the British White Star liner RMS Olympic in heavy fog. Four men went down with the ship and seven survivors were picked up by the Olympic. Three survivors later died of injuries sustained from the collision. The sunken wreck still lies in 200 feet of water 50 miles south of Nantucket Island.

The Error Chain

Rapidly changing weather conditions create hazardous conditions. In many accidents, weather is a factor, but not necessarily very bad weather because it seems most people are alert to treacherous weather. The subtlety of poor visibility apparently doesn't slow people down. It should.

Going too fast is often motivated by a small delay: we must make up time —time is money. In the case of the Andria Doria, she reduced speed from 23 to 21.8 knots (less than 5 percent) when she hit the fog bank. The rule is to be able to stop within the distance you can see: in zero visibility that means anchor. That was not the practice in the open ocean.

However, there were yet stranger mistakes made. For example, the misinterpretation of the radar was caused by poor lighting, which could have been rectified by the installation of a small light. The crew of the Andrea Doria couldn't hear horns, yet there was no radio contact. Poor communications is a very common problem in all catastrophes, and apparently this problem doesn't go away after them. Evidently we don't always learn from catastrophic mistakes. The lessons aren't recognized or communicated. The crew also turned left instead of right —swerving in front of oncoming traffic is always a very bad bet —and they had no ballast because they wanted to save money.

Because the parties involved reached an out-of-court settlement, thus avoiding the resulting intense scrutiny that full litigation would have recorded, no one will ever be sure of all facts and circumstances surrounding this great collision. Covering up the truth and burying the opportunity to learn from the mistakes compounds mistakes into a sin.

5.

"Duty is the most sublime word in our language.
Do your duty in all things.
You cannot do more.
You should never wish to do less."
-Robert E. Lee

Someone once asked Confucius what he would do first if he was put in charge of the world, and he said, "Fix the language." In OCS we were told that 90 percent of all problems in organizations are communication problems, so for clarity we had to use the nautical vernacular. We couldn't say floor, instead we had to say deck. Walls were bulkheads, stairs were ladders, rope was line, a toilet was a head, sideways was athwart ships, and maps were charts. When OC Jewel was describing his work history as cartographer for the state, he said he worked on maps, and everyone tried to correct him to follow our new Orwellian language that substituted charts for maps. He correctly replied that recordings of land and roads are maps. But don't ever get caught calling a chart a map on a ship.

We were never to refer to the left or right side —left is port and right is starboard of a vessel. When I was a child, I learned to form an "L" with my fingers and thumb, and the one that looked like an "L" was left. To figure out which side was port, I memorized that both port and left have four letters. The word starboard arrived over a thousand years ago as a contraction of "steering board," which was on the right side near the stern. With the steering mechanism on the starboard, a ship would have to dock in port on its left side: thus, going to port (which was changed from larboard —loading board —in the nineteenth century).

On the parade ground, we were grilled on the things we had to memorize from "The Spindrift" in our manual. We were asked questions like, "What is spindrift?"

"Sir, spray blown from a rough sea or surf, Sir."

"How long have you been in the Coast Guard?"

You wouldn't want to say five days, four hours, and twelve minutes, although we all knew exactly how many days, hours, and minutes we'd been in. We were required to say:

"Sir, all my blooming life;
my father was King Neptune; my mother was a mermaid;
I was born in the crest of a wave, and rocked in the cradle of the
deep; my eyes are stars, my teeth are spars,
my hair is hemp and seaweed.
When I spits, I spits tar,
I's tough,
I is,
I am,
I are [this ditty should have ended in Aargh], Sir!"

Note: this verse comes from our roots in the British Royal Navy, as indicated best perhaps by the use of "blooming." The Royal Navy had a marine revenue cutter service 200 years earlier than the U.S. Marine Revenue Service, the Coastguard, and the Spanish had the Guarda Costa. The hyperbole —"My father was King Neptune and my mother was a mermaid" —was eloquent and amusing. In high school I was one of the nerds who loved history. I had a good memory, so it was fun. I had thought about majoring in history in college, but Uncle Frank told me that, with that kind of education, I could work for IBM in its history department. I got the message and majored in economics.

One OC was named Neptun, and we accused him of changing his name just to suck up, but he was quick to remind us that he sired us all. Now he is a rear admiral; it must have worked.

I had a lot of time to think about the meaning duty, a word that was thrown about quite a bit. "Duty is the most sublime word in our language, do your duty in all things, you can do no more, you should never want to do less," was an oft-heard quotation by Robert E. Lee (I used to think, "But wasn't he the enemy?"). It is remarkable how ingrained that word was in the Coast Guard. If you ever thanked someone in the Coast Guard, the terse reply would be, "Don't thank me for doing my job." If you were overly polite to a chief petty officer and called him sir instead of chief, he would come back at you with, "Don't call me sir! I work for a living!" In other words, I do my duty. I guess in the Coast Guard we were expected to live a life of demerits without merits, like a hockey goalie that can never score, only screw up because he's expected to make every save.

Another bit from our Spindrift was: "What is the Coast Guard?" "The Coast Guard is that hard nucleus around which the Navy forms in times of war." But that's just an intricate way of claiming that, "The tail wags the dog."

Today one of the questions asked in "The Spindrift" is, "What is the Cuyahoga?"

"Sir, the CGC Cuyahoga was an officer candidate training vessel. On the night of 20 October 1978 she collided with the Santa Cruz II in the Chesapeake Bay at the mouth of the Potomac River. She sank quickly and eleven shipmates were lost, Sir!'" I have a paraphrased version of this in my mind and have been reciting it in my nightmares for thirty years.

We OCs had to memorize the many missions of the Coast Guard. One was particularly dear to my heart. Traditionally, the Coast Guard enforced and monitored the fishing grounds of the United States and protected them from foreign encroachment. Two years before I joined the Coast Guard, the service's mission had been expanded by passage of (this was a mouthful) the Magnuson-Stevens Fishery Conservation and Management Act, which followed the lead of Peru and some other nations to established an exclusive economic zone extending 200 nautical miles out from the coast. The act extended the U.S. fisheries management's authority way beyond the three-mile territorial jurisdiction that had been in effect for some 400 years. The Coast Guard now had to patrol and police 4,383,000 square miles of sea.

The exclusive economic zones (EEZ) were a direct result of the principles of economics I had studied in college, in this case, "the tragedy of commons." In seventeenth century Europe, land was often shared in common, which provided incentive to every single shepherd to extract every single piece of grass before his competitor could. The grass was eventually consumed beyond sustainability, and the commons became barren.

The same was happening to the world's fishing grounds, especially the most productive and accessible fishing areas in the world, the

Grand Banks of Newfoundland and Georges Bank off Cape Cod. Fish that could hide from fishermen in remote canyons were now sought out using advanced electronics and then captured using sophisticated netting and trapping technology. Fish used to be able to run and hide but not anymore.

The fisheries were fished beyond sustainability, and that slippery slope is extremely steep. Further, Soviet-bloc factory trawlers were taking what Yankees considered garbage fish —herring, bunker, alewives, and mackerel —to be turned into fish protein for home consumption and extruded pellets for fish farms in the highly subsidized Norwegian salmon fish-farming industry. The Norwegian government subsidized fish-farming because it was concerned that Russian submarines were using Norwegian fjords to hide from the U.S. Navy. The fish-farming subsidies provided incentives to citizens to occupy the many fjords along the 50,000 miles of Norwegian coastline where they served as an early warning system for Russian subs.

Fish-farming which may seem more sustainable than actual fishing, relies on about three to five pounds of food to create one pound of flesh. The trash fish were being scooped up by the Russians for fish feed, and the striped bass and other fish that lived off that prey in the wild were facing commercial extinction. As with any complex biological systems, there were certainly other factors that contributed to these fisheries' detriment. Co-conspirators were the use of pesticides and fertilizers and the loss of wetlands in three primary breeding areas: the Chesapeake Bay, the Hudson River, and the Roanoke River.

The U.S. Exclusive Economic Zone is now the largest in the world. Canada, which on most maps looks a lot larger than the United States, has less than half of the U.S. allocation of EEZ. (It's good to be the superpower.) Surprisingly, France has the second largest due to the many islands it controls in the South Pacific.

By 1976, the Coast Guard's mission had expanded exponentially, but its resources in both manpower and assets remained constant. But now every foreign fisherman was "stealing" fish from Americans even though they may have been fishing these waters for centuries. Negotiations had to take place, and they did. The Coast Guard took on the extended duties with its usual gusto; in fact, maybe with too much of a "can do, get outta my way" attitude.

∞

Everyone I knew had the utmost respect for the Coast Guard except for my grandmother who would have liked to see one commandant of the Coast Guard hung from the nearest cherry tree in Washington. My father's mother immigrated to the United States from Lithuania in 1905 at age fourteen. Her family hated Russians so much they refused to send their children to school because they taught in Russian. Consequently, she never learned to read or write. But she was smart.

In late November 1970, the U.S. Coast Guard cutter Vigilant was anchored alongside the Russian fish factory ship Litva off Martha's Vineyard. The Russian vessel was hosting a negotiating session between angry Massachusetts fishermen and their Russian counterparts. A Lithuanian sailor aboard the Litva, Simas Kudirka, sent a clandestine message to the cutter crew asking for asylum. The captain of the Vigilant sent a coded message to the Coast Guard District Headquarters in Boston: "What do I do?" No one was sure how to handle the situation but if Kudirka jumped into the water the Coast Guard would have to pick him up and could turn him over to the State Department. A forty-two-foot patrol boat was summoned out of Group Woods Hole to pick up the prospective Oscar (Man Overboard). The patrol boat would then race back to Woods Hole where a representative from the State Department would meet them.

Then, without further warning, Kudirka jumped the twelve feet from the Litva to the deck of the Vigilant landing on deck without being seen by the onboard KGB agents. Now what could the Coast Guard do?

    A) Suddenly call off the negotiations and hightail it back to New Bedford?

    B) Keep silent and have him jump off the Coast Guard ship when the 42-footer arrives?

    C) Notify the Soviet authorities and have them formally ask for him back -then give the guy back and let him spend the rest of his life in prison?

If option "C" appeals to you, you're qualified to join the ranks of the Puzzle Palace, better known as Coast Guard headquarters. Since it was late afternoon and the week of Thanksgiving, many people in the chain of command were either on vacation or had left for the day. As my father always said, "Never get hurt or sick on a holiday because all the experienced people are on vacation."

The commander of the Vigilant couldn't reach the acting commander, and so he called the district commander who was at home recuperating from an illness. The convalescing district commander, in the fog of illness, advised the captain that the negotiations were too important to be jeopardized. He told the captain that if the Russians made a formal request to get the defector back, we should probably return him to the Soviet ship.

The acting commander got back in the loop and tried to contact both the Coast Guard Headquarters in Washington and the State Department, but it was after- hours and only duty teams were available. The senior people couldn't be located, and the duty staff was unable to make decisions or give advice. Later, the State Department staff claimed that they thought the commander's question was still theoretical and they didn't realize a defector had actually boarded the cutter.

In any case, the acting commander took the district commander's advice as an order and told the Vigilant's crew to seek a formal request and then return the defector.

The crew members were sensitive to the fishing negotiations but returning the defector wasn't all that easy. Simas Kudirka who now knew that he was facing life in a Russian gulag refused to jump back on the Russian vessel. The commanding officer of the Vigilant didn't want his men to force the Lithuanian sailor to return so he took the next logical step: he allowed Russian thugs on board. They chased him around the ship, caught him, beat him, and dragged him back to his ship.

Imagine allowing your enemy to repatriate a person whose only crime is wanting freedom. Imagine allowing this on a sovereign U.S. man-of-war vessel near the coast of Massachusetts, the place where they practically invented freedom. Sam Adams would never have approved.

Although the Coast Guard distributed a press release on the successful fishing negotiations, the service decided that the Simas Kudirka event wasn't newsworthy and they didn't disclose it to the press.

However, one of the negotiators, a Latvian-American who had successfully escaped from the USSR years earlier, shared the story with the Baltic-American community. The Latvian, Estonian, and Lithuanian

Americans were outraged. The story soon became front page news. Congressmen, senators, and members of the Nixon administration all condemned the act. Even the United Nations filed a formal protest. Conservative columnist William F. Buckley Jr. thought we should send the Coast Guard Officers involved to Russia —and make them swim there.

My Lithuanian grandmother attended rallies and helped raise money for Simas Kudirka's defense. The made-for-television movie starring Alan Arkin won two Emmys, and indeed Arkin's portrayal of Simas Kudirka was compelling. You could feel that returning him was wrong in every bone of your body. How can people act in direct conflict with their ingrained common sense? Was there something wrong with the system that turned normally rational people into idiots?

At first, the Coast Guard was going to court-martial the commanding officer of the Vigilant, the district commander, and the acting district commander. But then the Coast Guard brass figured they had suffered enough; they just allowed the commanders to retire while the Vigilant's commanding officer was relieved of his command and received a written reprimand.

Simas Kudirka didn't get off quite so easily. He was imprisoned in Perm, Russia, far from his family. He did eventually make his way to the United States after many pleas from senators and congressmen and finally the personal intervention of Henry Kissinger.

The fisheries' negotiations were important, but not more important than one person's freedom. To the Coast Guard's credit, every officer in the service for many years to come was forced to watch The Defection of Simas Kudirka, to understand what went wrong and recognize the lessons learned. The film was also far less boring than most training sessions.

Members of the Portuguese community, who hated the way the Russians had decimated the fishing grounds, harassed the Vigilant crew and their families. As a result, the cutter Vigilant eventually had to be reassigned from New Bedford, Massachusetts to another port.

My entire family witnessed firsthand the decimation of the fish and shellfish stocks. My father spent his vacations pursuing the scallop, a marine bivalve mollusk of the family Pectinidae, in Waquoit Bay. The bay scallop was far better tasting than its cousin, the sea scallop, and could be found in abundance in a number of bays and harbors on the East Coast.

Waquoit Bay is a wide estuary that separates Falmouth from the town of Mashpee, a former Indian reservation. Scallop season started on October first of every year, and dozens of boats would head out at the crack of dawn to gather the scallops. When not resting on the bottom, scallops actually swim by opening and closing their shells by means of the muscle that we eat.

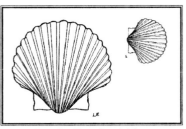

∞ Bay Scallop (Pectinidae) ∞

Bay scallopers use a window box, a small glass box that is covered in a hood to block out the sunlight, to spot the scallops on the bottom in the shallow water.

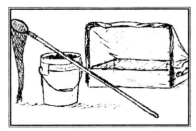

∞ Scallopers Tool Kit ∞

With a dip net that can extend as long as twelve feet, scallopers drift over the eel grass beds and scoop up the mollusks. My father loved looking at the wildlife in Waquoit Bay, but more importantly, he liked the fact that, within a few short hours, he could gather his legal limit of ten bushels, which would shuck out seven pounds of scallop per bushel and fetch two to three dollars per pound. My dad could make more money in one day than he could make in a week at his regular job as a meat cutter.

Because the boat was small and the scallops took up a large part of it, only my brothers would go out with Dad but at 6:00 or 7:00 p.m., when the scallops reached home, the whole family pitched in and shucked. We used to shuck them down in our cellar, and the shucking would go on until 1:00 or 2:00 a.m. with five or six pairs of hands doing the work. After a few seasons, our house started to smell like dead fish, but because of olfactory fatigue, none of us could smell it. We did eventually notice that although we were very popular with cats from the neighborhood, friends only wanted to visit the house for a short time. We soon moved the shucking to a Sears aluminum shed in the back yard, which became the new gathering point for the neighborhood cats.

In the first years, my dad would get his limit almost every day. Soon however, he was getting his limit on the first day only. After about ten years, he was lucky to get two bushels on any day. We don't know what happened to the scallops. Perhaps it was the tragedy of the commons: because there was no clear owner, no one took responsibility to maintain the resource and the scallops were over-harvested beyond sustainability. Or, perhaps, as some researchers suspect, a blight in the eel grass removed an important element in the successful spawning of scallops.

While I wasn't much of a fisherman, my brothers loved to fish. Tackle was expensive so they carved lures, painted them a bluish green to look like fish, and painted on gills and fins. My brothers also made sinkers and lead weights for diving by melting lead and pouring it into molds. Pouring molten lead in our cellar and breathing the fumes ensured that none of us would go to MIT which was just as well, we couldn't afford it.

My brother Chris fished in the pond by our house. The pond had been recently reconnected to the ocean but qualified as a freshwater pond. My brother entered a sea trout he caught in that pond into a trout competition, and he beat the nearest competitor by nearly double the weight. When his picture appeared with the fish in the newspaper, knowledgeable fisherman cried, "Foul! That's a damn sea trout!" They had been much more plentiful twenty years prior but had practically become extinct, so only the old-timers knew it was a sea trout.

My brothers and I were also fishing entrepreneurs and we pursued herring, (actually alewives (Alosa pseudoharengus)), that spawn in the many estuaries on Cape Cod. These fish spend their adult lives traveling the Atlantic Ocean and feeding off plankton. Like salmon, they return to their birthplace to spawn and die. In the late spring, the alewives form large schools near the herring runs along the coastline of the southern Cape. These herring runs are small streams that allow the tidal flow to go back and forth between the open ocean and the estuaries. Herring only enter an estuary on an outgoing tide because they need to smell the water. I always thought it would be more efficient if they went in on the tide rather than swimming against the current, but that's their choice.

As young fishing entrepreneurs, we found three sources of income from herring: a few older people would pay three dollars per bushel and salt/pickle them; we would clean the herring roe (eggs) and sell roe by the pint (we had a local buyer -the A&P meat manager); and selling the herring to fishermen as live bait.

The third option was the most lucrative since these huge schools of fish would be followed by "blues" (bluefish) and striped bass. A netted alewife with a big hook through its back was perfect bait for a fisherman stalking blues and stripers. We, and by "we" I mean my brother, built a cage for herring and we would net them right after school when the older men got out of work to go fishing for stripers, and sell them for twenty-five cents apiece. On days when the tide had changed and there was no longer any opportunity for a fisherman arriving late after work to net a herring, the price went up to fifty cents.

∞ Striped Bass (Morone Saxatilis) ∞

Once when I was manning the cage for my brother, the cage got away from me and started floating out into the ocean. I ran down the jetty to grab it, and I just about had it when an older man and his two sons pushed me out of the way and pulled in the cage. I was about to thank them for their assistance when I realized that they were going to steal it. The man took the cage, took the herring out and put them in his bucket, and then walked with the cage to his truck.

I followed them all the way to the truck where the father finally turned to me and said, "It's the law of the sea. It was lost and we found it. Now it's ours." While no experts in maritime law, my brother, who was eleven, and I, seven at the time, offered strong counter arguments; but we were no match for this older man and his teenage sons. Our arguments were in fact trumped by the ultimate maritime law: might makes right.

We watched as my brother's winter project of cage fabrication was carried down the street in the back of a truck. I wondered whether those teenage boys would grow into adults who modeled their behavior upon their father's gross misrepresentation of maritime law. I would be surprised if they are now legal advisors to Somalian pirates.

The most exciting time of "herring-ing" was the time a big school stayed outside of the herring run for almost a week. Each time a few brave scout-fish would enter the herring run they were immediately pulled out by fisherman. Somehow sensing the scout's demise, the herring school stayed out to sea.

We knew we would have a favorable tide on Friday at 1:30 a.m. so my brothers, a couple of friends, and I waited for our opportunity. Scouts came in and we sat quietly. They went further in but we stayed still. Finally, they went all the way into the small estuary. Then, like halftime at an NFL game when the masses, holding their bladders, rush in here they all came.

∞ Alewife (Alosa Pseudoharengus) ∞

The fish were so thick that you could walk on them. We scooped them up with our nets and just flung them to shore, and soon our nets were torn to shreds. With our bare hands and feet we just threw them or kicked them onto the shore screaming and cheering all the while.

A car stopped, obviously coming from a closed nightclub, and two guys and their fancily dressed girlfriends got out to investigate. Within seconds the two guys were in the water in their blue suede shoes catching the fish with their hands, joining in on the furious fishing frenzy. They clearly had no commercial interests because they promised all the fish to us. Their girlfriends stood in the parking lot staring in disbelief.

At this early point in my life (age seven), I came to a realization that most fishermen don't discover until after puberty: fishing is better than sex. While I watched the fish, my brothers went home and gathered wheelbarrows, bushel baskets, trash cans, and buckets, and within an hour we had all the fish back in our yard. By 4:00 a.m., without a shower, we were all sleeping in our beds with salt and scales still plastered to our bodies.

At 5:10 in the morning, we heard a scream from our mother. "Get down here! NOW!" The scene outside was right out of Alfred Hitchcock's The Birds. There were more seagulls in our yard than at the dump. Soon a fight ensued, boy against hungry bird. Rocks, BB guns, sticks; no weapon was held in reserve against the overwhelming numbers we faced.

Our reinforcements trickled in: first Dodigan's dog Jet, who ran full-speed, barking and jumping and snapping at the gulls and occasionally at our elbows. Then the neighborhood cats ambled in, thrilled at the possibility of surf and turf. It was like the final battle for the Kingdom of Narnia. When the battle for our catch was over, we still had more fish than any of us had ever seen, and we cleaned and de-roed them, yielding over three gallons of fish eggs.

My father had been building a small cottage, and the foundation was halfway done, laid with open cement blocks. More than a few herring fell into the foundation, and for years people complained of a strange odor that was most noticeable in the basement. This memory called to mind one more use for herring: odiferous revenge. There was a guy who always parked his car in the middle of our street-hockey game. He could have easily parked forty feet down the street, but no, he always had to park right in the middle of where we were playing. We found a new place to play, but we revisited the scene of his intrusion and put de-roed herring into each of his hubcaps. Stink! My eyes water just thinking about it. For about two days, his wife had him cleaning every part of that car, over and over. Sadly, he eventually found the source. Fortunately, because of his stinking attitude, nearly everyone in town was a potential suspect, although the dead fish might have pointed a fin in our direction.

As I tossed and turned in my OCS rack, I thought about where I could find a dead fish and wondered where Emory parked.

The Error Chain

The New York Times described the Kudirka affair as "one of the most disgraceful incidents ever to occur on a ship flying the American flag." The entire chain of command was in unfamiliar territory -there was no standard response for what to do with a defecting Lithuanian sailor. Holiday communications run by the juniors screwed up efficient information transfer to people who were in a position to apply reason. Because of one man's illness, the chain of command was broken, and that illness must have caused poor judgment.

The cutter's captain faced three very bad options: disobey a direct order, make his men return a freedom-seeker, or let Russians onto his ship to drag the poor guy to a totalitarian prison. The captain chose the easiest option at that moment which happened to be the worst of the three.

In short, bad options produce convenient bad choices, But there was a bigger lesson to be learned from the sad case of Simas Kudirka: basic humanity didn't figure into these decision-maker's final decision. Expediency had won the day.

6.

"Now it's all designed to blow our minds,
But our minds won't really be blown"
-"On the Cover of the Rolling Stone"
Shel Silverstein, Dr. Hook & the Medicine Show

I was the undisputed leader in acquiring demerits. I accumulated demerits like a boat without antifouling paint accumulates barnacles. My rap sheet was extensive. Crimes like lint on pants (even when they were in my locker), waving an unauthorized Irish pennant (a term borrowed from the British for a frayed line or any piece of thread hanging from your clothes, both indicating poverty -and you wonder why the Irish wanted freedom from the Brits so badly), talking in line ("you're standing on my foot!"), scuffed shoes ("he stepped on my shoe, while standing on my foot"), talking back to an officer ("he stepped on my shoe"), wrinkles on sheets (under the covers), dusty dados (I had to look up what a dado was (floor molding) so I could seek them out and dust them), and books out of order.

The books out of order demerit put me over the top, and I lost my first chance at Sunday afternoon liberty. When I first received my books, I was thrilled. Among them was my first Bowditch, the bible of navigation, that didn't have water-swollen and stained pages. I put the books in the bookshelf in my locker, in order, utilizing the Dewey decimal system basically by subject. It turns out that the books' correct order is tallest to shortest from left to right, and in the case of a tie, the thickest to thinnest. I argued that the Dewey decimal system was a bit more logical and universal,   but I was told unequivocally that there was a right way and a wrong way and the Coast Guard way.

There are two kinds of inspection: room inspection and parade ground uniform inspection. After the first week, room inspection settled down to once a week and the square meals ended. The uniform inspection was every morning before breakfast. The room inspections were done by the officer of the day (OOD). This OOD assignment rotated each week, and each inspector had a pet area of focus. One officer might be checking for the tuck of the bed, another checking to see if the sneakers in the locker were neatly tied and yet another would look under the bed, searching for a piece of unpolished floor.

The proud members of the class 06-78 were shooting at a moving target. That is, until one member of the class ahead of us, 05-78, started to tip us off. Unfortunately, this tactic didn't last as long as we'd hoped: "This week they will be looking at the outside window sill." Most people don't normally clean their outside window sill on a daily basis, and because we all had clean outside window sills that day, the officers started to suspect we were getting tipped off. The senior class was reprimanded, and our insider information ended.

At morning formation, the training officer of the day asked for a volunteer to organize our platoon's recreational activities. The job consisted of organizing two evenings of athletics per week and coordinating with the rest of the base. As a kid, I was told NAVY was an acronym for "Never Again Volunteer Yourself," and I also knew that no good deed ever goes unpunished. Despite this abundance of knowledge, I volunteered and was subsequently awarded the title of chairman of the recreation committee, a committee of one: me. My fellow classmates didn't like basketball, and so we settled on two other "Olympic" sports, dodge ball and street hockey.

I loved street hockey, and I probably had 2,000 hours of experience playing it. As a kid, I used two open Sears and Roebuck catalogs, one taped to each shin for protection, and I'd play for hours. I played hockey more like Dick Butkis than Bobby Orr, and in one game, both OC Williams and I went into the corner to dig out the puck -I came out of the corner with the puck, he came out with a dislocated shoulder. After that act of stupidity, I became the full-time ref.

∞

On the fourth day of training, while I stood at attention in the lunch line, one of the petty officers who had been laughing under his breath at us decided to take it up a notch. He got right up next to me and started to wave his hand in front of my face like so many obnoxious Americans do to the Royal Guards at Buckingham Palace. His two friends were amused, but they didn't join in. Taunting a big person is a lot of fun if you are sure that big person is not going to retaliate.

If I confronted him I knew it would cost me more demerits. I wondered whether this was some kind of test, if the guy had been put up to this by my superiors. I had given some thought to quitting but realized it would be too embarrassing; now I had the perfect out. If I just went after him and started a brawl and got kicked out of OCS, at least everybody back

∞ OC Larry Williams' hockey injury ∞

at the bar would be impressed. Of course, someone could get hurt or even kicked out with brig time, and that would be stupid and selfish. I recalled an old quote from one of the classics: "Violence is the first resort of the incompetent." Well, actually, that was from X-Men, but I dropped the idea and just looked forward and remained silent. Then he started to push his pelvis into the side of my hip, like a rude dog humping his master's leg.

Now, I'm from New England, and we don't like to get too close to each other, not even during sex, but especially not in the lunch line. Unfortunately, my hand was down by my side and I could actually feel something dangling under his pants. I've been in a few confrontations, and though I have never done it, a couple of times I've seen a guy grab another guy by the balls. Usually, the grabbee becomes very compliant and humble because, after all, the grabber has him actually and factually by the balls. The trouble is, when you finally let go he will either slowly walk away (bow-legged), or give you an indignant punch in the face. I decided the demerits would be worth it. This had to stop.

Just as I was about to confront the guy, I heard a very loud, "WHAT THE HELL ARE YOU DOING?" In a split second, Lieutenant Emory was five inches away from the face of my tormentor, shouting, and "Stand at attention when I am talking to you! Do you think OCS is a joke: yes or no? These men worked their butts off to get into OCS and you think it's funny? You think it's a joke? What's your name? Who's your section chief? I want to see all three of you at OCS offices with your section chiefs at 1330 hours! Do you understand?!"

My tormentor and his entourage were very compliant and humble. Former Army drill sergeant Emory kicked ass and took names. He looked at us and said, "Good job, men." It occurred to me we were his bitches and he wasn't the type who shared.

Right after lunch, we had a short break. Clark and Heistand came up to me and said, "I thought you were going to slug the guy." I replied, "Are you kidding? I didn't want it to stop. That's the best sex I had all week!" It's ironic, but when a big guy kids about his sexuality it's perceived as absurd. If a small guy does, it confirms all doubts.

∞

The Coast Guard has two primary sources of officers: graduates of the U.S. Coast Guard Academy who attend a beautiful campus on a hill overlooking the Thames River in New London, Connecticut, and the graduates of the Reserve Officer Training Program, or Officer's Candidate School, located in a swamp in Yorktown, Virginia. The Academy had bricks covered in Ivy, and Yorktown had lime-green asbestos shingles covered in mildew. At that time, both programs were producing around 175 officers a year. In theory, the graduates of both are equal and start duty after graduation as ensigns.

However, the Academy program is a four-year program and provides graduates with a commission in the U.S. Coast Guard and a top-rated bachelor of science degree upon graduation. The program is absolutely world-class and costs the government millions to maintain. The OCS program, on the other hand, costs significantly less to produce officers -by some estimates only one-fiftieth of what it costs to run the Academy. This bears repeating: the Coast Guard spends about 50 times more on Academy graduates that on their OCS counterparts. The Academy's training vessel is a beautiful tall ship called the Eagle that was taken as war booty from Germany after World War II and has hosted tall-ship regattas. In stark contrast, the Officer Candidate School had the Cuyahoga, a fifty-one year-old ex-patrol boat, which at the time was the second oldest commissioned vessel in U.S. government service. (The oldest was the USS Constitution, Old Ironsides, launched in 1797 and long a museum ship in Boston Harbor.)

The U.S. Coast Guard Academy's mission is "to graduate young men and women with sound bodies, stout hearts, and alert minds, with a liking for the sea and its lore, and with that high sense of honor, loyalty and obedience which goes with trained initiative and leadership; well-grounded in seamanship, the sciences and the amenities, and strong in the resolve to be worthy of the traditions of commissioned officers in the United States Coast Guard in the service of their country and humanity." The OCS mission is all of fourteen words: "Prepare Officer Candidates to serve effectively as officers of the United States Coast Guard." We were short-changed even on the mission objectives.

Unlike the merchant-marine academies, which attempt to license their graduates as merchant marine officers, the Coast Guard simply gives the fundamentals of navigation, piloting, and seamanship, and it then takes typically three months of underway time to qualify as a deck officer. Interestingly, prior-enlisted boatswain's mates who have already served afloat before going through the OCS program typically qualify as an OOD (Officer of the Deck) in less time than an Academy graduate.

This dichotomy within the Coast Guard between Academy graduates and OCS graduates creates some resentment. Academy graduates are called "ring knockers" because they wear oversized class rings and tend to annoyingly knock them at meetings as if to say, "Remember who I am." I got a first taste of this resentment when I was double-timing around one day with a fellow OC, who was a mustang, and I was redressed for some infraction by an officer with a ring. After the Academy graduate was out of earshot, the OC asked me if I knew the three most overrated things in the world. I said, "Tell me."

He said, "Home cooking, home fucking, and Academy graduates."

A little shocked by his profanity, I asked, "In that order?"

Of course, anyone insulted by this joke must reply in kind, and the Academy graduates show their respect for OCS "reservists" by mimicking our ostensible salute: both hands upturned at the forehead and a "What, me worry?" shrug of the shoulders.

My comparison of the two tracks is not a complaint that too much is being spent on the academies -in my view it is nearly impossible to spend too much on education and training. My complaint is that, in theory, OCs of the ninety-day wonder variety and Academy graduates were supposed to be equivalent. It is impossible to put the same amount of training into a seventeen week program as in a four year, 200 week program. Nonetheless, the Coast Guard tried this strategy, and they tried to do it on one-fiftieth the budget.

The Coast Guard's first officers' training school was initially on a twenty-three-year-old schooner, the Dobbin, where cadets spent two years harbored in New Bedford and sailing coastal cruises, learning seamanship and navigation. While most of their curriculum was math, there were also classes in law, English, French, and history.

After the first two years, the inaugural class graduated and the Dobbin was replaced by the Chase, a bark in service until 1890. While bark Chase may sound like a dog's bad habits, the Royal Navy started using the term bark for a nondescript vessel that didn't fit neatly into a category (though by the nineteenth century a bark was defined as a three-masted square-rigger with only fore-and-aft sails on it's after mast). Treasury Secretary Salmon Portland Chase graced this particular bark with his last name. Many Coast Guard vessels carry the name of treasury secretaries. Sucking up to the guy who pays the bills is always a good strategy. Eventually the government's auditors decided the program was too expensive and the training ship was dry-docked. The primary source of Coast Guard officers became the Naval Academy: the officers in training who were unable to pass the final test for the Navy -not the best way to get the cream of the crop.

It wasn't until 1910 that the Guard went aground and utilized land-based classrooms, courtesy of Congress transferring waterfront property in New London to the Coast Guard.

Many officers received direct commissions from the mergers of the pre-Coast Guard services based on their education and management positions. When the Revenue Cutter Service merged with the Life-Saving Service, there were 2,000 Revenue sailors and 2,300 Life-Saving surfmen. Nearly all the top brass and most of the commissioned officers came from the Cutter Service. Being master or officer of a ship was a prestigious calling that required education and breeding, and the Life-Saving crews were surfmen who came from humble backgrounds: fishermen and small-boat operators. The cultures clashed, and just five years later, after World War I, over 90 percent of the Coast Guard officers petitioned the executive branch to stay in the Navy. The pay was a lot higher in the Navy, too.

Although it is somewhat rare now, in the past many people were awarded direct commissions based on experience, leadership skills, and political connections. Colonel Sanders didn't go to West Point. The Coast Guard still awards direct commission to lawyers, engineers, and graduates of maritime academies.

The Coast Guard's relationship with the merchant marine has been close. In 1916, the Coast Guard took over the responsibility of licensing the merchant marines' ranks. After World War I, U.S. leaders knew that economic and military security depended on the transportation of goods and people over oceans. The U.S. merchant fleet wasn't growing fast enough and, moreover, most of its workers were foreign and poorly trained. The politicians wanted trained able-bodied seamen and officers who could be quickly integrated into the Navy in a time of war. During the build-up to World War II, the Coast Guard was given the assignment of training merchant mariners. By 1941, they had trained 5,000 merchant marines, and as American involvement in World War II increased, merchant marine academies went from eighteen-month courses to twelve- month courses, and finally to six-month courses. Obviously, students learn quicker under pressure.

My brother Bill graduated from Massachusetts Maritime Academy in June 1975, receiving a degree and a commission as an officer in the U.S. Navy Reserve. "Mass Maritime" produces officers for the merchant marine. A merchant marine is not a jar-head who likes to sell stuff, and the term itself is actually incorrect despite common usage. The merchant marine is the fleet of commercial ships registered in the U.S. that become part of the naval auxiliary during times of war. The people who man these ships are merchant mariners, or just mariners, seamen, or simply seafarers.

After graduation, my brother chose to work in a non-union job with the Woods Hole Oceanographic Institution on the research ship Knorr. The chief engineer, Buzzy McLaughlin, was our next-door neighbor, and it was Buzzy who was the inspiration for my brother to join.

Buzzy McLaughlin was a tall, dark-haired, good-looking man, the strong, silent type. Mr. McLaughlin spent his free time carving whale's teeth into scrimshaw and putting together one of the best HO train model sets I've ever seen in my life. Once, the Falmouth Enterprise published an article about both his scrimshaw work, a collection of more than 400 priceless pieces, and Nantucket baskets woven by the men who manned the Nantucket lightships to fill their time while they rested and waited for the rigors of duty: maintaining the ship's light bulb. Bill ended up learning how to carve scrimshaw, plus learned the ins-and-outs of the merchant marine trade and the science of diesel engineering from Buzzy.

On Bill's first trip down the East Coast, the Knorr had a port call in Miami. Bill wired me a round-trip ticket to visit him there, and when I arrived at port to stay on the Knorr, I walked by a guy carrying a TV set and really didn't think much of it. Soon I found out the TV set belonged to Bill's shipmate, who was not overjoyed by the fact that a stranger permanently borrowed his TV and walked by me and the guard with it. I was twenty-two, and this was the first time I'd ever been to Florida and the first time I ever slept in a ship. I spent some liberty time with Bill and the crew and realized how much fun it was to party with sailors instead of just bouncing them when they'd partied a bit too much. I once thought fraternity guys could party but these merchant mariners made us look pathetic. I knew then it was a sailor's life for me. When you only have a few days in port, you tend to make the best of them, and that urgency of purpose gives sailors a reputation that they well deserve. For a twenty-two-year-old, the opportunity to work hard, play hard, and balance risk and adventure was alluring.

Bill sailed on the Knorr for thirteen straight months, which is highly unusual for a merchant mariner. Most work two to three months on and then two to three months off. For sanity's sake, they need as much time off as possible. But my brother was never one who sought sanity.

Research Vessel Knorr was run by the Woods Hole Oceanographic Institution (WHOI, pronounced "hooey"), but the boat was owned by the U.S. Navy, which leased it to WHOI for one dollar a year. This arrangement stipulated that the Navy could use the R/V Knorr and other nautical research assets in cooperation with WHOI on research projects and other requirements. The Navy's relationship with WHOI paid huge dividends when WHOI's famous manned submersible, Alvin, was involved in the recovery of a sunken two-billion-dollar hydrogen bomb lost in a midair collision over the Mediterranean off the coast of Palomares, Spain, in 1966. An H-bomb is something you don't want to just leave lying around.

While a lot of people presume the Alvin was named after a chip-munk, it was named after its designer and inventor, Alan Vine, al-though now things are really invented by teams rather than individu-als. Alan Vine Jr. was a regular at the famous Captain Kidd.

WHOI submersibles, including the Alvin, were used in the dis-covery of the Titanic. While the Alvin was not involved in the initial discovery, its later exploration led to some of the most spectacular pictures of the sunken liner. While many people would agree that the discovery of the Titanic in 1986 was an incredible event, in fact, Cap-tain Bob Ballard's greatest discovery was on a Pacific cruise.

I remember Bill telling me about his second cruise with WHOI, off the Galapagos, when the research team uncovered a vast array of life nearly two miles under the sea. At the time, most scientists thought that food systems and the basis of life itself couldn't penetrate more than 400 feet down, but on Bill's trip the research team discovered that the black smoker vents (undersea hydrothermal vents that produce superheated seawater, the result of tectonic collisions of plates, releas-ing the earth's molten lava) produce life-sustaining heat and sulfuric acid. This warm acidic brew is used by bacteria to create carbon-based energy without sunlight.

Chemosynthesis, as it's now known, showed the world that life doesn't necessarily have to depend on photosynthesis. Some consider this one of the greatest discoveries of the twentieth century. Astrono-mers can now look at planets far away from the sun and search for life that is chemical- and heat-based. Europa, one of the four Galilean moons of Jupiter, is completely covered with an ice sheet, under which many astronomers think water flows due to heat from tectonic activity. Astronomers hold out hope that Europa could be producing chemos-ynthesis-based bacteria. In contrast, most mothers across the world cringe at the idea of finding yet more bacteria in the hidden corners of the universe.

The flora and fauna in this underwater universe were not as ap-pealing as those found in a coral reef. There were twelve-foot-long tube worms and giant clams. The clams got Bill's attention because he envisioned that, while unattractive, each clam was probably capable of producing a dozen pots of New England clam chowder —although he imagined they would be quite tough. When the clams were brought to the surface, the very distinct odor of rotten eggs made him conclude that they could only be used for a good Manhattan clam chowder —although he would consider that an oxymoron, as any chowder connoisseur would.

After the Galapagos, Bill and the R/V Knorr headed down to the Antarctic Ocean. The low-pressure storms they endured were relentless and terrifying. Once past the lows, they encountered the polar highs of the South Pole. As the southern latitudes increase, sailors refer to them in ascending order of ferocity: the roaring 40s, the furious 50s, and the screaming 60s.

The 279-foot Knorr is a relatively small ship, but it contains almost 3,000 square feet of lab space. The vessel is underpowered, with eleven knots maximum cruising speed, but it has a unique form of propulsion: instead of using screws or a normal propeller, it has an eggbeater-type prop, and its variable pitch can make it turn practically on a dime, which is great for staying on an exact spot, but not so good for fighting high seas.

The storms of Antarctica started to take a toll on the crew and the ship. The relentless vibration from the high seas seemed to cause every bolt and screw to loosen. A piece of machinery that came loose in the engine room on the high seas would be a deadly projectile, destroying other equipment and causing the immediate and certain demise of the ship; the crew went around tirelessly, day and night, retightening every nut, bolt, and screw to keep the ship from falling apart in the middle of the ocean.

One day, in particularly high seas, Bill got a call from the bridge to go to full power. He pushed the throttle up to full. After he was relieved from watch, he went up to the bridge to witness the sea's fury firsthand. Wave after wave towered over the Knorr, and then the vessel started to broach, to roll broadside to the waves. Bill heard the mate tell the able-bodied seaman to set the cycloidal pitch to full right rudder, but it already was. Then he called the engine room for full power, but the engine already was at full power. There was no more juice left to fight the storm.

At that point, Bill concluded that he was about to die, so he grabbed his life jacket, went back to his bunk, wedged himself against the bulkhead with his life jacket under his chest, and decided he'd rather die asleep in bed. The waves eventually subsided a bit, however, and my brother woke up alive.

Almost every day the scientists complained vehemently that they couldn't run their experiments. My brother knew they should thank their lucky stars that they weren't running their after-life experiments in Davy Jones's locker.

∞

While supporting scientific research has never been an exclusive Coast Guard mission, the service has traditionally supported various other organizations in furthering their research. Around 1970, however, there was movement in the government to create the National Oceanic and Atmospheric Agency, which would have included the Coast Guard, in order to administer the nation's civil marine and atmospheric programs. Instead, the president and congress created the National Oceanic and Atmospheric Administration and the Environmental Protection Agency.

One of the primary duties of the Coast Guard in the postwar period has been to use its vessels as ocean stations. Cutters would be employed along major air and shipping routes in the Atlantic and Pacific Oceans to provide navigation, communications, and search-and-rescue services. Sometimes it worked. Back in 1947, the Coast Guard cutter Bibb rescued all sixty-nine crew and passengers of the American-owned flying boat Bermuda Sky Queen. En-route from Ireland to Newfoundland, the plane had run low on fuel battling fierce headwinds and, despite thirty-foot seas, had to be ditched in the North Atlantic. While oil on water has been used since biblical times to quiet the seas, it is now frowned upon, sometimes with the imposition of fines that approach the GDP of a small country; but the Bibb dumped oil to smooth the water and managed to rescue everyone without injury. The Bermuda Sky Queen crash resulted in one of the Coast Guard's most outstanding rescues.

Cutters on ocean station duty collected meteorological and oceanographic data on patrol vessels called weather stations. While some people missed the ocean station duty, I was glad that boring function had gone the way of the lightship.

The Coast Guard has also been involved with scientific research in polar regions, thanks to their fleet of icebreakers. The Coast Guard's involvement in polar operations dates from the purchase of Alaska in 1867. In fact, for nearly seventy years, revenue cutters represented the only regular U.S. government presence in Alaska. During the pandemic of 1918, the Coast Guard brought supplies, medicine, and doctors to remote Alaskans struck down by the illness. The Coast Guard also buried the dead. During my lifetime, when scientists were trying to identify the nature of the bird flu epidemic, they decided to compare it to the Alaskan pandemic virus and went to the Coast Guard logs to locate the graves in Alaska. They were able to extract the virus from the permanently frozen corpses and concluded that the 1918 pandemic virus was very similar to the bird flu virus, which of course raised alarm worldwide.

Leading up to World War II, the U.S. Coast Guard oversaw the design of seven deep-draft polar icebreakers, and these wind-class breakers had a long distinguished history -most served until the late 1970s. Three served the Soviet Union in World War II as part of the lend-lease program.

Another venerable icebreaker, the Northland, was sold shortly after World War II. Renamed Jewish State, she was used to run the British blockade of Palestine, transporting Jewish immigrants. After the creation of the state of Israel in 1948, the Northland, now renamed Matzpen, became the first warship of the new Israeli Navy. She later served as a training ship and then as a tender to the Israeli motor torpedo boat fleet. The ship finished her career in 1962 as an accommodations ship for the port command at Haifa.

In 1975, the Coast Guard commissioned two new icebreakers to replace its aging fleet of World War II -vintage vessels, the Polar Sea and Polar Star, which were painted red to be visible in the ice. Both vessels were plagued with mechanical problems, but these ships were preferred duty for many of my OCS classmates.

The Coast Guard was involved in the negotiations for the founding of the International Ice Patrol. While many countries signed on, the Coast Guard did nearly all the patrolling. The Ice Patrol allowed the Coast Guard to be the first U.S. service to enter World War II, which they did clandestinely, supporting Greenland's defense forces and chasing away a German weather station. Germany wanted weather stations in Greenland to better predict the weather about to hit the

European continent, but the Coast Guard effort kept the Germans out of Greenland.

In general, duty aboard an icebreaker was popular because you received extra pay and visited exotic ports. My classmates told me a particularly interesting story about polar exploration. About a year before I joined the OCS, a Coast Guard icebreaker finished its research mission to the Antarctic and stopped over in New Zealand for liberty. A few of the sailors decided to take a souvenir back with them, a teen-age Kiwi girl, and hid their enthusiastic stowaway in the paint locker. Incredibly, no one with a lick of sense found out about it on the entire voyage back. I imagine for a few select sailors, the return 8,000 mile trip across the Pacific to home port was a lot less tedious.

The sailors smuggled the young woman off the boat, and she lived with one of the Coasties for a short time, but she apparently grew bored and hooked up with a rock-and-roll musician and became a groupie.

The Kiwi teen finally turned herself in at the Australian consul in Phoenix, and, much to the chagrin of the naughty nautical crew, it turns out she had kept a diary. The crew was court-martialed, but the girl refused to return to testify, and her diary was excluded as evidence because what it contained couldn't be verified without cross-examining its young writer. Without this crucial evidence, the charges were dismissed, and the outraged captain called a ship movement (legal orders to be underway), took the crew out to sea, and held a captain's mast.

A captain's mast comes from a long tradition of the captain standing in front of his ship's mast conducting inquiries and, when appropriate, dispensing punishment. The mast was at a convenient location because the punishment was often being strung up on, or tied to, the mast and beaten or lashed. While the beatings have stopped since the 1850s —the tradition of non-judicial punishment is proscribed in Article 15 of the Uniform Code of Military Justice —all commands have the option of holding masts. But a serviceman has the right to refuse a mast if he is on land or in the middle of a battle. By taking the ship out to sea, the captain insured that his men did not have the right to refuse the mast. When they returned, the captain's mast was dismissed because the lawyers concurred that the rules of evidence in this case applied to the mast, too, and the diary still couldn't be considered. Surprisingly, the culprits stayed in the Guard, but as persona non grata.

The Error Chain

It would take a real libido-driven risk-taker to smuggle a female stowaway aboard a crowded military ship traversing the Pacific Ocean, but that's simply the pirate in the man who has to go out but doesn't have to come back. Or maybe that is simply the definition of a sailor. It's hard to know how many people knew about the girl. Those who knew should have blown the whistle on the wildly bone headed decision; maybe they screwed up as badly as the perpetrators. In the parlance of the time, you're either part of the solution or part of the problem. Silence is consent. On so many levels, the silence that allowed a breach of good sense as well as standard military practices was indicative of something very wrong.

7.

"Clowns to the left of me,
Jokers to the right,
Here I am,
Stuck in the middle with you."
       -*"Stuck in the Middle with You"*
Joe Egan, Gerry Rafferty, Stealers Wheel

My brother Bill graduated from Mass Maritime Academy. Having been through the rigors of military training, he warned me that OCS was going to be tough for me. His advice was simple: "Keep your head down and don't stick out." Excellent advice. I've never been able to just hide in the shade. In the military, sticking out becomes an immediate high-profile problem. After my first five days in OCS, I was almost totally demoralized.

I was the demerit king and could barely remember the reasons I joined or what it felt like to sit and enjoy a meal without harassment. In fact, I was starting to feel like a failure in everything. Clearly, every activity cherished by the military, from bed-making to shirt-tucking, was beyond my capability, and I was rapidly coming to the conclusion that everything I had learned in my life up to the moment I joined the Coast Guard was wrong.

I found myself daydreaming about running away into the night, catching a cab or thumbing a ride until I finally wound up at the Kidd, ordering a beer. Maybe nobody would miss me for hours. OK, they took roll call every ten minutes, but I could dream.

One evening, the OCS officers offered us a small break from the unrelenting head games they played. We all sat in the lobby of our barracks, which was normally off limits, and the officers broke out Coca-Cola. I found myself relaxing on upholstered furniture sucking down a Coke, and was almost giddy.

Lieutenant Emory, who was in his early forties, of medium height but with a big frame, his dark hair combed to the side, was a drill sergeant for officers. He walked with a limp when no one was watching. He was from West Virginia and had a Southern twang that had been tempered by living outside of his home state for many years.

He went around the room asking each of us to tell our stories of why we joined the Coast Guard OCS program. Some among us had been enlisted for years and applied five or six times before finally being accepted. For others, being in the Coast Guard was about tradition. One candidate's grandfather, father, and two brothers were all in the Coast Guard, and he was the first college graduate in his family. After college, he applied for OCS. After three years of applying, they finally accepted him. Three of my classmates were focused on becoming pilots, and being accepted and doing well at OCS was an essential first step to getting accepted into the Coast Guard flight school track. Three other OCs had attended boatswain's mate and quartermaster schools. These guys already had boot camp and navigation down.

While all our paths to OCS were different, OC Rick Riemer's life-track was indicative of the quality of officer candidates in the room. Rick was a few years older than I was and shorter than average, and his demeanor was similar to that of my oldest brother. He was introspective and talked like that one high school teacher whose insights and anecdotes stick with you and pop up like warning buoys throughout your life. He had vision and purpose and was all too willing to share those with all of us.

He began his explanation for being in OCS as follows: "I graduated magnum cum laude from college and went on to the New England School of Law. By the end of my first year, I felt time slipping by too quickly. My money had already left the scene. I happened to see bumper stickers with the Coast Guard's iconic racing stripes: 'Small Service. Big Job' and 'In the Coast Guard, Good Enough Isn't.' I was in precisely the right frame of mind for such messages. I needed a steady income because my family had grown accustomed to living indoors and eating. The Guard hooked me by offering a combination of adventure and family security. The poster image hanging on my recruiter's office wall was of a forty-four-footer smashing through the waves. That image alone had me signing on the dotted line, and health insurance for my family and a shot at OCS just sealed the deal."

Riemer told us his grandfather was in the Navy in World War I and he had grown up captivated by the old man's stories, by the story of JFK and PT-109, and a little bit by McHale's Navy. He had considered joining the Navy, but he didn't want to be away from his wife for months at a time. His station was search and rescue in Scituate, Massachusetts, between Boston and Cape Cod. A year after being assigned there, he was accepted into OCS and tried to put off his matriculation because his wife was pregnant. Needs of the service came first, and so here he was 300 miles away from his wife.

Clearly, almost all of my fellow candidates were dedicated and incredibly well qualified. We were all in for very personal reasons, some less romantic than others.

∞

As I learned later, the Coast Guard became the haven of college graduates with low draft numbers. During the Vietnam War, many who faced the inevitability of being drafted after their college deferment ran out enlisted in the Coast Guard. Ultimately, fear of the draft inspired more voluntary enlistments than actual draftees in all the services. The Coast Guard, National Guard, Navy, Air Force, Army, and last of all, the Marines, were the pecking order for enlistments or officer candidate programs. The deal offered to volunteers was usually better than forced conscription, and a few surprised random conscripts ended up in the Marines.

During those years, the Coast Guard became picky. While the other military services recruited college graduates for officers, the Coast Guard already had the luxury of college graduates in its enlisted positions. After college deferments ended, some say that the Coast Guard was harder to get into than Harvard. As one jaded boatswain's mate later told me, he'd rather face the onslaught of drunken yachtsmen coming out of the Lamp Post Bar in Oak Bluffs on Illumination Night than starving Viet Cong coming out of the jungle during the Lunar New Year celebration.

While it was true that some Coast Guardsmen volunteered to serve in very hazardous duty in Vietnam, most were happy defending the inner circle of the hard nucleus. Seven Coast Guardsmen voluntarily risked their lives and paid the ultimate sacrifice. The other services gave up more than 50,000 of their own.

Company Officer Emory told us about the Coast Guard's pivotal role in Operation Market Time, the most significant naval victory of the Vietnam War. He was proud to have served under OCS Commander Loy, who had been decorated for skippering an eighty-two-footer during that campaign. The Viet Cong were being supplied by boats traveling along the coast into the Mekong Delta. Most of the Navy ships drew too much water to intervene and break the Viet Cong supply chain, and so the Navy commissioned the building of fifty-four swift boats.

Since it would take nearly a year to build and deliver the boats, the Navy called upon the Coast Guard and their shallow-draft eighty-two-footers to start the campaign. During the campaign, thirty-six of these craft with all-volunteer crews specially trained for combat engaged in the battle. Inspections on junks and sampans were always dangerous, and every bend in the Delta had a potential for ambush, as depicted in the movie Apocalypse Now.

According to the best estimates, the Coast Guard was able to catch 90 percent of all the wooden boats and 100 percent of radar-detectable metal boats and ships. When the swift boats arrived, the Coast Guard brought in high-endurance cutters to augment the campaign. Market Time effectively cut off the enemy's supply by water, forcing them to re-supply over the much more arduous and less efficient Ho Chi Min Trail.

John Forbes Kerry participated in this successful battle, and his involvement would first be an asset and then a liability in his quest for the presidency. Swift boat politics would eventually enter our vocabulary as a pejorative.

The Coast Guard also assisted in buoy-tending and port security, and augmented the crews of the swift boats. The Coast Guard claimed that this destroyed almost 2,000 vessels and killed or wounded 1,827 Viet Cong and North Vietnamese. Keep in mind, however, that high body counts were essentially guesses that received great "attaboys" from superiors, and the numbers were rarely verified.

Back on the home front, there were a few underestimates of a different nature. "We have spotted three bales of marijuana. No, wait… Belay that. It's just two; that's it, just two." Two would be entered into the evidence log and the other bale would become available on the local market. There were countless rumors of such incidents, and a few Coast Guard crewmen got caught and convicted. They were severely dealt with when caught, but small and isolated crews, a relaxed attitude toward drugs, and the temptation to make a little money on the side nevertheless caused some to stray.

Everyone understood the Coast Guard's contribution on the home front during World War II —it was the last line of defense. The Coast Guard was in nearly every town and port on both coasts. Growing up in Cape Cod, I thought that the Coast Guard was everywhere.

The Coast Guard's most significant contributions in the two World Wars were sub-hunting, rescuing crews and passengers from attacked ships, and escorting convoys. But Coast Guard vessels were generally slow and under-gunned, and in World War I, the Coast Guard lost a third of its ships. In World War II, planes proved to be superior in hunting submarines, and the Coast Guard protected convoys outside of land base aircraft range. Surprisingly, the Coast Guard ended up sinking more German U-boats than the better-equipped U.S. Navy vessels. The Coast Guard would either disable the subs with depth charges or cannon fire, or use cutters to ram the subs before they could submerge. An intentional collision at sea is not for the weak of heart, and during World War II intentional collision was the most desperate measure a crew could undertake. U-boats sank 2,900 ships and killed more than 80,000 sailors, most of them merchant sailors, but America was turning out ships faster than the Germans could sink them, and the Germans damaged less than 2.5 percent of our capacity. This gave rise to the belief that the U.S. out-produced, rather than out-fought, the axis powers. By contrast, the allies sank 800 subs and killed 30,000 German sailors —an incredible 75 percent of all German submariners.

∞

During the short silence in which all of us were thinking of collisions and drowning sailors, I interrupted to offer that, during our family's annual viewing of The Sound of Music, my father used to say, "It's a good thing Baron von Trapp relocated to Vermont. Otherwise, he'd be singing to Davy Jones." I then had to explain that Georg von Trapp had received his baron's title as a direct result of his heroic exploits as a submarine captain during the first World War, and perhaps he didn't want to press his luck again. The Coast Guard training materials refer to it being the first U.S. service to capture German POWs in a manner of speaking. In June of 1942, German U-boats put two teams of four saboteurs with large weapon caches on the beaches of Amagansett, on New York's Long Island, and Ponte Vedra Beach, Florida, with the intention of blowing up factories and infrastructure on the East Coast.

The saboteurs invaded in their uniforms so that, if they were caught, they wouldn't be tried as spies, but as soon as they arrived, they buried their uniforms along with their cache of weapons and supplies. A lone unarmed Coast Guardsman patrolling Long Island encountered one of the groups of four men dressed in civilian clothes. The Coastie was highly suspicious of their activities, and the saboteurs offered him a bribe. He didn't accept it. Instead, he returned to his station and reported the sighting. When the Coast Guard returned to the beach in force, the saboteurs had already made it to the Long Island Railroad, but they were eventually caught. Information was extracted from them, and within two weeks, the FBI caught up with all eight.

The discovery of Germans working to blow things up on home soil made America paranoid. People on the coast realized that, if our manufacturing capability became vulnerable, we could lose the war. Six of the eight potential German saboteurs were executed. They should have kept their uniforms on.

The Coast Guard eventually put over 25,000 men and 2,000 dogs to work patrolling the beaches, but they only encountered one other plot and captured two more Germans. My German neighbor, George Kirkman, used to say that ten soldiers tying up the attention of 25,000 soldiers was really a victory for the Germans. The beach patrols were considered boring and tedious, although I bet they had neat shell collections that could beat any octogenarians on Sanibel Island.

∞

My friend's father served in the Coast Guard during World War II and had a much different experience. Soon after the bombing of Pearl Harbor, Bill McKenna's dad and two friends went to the recruiting office in New York City to enlist in the Marine Corps. They didn't accept him. He was a bit farsighted and had a bum knee from playing one season of football in college. His friends all joined. The Navy wouldn't take Bill's dad either, so he joined the Coast Guard.

After basic training, he spent some time in New York Harbor as a deckhand aboard a Coast Guard tugboat. In April 1943, as the Panamanian steamship El Estero loaded 1,400 tons of high explosives in

Jersey City and was preparing to sail, a fire started in the bilge of the engine room. The ship could not be scuttled and had to be cut loose. Mr. McKenna's tug helped tow the flaming ship full of explosives down the bay while New York City fireboats flooded her with water.

Air raid alarms rang and radios broadcasted warnings of a possible explosion as lower Manhattan, Brooklyn, Staten Island, and the ports of New Jersey were under attack by a Coast Guard-towed Panamanian freighter. The ship was finally sunk four hours later, and a half-mile northwest of Robbins Reef.

Had the cargo aboard El Estero ignited, the resulting explosion would have rivaled the 1917 Mont-Blanc disaster at Halifax, Nova Scotia, which killed 1,635 people. There were 5,000 tons of explosives onboard the ship, but luckily the explosion was not in a high-population-density area like Manhattan.

Having skirted major disaster, Mr. McKenna was then assigned as a machinist's mate aboard the Coast Guard-manned destroyer escort USS Kirkpatrick (DE-318). On his third crossing, the Kirkpatrick's sister ship, USS Leopold (DE-319), was torpedoed off Iceland in March 1944 by a U-boat and lost 171 members of her crew, the largest single loss of Coast Guard lives ever.

Bob's dad made about ten more crossings. He was in the English Channel for D-Day, and he was sent to the Pacific for the dropping of the big ones. After the war, he compared notes with his Marine Corps buddies. They spent the entire war in Kansas. I wondered whether I would be like Bob's father, tracking a seemingly safe course only to could take a deadly, unexpected turn.

∞

Many enlisted guys with college degrees fell in love with the Coast Guard and wanted to take leadership positions. They were called mustangs: enlisted men who became officers. More than half of the guys in the room were mustangs. There were only eight candidates like me, fresh college grads, and there were no women in our class. There were two women in the class before us, but both had washed out before we arrived. There were two women in the class after us, and one is now Captain.

In fact, the Coast Guard was the first gender-integrated American armed service. In 1973, Congress ended the Coast Guard's Women's

Reserve as a separate entity and made women eligible for active duty in both the regular Coast Guard and the reserve. Men and women were to serve side by side. That same year, the Coast Guard opened OCS to women.

Going back even further, lighthouse service has always been a family business. When men left to fight during the Civil War, wives took over the responsibilities of preventing accidents and saving lives. One such woman was Ida Lewis, a lighthouse keeper and a life saver. Over a life saving career of 50 years, she pulled 23 people and one sheep from the water. When President Grant came to honor her, he ended up getting his feet wet, which his aides worried might reduce his enthusiasm, but he quipped, "I've come to see Ida Lewis; and to see her, I'd get wet up to my armpits if necessary." When she died, every ship in Newport Harbor tolled its bell for Ida Lewis, for the lives she saved and her long tradition in the service.

The Coast Guard led the other U.S. military service academies in gender integration of their academy as well. In 1976, the first female applicants entered the CGA as part of the class of 1980. This meant the class of 1979 was the last all-male class, or the "Last Class With Balls," LCWB —apparently a source of deep pride for some.

While the Coast Guard attitude was by and large progressive, more than a few sailors didn't want to sail with women. This LCWB tried to leave a lasting legacy. The official U.S. Coast Guard buoy system scheme, carried on placards and official navigation texts on the bridge or pilothouse of all U.S. documented and registered vessels, pictured buoys with the numbers 7 and 9 (for the '79 class), the lettered channel markers L, C, W, and B, and the two buoys 8 and 6. As in: "1979, the Last Class With Balls, 86 the women." When the Coast Guard leadership discovered the subliminal message, they 86'd the perpetrator.

I remembered first hearing the term 86'd back at the Kidd when Bill Wixon yelled, "Eighty-six that guy!"

I knew exactly what he meant for me to do, but I had no idea why it was "86." I remember Bill sharing a little liquor-lore with me: "There was a speakeasy back in the Prohibition called Chumley's, which was up the coast in New York. In those days, the entrances were private, and this one was at 86 Bedford Street. During Prohibition raids, the New York cops on Chumley's payroll would give a heads-up just before the raid and the bartender would announce "86 everybody!" This meant that the patrons were to run out of the 86 Bedford entrance while the cops came through the courtyard door."

I'd seen guys 86'd from the Captain Kidd, but they usually didn't leave on their feet. The military adopted the term 86'd for anything that should be discarded. Most seem to think it referred to Article 86, but no Article 86 exists.

∞

Looking around the room again, I realized there were no minorities among our OCS class. However, our OCS class did take two exchange students from Indonesia and three from Costa Rica who were going to start coast guards in their countries. The Coast Guard has long served as a world model and has always taken great pride in training other nations' coast guard officers, and the Coast Guard often went out of its way to be accommodating. Perhaps, in this case, they were too accommodating.

We had one warrant officer, Tim Stone. A CWO, or chief warrant officer, is a specialist who has most of the privileges of an officer but is technically lower in rank than an ensign. An ensign is the most junior officer, and it was the lowly ensigns who used to carry the flag into battle —they were essentially poorly armed targets. There is an old saying in the Coast Guard: "Ensigns and warrants call each other sir, and the ensigns mean it." The next rank is lieutenant, and, like gas, there are multiple grades: junior grade (jg) and full lieutenant. The warrant officer and the exchange students only had to take the classes; they stayed in the bachelor officer quarters and ate at the officer's club.

Finally, the room turned to me and I was jarred back from my usual state of daydreaming with a subplot of reality. "OK, Officer Candidate Eident, why did you apply for OCS?"

To this day I don't know why I said it -maybe because of a sugar high from the Coke —but I said, "Well, lieutenant, the judge said to me, 'Either join the Coast Guard or go to jail,' and here I am."

No one laughed. The lieutenant glared at me and muttered, "Smart ass."

I flashed back to my brother Bill's advice. Damn, I just made myself the lightning rod for every ill deed our platoon could commit. The other response I'd considered was as follows: "I was very interested in the environment, and I wanted to be part of the 'Clean Water Act Super Fun' that the Coast Guard manages. But I didn't realize there was a 'd' in the word." That might have gone over a little better.

I was, in fact, very concerned about the environment. Everyone on the Cape and Islands had had a wake-up call on December 15, 1976, when the Liberian-flagged oil tanker Argo Merchant ran aground twenty-five miles southeast of Nantucket with a cargo of 7.7 million gallons of fuel oil, enough to heat 18,000 homes for a year. The Argo Merchant was more than twenty-four miles off course, and she carried two unqualified crew as helmsmen, a broken gyrocompass, inadequate charts, and an inaccurate radio direction finder. The ship had recorded fourteen marine casualties and had logged two small spills in both Boston and Philadelphia. The Coast Guard commander of the First District tried to have her banned in Boston and in the rest of the U.S., but international treaties wouldn't allow it.

Group Woods Hole and the Cape Cod Air Station rescued the crew of thirty-seven and were planning to try to either refloat the Argo Merchant or pump the oil out of her. The economic life of Cape Cod, Nantucket, and Martha's Vineyard depends on pristine beaches and fertile sea beds, and now all of the beaches and the sea beds were in jeopardy. For six long days, Cape Codders and Island residents stayed glued to their TVs and radios, hoping the Coast Guard would save day. The high winds and ten-foot seas hampered containment efforts, and on December 21, the Argo Merchant ripped in two.

Fortunately, northwesterly winds blew the 6,000-square-nautical-mile oil slick offshore and coastal fisheries, beaches, and my prized shellfish beds were spared the worst. Nature saved the day by providing the ultimate solution to pollution —dilution. The floating pieces of the ship itself became a hazard to navigation, and on New Year's Eve, the Coast Guard cutter Bittersweet sank the battered wreck with twelve shots from her forty-millimeter gun.

One of the main duties of the early Coast Guard was taking care of derelicts, not the kind that sleep in parks but rather the shipwrecks that hamper navigation, which is not an easy job when you consider that most shipwrecks are near whatever sank them. The Coast Guard would either tow them out or blow them to smithereens. What young guy wouldn't think: "Cool, and you get paid, too?"

∞

I should have told that story. When Lieutenant Emory's turn came, I realized just how offensive my irreverence had been. He slowly came to his feet and said, "I served seven years in the Army, working my way up from enlisted to officer, and I served two tours in Vietnam. On my last tour, I was wounded, along with five of my men, by 'friendly fire,' which forced my medical evacuation from Vietnam for surgery stateside. I was stationed in a recruitment office as the officer in charge of notifying families, flights for the bodies, and helping loved ones deal with the services and funerals. These duties were broken up by time I spent in the VA Hospital. I had more than a half dozen leg operations and months of physical therapy to restore use of my leg. The leg wasn't perfect, and so I was handed a medical discharge from the Army.

"I found a civilian job, but my daughter had cerebral palsy and I needed better medical insurance than my job would provide. I kept up pretty intense training on my leg. With my body doing its best to recover completely, I really felt I'd be able to get back into the military. I applied to the Army, Navy, Marines, and Air Force; but they were all cutting back and didn't want to take a chance on me. Thank God and the Coast Guard, after two years of applying, the Coast Guard took me in as an enlisted, a second class petty officer (E5)."

I thought to myself, here is a highly decorated soldier, former drill sergeant, and veteran who was wounded in action, and they didn't want to take a chance on him? He had to go back through boot camp? At least he must have made it through without any demerits.

Emory went on. "I applied to OCS, but there was a regulation against former officers from the other services going to the Coast Guard OCS. I guess I'm not the kind of guy who takes 'no' for an answer, so I appealed, and appealed again, challenging the rule. I finally got the article changed. I went to OCS and served for two years in a marine safety office."

The scuttlebutt was that Commander Loy, who had just taken command of OCS, heard about this kick-ass former drill instructor and wanted him as his tactics officer. Commander Loy wanted to take the "wavy" out of the "Wavy Navy," and there was nothing wavy about Emory.

∞

It seemed clear why Emory was here. So, why am I here? Was this in my blood? Was the connection with the sea so deeply embedded in me, in my childhood, that I've made decisions based on things I barely remember? Was it the sea chanteys we used to sing when I went out as a four-year-old fishing crewman with my dad and uncle? None of us could really sing, but the shanties kept me from getting seasick and bored. Sea shanties are songs that are sung when the crew is working together to haul up anchors or batten the sails:

Cape Cod girls ain't got no combs
Haul away, haul away
They brush their hair with codfish bones
And we're bound away for Australia

So heave away, me bully, bully boys
Haul away, haul away
Heave her up and don't you make a noise
And we're bound away for Australia

Cape Cod kids ain't got no sleds
They slide down the hills on codfish heads
Cape Cod girls ain't got no frills
They tie their hair with codfish gills
Cape Cod cats ain't got no tails
They lost them all in the northeast gales

I had to sing these words in the third grade, and I thought the song made us look like hopeless, stupid idiots. My Uncle Frank, who lived in Worcester, used to say that Cape Cod girls didn't actually comb their hair with codfish bones —they just smelled like they did.

When I was ten years old, Steve Dodigan passed his paper route down to me, and I began hawking papers at the Falmouth Harbor. Along with the route came his delivery assistant, his dog Jet. Jet would make the trip with me any time Steve wasn't around. I made three cents a copy, and with twenty papers, I should have made only sixty cents, but I never failed to come back with less than five dollars. The boaters frequently gave me a quarter for the ten-cent paper, and the people in the moorings used to give me anywhere from fifty cents to a dollar. It probably helped that I never wore shoes and usually had cutoff jeans and a well-worn T-shirt. Accompanied by the black dog Jet, I probably looked like a salt-covered version of a Norman Rockwell print.

I swam out on my back and doing a one-arm backstroke, with my other hand holding the newspaper up high. One guy just gave me the dollar and said, "I didn't want the paper." The next weekend, he called me out just to show his friends. I felt like a performing seal, and when Jet was following me, we were a full act. It's amazing how much a black dog swimming looks and sounds like a seal.

I also used to hang out at the landing and help boaters, many from Boston and Worcester, launch their boats. These proud boat owners would see water action about two weekends in each year on average. There are really only nine weekends between the Fourth of July and the last week in August, and three of those are bound to have bad weather. The average guy has to go to at least one wedding and one office picnic knocking out two weekends. His remaining four available weekends usually include two weekends when his motor doesn't work or his trailer is broken, and so, when he DOES go out, he better have fun because it's probably costing him $1,000 an hour.

This absolutely desperate intention to have fun caused most captains to become somewhat less than human. These people often didn't know they could jackknife their trailer, or at least didn't want to go down and release it, and so they were more than happy to pay me a dollar or two to hold their boat while they parked their cars.

I've always been interested in statistics, and I've generally found that those weekend boaters with just two chances to launch the boat in the course of the summer forgot to put the drain plug in the boat about half the time. I used to remind them before they launched their boats, but despite my noble intentions, I came off as a smart-aleck kid who was making them look stupid in front of their wife and friends. That usually didn't result in a tip. If I told them just after they launched their boat and then scrambled onboard to put the plug in, the tips went up exponentially. If I told them what to do after the boat began to sink, the tip often went up further.

∞

Uncle Frank said to me, "The Coast Guard already has had over a hundred Midgetts, and now they have a clown." What my uncle was referring to was the fact that hundreds of members of the Midgett family from the Outer Banks of North Carolina —note the extra "t" —joined the Coast Guard. In fact, the Coast Guard never really worried about nepotism. The powers-that-be in the Coast Guard figured that seamanship was in the genes, and so, if one member of the family had the good sea genes, they all did.

The Midgett's claim to Coast Guard fame came in August 1918 during World War I, when they rescued the crew of the torpedoed British tanker Mirlo. Through heavy surf, dense smoke, and burning debris the crew rescued forty-two merchant mariners. The entire crew received gold lifesaving medals from the British government. All but one of the crew were Midgetts. Legend has it that anybody who's ever been in the Coast Guard has met a Midgett.

The Coast Guard always valued local knowledge, too. So much of navigating is almost instinctive knowledge of rocks, currents, weather, birds, fish, and tides; the Guard has always allowed Coasties with local knowledge to stay in one place. Unlike the military families at the Otis Air Force Base in the northern part of Falmouth, who stayed no more than three years in any one location, Coasties could often stay for nearly their entire career in a general locale.

I thought to myself: I'm tied to the sea, but why was I drawn to the military? I remembered that I constantly heard war stories from my dad, Uncle Arthur, and my brother's friends coming back from Vietnam. Of course there were war movies and popular TV shows set during World War II, and documentaries and endless docudramas of the American fighting forces barely winning, always on the ropes but always coming back for the last-minute knockout punch. My childhood recollections were wholly devoid of peace.

The world had been at war since 1939: some wars hot, like World War II, Korea, and Vietnam; some cold, like Berlin and Cuba, the continuing struggle with the Russians that we expected to continue forever. War was obviously a growth industry, which made the military a solid career choice without fear of layoffs.

While the military was a good career option, my nationalism went deeper than that. My dad and my closest friends' fathers were all second-generation Eastern Europeans. John Uchmanowicz, Jim Godlewski, and Mike Peter and their fathers were in the military, and they all Americanized their names. Eident was originally Eidentius.

Because they were all Eastern Europeans, they were not particularly anti-Communist, but they were wholly anti-Russian. The other reason our fathers were drawn to the military was because it didn't discriminate against Eastern Europeans, and so was the quickest way for them to get integrated into society. John and Mike's fathers were in the Air Force, but Jim's dad was in the Coast Guard.

Jim's family lived down the street and owned a large guest house across from Falmouth Heights Beach. Jim's dad must have worked in Group Woods Hole for ten straight years. I thought about how sweet it would be to be stationed right there in Group Woods Hole; it's not only a big exciting base but it's just up the road from the Captain Kidd. In fact, Group Woods Hole is one of the largest Coast Guard groups in the United States, with approximately 350 active duty, 150 reserve, 6 civilian, and 1,600 auxiliary personnel. It consists of 15 subordinate commands, including 9 multi-mission stations, 2 aids to navigation teams, and 3 patrol boats. It is essentially the operating unit for the First Coast Guard District headquartered in Boston.

Presuming I survived basic training, my commission from OCS wouldn't actually get me into the Coast Guard but rather the Coast Guard Reserves and I would be a reservist on active duty. Prior to World War II, reservists were comprised of two groups: volunteers who were similar to the other military reserves and volunteers who had special skills or equipment. When World War II broke out, the Coast Guard immediately called upon the reservists to protect the coast of the United States. Yachts were fitted out with depth charges, and their crews were given military issue rifles.

While no German submarines were ever sunk, many submarines were scared off and the auxiliary saved many merchant mariners and passengers who were victims of submarine attacks on the East Coast. As the Coast Guard rapidly grew in World War II, the auxiliary's mission was shifted to close-in patrols for small harbors and on-land port security.

Humphrey Bogart carried out weekly patrol duty on the Los Angeles Harbor while, on the East Coast, Arthur Fiedler volunteered his yacht and personally captained his vessel for patrol duty in Boston Harbor. Every red-blooded young American who has piloted a small vessel could imagine being a part of the great boat rescue in Dunkirk.

If that emergency rescue operation had been called for in the United States, the Coast Guard Auxiliary members would have been the ones to organize and carry it out. Falmouth was the first Coast Guard Auxiliary Unit in the U.S. to create a training program for teenagers, and I had been part of those Sea Scouts, a branch of the Boy Scouts.

Since the end of World War II, the pleasure-craft fleet has grown exponentially along with the Coast Guard's requirements to regulate and protect them. The Coast Guard has actually turned this increase into a net advantage. The Coast Guard Auxiliary's responsibilities have grown and complemented the Coast Guard. If the U.S. ever needs the assistance of privately owned small boats and airplanes, the Coast Guard Auxiliary is ready and available to help with search and rescue, port security, and events organization. This is a refreshing model of military interaction with civilians: cooperation rather than collateral damage.

Since our dads joined the military specifically because they didn't discriminate, all of my friends respected the way the military led the integration movement in the U.S. On July 26, 1948, President Harry S. Truman signed Executive Order 9981 establishing the President's Committee on Equality of Treatment and Opportunity in the Armed Services. The day after I was born, October 30, 1954, the secretary of defense announced that the last racially segregated unit in the armed forces of the United States had been abolished.

Prior to World War II, the Coast Guard, like all services, was lily white. Except for time of war, when they were allowed to die for their country, the only positions blacks held were in the mess halls and latrines. A very notable exception to this was the surfboat station at Pea Island on North Carolina's Outer Banks, which was entirely manned by black crewmen, a crew that gained a reputation for smartness and discipline.

In 1942, President Roosevelt ordered the Coast Guard to integrate. Because Coast Guard vessels were small, there could be no separate berthing or mess areas for whites and blacks, and so pragmatism forced integration. While there was significant resistance from some senior officers, the Coast Guard, perhaps under its greatest commandant, Admiral Russell R. Waesche, pushed ahead and became the most meaningfully integrated service. While in the other services, blacks were still relegated to relatively menial tasks such as mess and sanitation, the Coast Guard opened all rates (specialties) to blacks.

In the year of the presidential order to integrate, the Coast Guard commissioned its first black ensign, two years ahead of the Navy and Marines. Despite being a leader in integration, however, the Coast Guard has had a difficult time recruiting minorities. There was one black OC in the class before us, Johnny Holloway, who retired as a commander, but none in my class or the class that followed.

There have been notable exceptions however. The most famous ex-Coast Guardsman in the world in the 1970s was a black enlisted man who spent twenty years in the Coast Guard and retired with a nice pension. His most memorable contribution while in the Guard was the creation of a rate around his abilities: he was the first journalist specialist. His shipmates —both black and white —remember him as the guy who would help write letters to folks back home. Alex Haley upgraded his ghostwriting assignment when JFK asked him to edit and stylize Profiles in Courage. In 1977, 180 million people tuned in to his miniseries, Roots, making it the most watched television event in history.

As Alex Haley's post-Guard accomplishments ran through my brain, I thought to myself, "Man, do I miss TV. In fact, I miss my whole former life, even my father." Grumpy as he was, my father was always an honorable man, which is not to say my dad's not a bigot. He is extremely prejudiced against lazy, ignorant, and ungrateful hypocrites.

∞

My father had two cottages next to our house that he rented out. Most of our tenants were from Otis Air Force Base, located between Falmouth and Bourne. Otis was one of the largest Air Force bases in the world and part of the detection and reaction network protecting the East Coast from a Russian attack. Because of our proximity to the beach, we often rented to young pilots, some of the coolest guys in the world. They had the fastest cars and the prettiest girls, and I wanted to be a pilot, but when I turned twelve and needed glasses, that ambition ended.

Once, my father rented to a special services sergeant who was a cook in the Air Force. Sergeant Payton had a small family and, like my dad, had two other side jobs. One of his jobs was mopping the floor in Woolworth's, which meant that he was able to get my brother and me all the comics that didn't sell each month. The comics were just like new, except half of their covers would have been cut off. I was nine years old before I discovered that not all comics were published with half-covers.

Sergeant Payton was our favorite tenant of all time, but not all of our neighbors agreed. He was black, not varying shades of brown like many of the Wampanoag and Cape Verdean citizens of Cape Cod. Some of our neighbors took exception to my dad renting to Sergeant Payton, and a banker who lived three houses down tried to explain the economic effects on housing prices to my dad. "There go the property values," he said, but my father was less than diplomatic, and he replied that anybody who served his country could be his tenant or neighbor. Besides, he said, "He's the best tenant I've ever had. If I had ten houses, I'd rent all ten to people like him." Clearly, my father was not making his neighbors feel any better. He saw it from a different point of view, in part because, in World War II, my dad was a lieutenant in a company made up entirely of black, enlisted men.

When our other, non-military, tenant complained and used the "n" word, my father barely kept his composure. One night, at 2 o'clock in the morning, someone threw rocks at the side of the house and yelled, "Niggers, get out." Since our other tenant usually left the bars about that time and the rocks came from his yard and because he was the only person we knew who used the "n" word and often got drunk and did stupid things, my dad jumped to conclusions and decided he was the guilty party. My police captain uncle warned my dad that with no eye witnesses there could be no presumption of guilt, but my dad didn't care and had the tenant, who was also three months late on his rent, evicted.

I remember hearing my father say, "You know what really burns me up? Mrs. Payton has been giving them vegetables out of her garden and giving them baby formula, even baby-sitting for them just to help them out. That ungrateful s.o.b. turns around and throws rocks and calls them names!"

When the Paytons left, they literally walked backwards out of the house, cleaning and sweeping so the place looked spotless. They really were our best tenants.

∞

Our family had a small aluminum boat with a 25-horsepower motor, which was way too powerful for a boat of that size. I took the boat through dozens of the inlets in Falmouth and the Elizabeth Islands, and sometimes I ventured to the Vineyard, which was a particularly unsafe trip for such a small boat. I pushed far beyond where, as my mother put it, "anybody with an ounce of brains would go." The more friends in the boat with me, the more chances we took.

My brother Bill, after he had boys of his own, came up with a formula for calculating the brain power of boys. You just take one kid's brain and divide it by the number of boys. Two boys had half a brain and five boys were down to 20% computing power. A dozen boys and you had to employ nanotechnology to measure the remaining crumb of brain. I figured I had a distinct advantage over anyone else who wanted to con a buoy tender in Woods Hole. Buoy tenders were desired sea duty because junior officers got a lot of experience maneuvering a vessel, which is what most of us wanted to do. Also, the tenders usually didn't stray too far from home port, usually getting underway in the morning and returning to port in the evening. It was one of the few seagoing duties conducive to family life.

Buoy tenders, while not as glamorous as the name would imply, are the teams that place buoys. They have one of the most difficult jobs in the nautical world. When you see a buoy marking an area that you shouldn't go near because of a rock or a wreck, you can be sure that a large Coast Guard vessel spent nearly an hour on station placing or maintaining the buoy. Coast Guard buoy tenders were known to intentionally run aground, without damaging the vessel, just to place a buoy.

Coast Guardsmen need to know every hazard, and they need to know the best time to work on aids to navigation. They need almost a sixth sense for wind speed, tides, and currents to properly place a buoy in order to keep ships and boats safe.

The Error Chain

Humans have an instinctive ability to calculate probability. In fact, most other animals do too. For example, every night a raccoon returns to the trash that is the most probable to be full of food and the least likely to be dangerous. If that one is empty, he's off to the next midnight buffet down a notch on his probability list until, if he's still hungry enough, he is forced to take a chance and cross a road or go where he might encounter an angry dog.

The odds are calculated based on one's own experiences, but to implement decisions that affect a large group based on one's own experiences can often prove detrimental for an industry or society. People who train pilots and deck officers find that negative reinforcement works better than positive reinforcement because they witness regression to the norm. If a trainer sees and then praises an exceptional docking or landing, he then expects the same level or better of subsequent performances from that pilot. Statistically, that next performance would be worse and closer to average. The trainer then concludes that praise doesn't work. Whereas, if he witnesses an exceptionally bad performance and chews out the trainee, the next landing or docking will also be closer to the norm, which in this case will be a better performance. Thus the pilot concludes that admonishment works and praise doesn't.

In fact, neither praise nor punishment can overcome the overall pull of regression to the norm. That's why we call it average. But in the long run, beyond the odds of our personal experiences, studies reveal that praise is more effective than punishment. Consequently, O'Connell's OCS now has a merit system in place.

Pre-judgments based upon our personal experiences are often wrong and become self-fulfilling prophecies. Even worse, they are often embedded into a culture and institutionalized, creating vicious cycles. Prejudice is the worst kind of pre-judgment and has held back individual men and, indeed, mankind from reaching true potential.

8.

Our courses included seamanship, navigation, and Coast Guard administration and leadership. This last was by far the best course, and Lieutenant Emory led the class in an informal setting. We covered popular management theories like transactional analysis —"I'm OK; you're OK" (my version was "They're OK; I'm not particularly thrilled") —and Abraham Maslow's Hierarchy of Needs (many of which I was no longer fulfilling, including my basic need for beer).

Lieutenant Emory talked of job satisfaction: "It is not doing the things you like to do but liking the things you have to do that make life worthwhile." It was clear he loved his job.

While the lieutenant got the big theories across, his examples and down-to-earth observations brought clarity to my new world. Everything I needed to know about management, I learned in OCS. No kidding: lead, follow, or get the hell out of the way; shit always rolls down hill and picks up speed. They didn't teach this in college. He told us that bad things happen; then more bad things happen. Risk creates risks.

We were introduced to the five Ps: Poor Planning Produces Poor Performance. My brother Bill told me it was really seven: Piss Poor Planning Produces Piss Poor Performance. I learned that when you ASSUME, you make an "Ass" out of "U" and "Me." We were told about the great sage Murphy and his belief that anything that could go wrong would go wrong, but I found out later that Murphy was really an optimist. Then there was CYA, cover your ass, and being bullet-proof —all terms and concepts with which a Coast Guard officer must be familiar.

We were told that the responsibility of a message was squarely upon the sender, but there were always 20 percent who didn't get the message, didn't understand it, or worse, didn't act on it. This derivative of the Pareto rule (80 percent of the effect comes from 20 percent of the cause) happens so frequently that it's almost scary. In the Guard, whenever someone said, "I didn't know that," the reply was, "There's always that 20 percent who didn't get the message."

∞

The lieutenant's war story of communication gone horribly wrong burned a memory into me that will never be erased: "In Vietnam, I was a recon patrol leader, and I'd take five men into enemy territory and scout where they were going to insert troops, finding the best way in and safest way out. After five months of this duty, I was called in by my commanding officer and told to take my platoon of 44 men and hold Hill 86, the only high spot in miles of rice paddies. I knew that the famous 101st Airborne had been defending the hill and had already lost 186 men, and that it was now my task to hold it with 44. For three straight weeks we defended the hill, sleeping only about two hours a night. The exhaustion was becoming more and more a factor on our performance.

"When another platoon finally arrived to relieve my troops, I told the platoon commander that he had to change the machine-gun placements every day. If Charlie knew where the machine-gun nests were, they would be able to focus direct fire right on them at night and rapidly overrun them.

"Just as my platoon was settling in for their first night of rest, I heard on the radio that the hill was being overrun. We immediately rallied and double-timed the ten miles back to the hill and retook it. There was only one survivor. He had rolled down the hill and was submerged in a rice paddy, breathing through a reed. I surveyed the hill. Amid the mutilated bodies were the gun placements — in exactly the same position as when we left. The new platoon hadn't moved them to disguise their placements."

He stopped for a moment, and in a voice I wasn't sure was for our benefit or for his own, he said, "Did I do everything possible to get my point across about moving the placements? I live with that question in my mind every day of my life."

We just sort of sat there for a few minutes. Then somebody said, "Is that how you hurt your leg?"

He said, "Well, that's another story. On my birthday, March thirtieth 1967, my platoon was heading out again and my CO said I could hang back. I wasn't willing to send those guys out without me. We soon came under fire and faced superior numbers; Charlie was right on top of us. Since we were completely surrounded, we had to call in bombing all around us. I gave the coordinates, ordered the call, and said 'fire for full effect, but don't fire the rear gun — hold the rear gun.' I heard the call being relayed with the correct coordinates and the full effect, but without 'hold the rear gun.'

"I immediately knew we were in trouble, and I yelled, 'GET UNDER COVER!' Five out of seven of my men were wounded, and my leg was torn to pieces, my ankle just hanging on by the ligaments. One hell of a birthday. Survival is all about communication, attention to detail, and being on the top of your game."

I would soon learn for myself what he was talking about. I had no doubt that I was listening to a genuine hero, someone who had been there, came back, and did it again. I remember thinking that if I looked up courage in the dictionary, there would be a picture of Emory. This wasn't the theoretical world of Ivy League professors. In Emory's tenets of survival, there were no competing theories or uncertainty.

∞

It is impossible to underestimate the effect that the Vietnam War and the very hot Cold War had on my generation. In high school, no thought of future plans could exclude what you were going to do about the draft. The first person I knew who died in Vietnam was the son of my hometown's bicycle repairman. His father was always grumpy, and I didn't like him for that, but after his son died, everybody figured he had a right to be grumpy, and I started to like him. The Vietnam War started when I was six years old, and by the time I reached high school, we were still in it.

My oldest brother, Paul, got a college deferment and later went to work at a nuclear research lab, which earned him a "critical industry deferment." My brother Chris tried to join the National Guard, but his eyesight was so bad he couldn't get in. Then he failed his draft physical for the same reason. He didn't seem too broken up about flunking that physical. Bill attended Mass Maritime and received a

Naval Reserve commission.

The nation was conflicted: most people thought the war was wrong and stupid and they didn't think anyone should die in the jungle for something they didn't believe in. I thought I should serve. Hey, while my name may start with an 'e' and an 'i', I ain't no Einstein.

In my senior year in high school, I received congressional nominations to both West Point and Annapolis with a hard-fought combination of grades and football. My dream was right there in front of me, but I started to have my doubts. One night at a party, an old friend who was a midshipman home from Annapolis on spring break (and had just lost his girlfriend to someone at a liberal arts college) was babbling to me in a drunken state. With his mouth two inches from my face, he kept saying, "You're stupid, really stupid." His spittle was hitting me in the face to accentuate the stupid.

So I asked him, "Why?"

He said I was stupid to go to an academy. He said college should be the most fun time of your life, and for him it was the worst. He went on to say that I could probably get a full scholarship to anywhere I wanted, so why go to an academy? I'm not sure how much you should rely on drunken people's advice, but that sounded pretty profound. Besides, the war was winding down, the army was getting smaller, and promotions were tougher to achieve. Most importantly, I wasn't sure that I was ready for that kind of discipline.

The midshipmen spoke the truth. I didn't have to attend a military academy. I was lucky. Generally, there is an inverse correlation between SAT scores and football ability, but I was an outlier. There is an old adage about football players: they have to be smart enough to know the plays and dumb enough to think they are important. I knew football was important because it was my only chance to go to a top academic school. I decided on Brown, the perennial cellar-dweller football team in the Ivy League. The midshipman was right in that regard, too: it was the best four years of my life. We were even the first team in Brown's history to win the Ivy League football title. Twenty years later, our team would be inducted into the Brown Athletic Hall of Fame.

But none of that mattered to Lieutenant Emory. He wasn't impressed with past credentials, like athletic accomplishments. He had seventeen weeks to tear us down and then build us back up. High self-esteem probably just meant more work ahead for him.

I remember being startled out of my usual daydream. Emory barked, "Eident. I'll give you one more chance. Why did you join OCS?"

I responded, "I think everyone should serve his country."

"With your economics degree, you could have joined the Peace Corps."

"I thought a little military discipline would be good for me."

"At what point are you planning to get a little military discipline?"

Some of my new classmates, fellow candidates, fellow inmates, laughed guardedly, and Emory glanced around the room, assessing his audience.

"So, why the Guard?"

"I grew up a few hundred yards from the sea, and I fell in love with it. I've seen its dark side, too. The sea already covers two-thirds of the world, and I've seen it look like it wants to cover a hundred percent of it. I mean, it has done that twice already according to geologists. Cape Cod was created six thousand years ago, and in my short life, I've seen houses and beaches come and go. I've also witnessed some species come and go. We spend more money researching outer space than we do our inner space. I think we're far more likely to find the next medical breakthrough, food source, or natural resource in the sea than we are on the moon."

Clearly, I had spent too much time in the Kidd talking to potential post-docs who were trying to get research grants.

"Besides that, guarding the coast seems like a noble calling."

"Why didn't you tell us that in the first place?"

"I didn't want to seem like an egghead."

"Eident, we've all heard that you were a bouncer and a football player. No one is ever going to accuse you of being intelligent." His audience laughed out loud at that one.

When I graduated from Brown, the Vietnam War was over, but I still wanted to serve my country and I had a longing for the adventure of the sea. There's an instinctive draw to the sea. I loved gathering the sea's bounty and I tended lobster pots and clammed for personal consumption and to sell. I didn't like fishing because we never caught anything. It's not that the fish weren't out there; it's just that I was an inept fisherman (at least that's what my father would say). It's hard to lose a clam -you have them cornered -but fish are another story.

My infatuation with the sea really kicked in when I started working at the Captain Kidd in Woods Hole. The best part of working at the Captain Kidd was that it had a dock and I was allowed to moor my skiff.

∞

Woods Hole, located at the southwestern corner of Cape Cod, is the Athens of the sea. It is the only deep-water harbor on the Cape; consequently, it is the jumping-off point for most of the ferry traffic to Martha's Vineyard and Nantucket. It is also the center of the world for marine science research. Woods Hole hosts the Marine Biological Laboratory, referred to as the MBL, the Woods Hole Oceanographic Institution, and The National Oceanic and Atmospheric Administration (NOAA), as well as a number of other small labs and high-tech marine science companies that have sprung up around this marine science cluster. It also is the summer home of the National Academy of Sciences. Woods Hole has the highest resident percentage of PhDs, Nobel Prize winners, and National Academy of Science members.

Woods Hole's industrial base has come a long way from its first big employer, the Pacific Guano Company, which processed guano (bird excrement) imported from Peru into either high-nitrogen fertilizer or a key component of explosives. After the company's demise, Woods Hole became a summer resort for old-money families from Philadelphia and Boston. People were attracted to views of the hilly and rocky coastline, a sharp contrast to the rest of the Cape, which is mostly flat.

The village is not actually a legal entity, but rather a sub-unit of working-class Falmouth, a fact the inhabitants vehemently deny. While Falmouth was named after the famous English port at the mouth of the River Fal, Woods Hole was named for the swift-flowing strait or passage between Vineyard Sound and Buzzards Bay (Quick's Hole and Robinson's Hole are similar passages further down the Elizabeth Islands).

Most people think that the center of Woods Hole is the landing for the ferry system that runs to Martha's Vineyard and Nantucket, but the center is really the drawbridge over the channel that leads from Woods Hole Harbor to Eel Pond, the inner harbor, which is chock-a-block full of beautiful sailing vessels and old wooden boats. The folks in Woods Hole consider themselves true Yankees, nothing like the people from the big city who wear pinstripes. Once, when the Woods Hole drawbridge-keeper, Tiny, who was anything but, moved a little too ponderously in pushing back the gates for the driver of a big, shiny Chrysler New Yorker, the driver honked, an act considered a last resort by most Woods Holers.

Tiny immediately imposed a bridge keeping work stoppage and lumbered over to the driver, yelling, "You know what you are? You know what you are? Do you know what you are? You're a New Yorker! You're a damn New Yorker!" Witnessing such profanity, which at worst would be muttered only under the breath by most Woods Holers, made the normally snobbish but polite Woods Hole blue-bloods gasp. Luckily, the driver never realized how deeply he was insulted. He did understand the intensity of Tiny's rage, however, and meekly rolled up his window. He had already hit the power lock on all the doors and his passenger had shortened significantly as she slowly slid down her seat, trying to be invisible.

A bridge tender is not a toll keeper who might drop a few quarters. The stakes are higher. If he were to crush either a foot or a mast, Tiny would have failed at his job. A bridge tender is a traffic controller who must synchronize the safe passage of sailboats, cars, and pedestrians in changing weather and tide conditions, and Tiny was uncompromising when it came to basic safety. When it was time to close the bridge, the bridge closed. If you were about to miss the island ferry, you would miss the island ferry. No one gets back on the bridge until it's fully down, and pedestrians cross first. Most of his job was routine, but occasionally Tiny yelled last minute instructions to "damn fool city sailors." If they followed his advice, they would avoid a collision. Today, there is a stone bench dedicated to Tiny's memory right by that drawbridge, a tribute to an attitude and a job well done, not to how much wealth he consolidated.

People who live on Cape Cod and in Woods Hole in particular, were lockstep with the survival of the natural environment long before "Global Warming" became a standard topic of conversation. Because of the funneling effect from Buzzards Bay and Vineyard Sound, storm water often piles up against Woods Hole, making it particularly susceptible to hurricane flooding and high winds.

In September 1938, three Coast Guardsmen from the cutter General Greene lost their lives in a rescue attempt in Woods Hole. It was the storm of the century. The last time a major hurricane hit New

England was in September 23, 1815. Throughout New England, the Coast Guard posted 1,011 rescues and for weeks after carried medical supplies and mail for hundreds of stranded coastal communities in New England. The storm destroyed numerous Coast Guard stations and the waterfront at the Academy in New London.

Sixteen years later, two more storms of the century, Carol and Edna, struck fifteen days apart, battering Falmouth and Woods Hole. My parents were victims of the aftermath, which often causes more problems than the storm itself. After a number of days without power, the local theater operator found a generator, and my whole family found a short respite from the boredom of the power outage by viewing a movie. During the film, the power came back on and everyone cheered.

On the way home in the car, all the Eident kids were excitingly talking about what they were going to do first with their newly restored electricity. My four year-old brother Bill, standing up in the front passenger seat, joined in the excitement with an exclamation: "Neat-o! Look at the fire trucks!" Fire trucks are neat, that is, unless they are parked in front of your own house. All Eidents older than four watched the raging blaze with far less enthusiasm. The power had surged on and off before stabilizing, overheating the refrigerator motor and burning the insulation, which burned the adjacent plastic trash can, which burned the wall, and so on, until our house was engulfed in a blazing inferno!

There my father stood, watching his home burn with his pregnant wife (pregnant with me) and his four small children, all of them now homeless. The first selectman walked over to my dad and handed him ten bucks. My dad, uncharacteristically, swallowed his pride and took the money, and said thanks. Thereafter he voted for that selectman early and often.

There was insurance, and like any Yankee, Dad did most of the work himself and bought supplies prudently. He expanded the kitchen and made a couple of bucks out of the disaster. He would say, however, that it was too little compensation for living with his in-laws for six months.

Then there was Hurricane Diane in 1955, Donna in 1960, Gloria in 1985, and Bob in 1991 -all storms of the century. Climate change had put New England in hurricane alley and provided the Coasties with steady employment. Whenever there was a nor'easter, my brothers and

I would go down to the beach and watch the waves. Unfortunately, or fortunately, depending on your perspective, we weren't allowed to go down to the beach when Hurricane Donna hit. For Donna, we taped the windows, secured the doors, filled every available container with fresh water, unplugged the refrigerator, and made forts under our beds. We went outside during the eye, and the world was dark and creepy.

I don't think there is anything more exciting than being near the sea in a hurricane, but only fools and those who rescue fools go out to sea in hurricanes. The Coast Guard allowed me the opportunity to go out to sea in a hurricane without being called a fool.

War stories and sea stories are closely related genres. Lieutenant Yarborough took over the floor and told the story of how he had to go out in a storm to save a fishing boat that belonged to an old Portuguese fisherman. Using a more Italian than Portuguese accent, he recounted the distress call: "Coasta Guarda, Coasta Guarda. Come'a save'a my ship. I'a sink!"

When they caught up to the boat, it was swamped and well on its way to becoming an artificial reef, but the old man didn't want to give up on his ship and asked for pumps and a tow. The ship was his livelihood, it was all he had. The cutter couldn't tow a nearly sunken ship in those conditions, and the fisherman was risking his own life, his crew's lives, and endangering the Coasties who were there to save him. The Coast Guard skipper was in a dilemma and oscillated between threatening and cajoling the old fisherman. The debate ended when a rogue wave washed the fisherman and his crew overboard. The cutter's crew quickly picked them up and rushed them to shore. While most people have a sense of gratitude when saved, the fishing captain was angry.

OC Reimer shared a similar story of a pleasure-boater who was depressed and suicidal. The pleasure-boat skipper, looking to fulfill a death wish, took his boat out on Cape Cod Bay in the middle of a nor'easter. The mayday was called in by his loved ones and the Coast Guard had to go out to save him. The Coast Guard had a hard time convincing him to come home, but after a few hours they were able to get him back to his senses.

∞

Next, OC Clark chimed in: "Peter, tell them about your high seas rescue attempt." I didn't need this kind of attention. During a midnight watch I had tossed in my rescue story among the real rescue stories, and it had seemed to generate an inordinate amount of laughter. The trouble was, the tale wasn't supposed to be funny. While many people have exciting sea stories, either dramatic rescues or fishing stories, my story involved tricking lobsters and gathering clams. Nobody ever talks about the clam that got away. I worked six nights a week bouncing or bartending in the summer, and seven mornings a week I cleaned the bar before it opened. This left the afternoons to stalk the wild and clever quahog (Mercenaria mercenaria), a hard-shelled clam that hides in the sand, often beneath eel grass, of all places. I went after "cherrystones" and "littlenecks," younger quahogs that are considered a delicacy when eaten raw on the half shell. The Wampanoag tribe used the polished, purple pearly part of their shell for trading with other tribes. Wampum became the indigenous currency and could be found as far west as Arizona. My father used the shells for our driveway and we had arguably the best-maintained shell driveway on the Cape.

I had a unique comparative advantage over other shell fishermen: I had a flat-bottom skiff that was seaworthy enough to cross Woods Hole Harbor but small enough to get into the gunk holes (small anchorages) and inlets of the Elizabeth Islands.

The Elizabeth Islands and Woods Hole were formed in the last ice age by the glacier grinding down over Canada and Maine, then across what is now the Gulf of Maine. The sea was hundreds of feet shallower, with the coast way out on the continental shelf, and when the glacier began to melt the runoff sediments (moraine) created the ridges that became Cape Cod and the Islands when the sea rose. Some half-buried chunks of ice melted later, leaving deep depressions in the moraine called kettle holes. After the glacier melted and the sea rose, one of those kettle holes became Woods Hole. This deepwater hole is open to both Buzzard's Bay and Vineyard Sound, and between tides the water rushes through in excess of six knots.

Each afternoon, I would cross Woods Hole and head to the Elizabeth Islands to find clams and to tend my pots. The Elizabeth Islands and Martha's Vineyard make up all of Duke's County, which was formerly claimed by New York (get a grip guys, you're a hundred and fifty miles away). Nantucket, 10 miles to the east, is its own county with only one small town.

Cuttyhunk, at the southwest end of the twelve-mile chain, is the only fully settled island of the Elizabeth Islands. Its claim to fame is that, in mid-fall, it is the place to catch striped bass (Morone saxatilis). The Cuttyhunk Island Striped Bass Club, founded by New York and Philadelphia millionaires, bought most of the island in 1864. Its members included President Theodore Roosevelt and William Howard Taft. The club broke up partly due to overfishing.

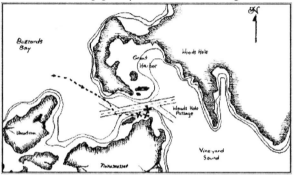

∞ Woods Hole Harbor ∞

Another island, Penikese, was once a leper colony that is now used as by a reform school. Nonamesset Island is mostly known for the Cape's least popular flora and fauna, poison ivy and ticks.

The two largest islands in the chain, Pasque and Naushon, are owned by the Forbes Trust. This Forbes is not the Stephen Forbes of magazine fame, but the family of John Forbes Kerry. The Forbes family of Boston made their fortune through trade with China when one family member became the world's leading expert in Chinese porcelain. Luckily, rich aristocrats have little interest in stalking clams. The Forbes family has assisted the MBL both through financing and in allowing scientists to use their facilities. The common sea star or starfish, Asterias forbesi, was named to recognize their contributions to science.

The islands also had a number of flocks of sheep, as well as herds of wild deer. What I liked most about the island chain was its unspoiled beauty. Unlike the over-developed Cape, these islands are pretty much in the same condition as when the Pilgrims arrived. Instead of barely squeezing out a bushel of clams in Falmouth waters in a day's work, I could extract over two bushels an hour in some of the key clamming areas of the Elizabeth Islands.

Of course, I gave my colleagues the short version. But I do remember saying, "The most productive part was Lackey's Bay."

Some smart-ass in the class mumbled, "Was that named after you?"

Undeterred, I continued. "It was so shallow and rock-infested that only a lackey could mistake it for the famous pirate hangout, Tarpaulin Cove, four miles up the coast."

There were numerous shallow areas where other lobstermen couldn't get their deeper-draft boats, so that's where I placed my pots. The second reason the Elizabeth Islands were so lucrative was that there was a very well-protected deepwater gunk hole near Woods Hole, between Nonamesset and Naushon Islands. While I collected my lobsters and clams, there were always thirty or forty yachts enjoying the beauty of Hadley's Harbor (considered the best of all the gunk holes). Many of the people on these yachts would signal to me because they could see the lobster pots and buoy stick in my bow, and they would ask whether I had fresh lobster.

Not only did I have fresh lobster, I had cherrystones and littlenecks. I was able to sell most of my lobsters at the retail rate, though there was frequently a wealthy sailboat occupant who asked for the wholesale rate. I was always taken aback by the fact that someone rich enough to own a boat like that would want to extract a discount from a college kid who was trying to make ends meet. Mind you, it was never those on the motorboats, it was the weekend sailors powering with free air.

Once, one of the yachtsmen waved me down and asked for a ride to Woods Hole to make a phone call. I ferried him across the treacherous channel, waited ten minutes while he made the call, and ferried him back to Hadley's Harbor. He gave me $20 and I felt like I was ripping him off. I tried to give it back because I thought it was too much, but then he told me he just saved $10,000 on a stock deal. Then he gave me another $20. I kept both of them, and thought, "Maybe there's another way to make a living besides clamming." But selling financial securities seemed so disconnected from what constituted real work by real people. Gathering clams and tricking lobsters was real work that satisfies a basic instinct. Saving lives and catching bad guys, that was a higher order of work that served the people. That's the kind of work that can make you get up in the morning; that was right at the top of

Lieutenant Emory's job satisfaction index.

I had to come up with a rescue story that had some weight to it, and so I launched into my best near rescue: "One day, when I was coming out of Hadley's Harbor on my way to Woods Hole, I saw the New York Yacht Club sailing from Buzzards Bay through Woods Hole to Vineyard Sound. They were on a reach with the push of maximum flow at outgoing tide, being funneled through Woods Hole. I saw four big yachts heading to the right of black can #5, which was nearly buried by the tide. I couldn't believe my eyes. Little did they know that to the left of the black can was a sixty-foot-deep channel, but where they were headed, to the right, was a rocky ledge covered by a little over two feet of water at low tide. I kept some of my pots in the area, and believe me I was the only one out there because the current in the channel, which some people claim goes six knots, was sure to exceed eight knots in these shallows that funneled the tides.

"I knew what was happening. While Woods Hole was treacherous for its narrowness and current speed, its buoys could be perceived as being backwards. We all know 'red right returning' -you keep the red buoys on your right and the black buoys on your left when you're returning from the open sea into a harbor and you can't go wrong. But, in Woods Hole, it's a little more complicated.

"According to the rules, if it's not apparent that you're entering a harbor or navigating upstream, you must go to rule number two.

∞ 'Red Right Returning' ∞

Based upon traveling clockwise around the Northern Hemisphere, you determine returning vs. leaving. Follow that? Neither did I. And neither did the New York sailors. This is why people only remember 'red right returning.' It's easy. The New Yorkers had been in the open sea and were now sailing down Buzzards Bay, which is over twelve miles across. When they saw the narrow passage through the Hole, they must have automatically assumed that they were returning into a harbor. In reality, they were leaving the shelter of Buzzards Bay and going into the greater Vineyard Sound.

"They also made another mistake: they were all just following the sailor in front of them. If he can go through there, I can too. It usually works. For a sailor used to a top speed of around seven knots, these guys may have been a little disoriented by their speed suddenly doubling."

Lieutenant Emory interrupted. "They were following like lemmings. I've seen that too often."

I thought to myself, "Aren't you training us to be lemmings?"

I went back to the story: "One after another, the four yachts ran aground on the shallow rocky ledge to the right of the channel. I quickly maneuvered my skiff to the nearest grounded yacht and saw the terrified expressions on the faces of the sailors, their crew, and families. The captain yelled out, 'Can you take my crew to shore?' As I got close, they could see inside my boat. Being so cheap, I always saved my dead bait and had a multitude of sea urchins and crabs lining the bottom. My motor had been covered in masking tape and sprayed over with two different kinds of spray paint to make it look old and useless, so it wouldn't be stolen; and at this point, the New Yorkers decided that staying on a grounded vessel in Woods Hole Harbor was preferable to a ride in my skiff.

"The captain then asked me if I could try to pull him off the rocks, so I grabbed his line, wrapped it around the cleat on the starboard side of my transom, and headed full-speed for the open water. When the line became taut, I came to a sudden and complete stop."

Lieutenant Yarborough interjected a quick observation: "Have you ever taken a physics course? Their mass was fifty times yours. They were beached on a rocky shoal, and you were surprised when you couldn't pull them?"

I thought to myself, "That's the first thing brother Bill said when I told him this story." But Bill both prefaced and followed up his comments with "you idiot." At least here it was just implied.

"OK, so I didn't bring my slide rule and vector diagram, but I thought maybe it just needed a 'nudge,' one of those small changes that have a big impact. Like you told us: make a two-degree course change five minutes before you'll need a 90-percent change." I was trying to use his own material against him, and that's why they all hated me.

Yarborough said, "It was too damn late for a nudge. Vessels on shoals need a change of tide and a lot of towing horsepower, not a nudge."

Emory jumped in to save me. "This is why experience and training matters so much. That's why we're here."

I thought to myself, "If I ever have an emergency that requires marching, I'm all set."

Needless to say, Yarborough was absolutely right. It was like tying your anchor line to the dock and then heading out as fast as you can. Not recommended.

"Now, because it was tied to the right side of my stern, the bow immediately turned to starboard, following the current. Suddenly, I was going at least six miles an hour in the current and my engine power was inadvertently supplementing the power of the current. I instantly headed for the rocks in an arc on my tethering line. I cut my motor and tilted it out of the water, and within a second my little boat was parallel with the current and directly down-current from the sailboat, taking water on at six-knots. The water was rushing over my transom, and I decided I'd take my chances drifting over the shallow seabed and released the line. As I drifted over the rocks, I immediately started bailing with my five-gallon bait bucket. The boat bounced off a huge rock, and I could see the aluminum on the second compartment cave in. I jumped to my feet and kicked the inward dent to its original position. She lost a few rivets, but was as good as old- though certainly not gold.

"I was over the shallow water within seconds. The boat was pretty much bailed out, and I tipped the motor back and returned to the channel to see if I could offer some more effective assistance. By that time, there were three or four motorboats in the channel communicating with the stranded sailors. Realizing I was the little engine that couldn't, I offered my services ferrying lines from the sailboats to the motorboats in the channel.

"Within a few minutes, the Coast Guard cutters from Group Woods Hole arrived, and there were dozens of other boats ready to lend a hand. Amateur hour was over, so I headed back to my dock in Eel Pond. It was one of the most exciting adventures of my life, like the fourth quarter in a tied football game. I was also proud of how quickly Woods Hole boaters responded to offer assistance to those in trouble, despite the treacherous current.

"I wondered if all boaters were like that. When I got back to Woods Hole, people eyed the carnage. Woods Hole residents hate to see a beautiful boat ruined, but they did derive a bit of schadenfreude from seeing rich New Yorkers screw up this royally."

∞

Perhaps inspired by my story, Bruce Wood followed with a Woods Hole story of his own, related to the ramifications of being a sound sleeper. Bruce said, "One really hot night, I was sleeping face down in my bunk with no covers or undershirt, and one of my shipmates printed Wood's on my backside in indelible ink with an arrow pointing towards, well, towards my hole. Included in this body art was a small diagram of Woods Hole harbor.

∞ Bruce Wood ∞

Word travels fast on a ship, and apparently the art was of such high quality and educational value that nearly the entire crew passed by my bunk for a viewing while I was sleeping."

That story brought down the house. Bruce's unassuming manner and deadpan delivery made him a very likeable victim, a kind of salty Bob Newhart. People who laugh together bond together. A person is thirty times more likely to laugh out loud in a group. It usually means, "I'm OK; you're OK." But sometimes it means we're OK, you're not.

The Error Chain

Strong winds, chop, reverse buoys, a lot of traffic, and an extremely fast current that dramatically increases speed: one by one, the big, beautiful, expensive sailboats ran aground on the rocks. One skilled yachtsman didn't follow the rules and made a mistake. The rest of the skilled yachtsmen followed. They were most likely high-paid Wall Street financiers, but the truth is, when one person makes a mistake, breaks or bends the rules, or takes a shortcut, the rest tend to follow. Shortcuts can usually work, but when they don't, it can be a disaster.

9.

"It's poetry in motion,
...as deep as any ocean,
...she blinded me with science."
-"She Blinded Me with Science"
Thomas Dolby

We were each assigned night-watch duty. We would wake up at 0145, put our uniforms on, and relieve the last watch at 0200. The watch consisted of walking around with a Detex watchman's clock slung over your shoulder. The Detex is a timepiece that you carry to five stations, each of which has a key attached to the wall that is used to punch the Detex clock.

Making these rounds would take about thirty minutes, and then we would go to the duty officer's deck and wait for 0300, take another thirty-minute walk, and wait to be relieved at 0400. It wasn't that the training center was a hotbed of crime that required around-the-clock security. This was just an exercise that simulated the watch cycle aboard a ship, though a watch on ship would be four hours.

I looked at the 0200 to 0400 shift as a welcome respite from the arduous task of sleeping straight through the night. There was always someone new on your watch, and the middle of the night is a good time to find out what others are thinking. One night I was on watch with Jerry Thomason and Bruce Wood, both mustangs, enlisted guys who worked their way up through the ranks and now wanted to become officers. Jerry was a Machinist's Mate 1st class and about eight years older than I was. His hair was thinning a little in the front, even without the OCS haircut. He was from Wichita, Kansas; I guess he didn't join the Coast Guard to be close to home. He probably said something like that to me; he had a sharp, dry wit.

Bruce was from Bellflower, California, married but separated, and from the way he talked, it appeared that after OCS he and his wife were going to get back together again. He was a radioman, but his last assignment was undercover work for Coast Guard Intelligence. He never told us exactly what he had to do, but you could tell that it affected his bearing and his family. My mother used to say that if you want to live a good life, "associate with good people and be honest with everyone," which is pretty much the opposite of an undercover agent's assignment.

Jerry and Bruce were about the same age as my big brothers, and with their experience in the service, I listened to everything they said. These guys were the real deal.

I remember spending many an evening in the Captain Kidd shooting the bull with scientists, sailors, and fishermen, but I enjoyed talking to the Coast Guardsmen the most. While they all had sea stories, there is something unusual about those who dedicate their lives to their country and to saving their fellow man. Bruce and Jerry had spent their entire adult lives in service to their country. There's something special about men who actually are their brothers' keepers.

∞ Jerry Thomason ∞

∞

During one of these early morning bull sessions, I said, "I'm really looking forward to being a part of a rapidly expanding organization like the Coast Guard."

They said in unison, "What!?"

I said with the new assignments, like environmental protection, stepped up drug interdiction, and patrolling the new economic exclusion zones, the Coast Guard must really be beefing up.

OC Wood said, "Our budgets are being cut and our manpower reduced."

OC Thomason added, "There is not a single high-endurance cutter on the East Coast that wasn't built before 1935. The Guard's "modern" ships are World War II hand-me-downs from the Navy and not specially built. Because of the age of the fleet and the speed of the vessels, the Navy declared the Coast Guard would be unable to perform its classic role: convoy duty."

"So what other duties are we giving up?"

"None. The Chief MK on my vessel said the Coast Guard motto has changed from Semper Paratus, Always Ready, to Semper Gumby, Always Flexible."

"You can't take on more responsibilities without more resources. Something's got to give."

"You're right: safety and readiness."

These people loved the Guard, but there was obvious concern in their voices. According to both men, there wasn't a single cutter that could pass a Coast Guard inspection. They told me that guys aboard slept with their life jackets on.

I said, "I can't believe a cutter couldn't pass a safety inspection. We must have much more safety equipment than the average vessel, because we go out when nobody else can or would. How can the Coast Guard not be obeying the rules? They wrote the rules. Why would they try to act like they're above the rules? I can't believe it."

"Believe it," they said.

As a machinist, Jerry knew firsthand how worn equipment wears down the crew, because of the extra hours required to keep things running and the stress from constantly questioning whether the equipment will perform in an emergency. I thought back to one of Lieutenant Emory's speeches that clearly showed the difference between the civilian world and the military: "Gentlemen, this is not like mis-ordering inventory or a marketing campaign that bombs on you; you make a small mistake at a critical time and people die. And there are no small mistakes; just mistakes.

Then I thought of one of Emory's mantras, so I blurted out, "Way to lead by example."

Thomason and Wood both grimaced at my comment, at a little too much pointed sarcasm aimed at their beloved Coast Guard from a virtual outsider.

They went on. Most weekend boaters had better electronics than Coast Guard boats. Everyone in the Coast Guard was asked to do more with less, and the "can do" Coast Guard officers just keep saying, "Yes, Sir. Right away, Sir." Those who dug in their heels would never make senior officer. The Coast Guard was reaching its breaking point and everybody but senior officers knew it.

I am sure the senior officers knew it, too, but what could they do?

The unpopular and expensive Vietnam War had drained the government coffers, and all budgets were being cut. In fairness, funding for flak jackets for soldiers in Nam would have had higher impact on safety than a new radar system on a cutter in the Great Lakes but... according to the frank and outspoken secretary of transportation, Brock Adams, the Coast Guard had difficulty obtaining funding for capital improvements because it was hard to convince Congress to buy a buoy tender "when there were more glamorous budget items like missiles and aircraft carriers."

OC Wood chimed in: "While everyone wants an aircraft carrier named after them, no one wants a buoy tender named after them. That's why we name all buoy tenders after my kind."

I asked, "What?"

Jerry said, "That's just a weak attempt at humor on the part of Mr. Wood. Buoy tenders are named after trees, like USCG Cedar, Beech and White Alder."

I said, "White Alder? Where have I heard that name before?"

Jerry and Bruce looked at each other the way parents look at each other when a child asks an innocent question about sex.

Jerry said, "The USCG White Alder is every Coasties' worst nightmare. On Pearl Harbor day in 1968, twenty-seven years after the 'day that will live in infamy,' we had our own day of infamy. We lost seventeen out of a crew of twenty.

"The White Alder was escorting a chlorine tanker up the Mississippi River when it inexplicably turned to port in front of a 455-foot Taiwanese freighter. It was T-boned and cut in two. This happened at night, and there was no warning for any of the crew below.

"Only three crewmen managed to get out of the ship before it went straight to the bottom, its final resting place. The three survivors clung to a navigation buoy that was on the deck transported back for repairs. Divers were only able to recover three bodies before the river sediment buried the cutter. The remaining fourteen bodies were entombed in the sunken cutter, which remains at the bottom of the Mississippi River.

"What the hell happened?" I asked.

"No one really knows for sure because the entire bridge crew died. The freighter had no damage, and they all just claimed the Coast Guard cutter cut in front of them. They did testify that there was no ship-to-ship radio contact."

"Why not?"

Radioman Wood replied, "The fact is, when travelling on a major shipping lane, you don't call every oncoming ship. You only call another ship in sticky situations, but often, by the time things get sticky, you're too busy maneuvering to try to make radio contact.

"The initial finding was that both ships were too close to the middle and the blame was shared; but eventually, the final finding was that it was the Coast Guard vessel's fault. Many thought it could never be the Coast Guard's fault. The three Coast Guard survivors never saw the vessel coming, so the only ones who could testify, the freighter's crew, had a vested interest in blaming the Guard.

"The physical evidence was buried forever along with fourteen guys like us. The uncertainty of not knowing what happened is the biggest problem. When you hear about an accident and then find out what happened, you can say, 'That won't happen to me because… whatever;' but when you don't know what happened, you can't say that and you lose your sense of control. That's scary."

Wood added, "That's why people sleep with life jackets, so if they die, at least they come to the surface and get a decent burial."

I said, "Being stuck in a sinking ship is bad enough for a bedtime story, but being buried in the mud for eternity? How am I supposed to sleep after that one?"

Then we all went off to punch our Detex clocks.

∞

When we returned, we still had thirty minutes to kill before our relief watch would arrive, so the conversation turned to blaming Washington for our woes.

We knew that the Coast Guard had more political problems than missions so mundane as to be easily fundable. The Coast Guard's biggest advocates were the gay representative from Cape Cod, Gerry Studds, and the liberal aristocrat senator from Massachusetts, Edward Kennedy. On top of this, Massachusetts was being punished for being the only state to vote against Nixon. The conservative administration had painted the Coast Guard as a service that catered to the rich eastern establishment and their yachts. There was certainly some truth to that. The Harvard-Yale boat race at New London, along with thirty other regattas, was all annual events patrolled for years by Coast Guard vessels. Today, this patrol is almost exclusively performed by the Coast Guard Auxiliary.

In response, the Coast Guard passed a rule that they could no longer tow any boat that was not in imminent danger if a commercial towing service was available. Senator Kennedy would feel the impact of these rules when he ran his yacht aground between Martha's Vineyard and Hyannis Port during the late 1970s, and a lowly Coast Guardsman refused to dispatch a cutter to his aid.

"Do you know who I am, young man?"

"Yes, sir, I do, but I also know the rules!"

Bully for him: no one was above the rules in his book! Senator Kennedy later complimented the Coastie for sticking to the rules.

The conversation that night on watch also revolved around the cultural divide between the new aviation branch of the Coast Guard and the Guard's maritime tradition.

The Coast Guard was introduced to the helicopter in 1942. On April 20 that year, the Coast Guard and Navy brass witnessed a simulated rescue with a man climbing a rope ladder into the cockpit of a Sikorsky prototype helicopter. The Navy overseers of the Coast Guard weren't impressed. As a Naval officer put it, "Hell, we're not interested in lifesaving. We want to get on with the business of killing the enemy."

The Coast Guard made their formal pitch to the Navy, selling the helicopter as sub-killer and convoy-protector, but the Navy was put off by the $250,000 price tag. The Coast Guard however, with its usual resourcefulness, was able to convince the Army to part with four of their order of seventeen. Ten months later, the Coast Guard performed its first aerial lifesaving mission when the U.S. destroyer Turner suddenly exploded off the New Jersey coast. Many believed it was torpedoed by a German U-boat. Fearing fear itself, the government wanted to play down the incredible effectiveness of German submarines, and the official report blamed it on faulty munitions. A Sikorsky R2 took off in an intense snowstorm from Floyd Bennett Coast Guard Air Station and flew to Battery Park to pick up desperately needed plasma to deliver to the Jersey beach where a Coast Guard sub-chaser and an eighty-two-footer had ferried the 167 survivors of the 200-man crew. The other 33 members of the crew haven't been seen since, and officially, no one died.

In the history of rescues, helicopters were game-changers. By 1978, the Coast Guard had ninety Areospacila Dolphines, each with a crew of five, able to cover 160 miles in an hour. Typically, it would take a cutter with a much larger crew ten times as long. New medium-endurance cutters with helipads were commissioned, but they were essentially rest stops and gas stations for helicopters. Officers were choosing between being a celebrated pilot or a gas-station attendant. Everyone wanted to be a pilot, and those like me, with glasses, were relegated to just driving boats on the sea.

I remember saying, "Given that most people who wear glasses are smart, the aviators must be a concentration of stupid people."

Wood pushed his glasses up and said he totally agreed with me.

While the Vietnam War draft drove a lot of very well-educated people into the Coast Guard, many of these college kids of the 1970s were free spirits who thought military stuff was bullshit. They planned to leave as soon as their commitment was over, creating shortages of experienced senior petty officers. These draft-avoiders took the place of people who joined for the love of the sea and their country and who wanted to make a career out of the Coast Guard. The dedicated Coasties were nicknamed by the dodgers: "Hard for the Guard!" The dodgers' unofficial rewriting of the Coast Guard service song tells it all:

Semper Paratus is a laugh
We joined to dodge the draft
We guard our shores
To protect our whores. . . .

The official version, which we sang every day while marching, was somewhat less cynical:

Semper Paratus is our guide,
Our fame, our glory, too.
To fight to save or fight and die!
Aye! Coast Guard, we are for you.

Once, during a late night bull session, someone asked if any of the Coasties present ever saved a life. Surprisingly, none of the experienced Coast Guard sailors had. I volunteered that I had, sort of, once rescued a Coastie.

One night, as I was beginning my bouncer duties at seven, the bartender warned me to watch out for a bunch of the guys in the middle of the bar. There were a few Coasties and some fishermen, and all of them had been drinking since one in the afternoon and were rowdy. There was a lot of banter between private sector and government and some of it was getting emotional. The Coasties were part of Group Woods Hole, and they were assigned to buoy tenders. Soon, two of the Coasties left because they had to make movement (legal orders to sail) the next day, and they asked me to keep an eye on their shipmate because he was "a little out of control."

Fishermen had a love/hate relationship with the Coast Guard. They were pissed off about inspections, but they liked the idea of enforcing the 200-mile limit on Russian fisherman, and when times got bad they counted on the Coast Guard to pull them out of whatever seafaring mess they had gotten themselves into.

The biggest of the fisherman, Jonathan, went to the head, and the remaining Coastie moved in on his girlfriend. I watched intently from the front door; when Jonathan returned, he and the Coastie exchanged a few words. I started to move closer to hear the conversation while gazing back at the door. The Coastie had BM3 Reilly stenciled on his shirt, a third-class boatswain's mate.

I heard the fisherman say, "What does BM3 mean, a third-rate bowel movement?" Reilly smashed his bottle across the fisherman's head. Jonathan staggered and fell against the juke box, making Gordon Lightfoot's Sundown skip.

I ran toward the middle of the bar and Reilly braced, but I ran right by him and he relaxed for a second. I then whirled around and ran at him. With one hand, I grabbed him by his shirt, with the other, I gave him a straight-arm shiver, planting the heel of my hand on his chin with my fingers wrapped around his face.

I had a theory: where the head goes, the body soon follows. I was now driving his head out the door as his feet were rapidly going backwards, trying to keep up with his head. When I arrived at the door, I gave a big push, and he fell down into the gutter. "Run," I told him.

Three fishermen led by the bleeding Jonathan, were now moving rapidly toward the door, and I thought I might impede their progress a little to give Reilly a head start. To gauge the amount of resistance I needed, I looked back to check on Reilly's escape progress only to find that he was coming back in to, in his words, "get the girl."

You had to appreciate this Coast Guard persistence, but not necessarily the level of intellect. The three fishermen ran by me, and soon a fight ensued in the street. Well, actually it was just a beating.

I was always leery of fishermen because when they fought they often used fids, a tempered steel rod used to splice the end of line (rope). Fishermen can't afford to break their hands on somebody's face —a one-handed fisherman is pretty much a danger to himself and his shipmates —so they take their fids and fashion ropes on them or put them in socks to make either brass knuckles or a blackjack. Fids are often used at blanket party's onboard vessels, which are not as festive as they may sound, especially for the guest of honor. A blanket party consists of holding a blanket over a shipmate's head and beating the crap out of him. This, I am told, only happens to people with "asshole issues."

Onboard vessels, the food is not fresh, there is seasickness, cramped quarters, no women, watch duties in the middle of the night, and a lack of alcohol; therefore, most guys act like assholes, so it takes an exceptional asshole to get the honor of a blanket party. These three fishermen were employing both applications of their fids and, judging by the thuds created on impact and subsequent groans, both seemed to be equally effective.

I had four years of crowd control engineering behind me and knew that my obligation ended when the fight went out the door. I was told never to confront anyone when the numbers were against me. But I also knew that the board of selectmen would take a dim view of a murder by bludgeoning on main street Woods Hole. I had been asked by Reilly's friends to watch him; watching him being beaten to death was probably not what they had in mind. So I executed a near perfect rolling tackle that took all three fishermen out. I have practiced the rolling tackle many times in football. A few times, in games, on a trap play I have knocked down the pulling guard, fullback, and tailback with the ball all at once. It's a rare move and it always makes the highlight films. This rolling tackle was a little easier because two of the guys were not facing me and all three were drunk.

This time, I yelled "Run!" and Reilly embraced my suggestion with great fervor and staggered to his feet. I sprang to mine and held onto the shirts of two of the fisherman to slow them down. Soon, the only thing we could see of Reilly was elbows and heels.

The three started to form a circle around me, and Jonathan said, "What did you do that for? Didn't you see what he did to me?"

My eyes moved up and down from their eyes to their hands. I was outnumbered, and I didn't like the odds. I said, "I didn't want see you guys go to jail for murder two."

One guy said, "Jail. I don't want to go BACK to jail."

They all laughed. An inside joke, I guess.

I said, "Besides, I want to buy you a round."

I am not the most free-spending guy in town, so you know when I offer to buy; it's got to be a desperate act. They knew that if they started a fight with me, they would be barred from the Captain Kidd for the summer, which would be like a homecoming queen missing twenty proms in a row. However, I also considered the possibility that maybe they weren't thinking rationally. It's funny what happens to packs of animals when they have adrenaline in their veins and they smell blood. You see this feeding frenzy in riots and police retributions. And then they started to move in on me.

Maybe I would get my chance to see firsthand if the blackjack was superior to the brass knuckles version. I raised my arms above my shoulders to fend off hits to my head and was about to follow the path of my future colleague —I knew I could outrun them. Then they all put their hands and fids in their pockets and started to head back into the Kidd.

I thought, shit! I made them back down! Then I heard the sound of a 420 overhead cam behind me. It was Officer Stone, a former teammate -a Boston University tight end -and fellow Captain Kidd bouncer, riding in a cruiser. He also had a shotgun.

I walked over to the driver's side and said, "What's up, Stony?"

"I heard there was a brawl going on."

"Nah, it must have been at the Leeside," I said, referring to our rival bar, in a voice loud enough for the fishermen to hear.

I said in a lower voice, "Maybe you want to drive toward the Coast

Guard base and see if anybody needs medical attention."

"How will I know who he is? Do you want to come with me?"

"I have to stay here and watch the door, but he should be the only guy bleeding profusely between here and Group Woods Hole."

Stony said, "I'll stay around here a few minutes."

"Thanks," I said.

He said, "Be careful,"

I said, "Thanks, but I'll be all right."

I went back inside, bought a round, and got an ice pack for Jonathan. We all laughed about the fight, and for years they complimented me on my tackle. Reilly made it back to base, but he was beaten so badly that he didn't make his ship's movement and was subjected to a captain's mast for damaging government property. So, that's how I saved a Coastie.

One of my fellow OC's knew Reilly and told me he was kicked out of the Guard a year later. They all agreed that my actions that night qualified as a "save," and that I would make a good drinking partner, if I ever got liberty. They weren't too optimistic about that prospect. I got my OCS nickname after that story: The Bouncer.

∞

Despite my heroics, I'd never be able to beat my sister Bethanie in total number of lives saved, however. Her day job derived its value from the sea. In 1970, scientists were studying a 350-million year old living fossil that has outlived the dinosaurs: the horseshoe crab (Limulus polyphemus), which has many unique attributes not found in modern creatures. Its blood is black-blue and uses copper to carry oxygen to its cells. In studying the blood of the horseshoe crab, a scientist discovered that the blood was constantly coagulating. He soon realized the coagulation was a direct protection mechanism to save the horseshoe crab from bacterial infection. Realizing that this may have some sort of medical application, he patented his findings in the name of the Marine Biological Laboratory, in Woods Hole.

Meanwhile, in Washington, for some unknown reason horseshoe crab research came under the purview of flamboyant politician, government-spending watchdog, Senator William F. Proxmire (Democrat from Wisconsin). Proxmire was the author of the Golden Fleece Award for governmental spending on seemingly useless projects that fleece the government out of its taxpayers' investment through nonsense such as horseshoe crab research. I guess it didn't occur to Senator Proxmire that we could actually learn something from a species that outlived practically every other species that ever existed on the planet.

Dr. Stanley Watson, a microbiologist at WHOI and a budding real estate tycoon, saw the potential of using horseshoe crab blood as a test for gram-negative bacteria in medical applications. My father always said that the wives of the scientists at Woods Hole constantly complained that if their husbands were so smart, why weren't they rich? Dr. Watson broke that particular mold by becoming rich while providing a great service to medicine through marine science.

∞Alantc Horseshoe Crab (Limulus Polyphemus)∞

Dr. Watson developed the process of taking horseshoe crab blood and freeze-drying it. After it was reconstituted with a swab from a material that had to be tested, it could identify gram-negative bacteria. Up until this point, the only test for gram-negative bacteria was the rabbit test, which involved raising a hybrid bunny, injecting a sample in it, seeing whether its temperature would rise, and then killing it. Dr. Watson's development of Limulus lysate proved to be more accurate, quicker (about ten minutes compared with twenty-four hours), and far cheaper. The price of horseshoe crab blood rose to $15,000 per quart, and horseshoe crabs became one of the most valuable marine species. Horseshoe crabs are mainly gathered from the Delaware River and brought to Watson's lab, the old Surrey Room Restaurant on Main Street in Falmouth, where they involuntarily give blood. I'm not sure whether they get orange juice and peanut butter sandwiches afterwards, but most are returned to the sea with less than 30 percent mortality.

My sister worked to coordinate overnight shipments to hospitals and medical centers around the world that needed the freeze-dried blood to test patients, equipment, vaccines, and heart valves. The test completely replaced the rabbit test, and researchers found other applications for horseshoe crab blood, like testing for hepatitis. The history of a great discovery often includes the "random walk and serendipity."

The Error Chain

Many error chains start with unforeseen consequences. The Vietnam War's draft improved the quality of the Coast Guard recruits, but in the long run, the Coast Guard couldn't retain enough of them and thus they suffered from high turnover. High employee turnover is detrimental to nearly all institutions.

Unforeseen consequences can be both good and bad. Who would have imagined that horseshoe crab blood could save someone's life, or that driving a gas guzzler could change the climate and put Woods Hole in hurricane alley?

Some consequences should have been predicted. Using old equipment and cutting back on funding is a recipe for disaster. But some cause and effect relationships are more subtle -moving the Coast Guard out of the Defense Department and the Treasury and into the Department of Transportation caused it to lose its political base.

While no one will ever be able to predict the future, the only way to reduce and mitigate unforeseen problems is to stick with the fundamentals: researching weird things will more than likely produce breakthroughs, and recruiting people who love the sea will lower turnover. And most fundamental of all, no matter what your budget, follow your own safety rules. Emory was right: no one is above the rules.

10.

"I see lights:
        Red over Green, sailing machine;
        Green over White, trawler at night;
        Red over White, fishing boat in sight;
        White over Red, pilot ahead;
        Red over Red, captain is dead."
        -"The Spindrift"

The piloting course was one of the most interesting and relevant classes for future deck-watch officers. Lieutenant Junior Grade Yarborough was the instructor, a young, fit officer who was almost underweight. He had been an underway deck watch officer and knew the pitfalls. In his classroom was a small poster with the following quotation: "A collision at sea can ruin your entire day —Thucydides." The ancient Greek historian made a funny.

Like Thucydides, I knew that sarcasm could often emphasize a message and make it even more real. When I was a bouncer, as the inebriated people were leaving at the end of the night, instead of saying "Drive carefully," I would tell them, "Drive as fast as you can, because you don't want to spend a lot of time on the roads when you're drunk." I am sure no one thought it was good advice, and my warning had a bigger impact through sarcasm.

Lieutenant Yarborough started the course with an old and incredibly relevant joke: A Navy admiral, commanding a ship, sees a contact ahead that he is approaching with constant bearing, decreasing range. The Admiral goes on the ship-to-ship communications and says, "This is Admiral so and so and I advise the contact dead ahead to change course."

The radio crackles, "This is Seaman Apprentice Smith, and I strongly advise you to change course."

Indignantly, the Admiral gets on the wire and says, "We're a 600-foot aircraft carrier with 3,000 sailors; I believe YOU should give way!"

"Well, I am alone in this small lighthouse, but I still think you should give way."

To those who have never been out on the sea at night this joke sounds ridiculous, but those who have been on the sea at night realize that relative motion is deceptive.

∞

A year and a half after my brother Bill graduated from Mass Maritime, he was sailing and making money. He bought a twenty-two-foot Balboa sailboat that we were able to dock behind the Captain Kidd. I soon learned that sailing was a lot more complicated than navigating a skiff. To get out of Woods Hole Harbor, you really had to sail with the tide, and while they say that sailboats have the right of way, technically a large vessel staying in the channel takes the right of way. The 250-foot ferries were on tight schedules, and if you got in their way, you had better watch out! The wake of these vessels could swamp you or create huge standing waves in the high currents of the Hole, and they could send you into a real scare.

The most feared vessel was the ferry that ran from New Bedford to Martha's Vineyard, the Schamonchi, which was small and didn't carry cars but used to cut through the Hole at full speed, sounding its horn as a warning to any vessel that might get in its way. I had a genuine dislike for and fear of the ferry that never slowed for anyone or anything, because my skiff took many a wave over its port bow courtesy of the Schamonchi, and each time I was reminded that the ultimate rule of the road is "might makes right of way."

One of the most important lessons I learned about sailing is to always determine whether the ships or other boats coming at you are going to pass in front or behind, and at all times, to consider the bearing, or relative position, of the other vessel from my point of view, and decide which way to go to avoid getting close. Because I was a self-taught sailor, I didn't know what it was called, but what I was always trying to avoid was constant bearing/decreasing range, and what I was hoping for was called bearing drift. For example, imagine your bow being 12 o'clock and a ship coming at you at 2 o'clock. If it starts to go to 1 o'clock, you have bearing drift to port and it is going to pass in front of you. If it starts going to 2:30, it's going to pass behind you. If it is at 2 o'clock and remains at 2 o'clock, it's time to change course.

I would be praying for that something I couldn't name but wanted desperately: bearing drift.

Lieutenant Yarborough gave us a very recent example of how quickly things can go deadly wrong. On November 22, 1975, the guided missile cruiser USS Belknap was severely damaged when it collided with the Carrier USS John F. Kennedy in the Ionian Sea.

The Belknap had a high probability, though we can neither confirm nor deny, of carrying nuclear weapons. It was nighttime, and the weather conditions were difficult: a strong chop and light rain. The carrier group was conducting flight operations, which required the aircraft carrier to face the wind for take-off and landings. The carrier's movement created a path like a big racetrack on the sea, with two "straightaways" and two horseshoe turns.

The carrier group consisted of one aircraft carrier, six destroyers, and a missile carrier. The Kennedy was experiencing some difficulty with one of its TACAN beacons, a tactical aid to navigation, and they called in the Belknap, which had the same beacon, to move into a closer position off the aft port side in case they needed to use the Belknap instruments and interpolate from their bridge. The young Navy lieutenant (jg) who was the OOD (officer of the deck) had never conned (commanded) the Belknap in the inner circle of the carrier group.

The first two laps on the race track path were to the starboard, and the Belknap had no difficulty keeping a safe distance, because it was on the outside of every turn. The third maneuver was to the left. Essentially, the Kennedy was cutting in front of the Belknap. The Kennedy informed the Belknap of its intention to turn to port, and the OOD then conferred with the junior OOD about what strategy they should take. The OOD suggested they slow down and let the Kennedy turn in front of them, and then follow the Kennedy around on the turn at an inner circle with smaller circumference, staying at the port position throughout the turn. The normal procedure would have been for the Belknap to slow down and turn to starboard to take a position directly behind the Kennedy on its turn, and then to follow the Kennedy's turn on the same circumference. At the conclusion of the turn, the Belknap would then return to port station. Because the junior OOD had never conned a ship or been on the inner arc of a carrier, he thought the OOD's suggestion sounded reasonable, and therefore, he agreed with him, reinforcing his decision.

Then the OOD became distracted. The Marine duty officer arrived on the bridge and gave him a weapons report of the watch. Because of the seriousness of their cargo, the OOD had to focus on making sure that weapons security was in order.

When the OOD refocused his attention, he noticed that the aircraft carrier was now directly crossing his bow and was confused with the lights due to the angle of the deck. The Kennedy's navigation lights were not properly placed on the ship and were actually in violation of maritime requirements (the lights were later changed with the application of duct tape).

The OOD couldn't figure out whether the ship was going in one direction or the other and made two false turns, one to starboard and one to port, to avoid decreasing range, constant bearing. Each time the young OOD of the Belknap made his turns, he accelerated the speed of the vessel to decrease the turning radius.

Just seconds before the collision, the captain burst onto the bridge and screamed, "Hard right rudder!" to avoid a near head-on collision.

The two ships ran parallel past each other in opposite directions, only a few yards apart, narrowly missing each other's hull. Unfortunately, the flight deck of the Kennedy extended far out beyond the hull and crashed into the smoke stacks of the Belknap. While no one was hurt from the impact, the stacks damaged the jet fuel lines of the Kennedy, and fuel rained down the stacks and into the engine room, creating Dante's inferno. The fuel also sprayed along the deck, and soon the entire mid-ship was engulfed in flames. Emergency calls went out from the Belknap and a top-secret "broken arrow" message was sent to the Pentagon, indicating the potential for detonation or burning of a nuclear weapon.

According to eyewitnesses, the fire burned so hot that it warped the superstructure and was so bright that those who were in the bow couldn't see the stern and those in the stern couldn't see the bow. Many thought the ship was going to burn in two. It took two and a half hours to put out the fire. Seven people aboard the Belknap were killed, and one sailor on the Kennedy was killed by smoke inhalation.

The OOD was a bright guy who had qualified as deck watch officer (DWO) quickly. The Navigator was a former DWO who was demoted to navigator. At one point during the watch, the navigator came out to talk to the OOD and asked him, "Why are you turning right?"

The OOD said, "Because the aircraft carrier is turning right, dummy." The navigator went back to the CIC (Command Information Center) and didn't come back out until after the crash. The navigator did send over twenty messages to the OOD, but these were not relayed by a twenty-three-year-old seaman apprentice, who was afraid to interrupt the brusque OOD with a message from the "dummy" navigator.

Onboard the Kennedy, there were more than twenty commissioned officers on the bridge and in the CIC room, but only one had ever been a qualified deck officer. They had never seen a ship in their convoy take that kind of course, but they still neglected to call the Belknap on the radio. They knew the CO of the Belknap was a seasoned captain who was in line for flag officer (admirals get their own flag) and they did not want to embarrass him.

At the beginning of the first turn, the captain was watching a movie with the crew below decks. With the two reversing maneuvers and engine acceleration, his calm must have been disturbed. Supposedly, the OOD had called him twice to inform him of the navigation changes, but there was confusion and at one point, the captain was handed the wrong phone and simply hung up. Both the OOD and the captain were court-martialed, the captain for not assigning a proper watch and the OOD for hazarding a vessel.

The captain's case was dismissed on a motion by the defense that the prosecution never established its case. The OOD's lawyer, Jay Flanagan, advised the young officer to try the case in front of a judge instead of a tribunal. The judge found the OOD guilty but could not see the benefit of any punishment.

The use of courts-martial to punish officers of the deck who commit navigation errors became highly debated soon after the case. Without criminal intent and in the absence of malice, why is a mistake of judgment treated like a criminal act? The other side of the debate was that you needed courts-martial to keep people on their toes. I'm not sure if any of us would drive better if we had a shotgun held to our heads.

The Coast Guard has found out that skippers generally treat communications as a distraction, not as a valuable tool to truly understand each other's intent. In a way, it's much like the male thing about never wanting to ask for directions. Maybe it's in our genes.

The Error Chain

Unfamiliar setting, distractions, not knowing standard operating procedures, misreading lights, not slowing down (in fact, going faster), and bad luck add up to unmitigated disaster. In this case, a bad thing happened, and then a very bad thing happened.

But at the core of the problem was communication. Some cultures, the military service culture in particular, rank high on Professor Geert Hofstede's Power Distance Index, which means these cultures are strict hierarchies in which people don't pal around with those above or below them in the hierarchy. People in high power cultures speak when they are spoken to and show extreme deference to their superiors. The incredible string of Korean Air accidents in the 1970s and '80s had a power distance issue at the core. Co-pilots (first officers) and engineers were culturally constrained from telling their captains that they were flying into a mountain, or into Russian airspace.

The Coast Guard had been putting the starch back into its military bearing for some time, and a higher Power Distance Index resulted. Combine this index with its traditional "can do" attitude, and the Coast Guard was saying "can do" when "no can do" would have been more appropriate.

11.

"So on we go
  His welfare is of my concern
  No burden is he, to bear
We'll get there
For I know
  He would not encumber me
  He ain't heavy, he's my brother."
        -*"He Ain't Heavy, He's My Brother"*
        Bobby, Scott, Bob Russell, The Hollies

One month into the OCS program we were scheduled to move to a new dorm location, and the base maintenance team was way behind schedule which had thrown the whole schedule off. The officers decided to take matters into their own hands. They postponed classes and had us paint our new barracks. Because it wasn't pre-programmed, the maintenance detail didn't have any built-in humility lessons and, therefore was actually a lot of fun and a welcome relief. We ordered pizza and listened to the radio.

We were also assigned new roommates. My new roommate was OC Clark, who was blond and tall, almost as tall as me but without the bulk. He too wore his hair short and favored crisp light blue shirts and dark blue pants with shiny black shoes. He had a quick wit, and was one of those guys to whom everything seemed to come easily. He was from New Mexico, and his parents were semi-retired and ran a bunch of laundromats. After he graduated from college, Clark got a job as a claims adjuster, but he was looking for a little more meaning in his life, and he fit right into OCS. He got it right the first time; he was a born leader.

OC Clark was nearly demerit free, and I asked him how he did it. After being sworn to secrecy, he told me (is there a statute of limitations on secrecy vows?): he and his roommate used to sleep on top of the covers of their beds, and pinned the covers so they were always

tight. That way they saved valuable time in the morning. They re-
varnished their belt buckles with nail
lacquer and could just wipe them off
each morning. Even when the up-
per class stopped tipping off our class,
they still managed to get us tips on
the demerit of the day. They had an
outlawed lint brush. I told him I wish
I had done some of those things, and
he told me it wouldn't have made a
difference because they were gunning

∞ James Clark ∞

for me and it really didn't matter what I did. I knew he was right. I had
always been the kid right in front of the mob yelling, "But the emperor
has nothing on!" Or worse, yelling "Hey, why does he have a wrinkled
flesh-colored robe with a short drawstring?" And my family and I
would have been hanged forthwith.

When we moved in, we quickly found out the air conditioning
wasn't working. This was a big issue because there were no screens on
the windows and we were having a September heat wave. It was so hot
that we left the windows open and, being located in a swamp, I was
being bitten incessantly. When the English settled Jamestown, which
was just down the road from our barracks, nearly three-quarters of
the newcomers died, many from malaria. While the lowlands of the
tidewater area provide good anchorage, living in a swamp has severe
drawbacks. A swamp is filled with mosquitoes, and it's hot and humid
in the summer and bone chilling in the winter.

My whole life I have been a mosquito magnet. I could be ravaged
by the blood suckers and everybody around me would be bite-free.
My brother Bill once suggested that the only reason people invited
me to their cookouts was to keep the mosquitoes off the other guests.
Of course, my roommate wasn't being bitten. He was too cool to be
bitten, but I was covered in welts. I put on my pants and a shirt and
covered my head with the sheet. The heat was stifling, and combined
with involuntary blood donations, I was in for a miserable night. I
woke up to a new surprise: our new digs didn't have hot water. I hate
cold water for good reason.

∞

When I was in second grade, I had a near-death experience. It was early January and I had just gotten off the school bus. Instead of going right and walking one hundred yards home, I headed left for Little Pond, a small tidal pond off Vineyard Sound.

I had noticed when the bus passed that the pond had frozen over in the wicked cold snap we'd just had, and it was now low tide. As soon as I got to the pond, I started jumping on the ice along the edge of the pond, which didn't have any water underneath. I was having the time of my life, cracking and crunching the thin ice. The bigger the sheets, the more fun it was. Crunching every ice sheet I could find, I was soon out of earshot from the road.

Then I spied a huge chunk, a real beauty. I got a running start and jumped on it with both feet. It didn't break, and my feet went out from under me. It was low tide, so all the ice around the edges slanted toward the middle. I slid further from the bank and promptly fell through.

I was only in about two feet of water, but I couldn't make it up the ice ramp that was formed by the low tide. I had nothing to hold on to, nothing I could use to pull myself out of the water. I tried breaking the ice with my second-grader fist, but it was too thick and it had water beneath it. I yelled for dear life, but nobody heard me. I was soaking wet, cold, and trapped.

I was there for what seemed like hours, and it was starting to get dark and colder. It was early January and the sun sets early at 41 degrees, 41 minutes North latitude —at about 4:20 p.m. I was starting to sink into hypothermia when I saw a big man who seemed to be running. He was coming at me with an axe and a blanket.

Normally, anyone would be terrified to see a stranger running at him with an axe, but at that point, being killed by an axe murderer would have been a welcome relief from the cold. Within seconds, I was wrapped in his blanket and heading for home.

On the way to my house, he kept saying, "It was the darndest thing."

I wondered, "What? My falling through the ice?

When he got me to my house, he told my mom the story: "My wife's father is senile and can't speak anymore. All he does all day is look out the picture window toward the pond. Today, just as it was starting to get dark, he started to pound on the window. He scared my wife half to death because he usually seems half asleep and he's never been violent. She thought he was having a fit, but she finally looked out the window and saw a kid trapped in the ice."

I really heard about this later, because when I was carried in the door, my mother put me right into a warm bath, which felt wonderful, but the next thing I knew she was pulling my arms and legs out of the water. It turns out she called the doctor and he told her that the blood needed to warm my body and vital organs first, and if the blood rushed to my extremities, the organs could be damaged. My brothers claimed that the time I spent in the icy pond caused brain damage, and I have spent the rest of my life trying to disprove their claim.

At least, now that my arms were out of the warm bath, I could hold the mugs she filled with copious amounts of hot chocolate. It turns out that giving hot liquids to people suffering from exposure is not a good idea either. I was blue, not sad but blueberry blue. It was half an hour before I warmed up enough to shiver.

The next day, my mother baked some blueberry muffins with "pretty near too many blueberries" and selected a jar of her grape jam. We had collected the grapes from Falmouth Heights Bluff. Nearly all the bluffs around Vineyard Sound are covered with grapes. That's how Martha's Vineyard got the last name. The tiny wild blueberries were gathered from woods that had recently caught on fire, the only place where blueberries grew on the Cape. We froze them in August for muffins and pies the rest of the year.

She made me go over to the old man's house with her to deliver the muffins and jam. I had never seen anyone like him before; he was a bit spooky. My mom, whose first love was acting (she was once on stage with Henry Fonda) sat down across from the old man and told him the story over and over again. In her dramatic voice, she kept saying he was a hero, a lifesaver, each time adding details that I couldn't even remember. I thought to myself, "I wish I could be a hero."

But there was no one home, as the saying goes. The old guy didn't have a clue to what she was saying. He just kept smiling and staring at her blouse. He loved the muffins. You could tell by his smile as he wolfed them down. Knowledge and experiences had been slowly stripped away from him, and all he had left were his basic instincts. Yet, the day before, he recognized that someone was in danger and needed help, and he acted. We thanked the whole family and left.

For years I thought about that day. I learned two things. In the very nature of man, there is an instinct to watch out for our fellow man. We are our brothers' keepers. The other thing I carried away from the experience was that I wanted to be a hero, and I spent about an hour each day daydreaming about saving people. In my daydreams, I was saving a child from a fire, pulling a drowning family from the sea, or rescuing captured soldiers from the commies —sometimes all three at once.

The daydream always ended the same way, with the mayor giving me the keys to the city as my parents watched (although we only had a town, not a city, and a selectman, not a mayor —but it's a fantasy, OK?). I do recall, though, that none of the fantasies included ice cold water. I also thought that if that old fellow could be a lifesaver, anybody could. It obviously didn't take a lot of thought.

∞

Sometimes people try too hard to be heroes. On September 5, 1934, the luxury passenger liner Morro Castle was traveling north from Havana along the East Coast toward New York. The ship encountered thirty-knot winds and heavy seas, and the captain, who was having stomach cramps, retired to his cabin, where he died of an apparent heart attack. Not a good omen.

At approximately 3:00 a.m., smoke was reported in a storage locker near the radio room. The newly promoted captain of the ship was slow to dispatch the fire teams, and even then they proved inept at battling the blaze. Without permission, and suspiciously early into the incident, the radio operator, George Rogers, transmitted a CQ: standby for an important message. The captain delayed the SOS for at least another fifteen minutes. The ornate wood paneling with its flammable glue and other expensive decorations all made great kindling, and when the fire alarm was finally sounded the passageways were filled with smoke and the crew was too busy getting themselves into the lifeboats to help the passengers find their way to the deck.

The crew quickly launched six boats that could hold 408 people, but only 85 climbed in, and most of those occupants were the crew. I can hear them now: "Did we forget someone, like the paying customers?" Then the lifeboats inexcusably headed for shore instead of hanging around the ship to pick up survivors.

While the Coast Guard did rescue 146 passengers and other commercial vessels picked up another 164, a total of 137 people died- by most accounts, needlessly.

Communication among the Coast Guard stations and vessels was completely screwed up, partially due to the fact that the Navy was in the process of taking over the Coast Guard East Coast radio network and partly due to the fact that the radioman on the nearest cutter was a striker, or trainee, and wasn't very vigilant. A few vessels didn't even realize that there were still survivors in the water. From inspection to rescue, the maritime system was pronounced broken.

George Rogers, that chief radio operator who began the radio communications before there was a clear and declared emergency, was identified as one of the few heroes in the debacle. Perhaps he knew about it first because the fire started in a closet to which only he had access. Later, working as a policeman, he attempted to kill a fellow officer, which started to raise suspicion. He later robbed and murdered a couple. His murder conviction raised further doubts about his character and his supposed act of heroism. Unfortunately, from what we have learned from forest fires, heroes who are "Johnny on the spot" are often the first arson suspects.

Congress created a special committee to study the accident, and after two years, in 1936, Congress took action and changed the name of the Bureau of Navigation and Steamboat Inspection Service to the Bureau of Marine Inspection and Navigation and rearranged some deck chairs. But the maritime industry was growing too fast, and the marine inspectors had more deep-rooted problems. I remember as a child hearing that "marine inspectors carry two briefcases onboard, one full of papers and the other empty. They leave with two full brief cases."

The Coast Guard reacted to the Morro Castle tragedy more intensely. Top leadership was changed and a new commandant, Commander Russell Waesche, took the reins and became Admiral Waesche. Policies and procedures were changed, manpower and resources were increased, and, most importantly, morale improved dramatically. The Navy decided to give the coastal emergency communications system back to the Coast Guard, and in 1942 most of the Bureau of Marine Inspection and Navigation was put under the command of the "can-do" Coast Guard.

In the incredible buildup to World War II, marine inspectors were overwhelmed and the Navy felt the entire marine inspection process had to be militarized.

Admiral Waesche would lead the Guard for ten years and supervise its growth from 20,000 to 250,000 at the height of World War II. Admiral Waesche commanded more 'man years' of personnel than all other Coast Guard Commandants combined. In the past, most commandants just stayed in Washington, but Waesche went into the field, met his men, and listened.

When the marine inspectors were being integrated into the Coast Guard many senior officers wanted to "throw the bums out." But Waesche knew he couldn't possibly train new people to be inspectors fast enough to accommodate the World War II buildup. He also thought that the corruption was due to systemic problems, not a wholesale loss of ethics. The clash of cultures between the civilian inspectors and military lifesavers, coupled with concerns that the civilians would corrupt the Coast Guard, presented Admiral Waesche with one of his greatest dilemmas: competent crook vs. honest incompetence. Which hurts more?

The Error Chain

We expect moral behavior from our government employees and the people responsible for our transportation, and we usually get it. The bending of rules can prompt a long slippery slide into broken rules and broken systems. Possibly, a displaced desire to be a hero drove George Rogers into an act that turned him into a villain -two sides of the same coin -on that slippery slope.

12.

On the first morning after our move to the new OCS barracks, I took a cold shower and shaved in cold water. My face wasn't cooperating, and the shave ended up being less than close. At morning inspection, the officer asked me if I had shaved that morning.

I said, "Sir, yes, Sir!"

He replied, "You didn't shave." He didn't say that it doesn't look like I shaved, but that I didn't shave. I was tired and angry.

I felt like saying, "Are you calling me a liar," but instead, I blurted out, "I did, too." I said it without the "Sir" at beginning and end.

He tore into me without mercy. I got demerits for improper grooming and talking back to an officer. After inspection, he told me to go back to the barracks and shave. I did, and the additional time it took me to shave made me late for class, and I suffered even more demerits. I made one mistake but compounded it into three two-demerit events.

I was now on the verge of extinction; another mistake and I would have to go in front of the fitness board.

Before I arrived at OCS, I wondered how hard it could possibly be. I had attended seven years of football camp with triple sessions in the August sun. A third of the participants would throw up out of exhaustion each day, and there was a list posted on the wall naming those who took the Greyhound home each night. But this was a different kind of torture. These guys got into my head.

I am ashamed of it, but I will say it: personal grooming was not my strong suit. I was a defensive tackle, and the nicest thing you could call me was a hog. As a matter of fact, the defensive line coach, Joe Wirth, a West Virginian, used to have us squeal like hogs. I squealed, and I enjoyed it.

At OCS, a sparkling clean uniform was somehow a sign of competence. In football, a sparkling clean uniform was a sign that you were sitting on the bench. As a high school sophomore on the varsity team, I remember rubbing dirt onto my clean uniform to give the impression to the girls on the cheerleading and pep squads that I had seen some action.

For twenty-two years, my Uncle Frank would say when he laid eyes on me, "Your hair looks like the dirty end of a mop." In retrospect, that was one of the nicest things he ever said to me. I am not sure whether I owned my own toothbrush or comb. I remember my two roommates in college protesting, almost violently, when they discovered halfway through the semester that there were only two toothbrushes in the holder and my teeth weren't particularly yellow.

"Hey, I rinsed out the brush both before and after!" I responded.

There had been a few times when I used a fork on my hair when I was going on a date. I rinsed the fork out before, but not after.

One Christmas, I received three cans of deodorant from three separate relatives. My father once commented that he thought I could grow a small garden under my fingernails. I hated showers, an aversion that I think came from the fact that I hated cold water, and every time I took a shower and used the hot water, a brother would inevitably go around and flush every toilet in the house.

The intense attention to hygiene at OCS was inherited from the British Royal Navy. One of the key reasons the British Navy was so successful was that it packed its ships with as many gunners, marines, and sailors as possible. With more men, their cannons fired faster and they always knew they could overwhelm another ship if they could board it. Conversely, with more men came greater potential for disease to spread rapidly through the crew.

The British Navy lost more sailors to disease than combat, Consequently, ships' surgeons, officers, and chiefs in the British Navy were emphatic about hygiene. They didn't know that the actual cause of disease was germs, however; they thought it was bad air (like mal-aria, "bad air"). So, if you smelled, you were treated badly, often with the boatswain's knot lash, and even sometimes fumigated —to death.

The OCs used to joke that, if they didn't make it at OCS, they could be professional janitors. I had spent five summers cleaning the toilets and the floor of the Captain Kidd, and two semesters each year washing and polishing floors in the cafeteria, but I can tell you that these OCs would be kicked out for inefficiency. If you took twenty minutes to polish a sixty-square-foot room, you would be pretty much thrown out of any janitorial service.

The mopping and cleaning were less a function of cleanliness than part of the concept of learned humility, however. Many of the college kids entering the officers' ranks had never done manual labor or taken an arbitrary order. Under the belief that you have to follow before you can lead, Ninety-Day Wonders were given essentially useless tasks to knock them down to size. I wasn't born with a silver spoon in my chops, and I'd pulled too many bar glasses out of toilets to need another lesson in humility, so I pretty much missed the point of these chicken-shit exercises. I suppose that attitude alone was counterproductive to my success in the OCS.

Because of the short duration of OCS, one goal is simply to test adaptability, because soldiers and sailors need to be adaptable to survive. Consequently, OCS overloaded us with work and nearly impossible challenges, testing our ability to just soldier through an assigned task and accept orders no matter how arbitrary. I was in fact trying to learn to follow blindly for I was not a complete idiot about the overall project, but it was hard.

∞

Luckily, the afternoon's agenda was much better — firing weapons. A Coast Guard

∞ Forty-five Pistol ∞

officer has a wider range of jurisdiction than nearly any other law enforcement officer. A Coast Guard officer has all the powers of a customs agent: the power to enforce warrants, subpoenas, summons, or legal processes, and the right to arrest without a warrant for any offense against the laws of the United States of which he or she has knowledge. These offenses include tariff infractions, drug and firearms violations, environmental hazards, fishing and maritime infractions, and illegal immigration. Of course, as a part of the military service, a Coast Guard officer must have the capability to defend the country in time of war or during a breach of security.

The Coast Guard officers and petty officers must also handle weapons that launch weights and lines across the bows of foundering ships. Picture the family of a weekend boater, already in a state of sinking panic. "The Coast Guard is coming! We're saved! Wait. One of them is aiming a shotgun at us. He's going to shoot! He's shooting! What the hell? Does he think we're a ganja boat?"

That afternoon, we went to the firing range to become weapons-qualified. I always loved guns, and this was one of my rare opportunities to shine. This time we had real guns, not the antiquated, unloaded, never-fired M1s we had to march around with. Here is a description of my supposed best friend:

"Sir, my best friend is my piece.
It's a U.S. rifle, serial number 5489471, caliber 0.30, M1,
gas-operated, clip-fed, air-cooled, semi-automatic shoulder weapon.
It is 43.6 inches long and weighs 9.5 pounds, Sir!"

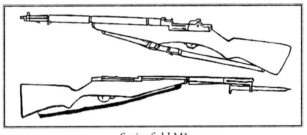

∞ Springfield M1 ∞

Coast Guard boarding parties were often armed with M16s and their officers had Colt .45 side arms. A number of boarding parties were fired upon during Prohibition, when the Coast Guard was chasing after rum runners, but the drug smugglers generally knew better than to shoot at a Coastie on a boarding party. They knew they would incur the wrath of a five-inch gun aboard the cutter, which stood at the ready, and if they did kill a Coastie and outrun the cutter and the five-inch guns, the operations officer could call a Navy F-15 piloted by a guy longing for target practice. The Coast Guard had also grown tired of firing across bows because the high-speed drug boats knew they wouldn't shoot them, so the Coast Guard came up with another strategy: sharpshooters in helicopters to take out the outboard engines. The strategy worked very efficiently.

The emphasis of the training was on gun safety, something I pretty much skipped over when I was kid. I had a Daisy BB gun and access to a .22; and don't tell anyone, but I also got a number of chances to try my skills with a government issue M16. When my father drilled at Camp Edwards, the Massachusetts National Guard Training Center near Otis Air Force Base, he took my brother and me along to pick up shells and load cartridges. We set up a firing range in our cellar with a platform to hold cans and a bale of hay behind it. Once, a friend of my brother, who "couldn't hit the broad side of a barn," completely missed not only the cans but the bale of hay, and the ricochet off the cement wall zinged by our heads. I am not sure there are too many people with firing ranges within the confines of their homes, and there is good reason. As a parent, I never had a gun in my house. I had a son, and I knew no matter where I hid the gun, the boy and the gun would eventually find each other.

Until I was fourteen, I played "guns" with my brothers and friends, pretend guns. We essentially played capture the flag, trying to ambush or outflank each other, in the woods behind our house. During the winter, we played among the hundreds of houses that were unoccupied in Falmouth Heights. There was one series of houses so close to each other you could jump from roof to roof.

Once, after a well-executed ambush during a snowball fight, I decided to make my getaway across the roofs, not realizing that snow provided an extra challenge while running. I lost my footing and slid off the dormer roof and onto the eve roof, bounced off the shed roof onto the porch, and then off of that onto a sloping Bilco door. Nothing broken, I got up and kept running. There was no doubt that, if the Russians tried to do a land grab and annex the Cape, the Eident boys were ready.

When I was older, I had a .22 and went with the "bad boys" on the football team to hunt crows on a farm. Joe, a linemen, was a member of the Wampanoags and part Cape Verdean. His uncle owned a farm. Joe was a super athlete, and while he never lifted weights, he looked like a bronze version of David. I remember that Joe could do a back flip on even ground, and that's an athlete. He conked his normally curly hair and always had a cocky Cheshire smile.

Joe and his friends had high-powered semi-automatic rifles with scopes. I had a vintage Remington .22 with a taped-on paper clip as a substitute for the original site. They laughed hysterically at my gun, and I took mild offense.

∞ There is nothing like the feel of an automatic rifle ∞

Crows are smart. We saw one and shot at it. Then we didn't see another. Apparently the one we missed notified the others. The Cape Verdean farmer told us why you never see dead crows in the road. He said there was always one crow on the telephone pole yelling "Caw, caw." That's a joke that can only be told in New England. Joe and his bad-boy friends were getting bored, so they started shooting everything they could see. Signs, fences, trees, cornstalks, and gourds were all fair game. We took a break in a small glen by a cranberry bog, and Joe and his friends started to light up their cigarettes. I pointed to a chickadee and said, "Well he's not afraid of us." No sooner were the words out of my mouth than Bam! One less Massachusetts state bird. Either the bird made the fastest getaway in history or it was vaporized by the .30-06. I realized at that point this would be my last hunting trip with Joe. Shooting at chickadees was a little too much gratuitous violence for me. We weren't going to eat it even if we could find it.

As we were standing around, I started to lecture Joe and his friends on the dangers of cigarettes. Joe seemed to be taking it in when suddenly he yelled, "Dance!" For some reason the order escaped me, but his friends also thought it was good idea, and they all started to shoot at my feet with a chorus of "dance." Wanting so badly to make the little spouts of dirt stop closing in on my feet, with one hand on my rifle and the other on my hip, I starting performing an amusing Irish jig to a song I called "Stop! Stop! Stop!" I thought about throwing in a chorus of "you assholes," but I decided I didn't want to further provoke three insane people with high-powered rifles.

It did the trick. They stopped shooting and were laughing their heads off. I didn't laugh with them. I was stuck somewhere between total astonishment and anger. I told Joe I just realized I had to go somewhere, actually anywhere else, and excused myself. I walked briskly toward my car, and when I was out of their view, I ran as fast as I could, vowing to give up hunting forever.

The next day Joe came by my football locker and sort of apologized. "Sorry about that, but we were all on acid." That was supposed to make me feel better?

Years later, I heard Joe died from gun play with LSD, I really liked the guy. What a terrible loss.

I learned two things from that experience hunting crows: I don't like it when people shoot at me; and when you drop acid, leave the guns at home. My other thought was that war was serious business and maybe I wasn't ready for West Point.

∞

I remember spending long hours discussing the relative merits of the M16 and the AK-47. Friends of my brother who came back from Vietnam would say the M16, with its tight tolerances, was far more ac-curate, but they never aimed at anything. They would hug the ground as close as they could and hold their rifles above their bodies and just spray bullets in the general direction of opposing combatants, and call in artillery support.

In that situation, the AK-47 was just as good, and it didn't jam like the M16 often did in the dirty, humid environment of the jungle. I imagined that jammed rifle in a tight situation would bring out some very creative profanity towards the designer and the officers who chose the weapon.

We had to take apart and reassemble the Coast Guard M16s and the .45s within a set time. OC Orr, who had been in the honor guard at quartermaster school, could do this with his eyes closed. I thought his sole purpose at OCS was to make the rest of look inadequate. I had never cleaned my gun, and therefore, I had little competence in taking a gun apart and putting it back together. I always ended up with spare parts. "Are you sure I need these parts?"

∞

I still managed to achieve "sharpshooter" on the M16 and just missed expert on the .45, receiving the sharpshooter designation on that one too. A few got "expert" on both, but some of the OCs didn't even achieve marksmen, the lowest designation. I thought, "Here are some objective measurements, and I am really not that bad —maybe I can do this."

The Error Chain

Guns begin and end a lot of error chains. Statistics suggest that gun owners are forty-three times more likely to have their gun used against them or a loved one than to use it to defend themselves. Consequently, I would feel confident rushing a man with a gun, knowing the odds were stacked dramatically in my favor, especially if the assailant didn't have any of his loved ones around. Lies, damn lies, and statistics.

We often mistake correlation with causality. After my daughter's fourth birthday party, she asked me, "Why is it some balloons fly and some don't?"

Invoking the Socratic method, I tried to focus her thinking on finding the root cause for floating or not floating. I asked her, "What do you think causes the balloons to fly?" She looked up at the flying balloons on the ceiling and then down to the lowly balloons dragged by gravity onto the floor and concluded, "It's the strings!"

I couldn't resist, so I replied, "Exactly! The more strings you attach, the higher you can fly!" She had perfect correlation and zero causality.

I then explained helium, and of course demonstrated its effect on ones vocal cords.

13.

"Sometimes I think it's a shame,
When I get feelin' better when I'm feelin' no pain,
Sundown ya better take care. . . .
Sometimes I think it's a sin,
When I feel like I'm winnin' when I'm losin' again."
-"Sundown"
Gordon Lightfoot

Each of the OCs had to be in charge of a colors (flag-raising) detail, which meant that we had to dress up in white gloves and leggings, and use a sword. I really didn't have a lot of experience with sword play except for the annual sword fight with cardboard tubes during Christmas wrapping sessions, in which I did quite well, especially against my sister. But my experience with non-cardboard swords was nil. Nearly all of the other OCs were chewed out because of sloppy execution, however, so I decided I was going to make this my turning point.

My roommate, OC Clark, had done an excellent job with his color detail; he looked like he belonged in one of those Marine commercials. He coached me and made me practice over and over. At lights out, I would pretend to sleep for a while and then go to the utility closet for some more practice. I discovered that use of this big closet as a post-lights-out study hall was not an original idea. When I arrived, there were already two other OCs studying there among the cleaning supplies. Apparently, for many OCs who were on the edge of academic expulsion, this was a regular ritual.

∞ USCG Officers were required to own swords ∞

I practiced my sword salutes over and over again in that closet for about three hours, and the next morning I was ready. My uniform was in impeccable order, and I was out there early organizing my first command, the color detail. When the time came for the actual event, I was nervous, but I pulled off all the moves in the correct order. As I was marching away, I thought, "Well, that seemed to go well. Nobody appears to be bleeding."

After I dismissed the color detail, an OC said the duty officer wanted to talk to me. I thought, "Maybe he wants to congratulate me on a job well done."

The duty officer started in on me. "That was the worst changing of colors I have ever witnessed in my life."

My thought: "Was I really the worst guy? Come on, think back. There had to be somebody worse. I mean, come on. While I didn't look like the guy in the commercial, I did all the right moves."

I instead countered, "Sir, I didn't make any mistakes, Sir."

He said, "You lacked crispness. It looked incredibly sloppy. You didn't practice. You just walked out there and, as usual, shot from the hip."

I was too embarrassed to tell him that that particular performance had about four hours' practice behind it. I felt like asking him, "Does this mean the next time our cutter is boarded by pirates I will not be able to hold my own in the ensuing sword fight?" But I stood there silently and took it.

I was beginning to realize that maybe this military crap wasn't my strong suit. Up to this point, the only thing I excelled at was playing defensive tackle. My key skill set was brute force and quickness. I had never heard a coach say, "I am disappointed in you! Your fifteen-yard sack on the quarterback lacked crispness." But this was a different world, a world with which I was really having trouble coming to grips.

∞ I was way beyond chewing my fingernails ∞

I decided to quit. I called my fiancée, Sue, and told her I was going to quit. She was very supportive because she knew I was out of my element. She wasn't overly thrilled that I had joined the Coast Guard in the first place, but she also thought that anything was better than that damn bar. Her vision of our life together was more in line with my passing the bar exam than working in a bar.

I had to make the dreaded call to my father. I started the conversation with, "Dad this just isn't for me. It doesn't play to my strengths. I am going to resign."

I waited for him to say something like "I'll be happy to have you home again," or something less sympathetic like "what do you plan to do now?" But he said nothing.

I filled the long void. "I think I would be better suited in a finance position. I'm going to apply to Merrill Lynch." I waited for him to say something, but the only thing that came from the other end of the line was silence.

"I am going to tell the company officer tomorrow. . . ."

And then he interrupted. "Your Uncle Frank was right. He knew you wouldn't make it through OCS. He said you weren't tough enough."

"Dad, you don't understand. This place is bullshit. They're cutting budgets and nobody sees a future in this outfit."

He was silent again.

I said, "I'll think about it some more, but I'm pretty sure I'm going to quit."

He just said, "Bye."

My dad loved the military. His time as an officer in the Pacific theater was the most rewarding and exciting time of his life. Although he made his living as a butcher at the A&P, he was also the National Guard commander for the Lower Cape. He was incredibly disappointed when I turned down my appointment to West Point and went to Brown. Although I am not sure many other parents would have been disappointed that a son ended up getting a full ride to an Ivy League school, he was. Now I was disappointing him again. He really did want someone to follow in his footsteps and share his glory days in the military.

Then I realized I couldn't quit. I had an epiphany. I had direction. I found my calling: I would dedicate my life to disproving Uncle Frank. But what would happen after my tour was up? I knew the answer to that one: I would find out what else he thought I couldn't do.

In my head, I could hear Uncle Frank say, "My nephew Peter won't ever make a living defusing bombs. He just doesn't have it in him." While not particularly fond of bombs, I would become a bomb de-fuser to prove Frank wrong. "It'll be OK," I reasoned. At least I had a raison d'être. I guess most of the decisions we make are purely emotional, and the rationale we use to justify our decisions are simply facades.

After the phone call, I had to go to leadership class. This day we left the classroom and went down to the OOD room, where the statistics of every class, about seventy classes over twenty-five years, were displayed. Make no mistake, the training officers prided themselves on washing people out.

There were three bases for getting kicked out of OCS. The first was health issues, including failing the physical fitness test, pregnancy, or weight issues. This category also included people who got past the medical screenings before the truth was discovered about a heart murmur or bad eyesight, and people who developed illnesses. The second was academics, for falling below the minimum test average. The third was military, for quitting or incurring the wrath of superiors for lack of discipline or military comportment.

Would our class be the first to have a 100 percent survival rate? That was what Emory challenged us with: Could we come together and achieve the so-far unachievable? Then Emory told us we were the first class in ten years that didn't have at least one washout within the first five weeks: he had thrown down the gauntlet. I was challenged twice within an hour. The first challenge was just my dad pushing the usual buttons, but this felt like real life. If I left now, I would be letting all my classmates down, and I was deeply surprised at how much that suddenly seemed to matter.

Shivers ran up my spine, and my mind flashed back to the days at Brown when the head coach, John Andersen, kept asking if we were going to be the first Brown football team to win the Ivy League title. Unlike my football memory, this time I had the unfortunate feeling that my classmates were looking at me sideways, eyeing me as the weakest link.

They say that heroism in battle isn't inspired by the love of God, family, or country, but by the bond of brothers in arms. In crisis, soldiers and sailors act to save each other. The trust and camaraderie that is required for sacrifice is what drill instructors seek to instill. Emory was right. We were getting compliments on our drilling; the officers grudgingly admitted that our academic average was the highest ever tracked; the senior class was even asking some of our boatswain mates and quartermasters for help on studying for their tests; we had become a world-class janitorial team. Clearly, our team of brothers had nearly coalesced.

∞

As OCS progressed, we were given more privileges. One privilege was the opportunity to sit at the head table with the training officers of the day. Just one OC from each class, each day, received this special honor. We were told that the conversation would be informal, that we could initiate conversation, and that we didn't have to start and end our comments with "sir." I was looking forward to talking with an officer and finding out more about how things really worked.

I was the last to be seated at the table. I put down my tray, sat down, and dug into the fried chicken. The other OC was in shock. The officer of the day just glared at me and said, "Don't you know that you don't start to eat until the senior officer at the table starts to eat? Didn't your mother teach you anything?"

Those were fighting words! I thought, "Don't bring my mother into this, you bastard." I said, "My mother taught me that, in an informal buffet or in cafeteria dining, it is OK to start without all guests seated at a table."

The officer shot back, "What makes you think this is informal?"

I replied, "Because of the trays and paper napkins. The manual even states that the conversation will be informal when dining at the head table; I concluded that the meal was informal."

I was ad-libbing. I knew I shouldn't have started eating before the officer, but the fried chicken looked so good that I just slipped up.

"You have an answer for everything, don't you?"

I replied, "I thought we were required to have answers or we'd be given push-ups or demerits."

"You think this whole thing is a lark and that you're better than all of us."

Then I realized the crux of all my problems. I was being accused of the most serious of the seven deadly sins, hubris. In the officer's eyes, I had yet to be broken down and be part of the team.

I told him, "I think this place is very serious, and in the first few days I may have thought I was better than everyone, but I was sadly mistaken. I am now in awe of my fellow classmates, and I realize that I am pretty much worse than everyone else in some very important areas. I am trying my hardest, but it doesn't seem to be getting me anywhere."

My honest and humble reply cooled the officer down and he started to salt his food, but I couldn't leave well enough alone. "My mother said that it is impolite to season your food before you taste it." Why can't I keep my mouth shut? The other senior class OC sat silently, looking down, and he just kept shaking his head.

The officer's reply surprised me. He said it was a bad habit and he probably should be cutting down on salt. We started to talk about nutrition, something I actually knew a lot about, and the meal ended up being a pleasant experience. He also said that the fact that I volunteered for the recreation committee showed the fitness committee that I was a team player and that I was willing to go the extra mile. Perhaps I had potential, he said.

The Error Chain

Most times doing less is less risky than doing something. This is what economists call a bias towards inaction: Managements' unwarranted predisposition toward not taking chances, even though their own well-diversified shareholders would benefit. In the 1950s and 60s, economists noted that managers tended to turn down projects with a positive expected value because the risk of failure was great and could have negative implications for their careers. Because these managers didn't benefit from the upside, why take a chance of getting fired? In the 1980s, management bonuses started growing in line with shareholders' gains. Now management is willing to take on more risk for their companies since, ostensibly, management and shareholders were now aligned. As the new millennium began, bonus schemes seemed to be working, so they got bigger and bigger, and management developed a bias for action, once again becoming misaligned with shareholders, which now meant taking on too much risk. This was just one part of 2007's worldwide economic error chain.

Those who ran the U.S. Life-Saving Service knew there would be a natural bias toward inaction on a stormy night. You could risk your life and win a medal, or you could say it was too rough to go out. To create a requirement for action, they instituted section 252: "In attempting a rescue the keeper will select either the boat, breeches buoy, or life car, as in his judgment is best suited to effectively cope with existing conditions. If the device first selected fails after such trial as satisfies him that no further attempt with it is feasible, he will resort to one of the others, and if that fails, then to the remaining one, and he will not desist from his efforts until by actual trial the impossibility of effecting rescue is demonstrated. The statement of the keeper that he did not try to use the boat because the sea or surf was too heavy will not be accepted unless attempts to launch it were actually made and failed, or unless the confirmation of the coast —as bluffs, precipitous banks, etc. —is such as to unquestionably preclude the use of a boat."

The only interpretation of the section is: "You have to go out, but you don't have to come back." And that stuck as a motto through generations of Coast Guardsmen, even becoming part of Coast Guard recruitment material during World War II.

But does this dictum make any statistical sense? There are conditions wherein going out will only create more victims. Are Coasties invincible, or are we disposable?

14.

"...and he's talking with Davy,
Who's still in the Navy,
And probably will be for life."
—"Piano Man"
Billy Joel

Our first real hands-on training was scheduled as a weekend short
cruise aboard the legendary Cuyahoga. The Cuyahoga wasn't large
enough to carry the entire class and crew, so the class was divided into
two groups: half would go out the first weekend and half the following
weekend. I was happy to go on the second weekend. We started "rules
of the road" —both inland waterway and international —that week,
and I figured the extra week would double my knowledge of piloting.
That second week would bring me up to 20 percent of the piloting
course, which I figured couldn't hurt before getting on the water. Also,
I figured that I could talk to guys from the first cruise and get some
tips on how not to screw up.

Ten other OCs was assigned to the second cruise, along with the
two exchange students and CWO Stone. It was a short trip: from Yorktown out the York River, then fifty miles up Chesapeake Bay, and into
the Potomac River. We would anchor in the river's mouth at around
2100. We were scheduled to go back into the Chesapeake the next
morning to practice man-overboard drills, steering-casualty drills,
and other maneuvers. After we would sail up to Baltimore for another
overnight in the port and return to the York River on Sunday evening.

We were looking forward to securing the anchorage watch, having a
good night's rest, and going off for a day of boating —followed by a leave
ashore in Baltimore. The guys in the other half of the class returned
with stories filled with libation and merriment in beautiful downtown
Baltimore. I found out that liberty would be exempt from the demerit
system; therefore, I was now scheduled for Liberty! Liberty! Liberty!

In fact, that is how liberty was announced every Friday afternoon

—in triplicate and with such gusto that it almost raised the hair on the back of the neck of those lucky enough to earn it. As an aside, I learned to say things in triplicate as was the Coast Guard way. Whenever you go on Channel 16 of a marine radio, you say the boat's name and anything else important three times. To this day, when leaving a phone message, I say the number three times.

The experienced quartermaster and boson mates from the first cruise told those of us in the second cruise about the handling qualities of the Cuyahoga, the finer points of the inland rules of the road, and the malfunctioning of the radar. Because most of their trip was in daylight and there was relatively good visibility, the radar didn't seem to matter. They described the malfunction as more of a nuisance than a safety issue. At times the talk became very technical and went sailing, no pun intended, over my head. I felt woefully inadequate and remember saying, "I'm not sure I'm ready."

MK1 Jerry Thomason replied, "Eident, you were born ready. This is just one more chance to have the officers show us how stupid we are before they send us back to the classroom to learn the right way to do things." Jerry was a machinist's mate. He ran the engines that powered the boats and ships and really didn't care much about what happened on the deck. His future laid below-decks, in the engine room as an engineering officer.

Imitating Scotty, the most famous engineer in the world aboard the starship Enterprise, I told him, "Aye, Cap'n. I'm giving it all she's got. She can't take any more."

Jerry said in a more serious tone, "Don't worry, Eident. They won't let you screw up too bad."

∞

When we got the schedule, we all got a little giddy because it said we would leave after an early dinner on Friday, and after a three-hour cruise, we would anchor. The words "three-hour cruise" were too much to resist and we started in on the Gilligan's Island theme. I am sure that some of my classmates thought Gilligan was my role model, but he wasn't: That honor fell to the professor. It was a testimony to the show's popularity among young boys in the 1960s that any man my age knew the theme song and could discuss the basic merits of the sitcom. The age-old questions remain: Why was there "an uncharted desert island" three hours cruising distance from Hawaii? Why did

Ginger and the Howells have so many changes of clothes? For that matter, why did Ginger have a tiara? These had been debated ad nauseam many times throughout our lives, but the real question we all asked ourselves was the most important: Ginger or Mary Ann? This amounts to the Veronica vs. Betty question for the Archie fans. Ginger was a voluptuous redhead who wore lots of make-up and beautiful gowns. She was a little stupid and very high maintenance; glamorous is perhaps the best descriptor. Mary Ann represented the girl next door, a cute brunette in pigtails who had a nice personality and was very practical. I had chosen a Mary Ann for a fiancée: while very pretty, she was practical and down to earth. We knew that these two archetypes represented a choice we all have to make. Jerry said that all Coast Guard men had been polled about the this question, and the results revealed that 45 percent went for Ginger, 45 percent chose Mary Ann, and 10 percent (all academy graduates) lined up behind Gilligan.

The discussion came around to Captain Robinson and the Cuyahoga. It should be noted that the captain of a ship may not be a captain in military rank. A captain's rank in the Navy or Coast Guard is just below admiral and is equivalent to a colonel in the Army or Air Force (a captain in the Army or Air Force is equivalent to a lieutenant in the Navy or Coast Guard). The other use of captain is any person who is in charge of a vessel —the "skipper." The skipper is also known as the commanding officer, CO, Charlie Oscar, El Jefe, El Supremo, etc. Robinson was captain of the Cuyahoga, but in Coast Guard rank he was a chief warrant officer. Warrant officers are highly skilled single-track specialists who have been promoted beyond the enlisted ranks. In theory, he was below an ensign, but he was held in high regard for his abilities as a skipper and for his teaching style.

Experience at sea is held in highest regard in the Coast Guard. Consequently, Coast Guard sailors bragged most about their experience underway. In bull sessions, everyone would try to outdo each other. One would say, "I have more experience backing down (going in reverse) than he has underway (going forward)." The banter would escalate. "I have more experience backing down while sitting on the head, while chewing gum," and so on. "I have more time pissing over the stern. . . ." These mock battles were absurd, but funny too, and emphasized that rank was far less valuable currency than experience.

Captain Robinson had twenty-seven years of experience at the con; he was a career boson mate —with all of the practical seagoing knowledge that entailed —and that made him almost god-like.

For my part, the news that we would be getting some liberty after our exercise was the best news I had ever heard. My first six weeks in OCS hadn't gone well, but maybe things would change. This would be my first weekend off in what seemed like six years. I had no idea what to make of the exercise, except that it was a prelude to time ashore.

∞

In 1978, unless you lived in Ohio and knew better, the name Cuyahoga conjured up a vision of a river so polluted that it caught fire in 1969. Although the fire was put out in thirty minutes, the press spread the story near and far. While this may sound pathetic, many rivers had caught on fire before this event but Time Magazine ran a cover story on it, and soon the late-night talk shows were all making jokes about it. "A guy who falls into the Cuyahoga doesn't drown, he decays."

Randy Newman came up with a song about the fire, and soon the Cuyahoga was the symbol of the decline of the U.S. environment and a "poster child" for the federal clean water legislation that followed, which the Coast Guard had to enforce. That name, Cuyahoga, would soon also be seen as a harbinger of the decline of the U.S. Coast Guard.

The Cuyahoga tied at the U.S. Coast Guard Training Center pier was not a very imposing vessel. She was 125 feet long, a "buck and a quarter," officially a patrol boat of the Active class. This class was originally designed right after World War I. At the tail end of the war, Germans sent a U-boat across the Atlantic that in July 1918 bombarded Orleans on Cape Cod and sank a tug and its barges, sending the whole East Coast into a panic. Realizing that it had to protect the coast, the government decided to build thirty-three buck-and-a-quarters, a class of vessels that soon found a new mission through the Volstead Act, the policy to enforce the 18th Amendment: Prohibition.

At first, rum-runners brought their cargo into ports. After the government became effective in enforcing Prohibition at the ports, they just took their booze to the three-mile limit (which was later a twelve-mile limit after a 1924 act of Congress) and anchored along "rum row" in international waters. Smaller, faster vessels that only required shallow draft fulfilled the last leg of a very profitable journey. Patrol boats like the Cuyahoga formed the outer line of defense to keep the smaller boats —which could often outrun them —from getting through.

Rum runners like Havana Joe and Bill McCoy became the Robin Hoods of their time. The longest rum row was off the New Jersey coast, supplying the New York and Philadelphia area. The ships vied for customers by offering a variety of price and quality of liquor and entertainment.

The rum-row ships were, by definition, lawless, and their cargo was often hijacked at gunpoint. The competition was so brutal that most rum runners were watering down their merchandise or labeling poor sparkling wine as champagne. Bill McCoy bucked that pattern; hence, his product was always "the real McCoy."

Prohibition had the negative impact of creating the roots of the Mafia, but it also had a positive impact by improving the navigational skills of a generation of sailors on both sides of the law, providing nautical experience that gave the U.S. merchant marine, Coast Guard, and Navy a head start in winning the battle of the Atlantic in World War II. Sailors on all sides of rum running engaged in running, hiding, and chasing -great practice for eluding German U-boats and protecting the coast and the convoys.

Launched in 1927, the Cuyahoga was the last of thirty-three buck-and-a-quarters to survive time and tide. She reached her penultimate place in history after Prohibition, when she was transferred to the Navy for escort duty for the presidential yacht, which wasn't as easy as it sounds. In 1933, President Franklin Delano Roosevelt decided to sail from Buzzard's Bay to Roosevelt's Campobello family retreat in New Brunswick, Canada. His trip took him through Woods Hole and to Martha's Vineyard and Nantucket. Neither his crew nor the crew of the Cuyahoga must have been pleased with that itinerary. It was the challenge course through the graveyard of some 3,000 ships. At one point, the crew of the president's yacht, the forty-five-foot schooner Amberjack, playfully ditched the Cuyahoga, and the Coast Guard had to send out an all-points bulletin: "Searching Massachusetts Bay for Amberjack; request orders." The fleet commander's response might have been, "Your only job was ...?"

∞

FDR was known for his sailing skills, and onboard he was the skipper. His reception from Woods Hole to Nantucket was wholeheart-edly American: flags waving from every boat and waterfront house on Vineyard Sound. The Amberjack anchored in Hadley's Harbor, and W. Cameron Forbes had a private conversation with FDR while the crew took a horseback tour of Forbes's private island. My mother used to tell us how hundreds of people gathered with American flags, horns, bells, and whistles on top of the bluff in front of Nobska Point Light, hoping to get a glimpse of their beloved president and be graced by his famous wave.

The Cuyahoga managed to twist its way through Woods Hole Har-bor and caught up with the Amberjack during their anchorage. The Amberjack's crew, by that time, was fondly referring to the Cuyahoga as "that little puppy." Perhaps looking for a big dog as backup, the Cuyahoga teamed up with the USS Indianapolis for the final open-ocean leg of the escort to Campobello. Who would have ever thought that these two ships would also share a common fate: being the worst tragedies of their respective service's history? The USS Indianapolis became Captain Quint's sea horror story in Jaws, and the Cuyahoga would become mine.

The day before our big cruise, we were marching to the Cuyahoga on the platoon leader's creative cadence, the off-color rhymes cranking our already high morale yet another notch higher. In the background we could hear the muskets from the battle reenactment of the 197th anniversary of the British surrender at Yorktown.

We were given an orientation by the executive officer (XO) of the Cuyahoga, who would not make the trip because of authorized leave. We had a quick tour of the vessel and were given an overview of safety procedures. We were briefed on details of the ship and shown the "correct" onboard traffic pattern. I didn't know a vessel could be so cramped that crew members had to move together in prescribed directions. Up on the starboard side, down on the port side: where were the one-way traffic signs? There was an exception to this pattern, however: The berthing area only had one ladder, and so you had to wait for the upcoming traffic before starting down the ladder.

Normally, two to three training officers go on the cruise to observe and help train the OCs. This isn't a requirement but certainly was standard operating procedure. Because we had three officers in the class as students (CWO Stone and the two Indonesian officers), the officer berths were occupied, which didn't leave any room for the OCS training officers. A few of the officers were going to catch up with the Cuyahoga each morning but not sleep over. Without the XO and two other officers, at least on the initial leg of the trip, the team was down by three key players: three qualified deck watch officers who taught navigation and piloting.

∞

We were briefed on the course of the cruise, which included turning off Smith Point Light. Smith Point in Virginia is where the Potomac River enters Chesapeake Bay. It is named after the great Captain John Smith: soldier, sailor, author, and ladies' man. John was a Lincolnshire native who went to sea when he was sixteen. His first real job was as a mercenary for the French Army and later for the Hapsburgs in Hungary. He was knighted by a Transylvanian prince after killing three Turkish commanders in duels, but later was captured by the Turks and sold into slavery. A Turkish prince gave the slave John Smith to his sweetheart as a gift to tutor her in English and French. Predictably, the prince's sweetheart fell in love with the dashing captain, and with her help, he was able to escape back to England through Lithuania.

Captain Smith joined up with the Virginia Company, but on the way over to Jamestown he was, like me, a pain-in-the-ass troublemaker, and Captain Christopher Newport ordered his execution. Newport changed his mind when he read the sealed orders making Smith one of the settlement's leaders, however. Good decision. Smith was a clever and experienced soldier and his being darn good with the ladies saved him more than once. Everyone knows the story of Pocahontas, who pleaded with her father and saved Smith from execution. Smith led the colony through its first two years, and without his leadership and a lot of luck, the Jamestown settlement would never have taken hold.

After the Civil War, a smear campaign was launched by Yankee historians to discredit Captain Smith and make Plymouth, not rebel Virginia, the real original root of America. After Jamestown, Smith explored New England: in fact, he gave the area its name. He wrote several books about America and urged the ambitious to become settlers in the New World. Generations of his namesakes are best known for checking into motels for short stays. Most importantly, however, Captain John Smith came up with my father's favorite saying: "He who does not work will not eat."

The Error Chain

Prohibition was a real test for American democracy. It was brought forth by a well-organized minority of voters that included the women's movement and the religious right, and it was fueled by the war. As usual, when religion mixes with politics, civil rights suffer. The law as so unpopular that smugglers of spirits –rum runners –became heroes and the American public started rooting against those who had to enforce the laws.

15.

When I climbed aboard the ship, I was elated —I was ready to chalk up sea time. This is what I had read about, what I had dreamed of. I was ready for my first seagoing adventure, despite the fact that it was Friday, the day that superstitious sailors refuse to start a voyage because of bad luck —which I didn't really believe anyway, but thought it a good excuse to have the weekend onshore.

The ship was manned by a crew of seventeen, with a warrant officer, a first-class boatswain who was acting executive officer, and a chief boatswain's mate, who was on leave. The Cuyahoga was at this point, also the purgatory of a few seaman and seaman apprentices who were awaiting discharge from the Coast Guard.

We each tossed our sea bag on a bunk to lay claim to it. OC Riemer noted that the top bunk in forward berth on the port side was not an optimal choice because the foredeck scuttle drained right into the bunk. "Not for me. I like to wet my own bed, thank you," I said. That didn't come out right.

To say space was at a minimum is a gross understatement. The question was raised, "What do we do with our gear when we sleep?" We were to put our sea bags on the deck and try to leave a small path for people to pass. The crew had even rebuilt the space under the ladder so that under each step there was an attractively varnished built-in drawer. While this was a clever way of increasing storage space, apparently no one had considered how difficult it would be to climb up if any or all of the drawers slid out in a violent sea.

After we claimed our bunks and stored our gear, we had to come topside for an abandon-ship drill. My assignment, in the unlikely case that the abandon-ship order was given, was to retrieve the navigation kit from the bridge, don a life jacket, and use the starboard lifeboat. I remember trying the clip-on light on the life jacket and noticing that it didn't work. I opened up the battery compartment to find what looked like a chemistry experiment gone awry. OC Clark checked his and found the same combination of corrosion and acid. I asked if there were spare batteries, but the permanent-party Coast Guardsman just laughed. "What the hell," I thought. "I guess we just wade to shore without lights."

The lifejackets weren't the kind you find under the seat of a plane. The Type-I orange jackets were huge, with two torso straps that came down from the back. The idea was to thread them under the crotch and strap them to the front belt. The key to putting these monstrosities on is to make sure all the straps are untangled and free before you put them over your back. Otherwise, they get stuck somewhere in the un-reachable expanse of your back. Putting on a life jacket was supposed to take two minutes. For a weight-lifting defensive tackle who hadn't had the flexibility to scratch his back for six years, it took about ten.

My watch didn't start until 2000, and it was now late afternoon. After drills, we engaged in the wait part of hurry up and wait. For six weeks, nearly every minute had been occupied, and it was nice to have a few minutes to smell the roses, or in our case, the salt air. After a prolonged period of waiting and the occasional round of signal testing, we heard the distinctive series of horn blasts that warned oncoming vessels we were about to be underway. The crew efficiently cast off the lines and we headed down the York River toward the great Chesapeake Bay.

Within minutes, someone reported that a piece of equipment had been left on the pier, and we had to go back and get it. That took about an hour and a half. I overheard a couple of crew members bitching to each other: "We'll be traveling in the dark for an extra hour and a half with that 'shitty' radar." It also meant that my anchor watch was actually going to be a navigating and piloting experience, too. The pit of my stomach tightened. Within a few minutes I detected the smell of chow. Subsistence Specialist First Class Petty Officer Balina had put together a delicious meal of roast beef with mashed potatoes and peas. We had choice of coffee or bug juice (Kool-Aid). Even Kool-Aid tastes better at sea.

Since the start of OCS, we had not been allowed to either lie down or sit in our beds between the hours of 0700 and 2200. I didn't have watch for another few hours, and so I decided to take advantage of this delicious "forbidden fruit" and climb down the ladder to take a nap. One of the drawers had slid open, and I almost stepped on someone's skivvies.

The berthing area had a unique scent combination: mildew, body odor, salt, and diesel fuel. My bunk was in the middle of a series of bunks stacked three high, and there were clothes and sea bags everywhere. I grew up in a bedroom with two sets of bunk beds and four boys, but this made that room look spacious. For a 240-pound ex-defensive tackle, it was a job just getting into the berth. I quickly discovered that I couldn't flip over, or for that matter even turn on my side. In response to my muttered profanity, I was told, "Make a decision: sleep on your back or your stomach. Then go for it."

I chose my back and surveyed the compartment. I had a habit for when I was lying awake in bed: I would lie there looking at the room and pretend that I was walking on the wall or the ceiling and map out my path.

Not able to sleep, and denied the luxury of tossing and turning, I went out on deck. It was a beautiful late fall night. While unusually chilly at about forty-five degrees, the night was clear and the sea calm.

∞

I remember approaching one of the permanent crew, Seaman Apprentice McDowell, who was standing by the wide, old-fashioned taffrail around the stern. He pointed to the wake of the ship. "What's that?"

I said, "That's phosphorescent plankton. I've only seen it a couple of times in midsummer on the Cape."

We stood at the rail marveling at the sparkling wake. McDowell said he was from Rochester and that they don't have phosphorescent plankton in the Great Lakes. I remember that he said, "Isn't this a masterpiece of God's creation?"

I replied, "I'm not really religious anymore."

McDowell told me how he had worked in a greenhouse for six years before joining the Coast Guard, and that he had spent every moment he wasn't at work out on his boat. It was his dream to make his living on the water. Then he told me he was going to take a nap.

We promised to get together for a couple of drinks on liberty, a promise he would be unable to keep.

I stayed on deck, watching the plankton trails in the water and thinking, "I don't know how much good religion has done me." My mother was highly religious, and I was an altar boy until I was eighteen —until my dad said that I looked more like the priest's bodyguard than an acolyte. At one point I was going regularly to daily mass, and my father wanted to know why I was trying so hard to suck up to the big guy. "What are you looking for? Special treatment?"

Then my mother died while I was in college and everything changed. I was mad at God and stopped going to church and talking to Him. As I stood staring out at the sea, I thought maybe it was time to move on and stop being angry. Maybe life on the sea would change things.

I thought that it would be interesting to see what the bridge looked like before my watch, and armed with my newborn sailor's enthusiasm, I headed forward along the starboard side and up the starboard ladder that led to the bridge wing. One of the lookouts on the starboard bridge wing told me that things were crowded up on the bridge and a little tense. He said that the skipper didn't want any excess people on the bridge tonight.

I went back down, but I wanted to get my eyes adjusted to the night darkness, so I decided not to go inside. I stayed out on the deck, wandering around and checking out the ship. She really was an old bugger. Just two years earlier there had been a ceremony to commemorate her fifty years of service, and at that time, she was the oldest seagoing vessel in service in the entire U.S. government.

Commissioned in 1927, two years before the last Model T came off the production line, she had been transferred into the Navy during World War II and armed with one three-inch, .23-caliber antiaircraft gun and two depth-charge racks. She served duty on the "Caribbean Front," guarding convoys against the possible German U-boats. Remember the movie? Of all the fronts in World War II, the Caribbean would have to be a close second to the Great Lakes for most remote likelihood of encountering enemy combatants. There was good reason for her soft assignment — she was considered old even during World

War II. Interestingly, most of her duty was escorting ships in and out of Guantanamo Bay. After World War II, she served as a platform for research and development work that the Coast Guard was performing. In the late 1950s she was given her last assignment: to serve as the training vessel for the U.S. Coast Guard Officer Training Program.

My watch started at 2000 hours, and we would rotate every hour. Technically, it wasn't a real watch because we were to shadow an experienced crew member for each position. We had been told we were just observers and should be aware that the crew may be busy, so we should try to either follow or get the hell out of the way.

∞

My first assignment was in the navigation room, just aft of the bridge. This station was most often called the combat information center or CIC, where radar and navigation work together.

In the CIC room was a large World War II vintage radar scope that looked like the ones I saw in scores of World War II movies. The screen was dull greenish gray and had a wide sweeping hand that created dots and long tails that eventually faded. I felt like Lieutenant Sulu on Star Trek monitoring comets. The radar had a mechanical cursor that could be used to ascertain distances. It also had two settings: one for relative bearing and the other for real compass bearing. There were no grease pens to calculate course on the screen, and no one was calculating direction and speed on maneuvering boards. We hadn't got to that part of training yet, and I was a little relieved. We were going to be piloting mostly by sailors' eye, as in "just watch where you're going" or as my Uncle Frank translated: "by the seat of your pants." There was also a LORAN "C," which is a land-based navigation positioning system.

My job was to record bearing readings from the bridge wing lookouts and ranges from the radar operator along with LORAN data, and plots them on the chart. We were navigating using Estimated Positions (EP), which consists of two lines of position. In our specific case, we were using ranges to Smith Point via radar and bearing to various fixed lights. This method results in an EP based on where we think we just sailed. The captain was not using dead reckoning, which isn't as ominous as it sounds. Dead reckoning is the process of estimating one's current position based upon a previously determined position, or fix and advancing that position based upon known speed, elapsed time, and course. Since we didn't factor in current and wind, we had to update our position every five minutes using plots to see if we were still on course or needed a correction. Most modern inertial navigation systems use the same concept but automatically update the position every few seconds, and have a directional symbol that tells the helmsmen which way to steer. For ranges, we had arcs, and for bearings, we had lines. Where the lines or arcs intersected told us where we were on the chart. We tried at all times to get a triangulation (all three points to line up), but the correlation was never exact. For the most part, however, the three points were very close.

I communicated with the radar operator and the bridge wing through a set of headphones with long wires plugged into the bulkhead. The headphones were the type I'd seen in World War II movies, dull green and bulky, and they utilized a hollow air tube for transmitting sound. The technology was a lot like the soup can with string that every kid plays with, but communication was much less clear. I thought to myself, "They just celebrated the hundredth anniversary of the phone two years ago, but it appears that the Coast Guard isn't an early adopter of technology: They're probably waiting for the telecommunications industry to get the 'bugs' out of that new-fangled technology that uses electric current to transmit noise."

The official reason for using air-tube phones was that, in case of flooding, the electric phones would short out. If the bridge is underwater, however, I don't think there is going to be lot of chatting on the phones. I was reminded of my shipmate's cynical observation of the Coast Guard: "A hundred and eighty years of tradition unhampered by progress."

While the lookouts and the radar operator were feeding me navigational bearings and ranges, their primary function was to watch out for other vessels. Since it was a clear night, all traffic and other objects could be viewed from the bridge. The radar was used to cross check what the lookouts saw. No one was calculating CPA (closest-point-of-approach). The OCs hadn't reached that part of their training, and the Cuyahoga navigation team just didn't do it on a regular basis.

I figured the ship probably had a new solid-state system on the bridge like the ones that I had seen on all the yachts and ferries. I found out later that I was half-right. The ship should have had a solid-state system, but it was going to be installed on October 25, 1978. The Cuyahoga was the only government vessel longer than sixty-five feet that didn't have wheelhouse radar —maybe the only one in the commercial fleet, too.

We were heading almost due north up Chesapeake Bay. The channel was well marked, and according to inland water rules, if everybody just stays to the right, nobody gets hurt. The only possible tricky situation would be if someone was overtaking us, we had to overtake someone, or if someone was crossing the waterway. We had to make two course changes to get into the Potomac, and each course change was dependent on predetermined bearings.

At 2045, I heard through the headphones that the lookout had spotted a light, and a few seconds later, CWO4 Robinson came into the chartroom and one of the OCs shouted, "Captain on deck." I came to attention. QM2 Rose told me that you only had to acknowledge the captain the first time on a watch, and you didn't have to do any more bullshit after that.

The captain used the radar to check the range of the contact, and I overheard him tell the OC Officer of the Deck (OD) that the vessel was 15,700 yards away. I knew there were 1,760 yards in a mile and an even 2,000 yards in a nautical mile, so I knew the ship was over eight miles away, or just less than eight nautical miles, about 10 percent less. Putting that into my own personal perspective, it was twice the distance from Falmouth to the Vineyard. I was ten years old before I crossed that vast distance to the Vineyard in a boat. I knew we would be making our first turn up the Potomac in a few minutes, and I didn't think we would be passing very close. The captain drew a conclusion about the size of the contact from the size of the dot on the radar. Seeing a very small dot, he hypothesized that it was a small ship. However, the radar dot coming toward us was the Santa Cruz II, a modern ship only two years old, far from a small vessel. Its bow was designed to cut through the water with minimum effort. If the ship was coming right at us, it is possible that most of the radar signal coming at them was deflected and didn't return to our radar scope, thus creating the illusion of a small ship. Unable to see more than one mast light from eight miles away, the captain further hypothesized it was a small fishing boat going up the Potomac.

∞

Because of another contact, we delayed our first course change by about a minute, making that first course change (heading 338) at approximately 2048. We had to immediately recalculate the correct bearing for our next course change (and by "we" I mean QM2 Rose did it and explained it to me).

After we told the OC OOD the next bearing change, QM2 Rose gave me some of the details of the anchoring procedures, which included taking a number of bearings to determine if the anchor was holding fast. A ship will move on an arc while anchored, and the navigator has to determine whether it's on the arc or dragging the anchor.

Slightly before 2055pm, OC Williams came back to relieve me as the OC navigator. I briefed him on what I was doing and the course changes and anchorage procedures. I waited for QM2 Rose to call in our hourly position (2058) before I went out to the wheelhouse.

Normal watches are four hours long with eight hours of rest in between, and most watch standers arrive fifteen to thirty minutes early to get adjusted and briefed; the relieved watchman will often stay on a few minutes to make sure all the information is passed and things are going smoothly. Since all of us were performing a watch and had to get to the next one, there was very little time to get adjusted and debriefed to relieve each other —the change of the watch was more like a Chinese fire drill.

When I came out on the bridge, I was surprised at how dark it was and how hard it was to see anything. I am nearsighted, and my left eye is 20-200, right at the limit of vision for admission to the Officer Candidate School. This basically means I can't read the big "E" without glasses. Pilots and deck-watch officers take pride in their vision and many claim to have better than 20-20 vision. On the sea, you need to have the eyes of a hawk. Piloting is visually oriented, and so onboard there are lookouts and sailors stand watch.

The problem with vision correction through glasses is reflection, and the thicker the glasses, the worse the reflections the less light gets through to the retina. There were also reflections from the windshield. A lot of progress has been made in glass technology and glass design since the 1920s. Unfortunately, the Cuyahoga didn't benefit from any of that progress.

OC Fairchild, the current OC OOD, went over the details of the next course change. When we arrived at a range of 5,400 yards and bearing of 199 degrees off Smith Point Light, we were to change course to 303 degrees northwest into the mouth of the Potomac. He told me there was one contact of interest and that he and the captain had determined it was a fishing boat, probably headed up the Potomac. He pointed it out and I could barely see it.

OC Fairchild handed me the binoculars, but I already had two charts in my hand. Our navigation chart was small-scale (covered a large area and lacked detail), and we were switching to a large-scale chart of the Potomac to have more detail. On a small-scale chart things are bigger, which seems contradictory that almost everyone gets the scale confused in the beginning. That is, large scale equals small area, and small scale equals large area.

There was no place to put the charts, and I fumbled around a bit. I also found it hard to focus the binoculars, so I took off my glasses and put them in my top pocket. I finally did see the vessel, and I could make out a number of booms. I had seen huge Russian fishing factory ships a number of times while fishing thirty miles east of Chatham, but this was one of the largest fishing boats I had ever seen. Because I was told it was a fishing boat and had no strong evidence it wasn't, I assumed it was a fishing boat. I thought that, since it was going up the Potomac as we were, it would pass us while we were anchoring. I thought that would be a point of concern when I debriefed the captain, especially if the anchor started dragging.

I was now ready to ask Captain Robinson for permission to relieve the watch. I had heard a lot about Captain Robinson, who had a reputation as an excellent skipper and great teacher. I finally came face to face with him. He was a short man and a little overweight, and it struck me that he looked worn out. He had that fourth-quarter, early-season exhaustion about him as he lumbered along, every step clearly an effort.

He was a chief warrant officer boatswain's mate and had more experience chewing gum while backing down than I had at OCS. Today people would call him "old school," but then we called him an old pro.

My big recital with the captain was delayed because he was on the port bridge wing working with an OC on taking a bearing from the alidade, a compass on a stand with a telescope mounted on top so one could read the bearing and see the object at the same time. The OC who also just relieved the previous bridge wing lookout was having trouble using the device for the first time, and the captain was helping him. Like me, this OC also wore glasses and his eyes hadn't had time to adjust to the dim night light. A hundred years ago, before the onset of electric lights, a lighthouse would be easy to pick out from a dark horizon. Today a couple parked in a beach parking lot to watch the late night submarine races could innocently throw off the search for that single point of light needed for navigation, just by leaving their headlights on.

I went out on the port bridge wing, but the captain was busy, so I waited until there was a break in the action before I talked with him. Remembering Lieutenant Emory's artillery story of misinterpreted coordinates, I kept repeating to myself the next bearings, ranges, and course while observing the contact off the starboard bow.

Finally I caught the captain's attention and recited the navigational information necessary to assume the watch, including the course change, anchoring plans, and current contacts, repeating what I was told about the fishing vessel contact. I then asked permission to assume the watch. The captain quizzed me a little on our eventual anchorage, and then gave me permission to assume the OC OOD.

The captain was very polite, but the briefing seemed labored and slow because he paused between each sentence to draw an extra breath. He then went back to his task of helping the other OC find the bearing.

It was 2102 -though I would have thought 9:02 p.m. at the time. I had been in the guard for six weeks and still didn't like the idea of time being demarcated in increments exceeding twelve hours.

I turned to the current OC OD and said, "Sir, I relieve you."

His reply was, "Sir, I stand relieved." I felt a great sense of pride.

A few seconds later, a voice came down as if from heaven. "Contact off the port bow." OC Riemer, the helmsman, saw my confusion and pointed to the voice tube, a tube that goes from the flying bridge to the wheelhouse, slightly above my head. I gazed into the dark, and the only contact in front of us was the same contact that I had seen for the last five minutes. I called up to the lookout, "The captain knows about it."

There were two guys on the flying bridge located above the wheel-house, and they reported on the voice pipe that there was a set of lights off our starboard bow. Everyone on the bridge had been tracking the lights for the past twenty minutes, and I had been watching them for the last five minutes.

∞

At 2104, OC Robinson announced that Smith Point Light was at 199 degrees, and the captain advised me to tell the helmsmen to change course to port at 303 from the previous course change a few minutes earlier at 338 degrees. I relayed the order to the helmsman, and we started to head up into the mouth of the Potomac. The captain asked me to show him where we were on the chart, and I did. He then told me, in a polite but distracted way, to report to the navigator and put the chart of the Chesapeake away. I went into the navigation room, put away the chart, advised the navigator, went back to the wheelhouse and stood near the hatchway to the starboard bridge wing.

The captain started to take a bearing on the ship. At 2104:30, the contact sounded a single blast, and within seconds the captain advised me to come left to 290, that he was going to sound one blast of the horn, a signal of intent, which if returned would mean port-to-port passage. The sound of the horn got my adrenalin flowing. I went to advise the navigator, and he asked, "What the hell is going on?" The navigator then went out to the starboard bridge wing to join the cap-tain. I stood behind them.

The ship was now within 1,200 yards, a little more than a half a nautical mile away. We were going to push over to the left so the ship could pass us on the right as we both went up the Potomac.

Now that we could see the vessel more clearly, it was obvious this wasn't a fishing boat. The Santa Cruz II was a 521-foot dry bulk car-rier, loaded with 19,000 tons of West Virginia coal, heading down the Chesapeake Bay from Baltimore on the way to San Nicolas, Argentina —and now it was aimed for the Cuyahoga. Captain Robinson still as-sumed it was heading up the Potomac.

∞

The Santa Cruz II was commanded by Abelardo Albornaz, a twenty-nine-year veteran of the Argentine merchant service. He was experienced, well-respected, fifty-one-years-old -the same age as the

Cuyahoga. However, he was not in charge at the time. Nearly every large, non-military ship bound into or out of U.S. waters is required to have an American pilot onboard. Pilots are licensed by states based on their skills in piloting, navigation and ship-handling, and their knowledge of local waters. Up to this point, the pilot onboard the Santa Cruz, John P. Hamill, a licensed Maryland master pilot, assumed the Cuyahoga and the Santa Cruz II were on a reciprocal course through the Chesapeake and would pass no less than one half mile apart. When the Cuyahoga turned to go up the Potomac, we had just cut across their path.

When Hamill saw the lights of the Cuyahoga change from port red (note to self: port wine is red) to starboard green, he immediately went to the wheelhouse radar and calculated the relative distance and bearing. Then he signaled with one short blast that he demanded a port-to-port passing.

∞

The guys on our flying bridge had occupied themselves with other contacts, and just about when they were going to report again on the vessel to starboard, the blast of our horn, about eighteen inches from their heads, made them put their hands over their ears. Recognizing that the wheelhouse knew about the contact, they did not report it again and stood watching the spectacle unfold.

The captain was taking more bearings, and I used the door frame as an impromptu bearing device. Standing back a foot and remaining steady, I lined up the ship with the door frame and counted to ten. I thought I could detect a bearing drift to the left, and even with the rapidly decreasing range, I was sure it wasn't going to hit us. I thought the other ship would easily pass in front of us. But, all of my prior experience was with vessels that went about six knots and could turn on a dime: the Cuyahoga and the Santa Cruz were closing in on each other at combined relative speed of twenty-four knots, and every two and a half minutes they were a mile closer. It was like a novice driver taking a left turn and suddenly finding himself on the Indy 500 track and facing the oncoming race cars in a Yugo with no brakes.

The freighter never heard our first horn blast, and investigators concluded their bridge was too far back from the bow and the ship's engines drowned out the sound. The freighter sounded another blast, again demanding a port-to-port passing.

∞

This is where the pilot made a common misinterpretation of the rules of the road. The pilot thought that his vessel was the privileged vessel and that he was obligated to hold the same course and speed. As soon as the pilot saw the starboard green light, he should have recognized that he didn't know our intention and, therefore, was obligated to sound five short blasts and make any course change that would avoid the collision, including slowing down. The pilot always has the right, and indeed the obligation, to slow down if he senses danger.

∞ The USCGC Cuyahoga 1927-1978 ∞

An analogy would be a pedestrian stepping off the curb into your "right of way" when you are driving. You wouldn't just keep your foot on the pedal and honk your horn. You would slow down, and if required, turn to avoid hitting the person. On the high seas, however, and with SUVs and trucks in my experience, might makes right. I used a pedestrian for comparison because, if it was a cement truck, everybody's first reaction would be to slow down.

∞

Chief Warrant Officer Stone was on deck smoking his pipe when he saw the freighter closing down on us. I watched him move toward the port side. I later found out that he went there to hang onto a stanchion and pray.

The Error Chain

This error chain started many years before the actual incident, but we need only consider the false start that delayed the trip by an hour and half, raised tensions, and made the captain a little more tired and therefore less alert. However, the antiquated and unreliable radar led in part to mistaking the size and direction of travel of the Santa Cruz in the dark. A fishing boat and cutter could easily dodge each at the last moment. A 521-foot freighter would have held everyone's attention. With this OCS class made up of experienced sailors, the long odds of having a training ship crew with no ship experience amounted to sheer bad luck. The only permanent crew member on watch was also a rank beginner. Other than Captain Robinson, there was not another set of eyes that could catch the mistake. Dual responsibilities of the captain acting as both teacher and pilot also diverted his attention. Then came one false move after another.

16.

"When in danger
When in doubt
Run in circles
Scream and shout"
-Unknown

At 2106:30, the freighter sounded five quick blasts on the horn. We were now "in extremis," which nautically means that two ships are in such danger of collision that neither vessel can avoid the collision by its own maneuvering alone —both vessels must act. The captain rushed to the engine-order telegraph and ordered "full reverse all engines." He correctly recognized that the ship was going to pass very close in front of us, and that taking speed off would increase the margin of safety. He ran back out to the bridge wing. My gut told me something bad was happening. The word "horripilation" sprang into my head. All my SAT cramming was apparently coming to my aid since I knew the word for hair standing up on the back of your neck.

I had observed bearing drift to my left, but now the ship was drifting back to the right, despite the fact that we were slowing down. This could mean only one thing: the other ship was now swerving to its left or slowing down. I remembered hearing that the Andrea Doria swerved to the left in extremis, and the captain lived to regret it.

∞

There were so many options for the Santa Cruz: maintain course and speed, turn to the right (which is the recommended course of action), turn left with full speed (a sharper turning radius), or turn to the left and cut all engines (the only combination that ensured collision: if the Cuyahoga had maintained its speed, it might have missed the Santa Cruz, or at least it would not have been hit by the bow of the Santa Cruz.)

I recalled my Spindrift: "What is a head-on situation?"

"Sir, when two power-driven vessels are on reciprocal or nearly reciprocal courses so as to involve the risk of collision, each shall alter course to starboard so that each shall pass on the port side of the other, Sir!"

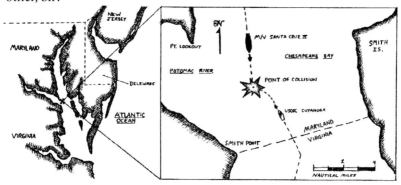

MK2 Baker was at the throttle station in the engine room and received the order. Although normal procedure would be to go in reverse at three-quarter speed, he somehow sensed danger and already had both engines turning in reverse at full speed. The full reverse engines made the whole ship shake and vibrate, and the noise of the quaking ship was deafening. The ship didn't like to be jerked around like this, and she was complaining loudly. I stayed on the bridge just inside the starboard wing, waiting for the captain's next order. Because of the increased noise level, I couldn't hear what the captain was saying to the navigator.

∞

The freighter was huge. Our bridge was lower than its anchor. I had been on the ocean a hundred times but never this close to a ship of that size. I tried to reassure myself that these guys were professionals and must really know what they're doing to be this close to each other. I thought it was somehow like the Blue Angels, fighter pilots so good they can fly within inches of the next jet's wing. I also remembered reading that, in the old seafaring days, ships often passed mail to each other. I figured these pros must be able to operate safely in close proximity.

∞

I did think that if I was out here with my dad or my brothers, I'd be scared as hell, and for sure my brother Bill would be yelling at me and everyone else. While usually soft-spoken, when we were out on the water Bill took on a demeanor that would make Captain Bligh look like an easy-going guy.

So danger for me was usually preceded by someone yelling, and there was no yelling here and so I saw no need to panic. Anyway, if we ended up in the life raft, we only had three nautical miles to go. No one else seemed to be panicking either, so I assumed things were going to be OK.

Then I thought, "Who ever heard of a Coast Guard ship having a collision in calm waters?" It didn't make any sense. I thought the odds of that happening were not even within the range of possibility. The freighter also seemed to be veering to our starboard, and it looked like it would pass behind us —I was sure it wouldn't hit us. Too bad Baker was so incredibly competent. Our engines, now stuck in full reverse, were starting to slow us down into the altered path of the freighter. I remembered walking down a narrow sidewalk when I was child and meeting a man coming towards me. Almost simultaneously we both stepped off the curb, then we both stepped up again, and then both stepped down, like a dance. We laughed and then both agreed to go to our right after these three false moves. (Later, my brother told me the guy was a child molester, so the story really stuck with me.)

∞

Much later I would find out that, onboard the Santa Cruz, the bridge had a VHF radio, and the pilot brought along with him a hand-held bridge-to-bridge radio that had both a one-watt low power for close-in communication and a high-power setting for other channels. While the radios were in good working order, the pilot had hung it on the other side of the bridge, and he didn't bother contacting the Cuyahoga when he first saw it because he anticipated that the ships would pass port-to-port passing and barely within a half a mile of each other. The pilot was used to dealing with non-English speakers on the bridge, and he didn't want anyone else to work the radio. When the Cuyahoga's lights changed from red to red and green, and then to green, the pilot went straight to the radar to determine how the two ships would pass. But he didn't want to be distracted trying to communicate with the Cuyahoga. It certainly wasn't second nature to him, or to the captain of the Cuyahoga, to pick up the phone and say, "What the heck is going on here? What is your intention?"

∞

The acting XO, BM1 Wild, who was not on duty, ran up the ladder to the bridge wing and said, "Oh my God, Captain. They are going to hit us!"

Then I heard it. The captain said, "Oh shit!"

My heart sank. This changed everything.

My mind jumped to the lyrics of "The Wreck of the Edmund Fitzgerald" when the cook said to the crew, "Fellas, it's been good to know ya." Later, the investigators would ask over and over again, "Are you sure the captain said, 'Oh shit.'" I asked them why it was so important. They told me if it was the captain's fault he would say, "Oh shit," but if it was beyond his control, he would say, "Oh, my God."

∞

I then heard somebody yell, "Brace!" I knew this was a real brace and not the chicken shit we had to do in the dorm. I held to the door jam and watched as the freighter hit the starboard quarter, creating a welder's arc of white fire, the color of melting steel. The screeching, grinding cacophony was almost deafening. This was the sound of dying steel. This was the sound of a dying ship.

Time of collision: 2107. These and the following times were pieced together by the Board of Investigation. But for me, time was rapidly expanding. My estimates were three times as long as reality. The freighter's impact immediately swung the Cuyahoga into an opposite but parallel course to the freighter. The freighter dragged us for about twenty seconds, a very long twenty seconds, raking us along her side until we broke free, and the Cuyahoga started to right herself a bit.

I went back to reassuring myself: I thought, "Well, that wasn't all that bad, a fender bender. Someone could put a dent puller on it, a little Bondo, good as new." From my angle, I couldn't see the gaping hole that extended well below the waterline.

Our engines went silent. Switching thoughts: "Damn, there goes our liberty." This whole mess would probably mean we'd have to limp into the next port and get stuck in a repair marina for the weekend. We lost electrical power and everything went black. We had a three-quarter waxing gibbous moon that night, so there was some light —not much. We started violently listing to port, and someone said, "Prepare to abandon ship." Blood rushed through my veins. Time expanded yet further: my thoughts were racing. I heard someone yell, "Where the hell is the back-up power?" Yeah, I thought, that's a good question. But despite Coast Guard regulations, the Cuyahoga had no emergency lighting that worked.

I darted into the navigation room, past everyone else heading in the opposite direction.

Someone said, "Where the hell are you going?

"Nav kit!"

"Forget it!"

∞

No way was the demerit king going to forget the navigation kit, a mistake that would probably mean a bazillion demerits and the breaking of my Coast Guard sword. I had been eying the nav kit while I was the OC navigator and I could just reach for it. The navigation room was pitch black, but with a little frantic fumbling I found the nav kit as I remembered my "to do" list for ship abandonment.

I scrambled back to the bridge. The ship was now listing at 45 degrees; it was impossible to walk. I literally had to pull myself up through the hatchway. I heard the port lookout yell, "What the fuck! What the fuck! What the fuck!" The wires from his headset were wrapped around his legs and he was struggling to get free as the water rushed in.

I thought, "Man, how would you like to have these famous last words on your tombstone. Couldn't he come up with something more profound?" In retrospect, I think that ends up on a lot of people's lips as last words.

A line from a Bee Gee's song started running through my mind: "Stayin' Alive… Stayin' Alive." It became my mantra. Years later, I heard that researchers concluded that "Stayin' Alive," with 103 rapid beats per minute and its simple message, was the ideal song to perform CPR to. As I climbed outside onto the bridge wing, the ship was now nearly on its side, and I walked on the side of the superstructure instead of the deck and headed aft for the life jackets.

As I was walking along the side of the boat, I remembered that we were supposed to drink as much water as possible before abandoning ship. I thought all that practice imagining a room on its side was coming in handy. Each passageway into the superstructure was a three-foot wide abyss that I had to jump over. I looked down into the passageway and eyed the water fountain. Within an instant, the incoming salt water gushed up around it and the water fountain was submerged. I thought, "Let's skip the water this time."

Getting a life jacket became job one. I turned around to look behind me and saw other guys helping each other to climb from the deck to the hull. Some were jumping right into the sea. My brain said stay with the boat; it's what I had learned in my Power Squadron course. When I arrived at the box that contained the life jackets, there was already someone trying to open it.

I said, "Hurry! Hurry!" as if I was offering some new insight on the current virtues of haste.

He said, "It's no use. It's no fucking use."

I thought, "I certainly could find a use for life jackets at this particular juncture."

He climbed onto the hull. I gave the life-jacket box a try myself. The box was almost completely underwater and the buoyancy of the jackets was pushing so hard against the door that the latch was jammed. I reached down and kept trying to pry it open.

I thought that maybe ten years of weight lifting would pay off and I could rip open the box. I was thinking I would be the guy who got the life jackets for everybody. There would be a parade down the main street of Falmouth and I would be given the keys to the city. It was such a clear vision of me being handed the key that I can still recall it today. Then it occurred to me that I couldn't be a hero with a parade if I was dead.

I kept reaching down into the water anyway. The water was ice cold and slapping me in the face. I looked over my shoulder and everybody was now on the hull but me. "Time to follow," I thought. My mental "survival hit parade" switched tapes to "Billy Don't Be a Hero," an anti-war pop song with a refrain that included "don't be fool with your life." I wonder how many lives in Vietnam that song saved.

I followed the lead of my shipmates and scrambled onto the side of the hull just when the ship started to turn completely over. I struggled to walk toward the keel, sort of the way a lumberjack walks on a rotating log. The ship stopped its rotation and seemed to stabilize in its capsized position. I kept reassuring myself, "It's only a movie. It's only a movie." I must have been in denial, but anything was better than this reality.

Later, OC Gordon Thomas shared his escape story with me and the rest of the survivors. Gordon was in the darkened radar room, two rooms behind the bridge. When the boats collided, the shaking didn't alarm him because he didn't have a point of reference on how much noise the ship should make. Just like me, he was on his first voyage and had no perspective on the abnormal. Suddenly, he found himself hanging by his neck, tethered to the starboard bulkhead by the short headphone wires that had wrapped around him like a noose as the ship rolled and plunged him into total darkness. He flailed around in the dark until he was able to grab hold of a pipe and take the pressure off his neck. He needed both hands to get the noose off, but one arm was busy keeping him from strangling. As the water filled the compartment, he floated up toward the bulkhead and got enough slack to escape from the headphone wires.

Gordon wasn't sure which way was up or which way was out, but he knew "out" was the only option. He figured that "out" was the direction from which the water was rushing in. Good assumption. His brain was working at five times the normal processing speed, and the only program on was "up, out, and air." When he dove down, he became entangled in the rubberized black-out curtain flapping in the watery breeze. He came back up into the air pocket and immediately tried diving again, but the curtain stopped him a second time. Then it struck him like a bell ringing in his head that the curtain would make a perfect rope ladder into the next compartment.

Gordon pulled himself into the navigation room and found he was one of many floating objects fighting for surface area. One of the larger objects was a heavy oak piloting table whose screws had been ripped out of the metal floor. Ever bang your shin against a table in the dark? He was banging his head and every other part of his body against an uncaring mass three times his weight as he bobbed unpredictably in the upwelling water.

He was now one room away from "out." He knew he had to dive down and swim through the doorway into the wheelhouse, but he was confused and couldn't get his bearings. Where the water was most agitated, by the door, the phosphorescent plankton was glowing. His mind flashed to the warning that to stay alive you don't "go to the light," but his high-speed logic overruled it and he dove for the light instead, pulling himself out hand-over-hand on the other blackout curtain. He emerged in the wheelhouse, where the water was rushing in much faster from the lower side of the ship. He swam up to the dwindling air pocket at the starboard side of the wheelhouse and was immediately struck by various pieces of equipment suddenly malevolent in their mindlessly buoyant quest for the surface. He and the ship's wheel, binnacle (compass housing), and the engine order telegraph all performed unsynchronized swimming right up to the solid steel door that was now above his head and shut tight. He tried to open it, but without leverage, he didn't have a chance.

He only had a few inches of air left. Earlier, during his short dinner-break relief watch, the captain had asked him to roll up all the windows on the bridge. Knowing the window was his only hope, he reached down into the water and found the crank. The windows were heavy and were geared for four turns to every inch. He cranked as if his life depended on it. With his lips pressed against the bulkhead, he cranked and cranked, periodically feeling the gap until he felt enough space to squeeze through. The window was fifteen inches wide and cranked to eight inches high. With the incentive of the moment, that was enough to get through while only slightly chipping his hip bone. OC Thomas was lucky to be skinny (or as he would say it, lean). If it was me, I'd still be cranking today.

Gordon took his last gasp and plunged through the window to the surface, then crawled onto the hull and what he thought was safety. He immediately heard voices telling him to get off the hull. He thought, "No way." Then one of the voices said, "You'll be sucked down." His mind raced to an old Sinbad movie where a giant squid was locked in battle with a ship as it was being sucked down in a whirlpool to Davy Jones. He jumped.

∞

Unfortunately, I didn't hear "sucked down." My thoughts flashed back to The Poseidon Adventure. I could almost hear Maureen McGovern singing "There's got to be a Morning After." The capsized Poseidon stayed on the surface for hours because air was trapped in it. I could clearly envision myself standing on the hull waving to a helicopter as it picked me up, flying me and my shipmates back to safety.

The eternal optimist, I would be saying, "That was a close one."

Then one of my shipmates yelled, "Jump in!" and the others started to jump in the water -that really, really cold water.

I said aloud to no one, "Why?"

All I heard in reply to my private query was: "Jump!"

I had lost some confidence in the overall wisdom of Coast Guard expertise, knowledge, and guidance. I thought, "I'm not taking any more blind orders tonight. My new policy is to question all orders. Besides, that water's cold. I remember being stuck in cold water. I hate cold water. I'm waiting for the helicopter up here. I'll tell them to pick up those morons yelling 'jump' next!"

I also remembered every boating safety lecture I ever heard, and it was always the same advice: "Stay with the boat!" There was only one other man on the hull by this time, and he seemed pretty intent on staying, too. Later, I found out it was Seaman Henderson. In retrospect, I was told to stay with the boat but to get the hell away from a sinking ship. As my brother Bill would later put it ever so delicately, "Even rats know when to leave a sinking ship."

I felt the ship start to move again, and I began to lose my balance. I realized that, since we were probably not going to be doing any more navigating that night, I could dispense with the nav kit with its sextant and charts. I had a pair of binoculars around my neck, and I tossed them over, too.

2109: Suddenly the ship sank under my feet, dragging me down with it. The water hit me from both sides and swirled around me — it was like being stuck between two huge waves. I knew from surfing that when a wave has you trapped, don't fight it. Wait out the fury and then find your way back up. The suction must have dragged me down fifteen feet before it lost its grip on me. I started to fight my way back to the surface. Being under the water was surreal: The phosphorescent plankton was providing light, and the glowing water was more than beautiful. Now it was useful. I actually remember quickly moving my arms back and forth to create contrails and thinking, "Cool! I can make this brighter."

I felt a sharp pain in my ear and knew I had broken an eardrum, but it was temporary pain and no big deal. I'd done that before. Bubbles and whirlpools were swirling around me as I thought to myself, "This is just what it was like when I was in our Maytag washer." I blame my brothers for that particular reminiscence.

I was also mad, anger being a prominent part of my morass of emotions. Ships weren't supposed to sink so fast. Every movie I saw had these long abandon ship scenes. Every reference to the Titanic I had ever heard made it sound like the passengers and crew had hours of time to rearrange the deck chairs.

I emerged back to the surface. I gasped for air and started to swim as hard as I could. I could see QM2 Rose and BM1 Wild near Captain Robinson in the water; I recognized that the captain was having trouble breathing. They had propped him up with some of the flotsam. I could hear him hyperventilating.

 I remembered an old rhyme that my father often used on us: "When in danger, when in doubt, run in circles, scream and shout!" The sarcastic poem had a message: don't panic . . . ever. But I was not sure if this situation even fit into the "ever" category. There was quite a chop, and my head wasn't very high out of the water, so it was difficult for me to see anything except blurry choppy waves. My glasses had gone down with the Cuyahoga, and my ears were ringing. With all senses malfunctioning, I was nearing complete disorientation.

I started to calm myself by thinking that as soon as I was rescued I was going to quit the Coast Guard. I started planning my exit interview: "Why am I leaving the Coast Guard? Because you fucking people tried to kill me!" My paperwork would be processed and I would be back in Falmouth the following weekend. I was disoriented, but I was pretty clear on one thing: I was now mad as hell.

The fuel tank must have burst open because I was almost overpowered by the smell of diesel fuel mixed with salt water. I couldn't ever remember being so acutely aware of smell before. I thought at the time it must be the adrenalin, but the memory stuck. Years later I was on a dock and someone spilled some diesel fuel into the water. As soon as I got a whiff of the mixture, my knees started to shake.

∞

I couldn't understand why the ship that hit us wasn't coming back to pick us up. I could see it the distance, but it didn't seem to be coming back. I also thought, "Aren't there supposed to be life rafts that surface after they are submerged? That would be nice."

∞

Some people have a phobia about swimming at night. I had some experience in this field. This wasn't the first time I engaged in nocturnal aquatics, but this time there were a few notable differences: it wasn't summer, I couldn't touch bottom, and as far as I could see there were no naked women. But seeing them would have been an issue had there been naked women because I had lost my Buddy Holly glasses. There was a backup pair in my duffle bag, but I knew they might be difficult to fetch now.

∞

Through my haze of disorientation, I could swear I heard Bill Cosby's impersonation of God asking, "Noah, how long can you tread water?" That really is a good question. I thought back to when I took my Red Cross lifesaving course. I had to tread water for fifteen minutes, and I probably could have done it longer. As a matter of fact, I even showed off by holding my hands above the water. I wouldn't be doing that this time. I thought, "Salt water is more buoyant than fresh water, maybe 20 percent more buoyant, and that should buy me a few extra minutes." But I realized that all the scrambling had really tired me out, so I would have to subtract, what? Maybe five minutes? But then, again, I had a lot of incentive to keep treading this time. I thought, "This is a complete waste of time. I know how long I can tread water. As long as it takes. That's that."

"Staying alive! Staying alive!" Barry Gibbs was back in my head. I thought, "Wait. I hate disco. Disco sucks. It would be pathetic to have lyrics of a Bee Gees' song on my headstone as my final thoughts. No, wait. Maybe my headstone should read 'Uncle Frank was right.'" Then survival mode kicked in. This was neither the time nor the place to contemplate tombstones or last words. I returned to the wisdom I had memorized from my Spindrift: "I's tough, I am, I are, I is."

I thought again, "Where the hell are those automatically inflatable life rafts that are supposed spring to the surface when the ship sinks? Certainly this would be an appropriate and well-appreciated time for them to inflate." Then my mind flashed back to the most popular book in the universe, The Hitchhikers Guide to the Galaxy, the book within the book had only two words: "Don't panic."

∞

How was I thinking all these random thoughts at a time like this? Believe me, this is a small sampling of the thoughts and images running through my head. I now understand what people mean when they say, "I saw my life pass before my eyes." I saw highlights from my childhood, my mother, my friends in school, my fiancée, random rapid-fire memories from kindergarten right through to that morning when I packed my sea bag for a three-hour cruise.

The brain is an amazing organ. When called upon in a life-and-death struggle, it uses every connection it can find to come up with a possible solution. For some reason, the lines "New York Life, of course. Why do you ask?" kept popping into my head.

∞

I thought, "Why did God do this to me? Why, God, did you do this to me? Why are you screwing me over again? What did I do that was so bad that I'm getting this raw deal? Again?" And then something hit me, literally: from underneath the water smashed into my boot and I thought it was a shark attack.

Being painfully struck from underneath the water is very disconcerting. Especially in the dark. It was a board with spikes sticking out of it. The teak decking had so much buoyancy that it was ripping off and shooting to the surface. I thought "Come on, God! Give me a break! Its bad enough you put me in the middle of the ocean without a lifejacket, but now you have to throw boards with spikes at me, too? Play fair, damn it!"

It occurred to me that these boards could hold me up, and I started to collect them with one arm while holding the other hand over my groin. The thought of flotsam hitting me in my tiny, blue, shriveled balls was a little too much to bear. I collected about three boards of varying lengths and wrapped my arms around them, avoiding the spikes.

Satisfied now that I wasn't going to drown, I had time to get back to being angry. I started going through the process of getting out of the Coast Guard; I could be home in less than a week. I then started shivering almost uncontrollably. I realized that while I might be able to stay afloat I could die of exposure.

∞

I heard a loud shushing sound. A small Boston Whaler shot out of the water like a Poseidon rocket and landed face up about ninety feet away. Could my luck be changing? I looked over my shoulder and said, "Thanks, God." The boat appeared to be high and dry, and it even had a motor on it. I now figured my luck was so good, the whaler probably had a case of beer in it, to boot.

Gripping the boards, I started to kick-swim toward the boat. After a few minutes, I realized the boat was getting farther away. The current was taking me in one direction, and the wind was pushing the Boston Whaler in the other. Pushing three long boards through the water while swimming with boots on was not particularly efficient. I started saying to myself, "Boards or boat, boards or boat, boards... boat... boat, boat, boat."

I knew that if I could get to the boat, I could act as a sea anchor and pull it toward the others. I decided to discard the boards and go for the boat. At first I just did a breast stroke, until I realized I wasn't getting any closer to the boat. You always hear about the kind of decisions that get you killed, and I had to ask myself: Was this one of them? I knew I had to pace myself, but I wasn't gaining on the boat at all -that's when I put my face in the water and tried to set the world record in the thirty-yard Australian crawl.

When I finally lifted my head, I was closer, but I still wasn't there. I went at it again. I remember reaching for the boat when it was just a few feet away, but at this point I was exhausted. Then NCAA swimmer OC Moser passed me and acted as a sea anchor to the boat. Somehow, with one last push, I reached out and grabbed the gunwale.

OC Moser told me to hang on with one hand and try and fight the current to drag the boat toward the others. While the boat was initially dry when it reached the surface, the drain pug was not in and the boat was starting to swamp.

Paddling as hard as we could with one arm while dragging the boat, we called out to others. Sometimes people would yell back at us. One by one the survivors made it to the Whaler, or the boat made it to them. I was exhausted, but I knew I was better off than anybody out there with nothing to hang on to. The initial energy from adrenaline was probably fading for all of us, but we pushed ourselves to keep finding survivors. We heard one fading voice, and we dragged the boat in that direction. I thought that some of us should swim out to him, but I heard an authoritative voice say, "Nobody leave this boat. Stick together. Just keep calling out. There is no way any of us can leave this boat and rescue anybody else right now —we bring the boat to them."

That is exactly what I remember from Red Cross lifesaving: the first rule is always bringing the victim something that floats. My mind was now cross-checking orders -besides, we had barely made it to the boat ourselves. Not knowing where the voice was coming from, and not being able to see more than a few feet, we had zero chance of rescuing whoever that voice belonged to, and we would have just added another victim if we headed out into the dark without the boat. I also thought that if someone had to do it, I would nominate Moser.

We decided that no one would get into the boat; we would just hang onto it. Three more arrived at the Whaler with injuries, and we got them into the boat. Chief Warrant Officer Stone had a gash on his head and OC Denny arrived in nothing but his underwear. OC Moser had also assisted the captain, and when the Whaler popped to the surface, they thought he was the best candidate to bring the boat to the captain.

∞

OC Moser and BM1 Wild joined Rose to get the captain to the Whaler, and they dragged him into the semi-swamped boat. He was hyperventilating between coughing spells, trying to catch his breath. I figured he must have swallowed a lot of water. I thought he might be having a heart attack. It was clear that he was under tremendous physical distress.

∞

The great thing about Whalers is they don't sink: I remembered seeing an old ad for the Boston Whaler that included a boat chain-sawed in half, and both sides were floating. That's a boat you want to stay with for as long as necessary. Stay with the boat. Abandon the ship. Too bad they don't teach that in class.

BM1 Wild was the acting executive officer of the Cuyahoga, but now that the ship was underwater, he took charge of the next largest vessel available. He found the Whaler's drain plug in the cold dark water, got it plugged in, and cut a hollow boat fender in half for a makeshift bailer.

∞

I had no idea how many people were on the Cuyahoga, but I was pretty sure we weren't all here. It was impossible to see who was hanging onto this little boat, but the entire crowded crew of a 125-foot ship couldn't hang on to a 14-foot Boston Whaler. There was no attempt to do a roll call because we wouldn't even know who was supposed to be onboard that night. We did know that men were missing. I could see silhouettes and hear heavy breathing and coughing. Any conversation was subdued. We could now see that the freighter was near us, but had pretty much stopped in the water. Someone said the freighter crew was worried about running us over and was probably trying to lower lifeboats to retrieve us right now. That was encouraging.

I thought, "I wish the Coast Guard was here... Oh shit, we are!" The Coast Guard had always been the cavalry charging over the horizon to save the day. Years later, I remembered this when I was stuck in an elevator with the worst guy you can imagine being stuck with —the elevator repairman. The only thing we could do was buzz the alarm to his empty office.

I wondered if anyone had a flashlight or even a lighter. I thought about the lifejackets that were stuck on the sunken ship. But even if we had them, the flashlights wouldn't have worked. The discussion turned to the fact that we were in the middle of an intersection of one of the most high-traffic shipping lanes in the world, and an unknowing ship moving at twenty knots would have a very difficult time seeing us floating here. I thought that would be adding insult to injury, just like Wiley C. Coyote avoiding the anvil and stepping off the cliff. What would I do if in Coyote's proverbial cartoon shoes? Maybe I'd swim underneath that anvil.

∞

My thoughts flashed back to when I was thirteen and plying my fourteen-foot skiff through a small saltwater pond in Falmouth. My friend, John Mitchell, was in the bow daydreaming, and I figured I'd play a joke on him. I stood up and said, "Think quick!" and dove over the side. I made two major miscalculations: John, while a straight "A" student, was not a quick thinker; and when I jumped off the stern, my push-off to the right set the boat in an immediate hard turn that, without correction, would put the boat in a tight circular course over the water I just dove into. I went to the bottom of the shallow pond and watched as the prop of the twenty-five-horsepower Evinrude passed over me three times. I held my breath for what seemed like an eternity. When John finally killed the engine, I came to the surface yelling,

"Why the hell didn't you turn the engine off sooner?"

His terse reply was, "Why the hell did you jump out of the boat?"

"Does anyone know where the love of God goes, when the waves turn the minutes to hours?" Gordon Lightfoot's haunting ballad came back to me again. I complained out loud that I was freezing my ass off, and the guy next to me said, "We are all freezing. Talking about it won't help." He was right. This was not the time or the place to be negative, and since we had so little to be happy about, there was very little to say.

After what seemed like hours, but what I later found out was less than forty minutes, a lifeboat from the freighter approached us. The master of the freighter, Abelardo Albornaz, had taken charge of the rescue. He called out, asking us if we were all right. I thought, "Do we look all right?" There should be a minimum prerequisite for "all right" that must include at least having a vessel under you when you're in the middle of the sea on a very cold night. One of the guys who were bleeding stood up and shouted to the lifeboat that we were all right but not all accounted for, and that they should go on and search for more people. I realized that "all right" is a relative term, and compared to the others still in the water, we were indeed all right.

We tried to pull ourselves as high out of the water as possible to reduce the water's efficient heat-draining abilities. All of us were breathing hard and coughing, but I could distinctly hear Captain Robinson fighting for his breath, coughing, and wheezing, which was really disconcerting. After a short time, the boat returned, and Captain Robinson blurted out between coughs, "Keep searching." When the lifeboat left, there was a small discussion and a consensus was reached: the next time someone offers us a boat ride, we better take them up on it.

The Error Chain

Pendulums swing constantly and, people and systems do too. One minute you're confident, the next you're not so sure. I started my watch thinking the Coast Guard was virtually infallible. Under water, I questioned everything they dictated. Perhaps the median is the best path but the channel markers are wide and the middle isn't always apparent. All things oscillate and the road to safety and improvement is often marked by ups and downs. Trend lines are never straight; they deviate from the mean creating variability and risk. In the world of systems, variability is risk and can be measured by standard deviation. There is little about standard deviation that is standard.

When an aircraft vibrates pilots sometimes cling to flight stick and can further induce the vibration. Worse, a pilot's corrections can often be an over-correction in the opposite direction, thus creating pilot induced oscillation. When a pilot's frequency of miss-corrections match the aircrafts gyrations, it all over but for the crying.

17.

"Sometimes the light's all shining on me
Other times I can barely see
Lately it occurs to me
What a long strange trip it's been..."
-"Truckin'"
Robert Hunter, Robert Weir,
Phil Lesh, Jerry Garcia, The Grateful Dead

I have no memory of getting into the lifeboat and boarding the Santa Cruz II. I think my brain said, "I have been working overtime for the past hour. Goodbye." I was told later by the other guys that the Santa Cruz II threw heaving lines toward us and Moser swam to get one of the lines and brought back to the Whaler.

All I remember is people asking me my name over and over again. They put us in a large shower room and had warm water poured over us, and had us drink warm water and whiskey. I didn't get any of the whiskey. I looked at my hands and saw that my knuckles were blue. I noticed the guy next to me had blue lips: blueberry blue. I recalled from my Sea Scout days that often people who suffer from hypothermia actually die from improper reheating after they are rescued. My mind recalled the 50-50-50 rule: a person has a 50 percent chance to survive in 50 degree Fahrenheit water after 50 minutes. I checked my watch: 9:09. That didn't seem right.

For a second, I felt euphoric. But then I got the sickening feeling in my gut that we didn't all seem to be on the rescue ship. Some of our shipmates must have been left behind in that cold water — or still in the Cuyahoga. I started to feel angry again -but at whom?

The crew members of the freighter were kind and supportive. While most didn't speak English, they all got their message across: Lo siento mucho. They were sorry. We were all very sorry. I turned to one of my classmates and commented that our hosts were awfully nice, but they seemed to be a bit timid. He said with a Southern twang, "Imagine you are a Massachusetts Yankee, which should be easy for you, on your way to Florida, and your Mercedes Benz just ran over a bunch of Georgia State Troopers because you were speeding. How would you act?"

"Lo siento mucho," I thought.

The U.S. Coast Guard was feared by the merchant mariners, especially on foreign ships. According to merchant mariners, the two greatest lies between a ship's crew and the inspectors were: "We're glad to see you" and "We're here to help." Coast Guard inspectors came onboard and always found both serious and what many thought were insignificant infractions: they were tough. The ship would breathe a collective sigh of relief when the inspectors left. The Coast Guard inspectors were self-righteous, nit-picking, and uncompromising, but I'll bet those self-righteous bureaucrats prevented thousands of merchant marine deaths. The Cuyahoga wasn't subject to such inspections, however. The Coast Guard vessels conducted self-inspections and also had inspections from the district commands. There were no third-party inspections from outsiders. There was no one in a position to say, "This ship is not leaving port until this is fixed."

∞

It felt as though people with pads of paper wrote down our names hundreds of times. I started to count how many people were listed, but one of the name-writers told me, "No counting!" I said I wanted to know how many people were missing, and he said, "Too many people are missing." I knew one was too many.

One of the Indonesian Navy officers, Lieutenant Jonathan Arisasmita, approached to ask if I had seen Captain Wiyono Sumalyo. He was desperately looking for his fellow countryman. When the ship turned on its side, he had straddled the hatch looking down into the passageway, hoping to find Captain Sumalyo. As the water rushed into the passageway, he only saw one person and pulled him out before the water started coming in over the top and the person wasn't Captain Sumalyo.

Arisasmita was totally distraught. I said his countryman was probably in sick bay, but Jonathan said he had just come from sick bay and only Captain Robinson, OC Robinson, and CWO Stone were there, and the Santa Cruz crew told him everyone else was here.

Then I noticed OC Clark wasn't among us. Neither was Heistand.

"Oh my God," I thought. Jerry Thomason wasn't there, and I couldn't see Bruce Wood. He had a wife. And I didn't see Seaman Apprentice McDowell. Tears came to my eyes, but I stayed composed as I said to Jonathon, "They're still searching, and they probably will be on the next lifeboat."

He said, "Sure." But neither of us believed it. His fellow officer, the future commander of the Indonesian Coast Guard, was not accounted for.

The last time I had seen Jonathan, he was operating the radar, so I asked Wiyono if he saw the contact on the screen. He said he did. He went on to say that he had followed it until it reached the center of the scope, at which point he decided to go out on the deck to see if it was actually a ship or a phantom dot. I thought to myself: "Good move." We hadn't had any training on the radar, and he barely spoke English, so staying with the radar screen would have been pointless. At least he got out of the ship alive.

While not required, a couple of the training officers usually went on the short cruise with the OCs. But a former training officer was getting married, and the training officers who had been displaced by the student officers were having a bachelor's party for him. Since there was no bunk space, they planned to board the ship at anchor early the next day. I know that most bachelor parties have a sad outcome (the guy gets married), but this would be one of the saddest on record. All the training officers must have thought to themselves that, if they had been aboard, another pair of trained eyes to recognize the danger, the accident wouldn't have happened. Everyone started the "if onlys". "If only if we hadn't turned. If only I had told the captain about the contact again. If only I hadn't joined the Coast Guard. My father used to say the only place that "if onlys" get you is on the road to madness.

Arne Denny came up to me and said, "It was unbelievable... " He was sleeping in the forward berthing area and heard the vessel shaking. He thought we might have started backing down or hit a shoal. He immediately got up, though he wasn't fully awake. I remembered what a light sleeper he was; there wasn't one time when someone came to wake him for a night watch that he wasn't already wide awake and getting ready, always up before the bugler played Reveille.

He instinctively walked toward the front of the bunks and into the open space. He heard the crash and was thrown against the port bulkhead. In the aft berthing space the men were thrown toward the starboard bulkhead, but the bow was pivoting in the opposite direction. When he got up, he saw a shipmate standing at the base of the ladder. Arne said he yelled, "Move, move!" Then the power went out and everything went black.

∞ Direct Impact ∞

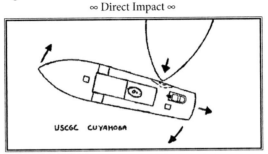

∞ When the collision occurred the Cuyahoga spun
clockwise throwing some of the crew against the starboard bulkhead
and others against the port bulkhead ∞

Arne saw some breathing space that was lit by a battle lamp, one of the few safety items that functioned that night. He immediately headed toward it, while tons of water was pouring in on him, pushing him down. Arne was amazingly fit. He was five feet ten and 150 pounds with muscles like cables, four percent body fat, the kind of guy who can do a hundred pull-ups and infinite sit-ups. There is no doubt that only his amazing fitness saved him.

Arne said, "When I hit the air space, I yelled back, 'CLIMB OUT'!"

The unidentified shipmate yelled back, "I can't make it."

The water crashing down the ladder must have been like climbing up a waterfall. While he couldn't see it, the stairs had become a series of pulled-out drawers, making it an even more improbable escape route.

The space filled with water and Arne called out to his wife, "Pat!" and his head went under the water. He said he was convinced he was going to die, and he felt almost serene. At that point, all he thought about was his young wife.

He felt something soft in the water, like a human arm. He grabbed it and started to pull himself up, but then he thought about the drowning victims who in their panic pull their rescuers down with them. He didn't want to do that and immediately let go. But it was already too late -the arm wouldn't let go of its grip on him. It was Lieutenant Arisasmita, straddling the hatchway and pulling him to safety.

Arne was the only guy in just his underwear, and here he was standing over me, telling me this incredibly horrible story —a worst nightmare —and I just didn't know what to say. I couldn't look him the eye; I was staring at his legs. I fell back on humor: I told him that he had very sexy legs. I wished I could be more comforting. He just kept shaking his head back and forth saying it was unbelievable. Judging by the fact that he was the only guy without pants, I realized that taking a nap had been pretty much a fatal act that night. I didn't know if I should be happy, sad, guilty, or angry. How the hell could this have happened?

Everyone was involuntarily shaking their head. When someone recounted a horrible detail, we said things like, "No... ," or "You're kidding," as if anyone would kid about any element of something this horrible. We were in denial and just starting the process of grief.

∞

OC Rutledge gave his account. He was on the mess deck watching the Rockford Files when he heard the ship start to vibrate. While a little concerned, he thought that maybe we were just slowing down to let a ship pass. It suddenly occurred to me that this would have been a much better choice than cutting in front of the freighter. Why were we so concerned with navigating instead of piloting?

He went on to say, "The bulkhead with the TV on it exploded, and the TV shot across the room and landed right beside my shoulder. I ended up swimming out of the twelve-foot hole in the mess-deck bulkhead that the Santa Cruz smashed through. Luckily she smashed all the way through. At least I had an escape route."

Three survivors initially found a Thermos cooler that shot to the surface; they clung to it until the lifeboat picked them up.

∞

BM1 Wild called us together and addressed us as a group. Yes, people were missing, but a full-scale search was on and every ship or boat available on the East Coast was now searching for additional survivors. Coast Guard divers were being readied, and they would search for any survivors still trapped in the ship. I did some mental assessment of the physics of a ship sinking. If the ship came to rest on its side or upside down, it was possible that there would be air pockets. But a human needs about four cubic feet a minute, or 240 cubic feet per hour. If it took a diver ten hours to get to someone who was trapped, one person would need a space of 2,400 cubic feet of trapped air. Anyone who found an air pocket would not run out of oxygen, but rather poison himself with his own carbon dioxide. It would take a space six and a half feet high, twenty feet long, and twenty feet wide that was airtight beyond the range of what seemed possible to keep one man alive. The biggest possible space was a corner of the engine room or the bow berthing.

Wild then asked us to pray, and we all got down on our knees and prayed that our lost shipmates would be found. In my previous prayers to God, I demanded fairness, but now I was praying for some form of mercy. As my dad always said, "There are no atheists in a foxhole." Tears filled our eyes, but no weeping could be heard. Everyone avoided eye contact until we recomposed ourselves.

∞

One of the crewmen of the Santa Cruz gave me a drink of warm water and asked, "What was it like?"

I said, "Bad. Real bad."

He obviously had a strong, morbid curiosity, and he persisted. He asked me in broken English if I was "ascared." Maybe it was just professional curiosity: a sailor must think about the possibility of such a thing happening, of a death by drowning. The meaning of his combination of afraid and scared was clear, but I wasn't really sure what I felt.

My mind was no longer travelling at warp speed. It was now sort of stuck in a tractor beam. I reflected for a moment; I didn't panic —no one panicked. Maybe my shipmates had experienced sudden overwhelming fear, but there wasn't any hysteria or irrational behavior. Maybe there had been some bad decisions -not irrational acts, just ignorant acts. For my part, not jumping off the hull could have been fatal. But I will never make that mistake again.

I didn't want to admit I was afraid, and I didn't want this crewman on the Santa Cruz to think I was bragging about not having fear. So I fell back to my old dependable crutch: stupid and tired humor. In my best Maxwell Smart (Don Adams in the TV series Get Smart) impersonation, I said, "No, I don't know the meaning of the word scared. Terrified, yes. I have that one down, and I was." The joke was lost on him because he actually didn't know what the word terrified meant.

At times like this the only people you want to talk to are your fellow victims, and it becomes an absolute imperative to just keep talking with the other survivors to see if they are feeling and thinking the way you are. For all of us, the experience was far more than the mind could handle —it was unreal. Did it really happen? I needed to keep talking just to regain a grip on reality. I would have done anything to feel better.

I tried to steer the conversation away from myself to the Santa Cruz crew. I asked one of them what it was like when they collided with us. He said he knew there was trouble when he heard the horns and felt the big turn and heard the collision alarm. "Collision alarm?" I wondered if we had one. Then asked about the impact itself. "No entiendo," was his reply, and he turned to his friend and his friend hit his fist into his hand and said impact. He said he didn't feel the collision. His friend, the first guy, said he felt something. It was like hitting a small wave.

"My God," I thought. "We were like a fly on the windshield." While we were only slightly more than one-fifth their length, we were nearly one-hundredth their mass. Materially, hitting the Cuyahoga was not much different than hitting a log in the water. I felt diminished and marginalized. I was angry at them, though I knew I didn't have the right to be angry —at these particular guys anyway. I hated the way big ships pushed ahead full speed, basically saying "get the hell out of the way." However, I did realize that we cut across their bow. A helicopter flew out to the Santa Cruz and airlifted the injured survivors. It turned out one of the bleeders was OC Robinson, the guy with the headset wire wrapped around his legs. His kicking and thrashing against the constraints of the wires created a series of nasty circular cuts on his legs. A launch was sent out to meet the Santa Cruz to take the rest of us to the Patuxent Naval Air Station.

∞

Unbeknownst to us, the Coast Guard had contacted the Navy, tugboat operators, and local police and rescue squads, including the Smith Point Sea Rescue Squad. One of the searchers on the Smith Point squad was Dr. Alfred Hunt, a local dentist. He, along with dozens of other pleasure-boaters, got a call from the squad's phone tree at 9:30. Dr. Hunt reported that, when the boats were launched, the squad was "running high on adrenalin," but in the pitch black darkness they had to slow hearts and motors to make sure they didn't run over anyone they were trying to rescue. He and dozens of other boaters were joined by fishing boats and tugs whose captains heard the SOS. Most spent the entire night and most of the morning searching. It wasn't just the boaters: Scores of people who lived along the shore left their homes and searched the beaches all night, joined by even more at first light.

∞

When we arrived at the station, photographers and reporters were already waiting. One of the pictures taken that day, showing me and two other OCs getting into a car, would end up attached to a front page article in the Chicago Tribune. I looked at my watch and it was still 9:09. I concluded my Timex watch was broken. While water-resistant, it didn't quite hold up to the Cuyahoga lickin' and didn't keep on tickin'. So, I had no idea what time it was.

At the Patuxent Naval Air Station, we were taken to what appeared to be some sort of administration building. We were given physicals, including having our temperature taken. While my body temperature was normally relatively low, the nurse wasn't even able to get a reading. "Well, you certainly don't have a fever," she quipped.

"Finally, a piece of good news," I thought. My blood pressure was a little higher than normal. I did not wonder why.

There were already a few Coast Guard officers there, and they started to interview us. My debriefing lasted about forty-five minutes. I asked if this was it. One officer said, "Probably not. There will be an official Coast Guard inquiry and maybe a National Transportation Safety Board inquiry, maybe more."

The other officer said: "Because you were on the bridge and talking to the captain, your testimony could be crucial. You shouldn't talk to other witnesses." I asked if I needed an attorney. He asked me if I thought I did anything wrong.

My immediate thought was, "Yes, I joined the Coast Guard!" But I said, "I really don't know."

He asked, "Did you tell us the truth?"

"Yes," I said.

He looked at me for a minute before saying, "Then I don't think you have anything to worry about... at least in that regard."

A Navy petty officer on duty unlocked a number of offices, and we were told that we should call our loved ones and family as soon as possible. I told him that I didn't have a credit card and that I wasn't sure my dad would accept a collect phone call from me. He said, "Don't worry about it. Call direct." During the first week at OCS we had been told that using a government line for personal use would be treated as a court-martialable offense, so I asked for reconfirmation. "No problem," he said. Cool -too bad I didn't know anybody in France. Maybe there was still a little pirate left in me.

The married guys and the permanent crew used the phones first. Judging from the scuttlebutt passed on by those who got off the phone, it was apparent that the Cuyahoga was big news across the country. The national networks issued news bulletins: "We are interrupting our regularly scheduled programming to bring you the report of a U.S. Coast Guard ship that has gone down in Chesapeake Bay with thirty men onboard. Many are still missing: News at 11:00."

It must have been around two or three in the morning when I got access to a phone and called my dad. I thought that maybe my father and my sister, along with my cousins and some neighbors, were sitting up with the TV, radio, and shortwave, perhaps with one candle burning and yellow ribbons around the old oak tree, waiting for "the call."

Then I thought, maybe my dad wouldn't know about the accident because he fell asleep around 9:15 watching TV and usually just woke up two-thirds of the way into the eleven o'clock news to catch the weather report, awake just long enough to turn the TV off and go to bed. So I figured that unless the Cuyahoga sinking actually had affected the weather, he would be totally oblivious to the tragedy. Just in case, I started with "Dad, I'm all right."

"Well, I'm not -you just woke me up in the middle of night. Don't you have a darn watch that works?" I didn't, but that was a long story. I tried to get the conversation back on track,

"I was on a ship and it sank."

I should have anticipated this one: "Did you wade to shore?"

"Actually, it's very serious and a lot of people are missing."

"Well, it sounds like a real adventure, but couldn't it have waited until morning?"

"It was in the news, and there is a lot of uncertainty about who is still lost, so our superiors told us to call our loved ones. I couldn't think of anyone who fit that category, so I called you."

"Well, I never worry about you; you're too mean to die."

My father once heard that only the good die young, and he thought that that was the best news he'd ever heard because that meant he was going to live forever. My dad hated "scaredy cats," thus his kids were expected to joke (and laugh) in the face of danger.

"Besides, what the heck were you doing out on a ship? Aren't you supposed to be in training?" I told him the cruise was part of the training program. He said, "That sounds like one heck of a training exercise."

I told him that I didn't think that the sinking was a preprogrammed part of the exercise. He ended by asking me if I knew where the socket wrench set was, and I told him I didn't.

After I hung up, I thought, "I really wish I did know someone in France. I'm sure they're a lot warmer and friendlier." But it was actually a good thing that I called: My dad got a phone call first thing in the morning from a reporter with the Falmouth Enterprise, our local paper, and at least he wasn't quoted as saying, "That's news to me!"

The next edition headline read: "Falmouth Man Escapes Capsized Cutter."

I called my fiancée. While she had heard on the radio about a Coast Guard ship going down, she thought I was safely sleeping in the Yorktown barracks. She knew that I had a training cruise scheduled, but she was sure it was in another week. "Are you sure the cruise is this weekend?" she asked.

In fairness to both of them, it's hard to wake up in the middle of the night and immediately have an intelligent conversation. In the Coast Guard, there is an unwritten rule that you are not responsible for any actions or words within the first five minutes of waking up. Some use that grace period to cuss out their shipmates.

My brother Bill was out on a cruise on the research vessel Knorr, and heard the news of the Coast Guard wreck across the shipping wire, but figured, "Why the hell would someone with six weeks of experience be out on a cruise?" The WHOI port office in Woods Hole wired out to him that I had survived though he never thought I was in danger.

I think there are two kinds of people in the world: those who expect that every bad thing they hear about will happen to them or their loved ones, and those who think nothing bad will ever happen to them. My wife and my family fall into the latter category, not because we are overly optimistic, but because we don't feel we're that special. Why would random bad things happen to us? Our response would always be, "Nah, that couldn't happen to us."

My father once told me that one day at officer training, during formation, his company commander said, "Look to your right. Either you or the man standing next to you won't make it back to the States alive." So my dad turned to the guy on his right and said, "Gee, I'm going to miss you!"

∞

For those with concerned relatives, the calls were a godsend. Many had heard the news of the sinking and knew that their love ones were onboard. They were hanging on to every piece of news they could find. Some were monitoring shortwave radio, the old internet, hoping to hear about the rescue of their loved ones. Some of the families of the permanent crew arrived at the base, and the Coast Guard kept them abreast of the latest developments. They spent the night praying and waiting for news.

I would find out much later that sometime during the early morning of October 21, while we were at Patuxent, the inflatable life raft finally decided to inflate, disproving the theory "better late than never." It was found on October 22 about twenty miles northeast of the collision site, high and dry and in good working order. Of course, no one was onboard. We'd taken an earlier option.

The other life raft was damaged by the collision and remained in its box. Inspecting and loading a life raft into a box is a tricky and delicate operation not dissimilar to packing a parachute. Coast Guard regulations for merchant marine vessels require inspections every six months, and unpacking and packing are done by a specialist at "approved service facilities." The Navy uses either dedicated teams or "approved service centers." The Coast Guard, up until that point, employed the cost-saving "do it yourself" concept used by the many homeowners who have running toilets and electrical shorts.

We heard that an early morning radio personality was searching for answers, and he was talking with an "expert" who had plied the water many times. His assessment was that both ships were probably on cruise control while their captains were drinking coffee below deck. How do people get designated as experts?

∞

After the phone calls, we went down to the galley —the base cafeteria —where we were told to get some chow and hot coffee. Because it was still a few hours before they would serve breakfast, they could only put some prepackaged food out for us. OC Thomas, who must have had the metabolism of a penguin, reached into the deep freezer and pulled out an ice cream bar, but the lunch lady declared that ice cream was only for dinner and weekend lunches and certainly not for breakfast. "But.. " said OC Thomas.

"No buts. Put it back."

As we took our lowly selections by the cashier, a Navy petty officer handed the cashier chits, and he tried to wave us by but she kept interjecting, "That's not covered and you don't have enough chits." He kept telling her it would be all right, but she said, "You're not the one who is going to be held accountable after the shift."

I wondered who was going to be held accountable for our incredible shift.

Just as we were about to sit down at the cafeteria tables, we were told they were about to wash the floor and we couldn't sit down. So we wandered over to the hallway and sat down on the floor with our backs propped up against the wall. The Navy's largesse had extended only as far as free phone calls. We were back to being treated like shit –though I admit it felt more natural.

I selected a Drake's crumb cake, a staple of military dining. For the last six weeks I had eyed the cake on the galley line but resisted, knowing that the crumbs would inevitably fall and linger on my shirt, continuing the onslaught of demerits. But now I couldn't look much worse. Our clothes had been dried but not washed or ironed, and they were blotted and stained with oil, seaweed, and now a fresh dusting of crumb cake. We all smelled like diesel fuel and saltwater. For sure there would be at least a short moratorium on demerits. Then we heard one of our OCs shout, "Attention on deck."

We all tried to jump to our feet, but our legs were not complying. We struggled to get up until we heard a deep warm voice say, "As you were. Please don't get up. For God's sake, don't get up." Our guest was our host, a rear admiral, the commander of this air station. He had been awakened in the early morning and had come down to offer his support. Despite his protest, we all struggled to our feet and stood somewhat at attention. The admiral was moved and started in on a moving speech.

"I've been a fighter pilot, wing commander, and squadron commander, so I've witnessed the downing of many flight crews. Whenever the Coast Guard was near, they did their utmost best to rescue the survivors. It didn't matter how dangerous or treacherous the conditions were, the Coast Guard never hesitated to go out. They were always there for the Navy. We were all brothers, and in times of need, we knew we would always be there for each other."

He continued, "I just got off the phone with the Commandant of the Coast Guard, and I've assured him that every Navy resource in the area is available and at his disposal. The Coast Guard is, naturally, leading the search as you have done so many times before for others. The Commandant wanted me to pass on his personal regards and prayers and tell you that the entire Coast Guard family is praying for you."

He closed by saying, "And if there is anything that I can do for you, please don't hesitate to ask."

I think most us thought that a somewhat rhetorical offer, but not OC Thomas who immediately said, "The lunch lady wouldn't let me have an ice cream bar, and I'd really like some ice cream."

The admiral, incredulous, "What!! Follow me," and we marched right into the cafeteria toward the lunch lady. I wondered if this would be the right time to ask for that beer I had been looking forward to. The admiral looked the horrified lunch lady in the eye and said, "These Coast Guard brothers are heroes, and they can have anything they want."

I could still hear the lunch lady saying, "Somebody has got to account for this."

At about 0530, I took my bone-chilled body to the impromptu ice cream line. I thought there was probably no food in the world less appealing or restorative at that moment, but the act was so incredibly gracious that I had to accept. I don't think I ever could have imagined a fully decked-out U.S. Navy admiral standing behind a food counter handing ice cream to lower-than-whale-shit Coast Guard OCs. Oddly enough, the admiral, with his amazing white uniform, actually looked a bit like an ice cream vendor. How did he end up here? How did I end up here! They let us sit at the tables.

∞

As I sat there eating my ice cream, I thought about the morning my mother died and how this day's losses would impact the families of my shipmates. Years later I heard Kate Carter's recollection: At 0822, Katie, a high school sophomore majorette on the pep squad woke up and realized she was late for school. She should be on the bus by now. She had a parade in Norfolk, and now

∞ YN1 William Carter ∞

she was late. Someone turned off her alarm clock. Coming down the stairs, she was whining, "Mom! Why didn't you ..."

There was a uniformed Coast Guard Officer in her living room talking to her parents, and she was stopped in mid-sentence by the look on her parents' faces. She had recently lost her grandfather, and Katie recognized the look on her mom's face. Katie's father was in the Army, so she knew what an unexpected uniformed visitor meant. Her mother turned to her, hugged her, and said, "We have very bad news: Bill's ship went down and he's still missing." She couldn't believe this could be happening. She and her big brother were supposed to work on his "wonder van" the next weekend. YN1 William Carter's dream was to be a Coast Guard officer. He worked his regular shift and then augmented the Cuyahoga crew on the weekend cruises, hoping to get the kind of experience that might improve his chances of being accepted into OCS. He acted in the local theater and liked to write comedy. He was twenty-two years old.

Bill's parents had been up all night, waiting, after they saw the report on the eleven o'clock news. They hoped they would hear from Bill before Kate woke up, so her mother snuck into her room and turned off the alarm clock.

The Coast Guard arranged to have a C-130 cargo plane bring us back to Yorktown. The seats on the plane faced backwards. The plane was not pressurized, or at least it didn't seem to be pressurized, and the noise was intense. We all had headsets that both blocked noise and provided communication if necessary, but we sat in silence, most of us with our heads down. I'd lost my glasses and my wallet, and my watch was broken. I felt blind and lost without my three most essential accessories. I could hear the wind whistling through one of my ears due to the broken eardrum, and my other ear was still plugged with seawater, and I couldn't clear it because of the hole in my other eardrum. One side of my head began to ache, but despite the discomfort, I really didn't want the flight to end. I didn't want to talk to anyone ever again.

When we arrived at Patrick Henry Airport, the family and friends of the permanent crew were waiting, and it was a tear-filled reunion. The crew were all hugging their families and friends and crying. They were giving each other some sense of reassurance, and it was clear to me that Captain Robinson had a crew who loved each other. I was envious of their closeness.

∞

The officer candidates were met by the company officers and driven back to the barracks. Our fellow officer candidates met us in the entrance way, and we hugged and cried. The company officer asked us to put our heads down and led us in prayer for our missing shipmates. This time you could hear weeping. There were no strangers. This was family, and we could weep as much as needed. As I looked down, I realized we were standing on the forbidden rug, the rug where it all began six weeks earlier. "What a long strange trip it's been," I thought.

The survivors had just gone thirty-six hours without sleep, and we soon found out that our fellow classmen hadn't slept either. They had kept an all-night vigil, hoping to hear some good news about finding more survivors.

∞

OC Uberti, one of the OCs on the previous cruise, recalled how he found out about the disaster: "We started noticing some unusual things happening. First, we saw Lieutenant Reynard show up in civilian clothes, then we saw Lieutenant Emory show up in civilian clothes as well." As a rule, we didn't look forward to seeing the company officer and the platoon commander, especially late in the evening.

Uberti continued: "When we saw the Chief of OCS come into Lincoln Hall in his civilian clothes, we knew something very serious had happened. We all mustered and Commander Loy told us that the

Cuyahoga was involved in a collision with a 521-foot Argentine freight ship in the Chesapeake Bay, and that the Cuyahoga had quickly sunk. We had been on the Cuyahoga the week before and spent a great sixty hours with them. Suddenly they were all gone."

It had been more than twelve hours since the ship submerged and each of us knew that the likelihood of finding someone alive was remote. But, of course, that thought could never be said out loud. Instead we just asked each other throughout the day, "Did you hear anything?"

The Error Chain

Shit happens. Mankind has refused to acknowledge this fact since the dawn of civilization. We accept fate or God's will, but not random chance. Even Einstein refused to believe that God plays dice with the universe. But quantum physics rules; randomness rules.

But if you accept that randomness rules, it's best to anticipate all possible problems —because if anything can go wrong it will go wrong. I can accept this fact as long as it's not on my watch. But then, it has to be on someone's watch. Someone has to be that one in a thousand, indeed that one in a million, the outlier, five sigma. Someone has to satisfy the statistic.

Sometimes we call it bad luck, and then we're back to the wisdom of bumper stickers: shit happens.

18.

"Do not go gentle into that good night,
Old age should burn and rave at close of day;
…Good men, the last wave by, crying how bright
Their frail deeds might have danced in a green bay,
Rage, rage against the dying of the light."
-*"Do Not Go Gentle into that GoodNight"*
Dylan Thomas

First thing Saturday morning, Coast Guard Commandant John B. Hayes ordered that all flags at Coast Guard installations be flown at half staff. A board of inquiry was convened with a newly promoted rear admiral as its head. The initial facts were not in the Coast Guard's favor. This wasn't going to be pretty. If I were the admiral, I would have been thinking, "Thanks a pant load! Why couldn't I be assigned to the Tall Ships Regatta?"

The press was clamoring for news, so the Coast Guard put the Cuyahoga XO, BM1 Wild, up front. He looked the part: thirtyish with dark hair, a big frame, a full beard, and a deep self-assured voice. The Washington Post reported this from BM1 Wild. "We… came out on the deck when we heard the horn blast and within seconds the ships collided." 'We were all operating on instinct. There was no chaos, everyone just came together and did what he had to do.' He stayed focused on the aftermath. He helped people get out of the wreck, and he was one of the last to make it to the Whaler. He said, 'Most everybody just fought to keep warm and prayed for their missing shipmates.'"

The Washington Post article also reported that Captain Blaha, the Yorktown Coast Guard base commander and official spokesman, said that the officer candidates had completed their eight weeks of classroom training and all the requisite survival courses.

Captain Blaha: "All the survivors were offered home leave yesterday, but many chose to remain at the base. We're trying to give them an opportunity to rest. Perhaps in a few days they'll be able to talk about it."

The training was actually only five weeks less the two days we lost to painting. We'd completed less than 60 percent of the material that was required, we had no survival swimming, the rules of the road class had just begun, and we had had no radar training. He was right about experience, though. "The Cuyahoga's last cruise was the first for many of the students."

To the general public, the captain sounded sure and comforting. Everything seemed like the Star Trek episode with two parallel universes, one with a good Coast Guard and the other with the Coast Guard that I was experiencing. I had been grilled and debriefed four times already, and there was no end in sight. I wanted to get out of the bad universe and into Captain Blaha's.

What wasn't said at the press conference, but could be inferred, was that Captain Robinson was initially hospitalized and now appeared to be persona non grata. The Coast Guard's strategy was to shift the blame for the accident entirely onto Captain Robinson. He became the "party of interest," which is a euphemism for "about to be screwed."

The Coast Guard could not be seen by the Santa Cruz's team of lawyers as having "systematically created conditions that endanger its men or another ship." Captain Robinson would be served up as the sacrificial lamb to absolve all sins. If the lawyers could say it was a single man acting against the rules, they could avoid what they thought would be millions of dollars in lawsuits.

Captain Robinson could spend his life in prison, but he made a smart move. He hired a world-class lawyer: Jerome Flanagan, a 1953 Coast Guard Academy graduate who went on to law school at George Washington University and became one of the premier maritime lawyers in the United States. "Jay" Flanagan was chief of the legal division for the First Coast Guard District during the Simas Kudirka case, although it should be noted that it was the ailing district commander who made the bonehead decision to return the asylum seeker. Flanagan was also the attorney for the OOD on the USS Belknap. Flanagan's son Brian had attended OCS a year earlier, and Lieutenant Emory had heard about his father's reputation and quietly recommended Flanagan to Robinson.

Robinson's lawyer wanted to lay the blame for the accident on the condition of the ship and the distraction of training OCs who were not ready to be part of such a training exercise. In essence, Robinson's attorney wanted to make the Coast Guard regret that it was crucifying Robinson. Anything that could be admitted into evidence that disgraced the service would serve Robinson by forcing the Coast Guard into a plea bargain. The strategy was pretty straightforward: dig up shit and threaten to throw it in the face of the Coast Guard so the whole world could be appraised, and then see if the Coast Guard would reduce the charges in lieu of making itself look bad.

The Santa Cruz's attorneys and Captain Robinson's attorney had the same goal: to discredit the training, the ship, and the Coast Guard systems in general. If the lawyers could prove the OCs onboard were not properly trained, then they could prove that the training itself was inadequate: Inadequately trained OCs were the distraction that caused the captain's error.

∞

Under government statutes, the families of the victims were only entitled to a $30,000 life insurance policy, and neither these families nor the survivors could sue the U.S. Coast Guard. However, they were coming together to sue the Santa Cruz and the pilot, who they thought must be at least partially to blame. Blame is often assigned in percentages; initial reports suggested that the Santa Cruz was 30 percent to blame and the Cuyahoga 70 percent. There was great incentive for both parties to make the Coast Guard training program look bad.

The logic against this argument was that the ship had a full crew on deck, and the OCs were there only to observe. We had no operational responsibilities. The OCs actually went beyond their prescribed observation-only duty by relaying orders, but they did that correctly and that was not the cause of the accident.

There was another conflict between what the Coast Guard training center thought the role of the trainees should be and what the Coast Guard district inspection team thought the trainees on the Cuyahoga were doing. The inspection team had noted each year that the Cuyahoga was undermanned and that the head-count shortages were stressing the permanent crew in their performance in navigating, piloting, and maintenance. They noted that the trainees were augmenting the crew, which helped alleviate the under-manning situation while underway. The question was whether the trainees actually augmented the crew or caused them more work than they saved. Our watch in particular had essentially zero experience.

I relived the final seven minutes aboard the Cuyahoga. Captain Robinson had given instructions and advice to me at least four times, and he spent most of the other time with OC Robinson, who was trying to take a bearing on Smith Point Light. Captain Robinson was the only person who had been on the bridge of a ship before that night. He had no back up, no one to cross-check facts or decisions, no one to say, "Hey, Cap, ya think we oughta hold off on that turn?" The flying-bridge lookout from the permanent crew had just been assigned to the Cuyahoga and this was the first time the seventeen-year-old had ever been on a ship.

A legal representative from the families of the victims and the survivors called to ask me if I wanted to be part of the suit. They were suing the Argentine freighter and its pilot for failing to slow down and not properly communicating the freighter's crew's intent until it was too late.

The families of the victims were only going to get $30,000 —not much to raise a family on. Beyond that, most didn't even have any insurance. All of the parents were seeking the truth, but some were seeking justice and a little compensation for giving up their son to a peacetime accident.

My situation was completely different from any of these other stakeholders; I hadn't gone through anywhere near what they had gone through. I thought, "My dad hates people who sue, and he is already mad at me because he thinks I lost the socket set."

∞

A large public hearing was scheduled in Baltimore. It would be a venue for Captain Robinson's attorney, the pilot's attorney, and the Santa Cruz's attorneys to make the OCs look like idiots.

We had to stand by in case the Coast Guard investigators needed to talk with us. We were told that the investigators were concerned about the quality of testimony, and they were afraid that we would be influenced by the discussions that we were having with each other. We were called into an all-hands meeting and given the simple message: "From now on, no one talks about the accident. Period. Are you all clear on this?" We said, "Yes, sir."

It was true that my own memories had started to include my fellow shipmates' recollections. In fact, we were starting to blend our thoughts together into one collective memory. It's natural and common for this to happen, which is why witnesses are not supposed to read the newspapers and jurors are not supposed to talk with each other until the final deliberations.

I was given the task of cleaning out the locker of my roommate, OC Clark. I was told his parents wanted his uniforms to be donated to others; they only wanted his personal effects from his valuables drawer. They knew that Jim had a camera and maybe some exposed film, and they were hoping to find some last pictures. We had to inventory everything, and there was no camera or film. I figured that Jim brought it along on the cruise and now it was on the bottom of the Chesapeake. There was nothing to pack except some letters, IDs, and a library card. Filling the box was heart-wrenching, but I thought how much more heart-wrenching it would be to receive the box. I also imagined what it would be like if my effects were sent home to my father. He would stick it in the back of the closet and never open it —unless of course he thought the socket set might be inside it.

∞

Our enforced silence on the subject was difficult for all of us, because one of the keys to getting over a tragedy is to talk things through. Our conversations with each other became stilted. Other than talking about the accident, what were we supposed to say? "Besides the sinking, how did you enjoy the cruise?"

I can remember a bunch of us sitting around the lounge with heads down, talking about how it affected our families and the Coast Guard family. Fred Fairchild told us about his wife's experience. The October 21st Miami Herald headline read that thirty crew members went down and that a local man, OC Fairchild, was still listed as missing. OC Fairchild was actually not listed as missing, and he called his wife the night of the accident before she heard any news in the press. Nonplused, she went to work like any other day, without reading the newspapers. At work, she got an unusually cool reception. Her co-workers figured she was either the bravest wife in Miami, or more likely, she hadn't heard the news. Her boss, not knowing which the case was, called her in and started by testing the water. "You really didn't have to come in this morning... "

We all laughed or smiled. It offered us an opportunity for a light moment in a dark time, a time devoid of anything even slightly funny. Then someone said, "If you were the boss, how would you break the news?"

One person suggested that the boss should have called all of his secretaries together and told them, "Everyone whose husband is still alive, please step forward; ah ... not so fast, Mrs. Fairchild" —very old joke customized to the moment. We laughed a nervous laugh; gallows humor was all we had.

Someone asked, "How would Captain Kirk have handled it?" One of my fellow survivors admitted that more than once "beam me up" was on his lips while he was treading water.

Another OC recalled one of our fallen shipmates, OC Heistand, marching alone with Big Mutha, out of step even with himself, and we laughed until we cried. Later, I found out that Lt. Emory had perma-nently retired the use of Big Mutha in memory of OC Heistand.

∞

The newspaper articles regarding the Cuyahoga proclaimed the collision the worst peacetime disaster in the history of the U.S. Coast Guard. The mustangs, however, reminded us that the Coast Guard buoy tender White Alder really held that distinction, but since the Vietnam War was in progress at the time, in spite of the fact that the White Alder's accident occurred far from the war zone, it was not a peacetime accident.

The weather on Saturday was rainy, windy, and cold. The OCS of-ficers had meetings all day; they looked more tired and haggard then the actual survivors. Toward the end of the day, the officers called a meeting and told us the news.

The Coast Guard had quickly set up a perimeter around the ap-proximate site of the collision. The wreck was found by identification of the hull, using sonar and visual confirmation. The ship had come to rest upright, and after narrowing the search and coming over the wreck, the mast was actually near enough to the surface to be seen. The fact that the wreck was upright reduced the chance for air pockets. Coast Guard divers made trips down to the hull to search for survi-vors. The divers quickly checked for air pockets and banged wrenches against the hull hoping for a reply. The divers were hampered by mat-tresses and sea bags stuck in passageways but persisted until they were absolutely sure that there was no possibility of survivors.

We then had a moment of silence. Even when you know bad news is going to come, it still hits hard.

We were told that everybody who didn't have duty would be allowed liberty that night after the investigators were through with us for the day. Since my anchor duty now seemed to be permanently postponed, I had my first chance for a beer in six weeks, but I decided to stay in. Not everyone wimped out like me and stayed in. A number of OCs decided to go out and drown their sorrows. That night the sorrows were deep, and they needed severe drowning.

∞

On Sunday morning at about 0300, I heard a commotion in the hallway as the OC officer of the day was waking the company duty officer. They had just received a call from the police -three of our fellow officer candidates were in an accident. The car was totaled and the occupants were being taken to the hospital. If my mother stubbed her toe she would curse, 'Jamais deux sans trois' —never two without three, or my dad would say, "bad things happen in threes." I knew risk was a dependent event. What next? There must be something to this run of bad luck. Why was I being punished by God? For what purpose? Any number of things, I guessed.

Within a few hours we heard that, while the car was totaled, there were no serious injuries, thank God. We also found out that the driver hadn't been charged with DWI. Of course, everyone in the Tidewater area was reeling from the tragedy, and we wondered whether our fellow law enforcement officers on the scene might have overlooked the driver's condition.

We were called in for a meeting in the morning, and Lieutenant Emory began yelling at us for the previous night's stupidity. It turns out the car belonged to one of our missing shipmates. The driver said he had been given the keys and permission to use the vehicle prior to his departure the afternoon before. Lieutenant Emory made a compelling argument: "Didn't you think that circumstances might have changed a little since he handed you the keys?"

The OC's family was flying in the next day on a one-way ticket, expecting to drive the car back. Who was going to tell them to reserve a rental car or make it a roundtrip ticket? With tears in his eyes, Emory said that he had just had one of the most difficult conversations of his life a few hours before, delivering the news that their son was presumed dead. They refused to believe it.

Now he was going to have to call again and deliver this shit news. The OC said he would call, but Lieutenant Emory said, "It's my job and I'll do it; I know what I have to do." Then his tone changed, and softly, "We all have to pull together and refrain from any more stupid acts. This is a very difficult time. We are all vulnerable and we need to be careful and watch out for each other. That's why I'm talking to you as a group."

∞

On Sunday afternoon we were told that three bodies had been found. McDowell's body was found in the passageway. This was probably the person Arne Denny had urged to "Move! Move!" Arne got up and left the room. I thought of Bruce Wood and how he cringed when MK1 Thomason told us about the White Alder's crew being interned in the Mississippi mud. Later I found out that MK1 Thomason was found in the engine room. He didn't have watch down there, and was probably just helping out or trying to learn a little more.

Later that afternoon, we were given details of the upcoming memorial service on Tuesday and what our roles would be. We were told that Monday's classes were postponed and that we were to be ready at 0900 with our swim trunks. I wondered why.

One OC didn't want to testify to anything anymore and tried to resign. The officers told him he could leave OCS but no one was going to leave the Coast Guard until all testimony was completed. All of us dreaded the idea of recounting the episode one more time.

∞

On Monday morning, we boarded a bus and were told we were going to a large pool for a course in survival swimming, now called drown-proofing. I was a little concerned. The last time I broke my eardrum, I was told not to go into the water for six weeks or until it healed. I hadn't told anyone that my eardrum was busted because I felt —there is no other word —ashamed. I had this image of going to sick bay and having a fifty-year-old nurse who looked like George C. Scott say to me, "ELEVEN PEOPLE DIED and you're complaining about an earache!" Then she would proceed to slap me over and over and tell me to be a man. But then maybe a little chlorinated water might be good for a busted eardrum.

I learned a lot from the course. I was especially attentive because I could now clearly envision the valuable application of these principles. I learned that you should get away from a sinking ship because the undertow could drown you, or the force of incoming water could smash your body against the ship, or the flotsam racing to the surface could crush your legs, or worse. I thought, "I sure could have used this information a few days ago." I didn't understand why the survival swimming class was scheduled after our trip to sea. There were lots of murmurs from others about closing the gate after the horse left the barn.

We practiced survival swimming, which is a motion and stroke that uses far less energy than treading water. In warm water, a survivor could last almost indefinitely —and be kept fresh for sharks. We were told over and over again that swimming intensely, as I had done when the Cuyahoga sank, was the quickest way to drown. Oops.

We also learned that when the water is burning, you swim under it, and when you need to come to the surface to breathe, you splash the water and the flames will extinguish. Given the Cuyahoga's name-association with the Cuyahoga River's burning water, and with all the sparks flying during the collision of our ships, I thought that we were damn lucky not to have been subjected to that particular inconvenience. Later, however, I learned it's almost impossible for diesel fuel to burn under the conditions we were in.

As we boarded the bus to the barracks, an officer asked me what we would say in response to the question, "Did you have survival swimming?" I responded, "Yeah, I had it days after I needed it."

He said, "Fair enough," and he proceeded to ask everyone else the same question. One OC said he would reply, "Yes, I had survival swimming." I heard someone comment behind me that the guy was a first-class damage-control man.

I thought, "Isn't he a college kid, not a mustang?" Then I got it. This was a junior officer's attempt at CYA, but there would be no cover up in Commander Loy's command, and the actual sinking/survived/survival swimming lessons sequence surfaced in the news.

∞

Right after survival swimming, I gave my account to the Coast Guard inquiry board and was told that a National Transportation Safety Board had convened a special investigation in Baltimore, and I had to go there immediately. The NTSB is an independent establishment of the United States government composed of five members appointed by the president, with the advice and consent of the Senate. No more than three members may be appointed from the same political party. At least three members must be appointed on the basis of technical qualification, professional standing, and demonstrated knowledge in accident reconstruction, safety engineering, human factors, transportation safety, or transportation regulation. The special investigation panel board was packed with Coast Guard officers, and the pilot's attorney was calling foul.

When I arrived back at the base I wanted to get a new ID card and some money, and order a pair of glasses, but I was told that I had to pack my gear immediately and take a car to Baltimore. They said I should take my books so I could study, because I would probably do a lot of waiting around. When I went back to my room, I put some clothes together and went in search of my books. At that point I realized that my books and notes were now being reviewed by lobsters- I had taken them to study on the cruise.

I was supposed to drive up with some of the guys from the Cuyahoga's permanent crew, but one of the guys took his own car and the other two went with him. I really wanted to talk to them. They'd been together on the Cuyahoga for months. Maybe they didn't want an outsider in their conversation; maybe they blamed the OCs.

Anyway, they left without me and I was assigned to a motor pool driver. I asked the driver to wait for me to get an advance, but the cashier was out to lunch and the driver couldn't wait an hour.

I rode in the front passenger side. According to our manual, I wasn't supposed to fraternize with anyone on the base other than OCs and staff, but by this time I was dying to talk. After we got on the Williamsburg Parkway, I started the conversation with, "Are you from here?" He looked over at me and said, "You guys really fucked up, didn't you?"

That was a non-starter for me. I told him, "I'm not allowed to talk about it," and I climbed into the backseat and tried to sleep.

The radio was playing, and I heard a news update that they had found three more bodies. I heard them say that it could cost over a half million dollars to raise the Cuyahoga, and that the wreck, search, and salvage were affecting maritime commerce on the Chesapeake.

When the broadcast cut back to the DJ, he remarked, "More expensive government mistakes screwing up the economy and the taxpayers have to pay for it."

"Turn that shit off," I said. "I'm not supposed to listen to news."

I was angry once again, but so was everyone else. People had started to feel the effect of huge deficits from the Vietnam War. Inflation was accelerating to double digits, mortgage rates would eventually climb to over 20 percent, and our year 1978, saw the highest jump in unemployment since the Great Depression of the 1930s.

In 1976, a character from the movie Network, Howard Beale, pretty much summed up Americans' feelings: "We're mad as hell, and we're not going take it anymore!" Just mention more taxes or spending and you'd be ousted from office. Both parties were blaming each other and were out to prove they were the cheapest bastards in the room.

∞

The driver switched the radio station. Although I was mad that he wouldn't wait for me to get some money, I felt I had no right to give him the silent treatment. I decided to start some small talk. My mom always said the best ice breaker is a compliment. I had noticed that SR was on his name tag. I had seen SA —Seaman Apprentice —and just SN —Seaman —but never SR. I thought it might stand for Search Rescue, or perhaps he was in some sort of officer corps and it stood for Sir. He looked like he was sixteen, so I started the conversation with, "You must have worked hard to have already made it to SR."

His reply surprised me. He said, "FUCK YOU," and in case I didn't hear, he almost completely turned around in the driver seat and said it again. "FUCK YOU."

I started to fall over myself with apologies. I told him I had no idea what SR meant. He calmed down a little and told me his story. He had made it through boot camp a few months before and was promoted from Seaman Recruit to SA. He also got a prime slot at Boson Mates "A" School. He was in the honor guard at boot camp.

Then he got caught smoking pot and the punishment from the Captain's Mast was as follows: busted one grade, thirty days extra duty, a fine, kicked out of "A" school, and a general discharge that would take another month. And so he was assigned to the motor pool. He told me he was "kind of a screw up" in high school, but the day he graduated from boot camp his father told him it was the proudest moment in his life. Now his dad had stopped talking to him. Tough love was the new parental craze sweeping the nation.

Jerry Rafferty's Baker Street came on and we stopped talking and listened:

He's got this dream about buyin' some land
He's gonna give up the booze and the one-night stands
And then he'll settle down in a quiet little town
And forget about everything

I blurted out, "That's what I wanted to do, go back to Falmouth and forget about everything."

He said, "My mom said my dad doesn't want me back."

When the song ended, he said, "Were you guys drunk or something? That's what everyone is saying."

"No one was drunk, but I can't talk about it."

He said, "It doesn't make sense. It's a huge ocean. How could two ships collide? Are you sure the captain wasn't drunk?"

That thought had never crossed my mind, and I had to think back. Having spent five years dealing with drunks, I could spot a drunk a mile away. The captain didn't appear drunk to me, but he did looked really tired and stressed, like someone who just came off a long voyage.

I asked, "What did you hear?"

"Most people say that he wasn't a drinker, at least not in public. But he might have been one of those closet drinkers -they're the worst kind. People say he looked like shit for the past year and had gotten into two accidents. He had two letters of reprimand on file, just from this year!"

That disturbed me. I had only spent a few minutes with him, but he was still my captain and I felt the need to defend him.

"No one was drinking."

When we passed Washington, the driver said, "You don't mind if I buy a six pack, do you?" While six weeks ago that might have seemed like an excellent suggestion, I realized this was exactly the kind of stupid act Lieutenant Emory was warning us about. But I was an officer candidate, not yet an officer, so I really had no rank or authority.

I said, "I would mind very much. I don't need to get into any more trouble."

"They are probably going to kick all of you out anyway, so why do you care?"

"Yeah," I told him, "but they could keel haul me before I'm discharged, so I don't want the charges to pile up."

"Can they still do that?" He didn't get my sarcasm at all, but at least he didn't get the beer.

After a five-hour drive, we arrived in Baltimore. There was a message waiting for me at the hotel desk: they wanted all OCs to attend the memorial service, so I had to immediately go back to Yorktown.

Luckily, the driver had told me he had to go to the head. I found him refilling in the lounge. I told him he had to drive me back to Yorktown. He had planned to spend the night in Baltimore, and was less than excited about heading back. He said he was entitled to a supper break and proceeded to partake in a liquid meal. Since I didn't have any money, I waited for him in the lobby. I walked into the bar about every five minutes, looking impatient.

After we got back into the car, he proceeded to give me the silent treatment, but about an hour into the drive he said he was tired and asked me to take over. Since I didn't have my glasses —and I am legally blind —or my driver's license, I told him I couldn't. He wasn't pleased. I stayed in the backseat with my seatbelt on and watched his eyes in the rearview mirror. He was starting to nod off. Tired and drunk, or bad vision and no license: who was the better driver? I decided to drive. I squinted my way down I-95 and we made it back to Yorktown safely at about 3:00 a.m.

∞

Our OC class had rehearsed the memorial service during my absence, and I was told just to go along with what everyone else did. It was a partly cloudy day that constantly threatened rain. More than a thousand people had gathered at the base for the service, including the commandant of the Coast Guard, the under secretary of transportation, the Indonesian ambassador, and perhaps fifty reporters.

All speakers made somber remarks or offered prayers, but it was OC Williams who read Psalm 107:23-30 (KJV) and brought us all to tears:

They that go down to the sea in ships, that do business in great waters;
These see the works of the Lord, and his wonders in the deep.
For he commandeth, and raiseth the stormy wind, which lifteth up

the waves thereof.
They mount up to the heaven, they go down again to the depths:
their soul is melted because of trouble.
They reel to and fro, and stagger like a drunken man,
and are at their wits' end.
Then they cry unto the Lord in their trouble, and he bringeth them
out of their distresses.
He maketh the storm a calm, so that the waves thereof are still.
Then are they glad because they be quiet; so he bringeth them unto
their desired haven.

It sounded like the ultimate Coast Guard Psalm; writing hasn't really improved much in the last 2,000 years.

We were seated to one side, and I noticed a commotion in the second row in the middle. Mrs. Balina, the wife of the ship's cook, collapsed in her chair, spilling her nineteen-month-old baby onto the person next to her. Captain Robinson was seated right in front of her and quickly came to her aid, knocking over a few collapsible chairs. The speaker stopped, an EMT gave her smelling salts, and they tried to escort her away, but she insisted on staying. As Captain Robinson started to unfold his chair and get resettled, I caught a glimpse of the saddest eyes I had ever seen.

At the reception that followed, we met the families of our lost shipmates. "I am sorry." "I am terribly sorry." "I am so sorry." "I am so sorry for your loss." These rejoinders were bad enough, but then there were a few questions from the bereaved. "Did you talk to him that day?" "What was the last thing he said to you?" "Was he happy?" "Did he say anything about me?" "Did he suffer?" "Was it quick?" I didn't have any answers. I felt like a zombie; I could offer no help.

As I was standing there, I overheard a thread of a conversation "... what did they expect, they had her sit behind the man that killed her husband." I realized then that sorrow and anger are unhappy bedfellows.

A few were crying uncontrollably, but there also were young children who looked dazed and confused, too young to understand that Friday's accident had changed their lives forever. I recalled a line from a poem by American poet Edwin Arlington Robinson: "They are all gone away, there was nothing more to say."

Immediately after the reception, I had to go back to Baltimore. I was on TAD, a military acronym for Temporary Assigned Duty. To some it meant Traveling Around Drunk. The base had basically been shut down for the day, so I couldn't get a cash advance, new books, glasses, or an ID. I was off for another five-hour drive without money or anything else.

∞ The Coast Guard experimented with a number of uniform styles ∞

Left: 'Disco Mike' (OC Moriarty) displays the disco look
Right: 'Captain Crunch' (OC John Brown) tries the minimalist look

When I went to check into the hotel, the hotel clerk asked for a credit card. When I told her that I didn't have one, she asked me how I expected to pay. I told her that I expected the Coast Guard to pay. She told me that the Coast Guard only made the reservation and that I needed a credit card to check in.

I tried to phone the contact I was given in Baltimore, but he was in meetings. I asked to speak to the hotel manager and told him my convoluted story. Out of sympathy, and because he wanted to get me out of the lobby, he offered me a room if I provided a cash deposit and an ID. I pulled out two wadded singles that looked like they had been through a shipwreck (they had), but I had no ID card. He said, "Well, I've heard a lot of stories, but this pretty much takes the cake." The ID was non-negotiable: "You can't stay anywhere in Baltimore without an ID —it's the law."

As I turned away, an older woman standing behind me in line said, "Oak, can you help me with my bags?"

I said, "Of course," and I followed her outside and started to grab her bags.

She said, "Oak is a strange name. What's it short for?"

I realized she was trying to pronounce OC and probably thought I worked at the hotel. It was that damn nondescript uniform: a light blue shirt, dark blue polyester pants, a polyester dark blue tie, and a name tag that said "OC Eident."

I said that it wasn't short for anything. My father named all seven boys after trees.

She said, "Well, your father misspelled the name."

"We're from West Virginia, ma'am." She immediately understood.

I dropped the bags at the desk and she brought out her purse. The desk clerk said, "Hey, he doesn't work here. He's in the Coast Guard."

She put her purse away; I thought, "Just because I'm in the Coast Guard doesn't mean I don't take tips."

After about three hours in the lobby and being told a half dozen times that I was the laziest bell boy in the western hemisphere, someone from the Marine Inspection Office arrived and secured a room for me with a Government Services Administration credit card. He said I should have come with orders and a cash advance, and that I shouldn't have gone even one day without a government ID. Maybe in a perfect world I thought, but my world had recently been turned upside down.

As he was leaving, he said that I was not allowed to charge alcohol on the card. I realized I couldn't use the phone for calls outside the hotel either, not even a collect call. Without a phone, I couldn't have anyone wire me money, but then, without an ID, I couldn't even pick up money if I wanted it, and without money I couldn't even buy a beer or a magazine to read. Without my glasses, TV was a blur. I was about to start a wait-fest, essentially a monk's life, nearly blind, and for all intents and purposes utterly broke.

∞

I'd never been in a hotel that had a minibar, and this was the first time I had a television remote control. I concluded that the minibar was one of the greatest inventions of the twentieth century: all this great stuff within arms-reach of my bed. But it was frustrating because here was this little refrigerator with three kinds of beer and all sorts of stuff to eat, and I couldn't have any of it on a GSA credit card.

I figured with my two dollars I could buy a beer or two and maybe strike up a conversation and be the recipient of a few free rounds. I headed down to the hotel bar bellied up, and ordered a beer. When it arrived, the bartender said, "That will be $2.50." I was fifty cents short. Hell, beers only cost ninety cents at the Kidd.

I turned to the guy next to me, who was wearing a five-hundred-dollar Brooks Brothers suit and told him my troubles. He looked at me as if I had just crawled out of a pond of scum and didn't say anything, but as he turned away he flicked two quarters in my direction with his little finger and ring finger. I felt like telling him off, but I didn't. I knew it was the cut of the cloth, the polyester —he immediately sized me up as a person who was not worth talking to.

The bartender wasn't sympathetic. "Hey, that came out of my tip!" I just went over to a corner table and ended the quest for that elusive beer I had so long sought. I felt sorry for myself. At the training center, I had company to share my misery, but here I was alone. I tried to tell myself that I was still breathing, but it seemed like cold comfort. My mind started playing and immediately got stuck on the "if onlys" track. If only I had said "hold off on that turn" or "I don't think that's a fishing boat." Why had I been so silent when most of my life I couldn't keep my mouth shut? I was disappointed in myself; I had failed my first test in the real world. If I could just wake up and find out this bad dream was over...

After the beer, I went back upstairs and tried to watch TV. I was still angry, sad, nervous, and lonely. I had no one to talk to.

The Error Chain

Many error chains begin by thinking you know what another person is thinking. Yet we have all seen that two people can look at the exact same picture and see completely two different things. We need to constantly cross-check do we really know what the other person perceives. I remember looking into those binoculars and thinking that one big fishing boat. If I had even joked 'that's hell of a fishing boat' maybe someone else would have taken a second look.

While normally I would have a low power distance index, the recent OCS experience convinced me that everything I said was stupid and everyone of a higher rank was unquestionably right. Boot camp creates an effective and obedient foot soldier, but a dangerous co-pilot. Certainly I wasn't in a state of mind that allowed me to break the error chain.

19.

"Set up like a bowling pin,
getting knocked down
gets to wearing thin..."
-*"Truckin'"*
Robert Hunter, Robert Weir,
Phil Lesh, Jerry Garcia, The Grateful Dead

The next day I got up early. Breakfast was included in the room tab, so I went to the restaurant, where they were serving a huge all-you-can-eat breakfast. As I sat there alone, enjoying my eggs, I remembered the unbelievable brunches that my mother made after church on Sunday: We had both sausage and bacon (it wasn't a choice but a complimentary set), scrambled eggs with mushroom and cheese, fruit salad that had never seen the inside of a can, cut tomatoes, baked beans, and last something special that was in season: maybe brook trout, fried herring roe, waffles with strawberries, or blueberry muffins.

My family had dozens of cousins and "almost cousins" from all over New England, and on hot weekends they would often decide to drive down to the Cape and stop by. My dad and mom never turned a guest down. More coffee was perked, more plates taken out, and occasionally "family hold back" was whispered so guests couldn't hear. Adults always had the beds, and there were many nights when I was happily displaced to backyard berthing.

As I remembered those breakfasts, I just wanted to go home. I could hear my mother say, "I've had just about as much as I can take from you boys." But she could never stay mad at us.

In the hotel dining room, I thought, "I've had just about all I can take," and tears streamed down my face onto the bacon.

The waitress, concerned, asked me if something was wrong. I had to cover in my usual humorous way; I told her, "I really like bacon, but I'm Jewish and I don't know what to do."

She said, "Well, you certainly took enough of it." Then she got away from me as fast as she could.

∞

After breakfast, I went to the Baltimore Marine Inspection Office, or MIO. The responsibility for certifying merchant vessels and personnel was the last piece of the five-part government-agency puzzle put together to form the modern-day Coast Guard. Despite this responsibility, the MIO still didn't have the authority to inspect Coast Guard vessels or require Coast Guard personnel to hold mariner licenses. Due to the training and special expertise required, the "M" track has always been somewhat separate from other Coast Guard operations. These guys don't log sea time, but they have marketable skills and can land a great job in the maritime industry when they retire, taking the revolving door within the great military industrial complex. These MIO guys are not the hardest working members of the maritime complex, however. Their unofficial motto seems to be: "You have to go to lunch, but you don't have to come back." Nevertheless, despite a few bad apples, the Coast Guard's marine inspection operation is considered one of the most efficient and well-run regulatory bodies in the world.

They put me in a conference room by myself and cryptically told me to wait. They didn't know when I would be called to testify. While I sat there, I spotted a set of Coast Guard marine safety manuals on the shelf and started to read them. The Coast Guard marine safety manuals have more volumes than the Encyclopedia Britannica.

I soon came to the conclusion that this was probably the assigned reading in hell, and since I would be reading these for eternity, why prepare ahead of time. Occasionally they needed to use the room, and I'd have to wait in the hall. At the end of the day, they sent me back to the hotel.

I was about to embark upon another night of unclear TV when my room phone began to ring. I was sure it was a wrong number because no one knew I was here. It was a grief counselor from the U.S. Navy's Special Psychiatric Rapid Intervention Team (SPRINT). Commander Loy had sought assistance, and the SPRINT team was activated to provide mental health services to the Cuyahoga survivors, their families, and others who had been affected by the disaster. They had been operating in and around Yorktown for the past week, and they finally tracked me down.

The counselor started in with, "How are you doing?"

I replied, "Fine, thanks."

He fired back, "No, I mean: how are you really doing?"

"I believe the accident happened. I am stuck in anger, and there is no one to bargain with —and I am so looking forward to depression."

He said, "Why are you looking forward to depression?"

"So I can get to acceptance."

"You've been through this recently." After my mother's untimely death, my sister and my oldest brother, Paul, sought counseling. I had heard them talk about the stages of grief. Of course, I never sought out counseling; I thought I was too tough and brave. Besides, pouring out your emotions to a stranger seemed scary to me.

"Yes," I said.

I was leery about talking with a psychiatrist. My father used to say you would have to be crazy to talk to a psychiatrist. He said, "Never talk to someone who can legally put you in a straight jacket." I think he really meant it. I had never heard of a rapid intervention team before, but I guess this was the kind of response that you would expect from the Coast Guard. I later learned that the Cuyahoga collision was the first opportunity the Navy had to use the SPRINT team. It had existed in another form as the Navy Critical Incident Stress Intervention Team, or NCISIT —not a great acronym. This team also responded to the Belknap-Kennedy collision, and nine months earlier they responded to the Navy's Barcelona collision -a liberty boat ferrying sailors from shore to the USS Guam and USS Trenton collided with a freighter less than 100 feet from the pier. With forty-nine lost sailors and Marines, it was the worst "boating accident" in the Navy's history.

The counselor asked me what I was angry about. I told him that I had been put in a situation that I shouldn't have been in. I ranted and rambled; I told him I felt guilty that I was alive. It made no sense that I was alive and my shipmates were dead. He asked about my religious upbringing. I told him I was Catholic, and I could practically hear him say, "It figures."

He told me that survivors frequently feel guilt, and that everything I was going through was natural. I would eventually come to under-stand and accept what happened. I asked him when. He said it would take time. We talked for a while, and we concluded that I was dealing with the aftermath OK. He said I should feel free to call him anytime. He called my fiancée, gave her my number and she called me.

Sue and I talked for hours; we focused on our wedding plans and our future. Years later, when the children were crying, my wife would soothe them by talking about how good tomorrow was going to be. The same strategy worked for me that night. I could order food from room service, and boy, did I —all sorts of food. Out of boredom, I started to eat five meals a day. Little did I know that there would be a day of reckoning -I would have to pay the government back after I received a per diem that could barely cover one good meal in a five-star hotel. The Baltimore Marine Inspection office finally secured me a government ID, and my resourceful fiancée gave me access to a credit card. The next day I got a pair of glasses, a new wallet, and some cash to put in it. Someone also drove up from Yorktown with a complete set of the OC curriculum books I had lost at sea.

∞

I later read that the SPRINT team considers the first twelve hours after a traumatic incident critical for therapeutic help. Apparently, the therapy-receptive frame of mind diminishes until, after seventy-two hours, the person becomes non-receptive. After that, the SPRINT team's most valuable assistance is helping with the range of difficult problems victims face, from funeral arrangements to emergency money for food and beer. Another finding was that, commanding officers, despite always trying to appear strong, are the most vulnerable to depression.

∞

I finally got to testify late in the afternoon on 25 October. Walking into a huge room filled with about 150 people felt like going from the dentist's waiting room to the dental chair. I suddenly realized that waiting wasn't all that bad. There was a row of gentlemen who appeared to be the board, and rows of tables occupied by the interested parties: the Santa Cruz captain and representatives of the ship's owners, Hamill, who had piloted the Santa Cruz, the captain of the Cuyahoga, the Coast Guard's team, lawyers for each of these parties, the members on the board and a separate legal team representing some of the victims who were all seated at tables. There were lawyers representing the agent of the Santa Cruz. It appeared that even the lawyers had lawyers. A sergeant at arms was in the galley as were court reporters, the press, and many concerned or curious people.

My mind flashed back to the sixth-grade school play: I completely froze. The girl next to me, realizing I wasn't about to earn a Tony, jumped in and recited my lines —showoff. After the play, my father said, "You looked like a deer in the headlights!" My mother's advice was, "If you ever have to do this again, find a reassuring face in the audience and just keep looking at him." My brother's advice was to never be seen in public again.

∞

After I was sworn in, the board chairman gave me a few instructions, which included not talking with other witnesses and not talking directly to the press. Then the lead attorney started with the interrogatives. Looking around the room, I saw just one smiling face giving me a nice reassuring nod: Captain Robinson. His nod seemed to say, "Don't worry. Everything's going to be all right."

The lead attorney started with some background questions and slowly got into the details of my watch. About an hour in, he asked me to stand and draw a diagram of the situation, to identify where the ships were and their headings. I did, and I explained what the situation was and what I said to the other OC and then to the captain. On another board, he asked me to show the positions after the Cuyahoga turned into the Potomac.

Periodically, I would look at Captain Robinson and he would give me a reassuring nod. The lead attorney asked me to label the first diagram as "time of relief," the exact time I took over as the pretend officer of the deck. Not the best speller in the world, I thought to myself "i" before "e" except after "c." I thought about writing, "How do you spell relief? R-O-L-A-I-D-S." I looked around the room and thought that maybe they wouldn't appreciate my humor, so I just spelled relief the correct way.

After I sat down, the captain's lawyer started with his questions, which took more than an hour. He seemed to re-ask every single question that had already been asked. In retrospect, he was probably checking my accuracy.

He said, "You have a fine memory, Mr. Eident, and you seem to have been coached very well."

I gave a bit of a "what the hell do you mean" look and said, "I wasn't coached at all."

He said, "Sure. Now how long have you been the guest of the Marine Inspection Office here in Baltimore?"

"About a week."

He then asked incredulously, "What you have been doing with your time here?" While watching TV and gorging myself should have been my answer, I chose waiting alone and studying. He asked me, "When the flying bridge called down and reported a ship off the port bow, why didn't you relay that information to the captain?"

"I had just talked to him no less than a minute before, briefed him on all the turns and all the contacts, and I didn't think there was a reason to remind him a minute later of something he already knew about."

He got up and walked over to my diagrams and said, "I want you to think very carefully about this question. After the bearing was marked, what did the captain say to you?"

"He said, 'I advise you to go west to course 303 degrees.'"

"Did he say 'advise,' or did he say, 'I order you to change to 303'?"

"He said advise."

"Are you sure?"

I could no longer catch the captain's eye. He was looking down. "I am sure he said advise."

"You then said or did what?"

"I told the helmsman to turn to course 303."

"Did you say, 'I advise you to turn to course 303'?"

"No, I said, 'Helmsman change course to 303.' He replied, 'Aye aye, Sir.'"

"So you gave a direct order to the helmsman to change to 303, correct?"

"I suppose it was an order."

"You, not the captain, ordered the helmsman to change to course 303?"

I looked at the chairman, and he immediately interjected. "It's been a long day; let's reconvene tomorrow."

"Thank God," I thought. I didn't like the way this was going. I made my way to the Coast Guard lawyer and he told me not to worry. He went on to say, "I don't know what that asshole was trying to prove. No one could even imagine that an OC could walk onto a bridge and start giving orders. There is only one guy who should give an order while the captain's on the deck, and that's the captain. All you did was relay a command, and you did it with accuracy, " No one is contesting that."

Next morning, on the way to breakfast, I passed one of those small newspaper boxes and caught a glimpse of the day's headlines: "Officer Candidate Gives Fateful Command." It was a reference to ME! While they say there is no such thing as bad publicity, I was at a loss as to how that saying applied to this situation. Certainly, a more accurate headline would have been "Officer Candidate Correctly and Accurately Relays the Order from Captain to Helmsman," but I am sure that would be too long, and I could hear the editor say, "Let's trim it down a little... "

The incredible all-you-can-eat breakfast had lost its appeal. For sure, the headline was true on one level, but really it was another "half truth," an outright prevarication even, that our press relies upon to keep their circulation numbers up. I thought to myself, "Do I know anyone in Baltimore? I hope no one I know ever reads this." The story was picked up on the wire service: It went national.

I went back to my room and called the Coast Guard lawyer. His immediate reaction was, "You were told not to read the newspapers." "I didn't," I said. "I just glanced at a headline and discovered that I was about to be served up as a patsy." He didn't press me on my infraction and reassured me that I had nothing to worry about. In any event, he would meet me at the Marine Inspection Office and walk to the courthouse with me.

While I am sure the lawyer had some idea how different that walk would be for me that morning, I didn't have a clue. The press was waiting for me —TV cameras and flash photographers surrounded me, microphones were jammed in my face. Apparently everybody wanted to hear my side of the tragedy. The lawyer did away with his normal politeness and whispered sharply in my ear, "Keep your mouth shut."

This time there would be no excruciating wait in a back room. I went directly into the hearing room. The captain's lawyer was scheduled to start where he left off the previous day. He greeted me with an ingratiating smile and said, "How are you today?"

"Angry," I replied.

His head jerked back, and with one of those bemused looks he practices. He asked, "What's the problem?" He already had the headline he wanted.

I don't remember my exact words, but the essence was: "I'm not sure that the whole truth is being revealed through the current process."

Murmurs spread throughout the room.

Since everyone in the room was part of this process, I had just offended everyone there. If my classmates had been there, I knew what they would be thinking: "There's Eident's mouth screwing things up again."

"Well, let's get to the whole truth today," the attorney said.

For continuity's sake, and for effect, the captain's lawyer began recalling yesterday's testimony. I interjected, "I want to make it clear that I simply, correctly, and accurately relayed an order from a superior officer." I looked at the chairman. "I don't think there is any question that I misinterpreted or changed the order that was given by the skipper, is there?"

The chairman looked at me and said, "Mr. Eident, you are not on trial here." Then, after a pause, he added, "No one here is on trial today."

That was another half-truth —the skipper was on trial; this process would decide if Captain Robinson would face a court-martial under the uniform code of military injustice.

The captain's lawyer changed his tactic. He looked down at his notes. "According to your application to OCS, you 'sailed and navigated some of the most treacherous waterways in the world."

"Damn!" That creative writing course I took senior year seems to have had an effect. I did what every college graduate did with a resume that essentially should read, "just graduated from college, still don't know shit from Shinola," a World War II phrase that my mother wished hadn't returned from the war.

OK, here is where I had bent the truth a little. Now I needed to downplay my alleged experience. "I had a fourteen-foot aluminum skiff that I used to tend lobster pots with and bring clamming. I also sailed on a twenty-two-foot Balboa. And yes, that sailing was in and around Woods Hole, arguably one of the most treacherous channels in the world, but these were boats with tillers and I never went out at night."

∞

While history doesn't actually repeat itself, there are certain waves that keep recurring. Thirty-five years earlier, my Uncle Arthur was a gunner on a destroyer in World War II. When his ship was passing through Woods Hole, someone had been checking the crew's personnel files and they called him to the bridge to share some local knowledge of the shoals and ledges. That was his first time on a bridge and he didn't have a clue. My grandparents never had a boat, and his experience in those shoals consisted of swimming in Buzzard's Bay and taking the ferry to the Vineyard. After a mildly embarrassing few minutes, the captain told him to return to his station.

"You took boating classes then?"

"Yes, a power squadron course."

"Did they teach you to turn to starboard in meeting situations?"

"Yes."

"The order you gave... " More murmurs arose from the crowd as they recognized the injustice of his half-truth. He qualified his interrogative in response. "The order that was given was to turn to port, correct?"

I thought, "It's like driving down the road: just stay to the right and nobody gets hurt." I said out loud, "There were two orders. The first order was to turn west up the Potomac to our destination. The next order was to turn to the left to avoid a collision. For the first order, no one realized that we were in a meeting situation because we didn't anticipate the other ship would be that close."

"What about the second order to turn to port? Why didn't you question it?"

"Having spent six weeks in the Coast Guard marching around, I didn't think I had the experience to question a respected superior with thirty years of experience as a qualified deck officer."

If Captain Robinson had told me to set course for Alpha Centauri at warp factor four, I would have repeated it, verbatim and without question. I learned later that QM2 Rose, the navigator who came out of the chart room at the last moment, was asked the same question. He told the court that, since he had been out to sea only once before the Cuyahoga, he felt he wasn't familiar enough with the ship's handling characteristics and, therefore, "didn't feel qualified to question the order." I wish I had said something as intelligent as that.

"Let's not forget this was an academic exercise designed to instruct, so why didn't you question it on an academic basis?"

"I realized this was an extremely tense situation and that all I should do was whatever I was told, and do it as efficiently and calmly as possible. I did not want to burden the captain with academic questions."

I knew this wasn't helping our captain; I added, "I also realized that we were in 'extremis' and in this emergency case a captain can turn any way that he thinks will avoid a collision." My testimony finally ended in the early morning. Afterward, I had to wait some more.

∞

When I asked the Coast Guard attorney if I could go back to Yorktown, he said, "We'll see." Late afternoon I approached the Coast Guard attorney and asked again, and he said that Captain Robinson's attorney was reserving the right to recall me so I needed to stay. I saw Captain Robinson leaving for the day, and I ran up to him and said I needed to get back to Yorktown before I flunked out, but that his attorney wouldn't let me. Captain Robinson nodded his head and turned and talked with his attorney; fifteen minutes later I was told I could go.

I was already packed. I jumped into the afternoon car headed for Yorktown. Figuring my testimony had ended, I bought the afternoon papers. The papers were getting tired of the story, and my clarification was five pages in —the damage was done.

A brash young Ivy League officer overstepping his bounds would make great press, but there was nothing about Captain Robinson that made him an appealing target for the press. He wasn't drunk, asleep, or reckless. He was sincere, kind, and hardworking. He was just trying to do his job under a difficult situation and he made a mistake, a mistake that would be with him the rest of his natural life.

As I stared out the window on the long drive back to Yorktown, I recalled what my brother used to say to me when I told him my problems. "Pete, it could be worse —it could be happening to me!" As you can imagine, I took very little comfort in that advice when he offered it, but shamefully, I must say Bill's advice was comforting as I headed back to Yorktown. I thought about the captain; at first I was angry with him, but from the little I saw of him and the way everyone talked about him, I knew he was a decent man. There was, however, more about him that I didn't know or understand.

The Error Chain
Many years later, I learned that I should have said, "Captain has the con!" —the maritime equivalent of "You're it, no backsies." It wouldn't have occurred to me on my own for I had no illusions that I ever had the con or should have been graciously given the con. While it sounds cutthroat, it does clarify the chain of command. Captain has the con. I will remember that next time.

20.

"We're at the best place around
            But some stupid with a flare gun
   Burned the place to the ground
   ...No matter what we get out of this
            I know we'll never forget
   Smoke on the water, fire in the sky."
                    -"Smoke on the Water"
Deep Purple: Ritchie Blackmore, Ian Gillan,
      Roger Glover, Jon Lord, Ian Paice

I returned to Yorktown and OCS. I had missed about a week of classes. I remembered that in the first week they told us that once someone had missed two days of classes they had to wash him out. I was behind and depressed and wanted to quit, until I saw a letter posted on a bulletin board among other letters and notes:

To all officers, crewmen, and especially the survivors of the Cuyahoga tragedy,

I have put off writing until now, hoping I could find the words, the unemotional moment, and the wisdom necessary to handle the task at hand. Time hasn't been any help. The heart hasn't healed, and the shock and loss is permanent. However, I must not think of my feelings and loss, but rather of the men who were there through God's grace were selected to carry on what our son died for.

It would be easier for me to write to you if I could remember one instance of displeasure with Bruce, some conflict of opinions and even the heartaches that some parents have—we were spared because Bruce was kind and sensitive to the needs of others, and had a deep love for us. Therefore, I must tell you how sorry we are that your class had to have such a tragic interruption and a dark shadow cast on your dreams. I can't let you feel sorry for yourselves or for us, or let this interfere with your aims and goals—I must ask each and every one from the bottom of my heart to continue with your ambitions, for me, with added strength and resolution. This was Bruce's dream, this is what he would want of his buddies and I would be so happy and so proud to know you carried his dreams to success. If yours was but a desire in the past, it should now be a dedication.

Look to Lt. Roger Emory and your superiors for guidance, and trust in their ability to help you through your trials —as we, parents of Bruce, have had to do recently. I will be in contact with Lt. Emory and will follow your progress and share all your setbacks, trials, and success.

If there is need for a letter from home, a word of encouragement, or just a friend, we have a vacancy.

With much love,
Ray and Laura Wood.

∞

I realized that through feeling sorry for myself I had lost the plot. My goal was to do my duty and serve my country; the world was far bigger than me. Besides, Uncle Frank would have had a field day with me if I quit: "Things get a little tough and you run home like a school girl." It was time to get back on course, and there was no turning back.

∞

The class had gone through fire fighting training while I was gone. According to OC Conklin, in the middle of the training, a football game broke out. My classmates, freezing cold and wet and wearing full fire-fighting gear, were still filled with pent-up emotion and anger. An officer threw a football at them and they took it from there; a full-contact battle disguised as a sporting moment served to vent their

∞ Football game breaks out during fire-fighting training ∞

negative energy. I was green with envy: they combine my two areas of core competence (other than eating) and I miss the opportunity to show off.

The Coast Guard must protect against fire on its own ships and be prepared to fight it on other ships, oil rigs, piers, and buildings adjacent to wharfs —and an occasional polluted river. I had really looked forward to this part of the training, but when I asked if I could make it up, they told me no and not to worry about it.

∞

A collision at sea can ruin your day, but a fire at sea can put a crimp in your cruise, too. When I worked in the Captain Kidd, there was a salty old fisherman who would drink until he started bragging, "I'm drunker than ten men!"

Then, somewhere between his tenth and twelfth drink, he would shout, "Fire in the paint locker! Fire in the paint locker!" Evidently, one day there had been a fire in the paint locker on his fishing boat, and the man who reported it seemed so frantic that his yelling defined "frantic"; apparently this had made a permanent impression on all ten of him.

During the second annual Earth Week, on April 19, 1971, Patriot's Day, I was headed to Washburn Island with seventeen so-called friends for another round of our pseudo-military skirmishes. Patriot's Day was a day off from school by a decree of the Massachusetts legislature.

The previous year's war games turned into a real debacle, so we had negotiated a set of strict rules that we had titled "The Washburn Convention." The convention observed certain protocols, such as: no torture. We were not totally committed to following the rules.

Washburn Island was a 330-acre, privately held, and totally unoccupied. It has since been purchased by the Commonwealth of Massachusetts to create a nature preserve, part of the Waquoit Bay National Estuarine Research Reserve. During World War II, the island was used by the U.S. military to practice amphibious assaults, and they left behind underground bunkers and other military artifacts. To the eighteen sophomore boys descending on the island to practice war games, this all added up to cool. Keep in mind that, according to my brother Bill's math, we're talking one-eighteenth of a brain practicing war in a sophomoric fashion. After one full day's battle, half the original landing party retreated to the mainland, citing war crimes. On the second day, having lost our detainees, we were overcome with boredom. So we started to torture each other.

Eventually, Dennis Rogers and I heard Kevin Payne yelling frantically. We ran up to the field where he was camped and found the two Godlewski brothers terrorizing Kevin with burning sticks. Kevin was concerned less with his safety than with the sparks that were dropping on the dry grass. It was a hysterical sight. Here was this six foot six, 160-pound lunatic in a state of what appeared to be total panic. In the middle of my laughter, I had a sobering thought: "Hey, these guys are playing with fire."

Dennis and I immediately began putting out the small grass fires. The Godlewski brothers also realized that their antics were getting a little out of hand, and they started to help us put out the fires.

It was always windy on the top of the hill, but an unfortunately-timed squall blew through and swirled the wind violently down the hill through our camp. Now every single one of us was desperately trying to put out the fire, beating the burning ground with our army jackets. We made excellent progress putting out the fire in the thirty-foot radius immediately within the reach of our jackets, but when we looked up, we realized the fire had spread 360 degrees around us. The fire had spread so fast that it spread like, well, wildfire.

When I felt the wind-blown flames singe my face and eyebrows, I knew it was a lost cause, and that we were in real danger. We grabbed some tarps, draped them over our heads, and ran down the fiery path to the safety of our fourteen-foot skiff. While we had made three trips to get everyone to the island, everyone insisted one sailing to get off the island. Even though we left much of our gear behind, the skiff rode dangerously low with all of us on board.

When Kevin couldn't get the engine started, I told him to pull out the choke. He did, and handed it to me: not exactly what I had in mind. We ripped the cover off the engine, and I pulled the choke manually. We got the engine started, but as we gingerly headed through the waves toward the landing, we knew we were in big trouble. It was April, and the water was still freezing cold. If the boat swamped, we would have been swimming back to the island for warmth. I don't think there was a happy medium. During our passage back to the mainland, we devised an ingenious plan: we would beach the boat and hide. Perhaps forever.

As we rounded the point of the island and the landing came into view, we saw three fire trucks, with lights pulsing, and perhaps twenty volunteer firemen.

We implemented Plan B: Wave and yell for help.

The fire had been spotted from six miles away by one of the fire towers in the town forest. This was one big fire, and the smoke on the water nearly covered Waquoit Bay.

On the shore, the fire team was led by the deputy fire chief, Dennis Roger's father. Deputy Fire Chief Rogers immediately talked to Dennis, and Dennis came back to us with Plan C: "Help put out the fire and keep your mouths shut."

We ferried the firemen to the island, and our whole group became instant volunteer firemen. We had to don hard hats and were given either shovels or Indian pump cans, five-gallon backpacks of water with a pump hose. It took us two hours to extinguish the fire —the one benefit was that the fire prepared about five acres of the ground for blueberries.

With our faces red, partially from embarrassment and partially from burns, our eyebrows burned off, and our semi-melted polyester shirts glistening and clinging to our torsos in an unpredictable configuration, we looked a little like drag queens. It was a proud moment for our collective dads, particularly Deputy Fire Chief Rogers. The irony of this happening on Earth Week did occur to us, the young patriots that we were.

It impressed me to see how quickly the volunteers arrived and how well-trained and organized they were. It was not just the trained volunteers who responded to the fire call. Anybody with a boat ferried volunteers; people who lived near the landing brought out hot coffee and cookies; and anyone who wanted to carry an axe or water pack helped. It was truly a life-changing experience to see people come together in an emergency. I wanted be a part of that —not the starting-a-fire part but the putting-out part.

∞

One of my fellow football players at Brown, Chuck Margiotta, wanted to be a fireman. He was the type of person who attracted nicknames: "helium heels" because he walked on his toes, and "pumpy" because he was a serious body-builder. Pumpy stuck with him his whole life. He played offensive line, often across from me, and while he was only five foot eleven inches, he was tough as nails and in practice he never let up.

People would ask him, "Why go to Brown and then just join a fire department?" Pumpy always responded that he wasn't just going to join "a" fire department, he was going to join "the" Fire Department —FDNY —the Fire Department of New York, the best fire department in the world. Chuck always talked in superlatives. He said he just wanted to be the best fireman in the world as well as go to the best college in the world.

Most of the men in his family were in the FDNY, and he loved to talk about it. It sounded like such an exciting job to me, and I told him I wanted to go into the Coast Guard. FDNY works closely with the Coast Guard to put out fires in New York Harbor, and he had great respect for the Guard. He thought it was the best service in the federal government, and the best Coast Guard in the world.

While he was just a sophomore and a back-up lineman, his positive outlook was contagious. While he may not have made any big plays that season, his attitude helped propel the team into the Ivy League championship. We weren't the biggest, the strongest, or the most talented team, but we were the most determined. As our coach, John Andersen, would always say, "Men, there is no doubt, absolutely no doubt —we can win this!" It was that positivity that led to our success.

I remember trying to motivate myself at OCS during the dark days following the sinking of the Cuyahoga, thinking often of Chuck's assessment. I would say to myself, "I am in the best service in the world and can help by just being positive. I am doing the right thing." But there was much going on to lower our morale.

On October 28th, Republican Representative Robert Bauman and Democrat Representative Barbara Mikulski, both from Maryland, were calling for Congressional hearings. Representative Mikulski said the crew's testimony was "chilling."

I saw the headline, and decided to read on. Was Representative Mikulski referring to how cold it was or to the terrifying testimony of OC Denny and OC Rutledge's escape from below decks? No, the crew's level of incompetence was what the congresswoman found "chilling."

"A seventeen-year-old boy who was on lookout... thought the radar scope looked like cartoons... Why was he teaching Officer Candidates?... The Officer Candidates had a shocking lack of knowledge." The captain's attorney was winning the public relations battle. The term "cartoons" was a reference to watching the radar screen. Since it was almost useless, and since it was displayed on a picture tube, the crew called it "watching cartoons" —thus the reference to the "cartoon watch." It was actually a very clever metaphor that illustrated how bad the radar system was and that the safety standards being observed were cartoon-like as well. Calling it the "cartoon watch" reminded everyone that the radar system was a joke, although I refrained from calling anything "cartoon-like" during public hearings.

I read on. Captain Robinson had submitted a report on the safety condition of the Cuyahoga. His report indicated it was between "poor and unacceptable." Captain Robinson was an optimist. The communications system was practically useless. I remembered the leadership lesson from Lieutenant Emory: communication is the cause of 90 percent of all managerial problems. The person on the radar scope couldn't be understood by the other crew members because he was Indonesian and couldn't really communicate in English. The captain and the crew were criticized for not using the radar, but reports indicated that it had broken down fifteen times during the last self-inspection period. A technical instrument with that level of reliability couldn't be relied upon; therefore, they didn't trust it at all.

The secretary of transportation rebuked the two representatives, stating that the Coast Guard "fundamentally was not at fault." He added that both criminal and civil judicial suits were anticipated, and that the Congressional hearings could damage the government's case.

The representatives backed off. Representative Mikulski announced, "We do not want to interfere with or subvert any judicial process." Thus, the Coast Guard was now free to fix its own problems. What I found chilling was the representatives' lack of fortitude in pursuing an investigation into something affecting the survival of U.S. military personnel, however costly or unpopular it might be.

I was angry when I thought about how without coaching and with no attorneys on our side, an arrogant attorney with thirty years experience in law and navigation was able to make us look like idiots. I liked Captain Robinson and was glad he had him for an attorney, however. I also thought that if I ever had a maritime predicament, Flanagan would be the first guy I called.

The newspapers reported that Captain Robinson had received two letters of reprimand in the past six months. Right after the accident, a petty officer from the Cuyahoga had blurted to the press, "This was an accident waiting to happen." He didn't elaborate on the reason.

It takes a big man to admit a mistake. Initially, Captain Robinson exercised his constitutional right to remain silent, but he later decided, against the public advice of his attorney, to issue a formal statement to the Coast Guard. He admitted that he advised the course changes and the move to reverse all engines on the mistaken notion that the ship he saw was going up the Potomac River.

That belief stemmed from a conversation with OC Fairchild. When they first saw the ship eight miles away, they only saw one white light and one red light. The captain had said to Fairchild, "Do you know what that means?" Fairchild replied that only one white light meant it must be less than 150 feet in length, at which point the captain said it was, and therefore it must be a fishing boat going up the Potomac River. When Fairchild reported to me that he and the captain had spotted a fishing boat going up the Potomac, I took that as a statement of fact. When I peered through my binoculars, the ship looked like a fishing boat because of all the equipment on deck. Santa Cruz II was a self-unloading bulk carrier and carried a series of booms and cranes so it could load and unload in ports that had no facilities. As I would learn later, this equipment can obscure certain navigation lights from certain angles. When I gave my recital to take over the watch, I told him that there was a contact: a fishing boat, heading up the Potomac River, as if it were an established fact. That reinforced his original hypothesis and perhaps turned it into an irrevocable conclusion.

∞

Rumor had it that Captain Robinson would face potential court-martial for homicide. Of course, none of us as young OCs were cynical enough to realize that this focus of blame was intended to save the Coast Guard liability in a lawsuit and keep Congress off its back. Congress knew they were underfunding the Coast Guard and didn't want to be blamed for causing the tragedy.

The potential punishment that could be meted out seemed absurd. I was officially notified that I would be a witness in this travesty, and I wasn't happy about it. There was no malicious intent or willful misconduct behind this accident. There was no gross negligence of duty, and there was absolutely no chance the captain would ever do it again.

The accident was simply the result of an error in navigation judgment that could be punished by many years in jail, a dishonorable discharge, and loss of all benefits. Captain Robinson was a very religious man, and he loved the Coast Guard. People in his church, his community, and especially the Guard, looked up to him. He was also a family man with six children and a loving wife, and his whole family was suffering. One day you're a respected member of the community and the next you're responsible for eleven wrongful deaths and you could spend the rest of your life in jail.

On October 26th, six days after the collision, Coast Guard and Navy divers pulled seven of the last nine missing bodies from the wreck. Two other bodies were still missing. We were told, rather matter-of-factly, that when a person first drowns, the body sinks. After a few days, depending on the water temperature, a body bloats and rises to the surface. This is information that every Coast Guardsman who per-forms search and rescue needs to know.

On October 28th, the body of YNI Carter was recovered, and final-ly, on October 29th, Senior Chief David Makin, the last of the missing, was recovered and brought back for a proper burial. The bodies were found by private boaters, and these men were pulled out of the water by their fellow Coasties.

∞

Ever since I was a paperboy, I had maintained a tradition of keeping the newspaper on my birthday: October 29. I picked up a copy of that day's Washington Post and there was a small piece noting that the Cuya-hoga was going to be raised that day.

Also in that edition was a write-up on the funeral of Seaman McDowell, titled, "Spartan Funeral for Cutter Victim." The article, written by a Wash-ington Post staff writer, said there was a fifteen-minute service. There was a single reference to McDowell and no mention of the Cuyahoga.

Mrs. McDowell was so distraught that she stayed in her car dur-ing the service, and she was the last person to leave the grave site at Arlington National Cemetery. "She clenched the neatly folded flag that had earlier been presented to McDowell's father. She moved away only after one of McDowell's friends put his arm around her shoulder and led her away."

The staff reporter asked the Navy chaplain (a captain) why the ser-vice wasn't personalized, and his explanation was that he wasn't able to talk to the family or friends prior to the service. The reporter implied that the Navy chaplain was derelict in his duty.

McDowell had joined the Coast Guard seven months before. Because he loved the Coast Guard and wanted to make it his career, he was buried in uniform at his family's request.

∞

Years later, Kate (Lemon) Carter described YN1 Carter's funeral. This military family had been bracing themselves for the dreaded knock at the door announcing that their loved one had given the ultimate sacrifice for his country for years. They just expected the uniform to be Army and the sacrifice to have been made by Lt. Col. Carter, Bill's dad, during his tour in Vietnam.

Bill had been in the Coast Guard and on a training cruise on inland waters. This just didn't make any sense to the Carters. After "Taps" was played, the flag was about to be handed to Lieutenant Colonel Carter, but his wife reached out and took it from the officer's hands, realizing that it would have been too hard for her husband to hand it to her. The officer said to her and her husband, "On behalf of the President of the United States, the Commandant of the Coast Guard, and a grateful nation, please accept this flag as a symbol of our appreciation for your loved one's service to our country and to the Coast Guard."

∞

Raising the Cuyahoga wasn't easy, but it was urgently needed. The ship lay in the middle of the channel and was a hazard to navigation. It was also needed for evidence. Two U.S. Navy floating cranes were brought to the scene, but for the next two days it was too choppy to raise the ship from fifty-seven feet of water. The press focused on the expense.

The New Haven Register, on October 30th, featured a front page photograph of the Cuyahoga being lifted from the Chesapeake Bay with the caption "Death Ship Recovered." I thought: all the years of service the ship and its crew had provided to this country, distilled down into this tasteless sensational headline.

The ship was brought to Portsmouth, Virginia, and inspected by the National Transportation Safety Board. On October 31st, the OC survivors were told to clear their personal gear out of the Cuyahoga. The assignment was optional, and two OCs decided not to go. Our car arrived at the dock at about 1900 at night. It was pitch dark, Halloween night. The Coast Guard obviously doesn't officially recognize

Halloween as a holiday of any significance.

As I was climbing out of the car, I could make out the ghostly shape of the ship. The Cuyahoga was standing out of the water on blocks with a huge hole gaping in her side. The night was damp and cold, and somehow the whole scene felt dramatically reminiscent of the haunted house my mother and older brothers used to set up in our cellar. They always had people dressed in ghoul costumes, heads and limbs hanging as they moaned and jumped out of the dark to startle their Halloween victims descending the cellar stairs. I was having second thoughts about continuing as I stood there in the dark, looking at this specter of a ship, but I followed OC Thomas up the ladder onto the deck. He headed off toward the bridge and I headed for the berthing area to get what I came for as quickly as possible. I remember walking down the ladder way into the berthing area where I last saw my duffle bag. As I feared, each step was an open drawer swollen in place, and it was very difficult to descend.

The interior of the ship was strewn with light bulbs in cages, but they provided only minimal light and threw grotesque shadows into the gloomy recesses of the wet compartment. The place smelled like diesel fuel and seawater. My hands were trembling slightly. I first found Clark's sea bag and looked for his camera and maybe a water-tight canister of film for his family. No luck. All his mother wanted was one last picture.

I rummaged around until I found my duffle bag. I was hoping that my laminated Massachusetts driver's license might have survived the sinking. When I reached in, I felt something move and jerked my hand back out, stifling a yell. I was wrong about lobsters reading my books; the new owners of my sea bag were tiny, quick-moving Chesapeake Bay crabs. I didn't find my license. The only salvageable thing I found was a brass buckle in serious need of polishing.

OC Thomas went straight to the window he had climbed through and just stared at it. Then he went through the navigation room and into the compartment where he'd gotten hung up. He viewed his noose and then looked down at the floor. Beneath his feet the Cuyahoga holiday ensign was sticking out of the mud. He stuffed it under his shirt and smuggled it back to OCS for cleaning and proper storage. He thought the flag might one day be an important relic to be kept in memory of the Cuyahoga.

I went through nearly every part of the ship and exited through the ten-by-six-foot hole in the hull. I'm not sure why I needed to see it. Maybe this was the wake and viewing for the Cuyahoga before she was buried at sea. I guess we all went back that night looking for closure.

Because of the upcoming court martial, we were reminded again not to talk to each other about the details of the collision. This didn't matter, we had already stopped talking about it. We had to push the experience into a closed corner of our minds, but sometimes the corner was not completely closed.

In one class about port safety, we saw an incredibly graphic documentary about the 1947 Texas City disaster. Two ships carrying ammonium nitrate fertilizer exploded near the Houston Ship Channel, leveling much of Texas City and killing at least 581 people. Exposing us to the carnage was designed as an object lesson in safety, but Arne Denny got up and ran out of the room, and Lieutenant Emory got up and ran after him. Arne evidently had exceeded his quota of object lessons. Years later, I found out that Lieutenant Emory caught up to him and held him as he cried, then gave him the rest of the day off. Lieutenant Emory had spent eight months in the Army on counseling duty while he was waiting for his medical discharge. His job was to inform parents of their sons' deaths and help make the appropriate arrangements. I'll bet he was a helluva lot better than that Navy chaplain.

The Error Chain

The Washington Post reporter was wrong when he wrote the headline "Spartan Funeral for Cutter Victim." While the headline conveys the idea that the event was a simple service without fanfare, when it came to funerals, the Spartans were anything but Spartan-like. In fact, the Spartan's most glorious events were funerals because they knew the importance of honoring their heroes.

My fellow football player, Charles Margiotto, instead of joining the fire department right after college, took an executive job at GM. Despite doing a superlative job at GM, he quit after a few years and joined the Fire Department of New York. Pumpy quickly rose through the ranks to become Lieutenant Charles Margiotto.

One day, he was heading home after a twenty-four-hour shift on the Brooklyn-Queens Expressway and saw the World Trade Center billowing out smoke. He called a friend and told him to turn on the TV. His friend knew exactly how Pumpy would react, and so he said, "You're off duty; go home!"

Pumpy's reply was simple: "Buddy, are you kidding me? I'm not staying away while something like this is going on. I'm going in. I'm going to call division now. I'll call you later."

There was no later.

I have absolutely no doubt that he reached his goal. He was the best fireman in the world. Five years later, when our team was inducted into the Brown Sports Hall of Fame, there were more than twenty of his fireman buddies there to see Pumpy's young son accept the Hall of Fame award in his name. They all stayed overnight to be there for the half-time ceremony the next day. Our whole 1976 team received an FDNY ball cap with Pumpy's name on the back.

Pumpy's positive legacy continues. There is a million dollar scholarship fund in his name and a website dedicated to him, and the FDNY has organized motorcycle rallies, running races, and the Charles Margiotta touch-football league. When it comes to honoring their dead heroes, there is no doubt in my mind that the FDNY is the best fire department in the world.

21.

*"I don't know what I'm searching for
I never have opened the door,
Tomorrow might find me at last,
Turning my back on the past
…You can never go home anymore."*
- *"You Can Never Go Home Anymore"*
Justin Hayward, The Moody Blues

It was Thanksgiving, and while we were originally scheduled to stay at OCS over the Thanksgiving holiday, liberty was extended and we had a four-day weekend. When I arrived home, my whole family had gotten together, and they were playing cards. Naturally, no one got up to greet me. I remember walking around the table and hugging everybody.

When I got to my Uncle Frank, he quipped, "I heard you had the shortest command in the history of the Coast Guard." He was relentless. "I never thought I would know a mass murderer, but now I am related to one." Ouch, that was brutal, and it required a comeback.

"After the sinking, I thought I should make it an even dozen. I had you in mind."

"Well, I guess I should never go out in a boat with you again."

"That, Uncle Frank, would be a very rare wise move on your part."

I am not sure whether Frank was actually his real name. I think one day he said, "Can I be Frank?" and no one could stop him. He was indeed brutally (Uncle) Frank.

My Uncle Frank had a heart of gold, however, and I loved him dearly; but the more he liked you, the more he insulted you. It's just what he and my father did. The most endearing thing he ever called anyone was the "dirty end of a mop." I think it was kind of a test —maybe a little like OCS or boot camp. My father and his brother would push people as hard as they could to see how much they could take. If a person can take it, that person can be trusted.

The first time Uncle Frank was introduced to his son's fiancée,

Peggy, he took one look at her and said, "God, what do you charge to haunt a house!"

The pretty Irish lass's quick reply was, "How many rooms?"

Frank's immediate conclusion, "She's a keeper."

Frank was the kind of guy who would have named his son "Sue" if he had thought of it at the time.

∞

He and my father always said the most outrageous things to people. Once, the son of the assistant meat manager at my dad's store arrived to pick his father up at work. The town had been plagued with a serial firebug. My dad said to this boy, who was leaving for six months of National Guard training the next day, "I guess, now that you will be gone, we won't be having any more fires."

The son replied sheepishly, "I guess not, Mr. Eident."

That night, the son was arrested for being the town firebug, and he confessed. I guess my dad had softened him up. He must have figured that if the meat manager at the A&P knows, everybody must know. But my dad didn't have a clue, and he apologized profusely to the assistant meat manager. He knew my father didn't have a cruel streak in him —it was just a random joke. Maybe there is no such thing as a random joke.

As the night of cards progressed and beers started to flow, I told a few parts of the tragedy. At one point in the discussion, I turned to my father and said, "You think that I was somehow to blame for this, don't you?"

He said, "Well, if it was me, I am sure I would have done something to avoid it."

Bill, my merchant marine brother, jumped in. "What would you have done? You've spent more time being towed than moving under your own power." This was only a slight exaggeration. My brother went on. "You've had two boats sink."

"Maybe it's in my genes," I thought.

"They put a uniform on these guys, march them around for six weeks, tell them how stupid they are, and then put them on a ship's deck at night. Let me tell you, in six weeks you know nothing. You're still stupid, ignorant, and a hazard. . . ."

I started to think, "Wait. You've made your point. Let's not go overboard on this."

My brother was mad, and I think he had been through this dia-
logue with his other shipmates. "Even merchant captains with twenty
years of experience wouldn't be allowed to take a ship through Chesapeake Bay. They would have to take on a pilot who could draw every
buoy and depth from memory. The Coast Guard has incredibly stringent standards, which include objective tests, and yet none of their
own people are required to take them. They just need a subjective 'OK'
from the commanding officer to be qualified as an OOD.

The Coast Guard cuts a corner or two, violates a safety rule and
they get away with it and sometimes they win a medal. But the only
thing it proves is you're an idiot. In the long run, the house always
wins... and the ocean is a one big house.

A Navy captain wouldn't enter a busy port without a pilot, but the
Coast Guard thinks their crews can do it, and I tell you they can't.
What was Pete supposed to do, walk onto the bridge and tell the captain, 'Hey, Cap, you go on down below decks and have a beer; I'll take
over from here?'"

My dad was now on the defensive, "I just think... "

My brother wasn't through. He interrupted the old man: "That's the
trouble. You don't think. You don't consider the impact of your words
or actions."

My brother was my drill sergeant growing up, and like Emory, he
was also my protector.

Uncle Frank said, "Shud'aap and deal." We went back to cards and
that was that. But my dad gave me an important piece of insight that
night. I now knew that there would be those who would say to themselves, "If I was in his shoes it would have been different." I would live
with that for the rest of my life.

∞

As an engineer on ship, my brother was concerned with safety. He
knew that if those lightweight deck officers screwed up, the engineers
below were often the guys getting the short end of the stick (he would
say "shit end of the stick"). No captain was willing to go down with the
ship. It's more likely that engineers end up with that undesirable role.
Engineers are blind to what is happening above, and they have to fight
their way to the deck as water pours in; they're lucky to get the last
available seat on the lifeboat.

My dad was profoundly guilty of lacking even an ounce of discretion. Once he was having trouble getting his National Guardsmen to attend drills. When he was well short of a full complement one weekend, he heard that some of the AWOL men were playing cards and getting drunk "over at so-and-so's house." He decided to take action and went down to the police station. He showed the night captain (his brother-in-law) a little-known law that allowed militia captains to petition the town constable to arrest or "leg iron" citizen soldiers who refused to attend drills or properly maintain their weapons, or those who gave aid or comfort to the enemy. My uncle Arthur (the former Navy gunner) was wise in the arena of local politics and reminded my dad that anybody who got into the Guard during Vietnam was a political appointee and had friends in high places. My dad didn't care. That was just all the more reason to make them fulfill their commitment. I can still recall my Uncle Arthur rolling his eyes each time he told the story and telling my dad that his cops were fresh out of leg irons —ever since the last Indian attack.

Nonetheless, my dad prevailed and my uncle had the card game raided. Those "AWOL" reservists were arrested and thrown in jail. Dad never got beyond the rank of major, largely reflective of this and his many other self-righteous actions. To his credit, however, he was by-the-book and would never let troops go out on ships that couldn't pass muster—he would have told his commanding officer in no uncertain terms to go to hell.

My dad spent nineteen years, eleven months, and twenty days in the National Guard, and he quit in a huff over something having to do with principles. He missed an important milestone that would have given him a hefty inflation-proof pension. My brother, "jailhouse lawyer Bill," clandestinely worked the system and was able to get him the extra ten days. Ungratefully, Dad now receives his pension.

∞

At about midnight, after being tormented by my family and winning at cards, I went to the Captain Kidd to meet my old friends. I didn't tell them that I was coming, so when I arrived, just Mike, the owner, was there with a few other people. He told me that everyone was at the Leeside and we decided to take the 300-yard walk over there. It was just about closing, and the place was packed. At the door, a couple of "unofficial doormen" were holding back a small crowd of a dozen people who wanted to get in. Jake, one of the two doormen, a thirty-year-old carpenter who was a regular at both the Captain Kidd and Leeside, said to me, "Didn't you join the Navy and 'fuck up' bad?" "Actually that would be badly," I shot back, emphasizing the "ly." I hate it when people don't use the proper adverb form.

Mike was talking to the other unofficial doorman, Stuart, and said to me, "They're turning people away because it's just about last call, but Stuart said he'd let us in the back door." We went to the back door and Stuart was there, holding it shut and laughing. "Suckers," he said. We went back to the front door; Stuart was already there and said, "No more people tonight." Mike just said, "Assholes," and we started back to the Kidd.

This was never how my hero's-return-to-Falmouth daydreams ended. I was being insulted and rejected from a bar in Woods Hole. This was pretty much the opposite of getting the keys to the city. I couldn't even get a beer in a second-rate bar.

Stuart wanted clarification on what Mike just called them, so he and Jake came out the doorway and confronted us. Mike was a short guy in his early thirties, way above his weight class with this group. I turned around and said, "Forget about it and go back in the Leeside and finish your drinks." I told Mike, "Let's go back to the Kidd." We started walking back, but Stuart and Jake were following us.

We were about twenty feet ahead of them and they were closing in. As they got within a few feet, I whirled around and told them, "We're going back to the Kidd and you should go back to where you belong."

Mike yelled something like, "Next time you come to the Kidd, expect similar treatment." Despite my size, they weren't afraid of me because they knew I would never pick a fight. Mike told me on my first day of work as a bouncer at the Kidd that if there was a fight, I had failed my job. If there was a fight —and there were many —it was not started by me. I was a peacekeeper who took shit from the drunks (like Stuart and Jake) for hours while I politely inched them to the door. This night, however, I wasn't on the Captain Kidd's payroll.

We were just about to the Eel River drawbridge, and they were still following us, yelling the nonsense particular to drunken belligerent people. Mike and I were no longer side-by-side; I was walking directly behind Mike, thinking, "If they touch me, I'm under no obligation to act with restraint." I could already feel the adrenalin.

Stuart tried to pass me on my left side. Good thing; my right arm was much better at delivering a blow than my left. There couldn't be any half measures because it was essentially me against two. I swung my right arm and landed it squarely on his chest while extending my left leg behind him. He went backwards over my leg and hit the ground hard. Either the straight arm or the collision with the ground knocked the wind out of him. My Marine cousin Franny taught me that one.

Jake came after me swinging. I put my head down, and his fist hit the side of my head. While I felt the impact, I knew that the blow hurt him more than it hurt me. He landed a softer punch to my side, but now I had my left arm firmly around his neck.

He was as tall as I was, and I couldn't bend him over (I had lost about twenty pounds at OCS) so I delivered a blow to his stomach with my right hand that made him buckle. I twisted his body and threw him on the ground on his buddy, with me at the very top. "Pig pile!" I thought. I had done that a thousand times with my brothers, but with me the unwilling participant on the bottom.

With my left arm around Jake's neck, my right arm was free to repetitively punch him in the face. I delivered soft blows; not hard enough to break anything but hard enough to show I cared. I was shouting, "It's the Coast Guard, asshole!" as I threw a barrage of rabbit punches to his face.

Mike, who hadn't seen Stuart come after him, asked, "What the hell are you doing?"

I stopped punching Jake and shoved his head away, got to my feet, and proceeded back to the Kidd. They didn't follow us this time. When I arrived at the door, I looked back and could see that they were just getting up. I was relieved as they appeared only to have flesh wounds. I could just image the headlines in the Falmouth Enterprise: "Local Pariah Continues his Reign of Destruction."

I iced my fist and took a couple of pints of liquid pain reliever. It didn't appear that I had broken any of my knuckles, so I hadn't damaged government property. Mike kept saying, "What the hell got into you?"

This wasn't the homecoming I expected. I remember when guys

came back from Vietnam. They were allowed to go to the VFW hall
and have fifty-cent cocktails. But when the older guys from World War
II and Korea got plastered, they would always bitch about how our
generation was only good at taking drugs and losing wars. Needless to
say, despite the fifty-cent drinks, most Vietnam vets stayed away from
the VFW.

The next day was the first Thanksgiving since my mother died.
It wasn't the joyous occasion that we had always experienced. As a
butcher, my father had always given advice to his customers on how
to cook a turkey, but in truth he had never actually cooked one before.
Our meal wasn't your classic Norman Rockwell scene. The gravy was
lumpy and the mashed potatoes even more lumpy, but we thanked
God for being able to be together that day and for all the joyous times
we'd had before.

∞

Later, Kate Carter told me what that Thanksgiving was like for
YN1 William Carter's family. Bill's mother, the classic steel magnolia,
politely refused to cook a Thanksgiving meal. For many years to come,
Carol McDonald Carter would tell her family, "It just seems a waste
when we're such a small group."

When we returned to OCS from Thanksgiving liberty, we were
told that CBS would be doing a story on the collision and that a
few of us would be giving interviews and we were to tell the truth.
Diane Sawyer was brand new to CBS, and this was one of her first
investigative reports. I saw her from a distance and I was captivated
by her beauty —she certainly had Walter Cronkite beat. Three guesses
why they didn't choose me as one of the interviewees. I don't think
anyone named Eident is ever going to be a press secretary. I would
have turned into a younger version of Uncle Frank: "Yeah, we really
screwed up that one, and covered it up to boot!"

I got wind of her questions, however, and they were focused on a
micro issue: OC training. She didn't go into the dire condition of the
U.S. Coast Guard's vessels and the under-manning of its ranks. Sadly,
she lost the plot. Moreover, the piece was shown on Christmas Eve,
not a good day for a hard-hitting investigative report. I think they
were looking for filler. I didn't watch it.

I stopped getting demerits of any kind, but I didn't improve. If anything, I was less diligent. Inspections became non-events. The screening process and accompanying chicken shit was over, and we were all anxiously waiting to move on. Many of the mustangs had calendars, and they were literally counting the days, checking each off as they passed.

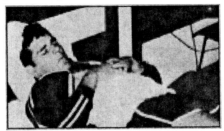

∞ Caught taking an illegal nap ∞

It's funny how people in the service mark and count time. You figure out how many days you have left and then subtract one. Everybody would say, "I have thirty-two days and a wake up," and then they would brag about how short they were. Coast Guardsmen were allowed to have pocket watches, and they often fashioned the chains with knots, one for each day left on their tour. These were short-timers. They worked the shortness metaphor into every dimension.

"I could win a limbo competition without bending."

"I don't even have to open the door. I can walk under it."

And my favorite: "I'm so short, I just did ten pushups under a dime."

It struck me as odd that some OCs cross off each day like a prisoner. I would tell them that, despite being closer to freedom, they are now one day closer to death.

Marking time wasn't confined to training or ships. Coasties would do it for hitches. They would say, "Three months in this hitch, and boy are things gonna be different. Great people . . . Good times . . . Only five months left." They all had plans that had nothing to do with the military, and as the time for departures got closer, all they could talk about was the future, and how short they were. Then about a week or two before their "wake up," they stopped talking about it. It would leak out that they were "re-upping" —reenlisting. Because it was difficult to recruit an all-volunteer service, re-up bonuses were instituted, and there was even a program that paid a Coastie a bonus for getting one of his friends to either re-up or join. This version quickly earned the nickname the "Judas Program," although you didn't have to kiss anyone on the cheek in the Garden of Gethsemane.

∞

After Christmas we returned to OCS and finished our classroom training. The OCS program culminates with a one-week cruise to nowhere aboard the 327-foot cutter Ingham, the most decorated vessel in the Coast Guard fleet and the only cutter ever to be awarded two Presidential Unit Citations. The ship was commissioned in 1936, provided distinguished service during World War II, Korea, and Vietnam, and was a mere forty-two years old when we boarded her. In fact, since the sinking of the Cuyahoga, she was the second-oldest warship in the U.S. fleet (the USS Constitution having been in commission since 1797).

The Ingham's crew knew that we were Jonahs —shipwreck survivors. Jonahs in the seagoing service are viewed with an unholy combination of curiosity, respect, and contempt: curiosity to know what it was like; respect because you survived; and contempt from the belief that (in spite of the reason for curiosity) it could never happen to them. In typical Coast Guard fashion, the person in charge of our orientation said he had an official announcement from the captain: "Special permission is hereby granted to any of us who wanted to sleep on deck —in the life-jacket bin (ha ha)." For sure I was going be the first one off this ship in the event anything went wrong.

We took off from Chesapeake Bay and headed to Charleston, South Carolina, in mid-January. The North Atlantic is not a particularly friendly place in the middle of the winter —certainly too cold to sleep in the life-jacket bin. I was assigned a bunk in lower berthing area under the mess deck. The smell of food wafted down, and I soon discovered that I was susceptible to seasickness. I was sick for the first two days out, and I also have to admit that I didn't get much sleep. Every time the engine slowed or accelerated, or the ship hit a wave the wrong way, I woke and eyed my escape route. Growing up, I had always been a sound sleeper. I could fall asleep on the living room floor, with the TV blaring and six people talking and laughing, and feel, well, incredibly safe and secure. I thought of Arne Denny, who jumped to his feet as soon as the ship was backing down. I realized that was what saved him. I internalized the sense that perhaps the key to staying alive is remaining in a high state of readiness even when you're sleeping. Ever since, I've been a light sleeper, and I am always tired.

None of us expressed any fear to each other. I expected the crew of the Ingham to ask about our experience, but they didn't, and we didn't offer to tell them. It was a sort of a "don't ask, don't tell" policy. It was not official, mind you, but simply an understood guideline. Remembering our shipmates and saying nice things about them was the only part of the Cuyahoga incident that was socially permissible. All other discussions were taboo.

Once, as I stood on a bridge wing looking for contacts, a boson's mate standing next to me and looking out to sea said in very low tone, "I was stationed with Bruce five years ago."

I replied, "He was a great guy."

"Yea, he was."

And that was that. Sailors don't like to see each other cry.

We had to stand watch, essentially shadowing a real crew member, and we had to fill out a huge list like a giant scavenger hunt that took us to every nook and cranny on the vessel to find obscure details, like serial numbers and PSIs of boilers. My every waking hour was spent either throwing up over the side or filling out the huge questionnaire.

If you've never suffered prolonged seasickness, you have no idea what I'm talking about; if you have, you must agree that death seems like a better option. Looking down at my Technicolor splatter pattern, I remembered watching my father's fishing guest suffer.

∞

One time, my father took one of his fellow butchers out for spring flounder fishing off Falmouth Heights. The fish were biting incredibly and we were pulling in one tasty flounder after another. Our guest started chumming for the fish by sticking his head over the side and sending small pieces of his lunch into the ocean. Just after he finished his final gag, as he was staring into the water over the gunwale, Uncle Frank and my dad tossed greasy Polish sausages into the water in front of him, immediately conjuring a new set of heaves. He so desperately wanted to go ashore that we started heading toward the inlet. On the anticipation of nearing solid land, our guest looked a bit less green, so my father decided to stop for one more quick round of fishing. No sooner were the hooks over the side than our guest went over the side, too — clothes, shoes, and all. Although he was a horrible swimmer, he decided to dog-paddle the 200 yards to the beach and walk a mile and a half to his car rather than complete his social obligations on the fishing expedition. We did keep a close eye on him to make sure that he completed a beach landing. We headed back out with a lighter ballast for more fishing in "middle grounds." I used to make fun of people who got seasick, but on those first days of the long cruise, I didn't have a nausea-free moment. I wonder if my body was trying to tell me something, like "get back on land, you idiot!"

∞

As part of our role in the Cold War, we shadowed a Russian fishing trawler that had about twenty-five antennae on it and never put out a net. Legend has it that, once, during the shadowing of a USSR vessel, a cutter's captain called his musicians to the bridge. Like many ships, they had an in-house rock band that played heavy metal. The captain told them, "Set up on the deck and don't spare the amps." When the budding international rock stars were ready, the captain maneuvered his ship as close as he could without violating protocol. The cutter's mission and intent was to harass the Russians, and the captain's intent was to thoroughly harass them by putting on a concert with "that awful music the young play." The Soviet reaction was completely unanticipated. Their sailors all came out on deck, waving, and all the Coasties started waving, which began a sort of happy little festival instead of the intimidation that the captain was looking for.

We rode close to our Russian object of surveillance for about twelve hours, and I think the people in the CIC room did some monitoring, but our general objective was just to show them how much we cared.

The second night, on the four-to-eight watch, we finally had a clear sky. We were woken and told, if we didn't practice celestial navigation right now, we might not get another chance. Finding latitude is easy: find the big dipper and follow the two stars that make up the outside of the front of the dipper. They point the way to the North Star (Polaris, the nineteenth brightest star). Put your sextant on the North Star, and measure the angle between it and the horizon, and that's your latitude. If you're on the equator, the North Star is on the horizon; therefore, you're at zero degrees latitude. If it's right over your head, you're on the North Pole, and that's 90 degrees.

Longitude is another story. One needs exact time and a celestial almanac. The first step is to make sure you have the right star; the next step is to record the correct reading from the sextant on a ship that is rocking on the North Atlantic, and to also record the exact right time and date. Then it's a matter of a number of calculations with the almanac, and finally, based on the latitude and longitude that you calculate, you check to see if your answer jibes with the chart. On my first try, my calculations indicated we were in Nebraska.

Of course, celestial navigation had become a back-up system because the world was using LORAN. (Now we take satellite navigation for granted, but LORAN was standard from World War II until the 2000s.) The Coast Guard developed the first long-range navigation system (LORAN) at the beginning of World War II, under a top secret project. LORAN is a radio wave system that uses the time difference in the reception of radio signals from a master and two slave stations to locate positioning along parabolic lines on the chart that represent the time differences. The technology was first developed at Cambridge University and was used to guide British Bombers to their targets and then home again. MIT scientists, in cooperation with the Navy, started the project before the war, but the Coast Guard was able to get the bugs out. By the end of the war, LORAN covered one-third of the world.

∞

Later that day, I got the opportunity to shoot a .40-caliber cannon with tracers. Those empty barrels never had a chance! Filled with a small amount of gasoline, they flamed up nicely when hit directly.

∞

After the cruise ended, only a few weeks remained before I got my gold bars and headed to my first assignment. Everyone was now focusing on the culmination of this sad chapter, heading onward to the future where we could live long and prosper. But for me this leg of the journey wouldn't be over until the paperwork was done. With all the lawsuits and the captain's court-martial, my mind couldn't get past the idea that my testimony could put a decent man behind bars. I also have to say that I was a little terrified that Flanagan would tear me apart on the stand, as in a Perry Mason episode when somebody ends up confessing on the stand. My only real crime, as far I could figure, was incompetence and bad luck: I would readily plead guilty on both counts, but with the extenuating contention that trainees are incompetent until they are trained and made competent. I would further argue that, in the law of averages, it's guaranteed that someone has to have bad luck. I did wonder whether lack of awareness that the Santa Cruz was a danger was a crime for which I was guilty.

∞

People always told me I was lucky, but what kind of luck put me on a routine cruise and, with million-to-one odds against it, the boat sinking under me? Certainly, however, among the twenty-nine of us sailing out on that night, I was one of the lucky eighteen.

Graduates of OCS are required to serve a minimum of three years in the Coast Guard. We had a choice of a serving on a cutter, flight training, or operations ashore. Due to my eyesight, flying was not an option. After the Ingham cruise I had given up my original plan of going to sea because I just didn't think I had enough visual acuity. At night on the sea, I couldn't see anything. I was once advised that if you don't actually believe you are the best pilot or captain in the world, you shouldn't be a pilot or captain at all. There was also the issue of my seasickness, although my brother told me that the great British naval hero, Admiral Lord Horatio Nelson, was prone to the malady and was sick for the first three days on every voyage.

So I had to choose a shore billet. We were given a list of available billets, and we were allowed to list three preferences. The detailers at Coast Guard headquarters in Washington, D.C., would consider our choices, but the final decision was theirs. The mustangs were calling around to their old shipmates, trying to position themselves for the best possible placement. I put in for three support positions, two in New York and one in Boston. Boston was highly desirable, but nobody wanted New York. It was a little intimidating. Small towns are over-represented when it comes to Coast Guard recruits. New York was also viewed as overly expensive, but I planned to immediately enroll in an evening MBA program, and New York had some of the best to choose from. I figured that I could serve my country and prepare for the future at the same time. After my three years of duty, an MBA would enable me to pursue a career in finance.

Billet night was a big event. The OCS leadership read the assignments one by one with all hands on deck. The guys who wanted flight school were all getting in, and Eric Fontaine got sea duty. Most mustangs were getting their picks. OC Thomas was later told that the detailers thought of the survivors as Jonahs who would never be on sea duty again in their careers. Then the recitation came to me. "Eident, Adak, Alaska."

I picked up my orders. I had seen Alaska on the list. The mustangs told me about it: Adak was a remote billeting where no dependents were allowed. It wasn't the end of the world, but you could see it from there. The place was actually west of parts of Siberia. It was cold ten months a year, and when it was warm, mosquitoes infested the place. Cold water and mosquitoes —right up my alley.

I was about to be married, and I would have to live away from my new bride for at least a year (remote billets only had a one-year tour). I tuned out the excited chatter over the other assignments and stared at my official orders. I just sat there dumbstruck.

After they finished reading the last billet assignment, Lieutenant Emory said, "What's the matter with you, Eident? It looks like you just lost your puppy." I had no brilliant retort this time. I was speechless. Then Emory told me it was a joke —they had actually fabricated false orders —and everybody laughed.

I was angry and I clenched my jaw so hard that my ear began to ache. That brought the Cuyahoga to mind. I thought about OC Heistand drilling with big Mutha and the grace he showed, and I thought, "Fair enough. I can take a joke." I laughed with them. There was no doubt they were good at torturing people. I was so happy I wasn't going to Adak.

My real assignment was the U.S. Coast Guard Training Center on Governors Island, New York City. I was assigned as both the security officer and the morale and recreation officer.

∞

My fiancée, my father, and Uncle Frank drove down for graduation. I warned them, "No Cuyahoga jokes." My fiancée brought me an article from the Washington Post about the Cuyahoga dated January 21st. Secretary of Transportation Brock Adams and the commandant of the Coast Guard held a press conference to announce the results of a comprehensive, "two-inch thick" study into the safety of Coast Guard training. The report recommended changes in procedures and the upgrading of equipment. Secretary Adams said, "We do not have that kind of exposure anymore, and if I thought there was another situation like the Cuyahoga out there I would pull it like that." Reportedly he snapped his fingers for emphasis.

The commandant and the secretary both emphasized that no additional money or manpower would be needed for those actions. The article's last line was a quote from the secretary: "Increased responsibilities in drug enforcement, fisheries, and pollution control had contributed to the (Coast Guard's) resources being stretched pretty thin."

I was stunned and disappointed. Sure, you can work smarter and harder and longer, but at what point do you start getting diminishing returns? It was complete BS. How do you upgrade ships and solve under manning without spending more money or adding additional personnel? But, of course, it was a two-inch thick study —so it must be right. Much of the study was dedicated to the Academy's cruise ship, the tall ship Eagle. The report cited the ship as a real source of danger. Sailing ships are dangerous because you're climbing high up and there are lines, yards, and sails that, combined with rocking and a surprise gust, can turn a routine cruise into a tragic event.

I read this just before the graduation ceremony, and it weighed on me while I listened to the speakers. It was a proud, bittersweet day for us all. My father was a retired military officer, so he was allowed to administer the oath and award me my bars. My dad never attended college, but based on his aptitude scores, they sent him directly from boot camp to OCS —instant upward mobility. He loved the U.S. military

and everything it stood for, and he had big grin on his face and twinkle in his eye when he handed me my bars. If nothing else, he had just proven Uncle Frank wrong, and that in itself was worth celebrating.

At the graduation, OC Moser received the silver lifesaving medal for his actions. He was not on watch at the time of the collision, but he had been so excited to be underway that he remained

∞ Checking to see if OC Michael Moser is actually a mortal ∞

topside. Instead of going to bed after he was relieved, he climbed up on the flying bridge and, along with SA Myers, acted as a lookout. OC Moser, along with QM3 Rose and BM1 Wild, came to the aid of Captain Robinson. All of us were very proud of our fellow OC. It was the first time any OC had ever won a lifesaving medal while at Officer Candidate School. Hopefully, it would be the last.

The Error Chain

It only takes a 20 percent list to put out the lights on a ship. The internal report on the Coast Guard's safety focused on training, but training was just one element in the overall issue: the condition of the Coast Guard. The equipment was old and outdated, and the manpower supply and training was inadequate. To keep operating under these conditions, officers had two choices: go along and get along, or fight it. Many fought it until there was an emergency, but when a mayday was called, they sent out everything they had. They had a motto to maintain: "We have to go out." Therefore, safety regulations required flexibility.

How many times did Captain Kirk, despite Scotty's warnings, violate the safety parameters of the matter/anti-matter reactor and end up saving the Federation? No guts, no flight medal. It seems there was an expectation of doing more with less, but that was an alchemist's fantasy.

22.

Immediately after graduation, I headed to Connecticut, got married on Saturday, and on Monday morning reported for duty on Governors Island in New York Harbor —not quite the honeymoon getaway island I'd promised my fiancée.

I was excited about having a real job in the real world besides being apprehensive about how my wife and I would fit in, and how the Cuyahoga might affect the way that I was perceived by folks on the base. But my wife and I made friends quickly and enjoyed the social cohesiveness of the Governors Island community.

As I made friends, eventually everyone had to ask the question: what really happened? I hadn't seen any of the reports and had managed to stay away from most of the media circus, and for the most part I hadn't talked about it with anyone. Usually, the questioner had more details than I did.

Most of my fellow officers had been out to sea, and to them the accident was incomprehensible. It made no sense. "Was he drunk?" was always the first question. Although they had had close calls, there was always a reason: thick fog, heavy seas, nearby shoals, equipment failures. The sinking of the Cuyahoga was inexplicable to them and to me. We usually got around to complaining to each other that things were "not good in the Guard."

∞

Governors Island had an amazing officer's club, and because of the proximity to New York we were able to arrange visits by famous speakers. At my first luncheon, G. Gordon Liddy gave a speech about how the real American heroes all ended up in jail. Gordon was asked why he didn't obey the law of the land and the will of Congress. His reply was, "Have you ever gone through a red light at four a.m. when no one was around? If you did, you disobeyed the law just like I did." Sophism: the art of making specious arguments sound like wisdom.

There was a well-lubricated warrant officer sitting at my table who wanted to further elaborate on the injustices of the day. He began with the unfairness of trying CWO Robinson for manslaughter. He didn't know I was a survivor. I agreed with him until he said, "A bunch of wet-behind-the-ears college kids screw up and, as always, a warrant officer gets blamed."

I wasn't going to let this slide. I said, "Does your head hurt? I figure anybody that ignorant must feel the pain of the severe vacuum in his head. Tell me one fact that says an OC screwed up. Just one fact." He wasn't aware of a single detail.

"Well I heard. . . ."

"You heard from another ignorant person, but you don't have a single fact. The OCs were in an observation mode and had no operational responsibilities. Many people much smarter than you sat for long hours discussing the facts and they decided to press charges against the captain. There is no doubt that the captain was at least partially to blame. I agree that the charges were excessive, but no one ever said any OC was to blame. You weren't there."

I got up and walked out, and he had the pleasure of picking up my share of the bar tab. My outburst was heard by many, and people seemed to cut me a wide berth on the island for a while. That was not necessarily the desired effect, but sometimes you have to get mad.

∞

Governors Island is located a few hundred yards off the southern tip of Manhattan Island, near Ellis and Liberty Island. Accessible only by a private ferry, the island has a fantastic view of the New York skyline. More than half of the land area of the island was created from fill excavated by digging the subways and Brooklyn-Battery Tunnel, but the island's name came from British colonial times, when it was reserved for the exclusive use of New York colony's royal governors. The Coast Guard moved to Governors Island in 1966, when the Army moved out and passed down their historic buildings to the Guard.

The island had two stone forts, and for many years one served as a prison —the East Coast counterpart of Fort Leavenworth and Alcatraz. According to local lore, the prison housed 1,500 Confederate soldiers during the Civil War and, ten years later, was used for World War II AWOL recruits, including the free-minded cartoonist Walt Disney and the tough-minded boxer Rocky Graziano.

The island also had the only golf course with a Manhattan zip code, with crisscrossing fairways that required a hard hat. The pin of the second hole, as seen from the tee box, was placed directly between the twin towers of the World Trade Center. GI, as we called it.

The security officer position meant I was in charge of discipline, but I was also in charge of morale. While these may seem on the surface to be in direct opposition to each other, these responsibilities were actually very closely tied. No, we did not have daily beatings until morale improved. Former heavyweight champion boxer Jack Dempsey served in the U.S. Coast Guard in World War II as a recreation and morale officer, so I thought I was fulfilling a proud tradition. The problem was that we were on a very crowded base and there wasn't a lot to do (besides the golf, of course). The Coasties assigned to the island only had to go left off the Governors Island ferry terminal into Battery Park to find a hundred purveyors of ten dollar bags of pot or cocaine. The enlisted guys not interested in controlled substances had two choices: a cheap drink at the enlisted man's club, or an expensive drink in Manhattan. I spent many a Sunday morning bailing Coasties out of New York City jails or signing them out of the Governors Island holding tank, which brought in the age-old question: "What do you do with a drunken sailor, earl-aye in the morning?" The options available, according to the sea shanty, were:

a. stick 'em in the bilge and make 'em drink it;
b. shave his belly with a rusty razor;
c. heave 'em by the leg in a running bowline;
d. stick 'em in the bed with the captain's daughter.

Unfortunately, the first three remedies were barred by the Uniform Code of Military Justice, and the last one would look bad on my fitness report. Interestingly, the tune to "What do you do with a drunken sailor" is Shostakovich's Piano Concerto #2 in F Major, and the background music for NFL highlight films. The music invokes a sense of teamwork and dedication.

∞

In February 1979, the newspapers published findings from the National Transportation Safety Board: Captain Robinson was held responsible for the collision. The findings concluded that he was "confused" and displayed "a total lack of perception" in the minutes before the collision.

The board concluded: "Had the turn not been executed by the cutter, the two ships would have passed at a distance of 600 yards." The first order I ever gave on a ship popped into my head: "Helmsman, change course to 303." Now it was official: we had cut in front of their bow.

∞

In March, they sank the Cuyahoga, making her part of the artificial reef off Cape Charles, Virginia, at the north side of the entrance to Chesapeake Bay. The reef was designed to protect the cape from erosion and to function as a habitat for sea life.

∞

In April, the admiral convened a board to indict Captain Robinson on three counts: manslaughter, destruction of government property, and negligently hazarding a vessel. The rumor was true. They were going to try the captain on the capital offense of manslaughter. It was shocking. Robinson was no criminal.

The Coast Guard's internal board of inquiry released its report in May 1979, concluding that CWO Robinson was primarily to blame for the collision. The official report stated, "The Commandant has determined that the proximate cause of the casualty was that the commanding officer of the USCGC Cuyahoga failed to properly identify the navigation lights displayed by the M/V Santa Cruz II. As a result, he did not comprehend that the vessels were in a meeting situation, and altered the Cuyahoga's course to port, taking his vessel into the path of the Santa Cruz II." The Coast Guard, however, also accused pilot John Hamill of having failed to sound the freighter's danger signal in a timely manner before the two vessels collided, and not doing enough to avoid the accident.

I received inquiries regarding my availability, and notified that I would be required at Yorktown for the court-martial. I stayed in touch with my classmates, and they kept me informed of the process. They said it looked bad for Captain Robinson, and they shared my outrage.

∞

In Massachusetts, the owner of the Santa Cruz, Empresa Lineas Maritimas Argentinas (ELMA), was sued by the families of the victims and four survivors. In turn, ELMA sued the United States to hold them liable for all claims against them. It's called a "back door" to get around the $30,000 limit in the Veterans Act.

The United States denied liability but asserted that, in the event it was found liable, its liability should be limited under 46 U.S. Code Section 183A to the value of the Cuyahoga: zero value. This law was passed to encourage maritime trade and limit liability, and thus insurance costs, for ship owners. Ship owners get to limit their liability to the value of the ship if there was no negligence prior to leaving port. In theory, a licensed captain is in charge in the open water and has full responsibility, and if he screws up, the ship's owners couldn't have done any better.

With the court-martial weighing on my mind, it was difficult to focus on my current duties, but I tried to maintain a positive approach on Governors Island. The officer who preceded me was a highly dedicated ex-high school teacher, Lieutenant (jg) Garneer, and he had actually started to turn the morale office around before I got there. I was able to build on his success.

We began to offer excursions to the New Jersey malls, skiing, white-water rafting, mountain hiking, trips to amusement parks, and even apple picking. I found an unused basement, and then ten dilapidated pool tables and five ping-pong tables in a warehouse and had them reconditioned. We built a first-class recreation hall with ongoing ladder tournaments.

The enlisted men's club was depressing because there were hardly any women and the music was canned. I contacted a nursing school and a secretarial academy and had women shipped in. Our few enlisted girls protested, but I was able to prevail. Guys drink a lot less when women are around; guys with girlfriends get into a lot less trouble. Dozens of bands would play for free, or next to free, but instead of paying for a band, we had a beat-the-band contest with a first place prize of $500. With the same budget, we could offer bands every week instead of once a month. It appeared the only basic criteria the bands had to meet was an ability to play "Free Bird" by Lynyrd Skynyrd. One band played it three times in a row, and even that wasn't too much.

We only had two softball fields, so we switched to single pitch and had three times as many games for three times as many people. I was able to secure the tennis courts for street hockey, and instead of having two people playing tennis, we had twelve playing street hockey. The officer's wives' club filed a formal complaint. The post used to close the gym at 1900 until we installed a volunteer watch and kept it open until 0100. Sometimes we had dodge-ball games with twenty on a side.

My wife had a job on Wall Street, and her boss was a Mason who was in charge of the greater New York Masonic blood drives. He offered a free steak and beer to every Coastie I could get to donate blood. The Coasties and Masons really got along well, and our guys gave blood until they were anemic. The Masons began to invite our men to their homes, and Coasties met real New Yorkers instead of just hookers.

As recreation went up, the need for disciplinary action went down and my job actually became easier. We assigned a uniformed Coastie to simply stand in Battery Park, which kept our guys from buying drugs there. Believe it or not, the drug dealers protested to the NYPD and an officer actually called me up and wanted to know why we had a uniformed Coastie there. For reasons known only to people far above me, we had to dismiss the Battery Park detail.

As security officer, I had to write charges and prosecute at Captain's Masts. My Uncle Arthur was town prosecutor, and he loved his job. He told me all the tricks he used to catch people lying. He knew how to get to the bottom of things. At first I really enjoyed uncovering the mystery and the motivation behind the crimes, but the cases were not all that big. Most involved alcohol and pot, and resulted in assignment of extra duty and fines. The motivation for these crimes was always the inexplicable need for sailors to get a buzz. Repeat offenders were sent to substance-abuse duty or, in the case of pot, sent packing. The Coast Guard invested a lot of money in recruiting an all-volunteer force, but wages that were lower than the commercial sector made retention difficult.

The Coast Guard had yet to consider routine urine testing, which eventually dramatically reduced controlled substance abuse. There is no easy way to hide from urine tests.

∞

One case in particular was a good example of our pragmatism: One of the training center's students was propositioned by one of his teachers. There had been a gathering in an instructor's room with trainees, and they all were drinking, which is not allowed in the barracks. The male instructor put his hand on the thigh of his male student, who ran from the room. The situation normally would have been an "oh, whoops, let's not talk about that anymore," but the instructor went to the student's room and threatened him with failure if he said anything. The student complained about being threatened and wanted to press the case. The case was pursued because it included teacher fraternization with students, and saying that special power-relationship of teacher/student that is ripe for abuse, and must be dealt with.

The instructor testified at the Captain's Mast that he loved the Guard, and that he was afraid of losing his job because was gay. He panicked and threatened the kid. The captain made him apologize to the student and invoked our usual solution: substance-abuse training. That ought to rehabilitate him!

∞

We set up another morale-building activity to help Coast Guard trainees get qualified in firearms. We decided to reopen the firing range, located in the attic of one of the dorms. We were told it was closed because of potential environmental concerns. There was asbestos on the pipes, and there was the potential for lead inhalation from the pistols and rifles.

I was able to get my brother Chris to come look at the situation. He was working for the Navy at the submarine base in New London as a certified industrial hygienist and a certified safety professional, AKA nerd. He was a world-leading expert on the effects of asbestos and other air quality issues. Prior to working at the sub base, Chris had worked at Cape Kennedy for the space agency with their health, safety and environment department.

In a submarine, the ship recycles the air, and airborne pathogens have many chances to infect the body. Asbestos was a leading cause of illness among merchant-marine engineers. Asbestos is a rock with very small crystals that, due to its small size and structure, is a fantastic insulator. Unfortunately, the fibrous properties that make it a great insulator also make it a substance that gets stuck in peoples' lungs, causing asbestosis, lung cancer, and mesothelioma, cancer of the lung or abdomen lining. The tiny asbestos fibers go right through the lung and intestine into the organ lining; asbestos is the only cause of that type of cancer.

Merchant-marine engineers were also assaulting their bodies with asbestos from another direction. The engine insulation was a combination of calcium carbonate and asbestos, and hung-over merchant mariners were eating small pieces of insulation to neutralize the acid that was causing their heartburn. Because of the possibility that it could cause gastrointestinal cancer, an advisory had to be published telling grown men to stop eating the damn insulation.

Chris brought up his two bags of equipment for testing of lead and asbestos, stacked with air pumps, filters, and the rest of the paraphernalia. Before he did any testing, he walked down to the target end of the range and moved a bale of hay. Behind the bale of hay was a wooden wall, though it looked more like Swiss cheese than an actual wall. I looked through one of the bullet-sized holes, and there, directly across, I saw a student through the window of his dorm room. My brother announced that having a firing range in a wooden attic was about the stupidest thing he had ever heard. While the Eident family did have a firing range in our basement, we were definitely not stupid enough to have one in our attic. Chris declared the range unusable.

∞

That evening we had a mini family reunion when my scientist sister joined us for a weekend in the Big Apple. After dinner in Little Italy, we were riding the ferry back to Governors Island, looking out over the starboard side at one of most spectacular views in the world: The World Trade Center on the right, Ellis Island 90 degrees off port, and the Statue of Liberty off the bow. I asked my brother, "Do you know anything about aspergillosis?"

"It's the next asbestosis," he replied. " Detecting mold and abating it is a real growth industry."

"I'm not thinking business opportunity here. I'm asking whether it could cause somebody to be confused. The papers reported that Captain Robinson had a complete lack of perception, and I've heard rumors that he was diagnosed with aspergillosis, and people are claiming that's why he wasn't on top of it. Supposedly it's caused by mildew."

Beth jumped into the conversation. "Mildew is a generic name for mold, but it's really fungus you'd be talking about. That's actually a subset of mold. Fungi can grow on anything from the skin surface to anaerobic host surfaces, but worst of all, it can grow in the lungs like you're talking about. Aspergillosis would cause inflammation of the airways and the air sacs in the lungs, and reduce the lungs' efficiency."

"But could a lung disease have affected his thinking?"

"You idiot," Chris said. Let's try putting a paper bag over your head, and I'll start a quiz in five minutes. We'll see how you do. Your brain needs oxygen —a nice steady supply. He was probably oxygen starved, day in and day out."

"Probably your only quiz answer would be, 'can I take the bag off now?'" Bethanie said.

"That's a good point," Chris replied. "An illness that affects your breathing not only affects your ability to think; if it's serious enough, it can leave you totally preoccupied. People don't go more than a few minutes without thinking about taking that next breath." Then he started in on a Colombo-like investigation: "Did the ship smell musty?"

"Just to the point that it made my eyes water."

"Mold likes wood paneling and insulation. Was there any of that?"

"There was insulation everywhere, but I think there was only wood paneling in the captain's quarters."

"Well that's it, then. Mold caused the accident."

"Come on," Beth said. You can't blame a shipwreck on mold." Chris said, "You're right. Mold is probably judgment-proof. You'd have to go after the ship's owner or whoever is responsible for the mold in the first place. Aspergillosis is rare, and doctors are trained to think horses, not zebras. They probably misdiagnosed him with asthma and bronchitis and prescribed antihistamines."

"But they couldn't have prescribed antihistamines because you're not allowed to operate heavy equipment while using them," my sister added. " Pilots can't take them, and with the changes in pressure on their sinuses and ears, they're the ones who need them the most. Pilots log a lot of sick days over that."

I said, "Well, the rumor is they prescribed three kinds of drugs for him, and they all were in the 'don't operate heavy machinery' category."

"Don't they have rules about being fit for duty on a ship?" Beth asked.

"You'd think, but they actually don't," I replied.

"Antihistamines could reduce cognitive abilities, but the real issue probably was his breathing problem," said Chris. "There are lots of complications from not breathing well: especially sleep disorders. Did he have to sleep sitting up because his lungs were filled with fluid?"

Beth chimed in, "Studies suggest that sleep deprivation is worse than being legally drunk."

"This just sounds like a cop-out to me," I said.

Chris replied, "This isn't the Mod Squad, you idiot —this is a health issue. You were a football player. Didn't you ever notice any effect from a health problem? Like maybe a twisted knee could affect a running back's performance?"

"Come on. That's different. You need your legs to run."

"A captain needs to see. People who aren't getting enough oxygen start to have blurred vision. He also has to collect data and analyze it, and he must set priorities and make decisions —all in real time. All of this requires a brain on oxygen."

I thought back to Emory's tenet of "being on the top of your game."

Beth added, "Sleep deprivation can do you in, too. If you're sleep deprived enough, you go beyond cognitive problems and start to hallucinate, letting the subconscious brain fill in the gaps in images they can see but can't really focus on properly. It works like a lost soul in the desert who is suffering from dehydration and sees a mirage."

"Or like just waking up and seeing apparitions," Chris added.

Beth said, "Or like overtired kids seeing monsters in the shadows. But hallucinations can be more subtle, like seeing a flock of birds and reporting a flying formation of planes. The brain needs its sleep."

"This sounds like a bunch of crap, just an excuse for the weak or incompetent," I said. " You know what people are saying about agent orange and battle fatigue or whatever they call it now —Post Traumatic Stress Syndrome."

"If you think that, you're a jerk," my sister said. " People react differently to stress and their environment. Until you've walked a mile in someone's shoes, you have no idea what it's like to be sick or depressed."

"Especially chronic illness," Chris added. " It just sneaks up on you. It's nearly impossible to know your capacity is diminishing. What you're thinking seems right at the time. It's only when you are competent that you can tell if you're screwing up. If you do notice that you're screwing up, you think maybe you're just growing old, and no one wants to do that. He was probably in denial."

"How do I know that the captain's smart-ass attorney didn't just look this up in the New England Journal of Medicine and use it as an extenuating or mitigating circumstance to get his client off?"

"Was there any evidence of the disease prior to the accident?"

"I don't know anything about his health record, but he had two accidents just before to this one."

"Do you really think he wanted to get into these accidents?" Beth said.

"Do you think he said to himself, 'Gee, why don't I have an accident today?' He should have had a full fitness physical after the first accident."

"There are no accidents, just a series of events that are caused by systematic failures, miscalculations, poor judgment, carelessness, or in rare cases, malfeasance," Chris said.

"I think we can rule out malfeasance," Beth offered.

"Suppose we reopened the Governors Island shooting range in the attic and someone got killed," Chris said. "Whose fault would it be?"

I said, "Yours. You're the safety expert, and I would be the first to blame you."

"If he really is sick, it would be a complete travesty of justice to try him," Beth said. " You have to do something about it. Talk to the commandant!"

He's not even supposed to know about this," Chris said. " I'm working for the Navy, and I can tell you, he's only an insect. That's what I hear the chief petty officers calling ensigns. Nobody is going to listen to him. He's not an expert in any of this crap. Nobody should listen to him."

I thought to myself, "Thanks, Chris."

Chris said, "If they have diagnosed it right, they could treat it. The right drugs will take his acute symptoms away pretty quickly. Of course, if he also had a preexisting condition like fibrosis, which is likely, his prognosis will be much less rosy.

∞

The next day I suffered from sleep deprivation as a result of this conversation. Two weeks later, I would get a firsthand look at what diminished thinking ability can do to a man. I received a phone call at around 1600 on a Sunday. They had just pulled one of our electronics students (ETs) out of the East River. He'd been swimming until some people on shore called the Coast Guard to go out and see why the hell anyone would be swimming in one of the most polluted bodies of water on the East Coast.

When they got out there, he was ranting, saying that the sky was starting to touch the ground, and he was afraid he was going to get crushed. I was convinced this guy was on serious drugs. He desperately fought his rescue. Finally, another boat arrived and they literally dragged him into the boat, scratching and biting. Because he was in my command and I was the security officer, I was called in to talk to him. He was worse than drunk; he was completely incoherent and hallucinating. He went from crying to screaming to laughing in a single sentence.

We gave him orange juice, got him into some dry clothes, and after a few hours he started to calm down. We informed him of his Article 31 rights, equivalent to the civilian Miranda rights, which he waived, and we questioned him. He told us that earlier in the afternoon he had taken acid, and because he was starting to feel paranoid, he began drinking to come off his high. He didn't remember much, except that he didn't want to get crushed by the sky, which didn't make much sense to him anymore -That's why he had decided to kill himself in the East River.

Thank God that his basic instinct of survival didn't allow him to breathe in the water and go under. We asked him where he got the LSD, and at first he was reluctant to tell us. So we beat him (just kidding). Soon he told us who provided the LSD and the booze -another ET student in an advanced course.

Coast Guard Intelligence (CGI) and base security were also involved, and with the name of the guy who sold him the acid, we went to the CO of the training center and got a search warrant. We briefed each other on how we would do the search. Coast Guard Intelligence was to lead the search and I was to inform the suspect of his Miranda rights and attempt to elicit a confession.

The Coast Guard team donned plastic gloves and Tyvek suits to make sure that the LSD wasn't absorbed through the skin and into the blood stream. The search was, of course, a surprise to the suspected LSD dealer. We pulled him out of his room, threw the cuffs on him, and read him his rights.

Meanwhile, the CGI team began their search. I had known the ET for quite some time, a brilliant Hispanic guy, maybe too clever by half. He clammed up immediately and demanded to see a legal representative. After about forty-five minutes, the CGI officer came out and said, "All we found were these bottles of wine. So all we can book him on is the illegal possession of alcohol."

I looked at the wine and noticed it had been re-corked. At the bottom of each bottle of wine were small pieces of paper. I looked closer at a bottle and saw that the paper was a small section of a sticker pad with Yosemite Sam's image on each of four perforated sections. "Let me take a look at the room," I said.

"Mr. Eident, you're not fully protected!" the CGI guy said. I walked into the room anyway, and on his desk, right in the front, were another forty tiny stamps with Yosemite Sam's pistol shooting in both directions. On each stamp was a slight discoloration.

I picked up the stamps, "Guys, do you know what this is?" They didn't. They replied that six months ago High Times Magazine had cancelled their subscription, and now they had no idea what the latest drugs looked like. I held up the small pad of stickers. "Guys, this is blotter acid."

One of them asked how I knew, and I told him I spent four years in college in the 70s. The CGI agent took the blotter from me very carefully, took a pair of tweezers, put the blotter in a double plastic bag, and wrote out the transmittal on the evidence tag.

I grabbed the bag of LSD with the tag and went out to confront the ET suspect. I asked whether he knew that the guy he sold to had just tried to commit suicide, and I asked him whether the people he gave the wine to understood there were four hits of acid in each one.

Within a few minutes, I pulled him back into the room and he broke down, crying. Clearly his career was over. I asked him whether he wanted to do something constructive and tell us where he got the LSD. His cooperation would be noted, but I couldn't guarantee anything. He agreed, and soon we knew the place where a few of the Coasties were buying their drugs in New York. Since all my past experiences in trying to work with the NYPD went nowhere, we decided do a little extra duty and see if we could stop the drug problem at the source.

We put him in isolation along with the suicide victim, and we ordered both to be kept under close watch. Then we went down to Soho with very specific directions. Dressed in jeans and a T-shirt, I walked into the candy store. I looked around for a few minutes, and then I asked for drugs. Under the candy counter was a whole display of recreational drugs. I negotiated with the clerk/dealer for a few minutes, told him his prices were too high, and left. We went back to the base and called the Drug Enforcement Agency (DEA). We also called the New York Police Department and gave them a rundown of what happened. We told them we wanted a bust of the candy store.

The NYPD was most under-impressed. Nonetheless, we put together an action plan and got a court order from a New York judge. He set up a sting operation that included one of our trusted Coasties buying drugs. It took the NYPD two days to get the search warrant and organize the sting operation.

The day of the operation, we noticed that kids were going in there and coming out very quickly. We knew something was up. We sent in our wired volunteer, who asked to see the stuff under the table. The man laughed and said, "I have nothing! What are you talking about?" We did the raid on the place after the Coastie left and came up empty.

The DEA agent sitting with me in the car said the guy was definitely tipped off by the NYPD. The police department had been going through a lot of corruption investigations; in fact, this was only a few years after Serpico (who, incidentally, stayed on Governors Island during his trial in order to avoid being murdered by his fellow police officers). During the debriefing I was mad as hell. I knew what LSD could do, and I knew what drugs could do generally, because my fellow football player ad killed himself while tripping. I think —but I'm not sure —that in my enthusiasm to make a metaphor, I made a statement about pigs being at the feeding trough, and soon the CGI agents and the DEA agents were separating us. It's probably not a good idea to insult a guy with a gun and a badge.

It was a disappointing end to an exciting, and potentially worthwhile, three days. Afterwards, the DEA agent told me that maybe the dealer was an informant and that NYPD needed to keep him on the street. I would have liked to have known that before I pissed off all of New York's finest. For the record, if the guy was spared arrest because he was an informant, I apologize. However, if you guys were paid off, my insult still holds.

I worked on a few other cases with the CGI unit and found them to be incredibly competent and dedicated. If I had stayed in the Coast Guard, I would have liked to have been part of that organization. Cops and robbers on boats — how can you beat that for a job?

The Error Chain

The individual's mind can have its own error chain that can begin with the data it collects and decide whether that data is right or deceptive. Even if the initial assessment is right, the mind can distort reality and create a wholly believable mirage: a dangerously misleading perception. The perception, right or wrong, is then sorted through the individual's learned or experience-driven paradigms. As an OC, the experience paradigm is that your superior officer is always right —even when he's wrong. The captain's paradigm might include the assumption that Friday night is when all the fishing boats are heading home for the weekend. We're trained to think horses, not zebras. On average, that's efficient. It usually works... until it doesn't.

23.

"Was there a man dismay'd?
Not tho' the soldier knew
Someone had blunder'd:
Theirs not to make reply,
Theirs not to reason why,
Theirs but to do and die."
-*"The Charge of the Light Brigade"*
Alfred Lord Tennyson

The proceedings leading up to the court-martial for Captain Robinson were an ongoing saga throughout 1979. I received many notices to stand by. . . to stand by. . . to stand by. . . .

In June of 1979, Secretary of Transportation Brock Adams, who the New York Times called the Carter administration's biggest disappointment, resigned. His replacement, Neil Goldschmidt, took office in September and vowed to keep inflation down in the transportation sector and to revive the automobile sector. I am sure the Coast Guard and its troubles were far from his mind.

Because I had been dealing with security violations, I had developed a few friends in the Coast Guard legal department, who were following the court-martial with keen interest. They explained to me that this was, in many ways, a unique case. The Article 32 hearing was convened at the highest level, by the Commandant. An Article 32 is somewhat equivalent to a grand jury and requires the board to examine the case and decide whether or not to indict and what the appropriate charges should be. Generally, the convening body is on a lower level and other districts or commands provide the officers. The Uniform Code of Military Justice requires that any member of these boards cannot be subject to submitting fitness reports by the convening authority. Since all fitness reports funnel upward to the commandant, Robinson's attorney, Flanagan, claimed that each the officers would have a conflict of interest. He said that the judges' fitness report which went to the commandant's staff, should be removed. This had never been done before.

The original trial date was in May, but Flanagan submitted a motion to dismiss the case due to unlawful command influence. Chairman of the House Coast Guard and Navigation Committee, Representative Mario Biaggi, stated that the collision was "so grievous in nature and so negligent a performance, that certainly an example should be made, a proper example." Flanagan cited the 1971 William Calley court-martial for the My Lai Massacre as his precedent. In that case, the president and the secretary of defense asserted civilian command influence to secure a conviction for Calley.

The Coast Guard claimed that Rep. Biaggi was not in the chain of command. Flanagan asserted that, when you approve the budgets, you have a lot of influence, and the "Coast Guard takes every opportunity it can to accommodate Biaggi's requests." He who writes the checks makes the rules.

Biaggi didn't know a thing about the situation but saw an opportunity to enter the news as a tough guy. Mario was in the NYPD for over twenty years and declared by his publicist to be "the most decorated police officer in the United States," and he loved to play for the crowds. He became an attorney at forty-nine and got a different view of the criminal justice system. At fifty-two, he was elected to Congress and saw how laws were made. Later I would find out that at the age of seventy, he got to experience yet another side of the legal system, when he was sentenced to two and half years in jail for bribery.

During the unveiling of the Cuyahoga Memorial, a reporter asked my shipmate, Ensign Fairchild, what he thought of the upcoming court-martial. The reply that made the newspapers was, "I kind of hate to see them do it to him. If it's necessary, then the people who run this country see something I don't." The first part I agreed with, but later I had no misconceptions about the people who ran our country.

Police and other former law-enforcement agents are usually excused from jury duty because they suffer from a well known and generally accepted bias: they tend to believe if the guy is arrested, he is guilty. My uncle, Captain Robichaud, firmly believed that, and likewise Biaggi, who was spearheading the persecution of the captain also saw things as black and white, and never delved into the deeper extenuating and mitigating factors. Nearly everyone in the chain of command in the Coast Guard had been in law enforcement at one time or another; they were all susceptible to this bias. Flanagan wanted another service to try the case, one that didn't have a command structure affected by the commandant's and Biaggi's pressure as well by law enforcement bias.

Someone had leaked a memo to the press who had a more authoritative voice than either Fairchild or me. In the memo, the chief of operations, Admiral Venzke, wrote to the commandant, "The record shows that there were clear indications for some time that the operation of the Cuyahoga was marginal, but supervisory commands did nothing, leaving the CO to go it alone. I strongly feel CWO Robinson should not stand alone if blame is to be apportioned." Clearly, the commandant was not listening to his highly experienced staff, but rather to his political superiors.

Flanagan tried to call the commandant to testify. He wanted to know why the commandant announced his decision to court-martial Captain Robinson three days before he had to testify before Biaggi. Flanagan also wanted to know if the commandant took into consideration the Coast Guard investigation that said responsibility for the accident should be shared and only recommended one charge of hazarding a vessel. The Article 32 board had added the two additional charges: involuntary manslaughter and destruction of government property.

Flanagan filed eleven motions, including dismissal of the judge. To be technical, the judge was a hearing officer and the jury or jurors were members of the court martial-board, in military-speak. The judge's fitness report was approved by the commandant's staff. It was the first time that a Coast Guard judge's authority had ever been challenged, and the first time a commandant had been asked to testify.

Flanagan also accused the Coast Guard of prosecutorial misconduct. Flanagan was able to uncover three more internal memos from high-ranking Coast Guard officers that all called for sharing the blame and not holding Robinson solely responsible. Flanagan contended that they should have been considered at the Article 32 hearing. The prosecution said Flanagan used "sinister juxtaposition of eye-catching words" from memos that were hearsay. Flanagan agreed they were not firsthand accounts, but he countered that they were "dynamite hearsay!" Indeed, this evidence could have blown the prosecution's case out of the water.

Flanagan wanted to take the fight back to an Article 32 hearing where he had more favorable rules of evidence and a chance at avoiding the court-martial. In an Article 32 hearing, the rules of evidence may be less stringent and hearsay could be admitted if the judge ruled that there were expert opinions.

After months of haggling, the defense and prosecution arrived at a negotiated agreement: The commandant agreed to be deposed in Washington, but he would not testify at the actual court-martial.

∞

Finally, in November, I got a temporary assigned duty order: report to the U.S. Coast Guard Reserve Training Center to be available as a witness for the court-martial of CWO Donald K. Robinson.

The officer's club confrontation was never far from my mind. "A bunch of wet-behind-the-ears college kids screw up and the warrant officer gets blamed." Would I be the smart-ass college kid who drove the last nail into Captain Robinson's coffin?

My commanding officer, Captain William Thrall —one of the wisest men I have ever known—called me in. He had heard through scuttlebutt that I was suffering. I started my reply to his query with, "This stinks!"

"We all have a role to play, and your role is to tell the truth."

"That they put us out on a death trap and then blame it on one man? This court-martial is a travesty." My thoughts raced back to Woody Allen's court scene in Bananas: This case felt like " a travesty of a mockery of a sham of a mockery of a travesty of two mockeries of a sham —of a mockery of a sham."

"That is an opinion, and at this point in your career, you haven't earned the right to have an opinion on a matter like this." He softened a bit. "It will all work out in the end, but only if we all do our duty."

He got me by using the most sublime word in our language. He, of course, was right.

∞

I knew it was coming, but I was never quite prepared. A court-martial was for conduct affecting good order and discipline, such as being absent without leave (AWOL), showing disrespect toward superiors, disobeying orders, deserting, and dereliction of duty, conduct unbecoming of an officer and gentleman, malingering, misbehavior before the enemy, spying, rape, larceny, drug offenses, assault, and murder.

I couldn't remember if I knew anyone who'd been court-martialed. I had watched the The Caine Mutiny and could picture Humphrey Bogart breaking down on the stand. But that was fiction. I also remembered coverage of the Calley court-martial for the My Lai Massacre. A court-martial didn't seem like a lot of fun.

Collisions with loss of life often result in a court-martial, right or wrong. Back in January of 1949, the Coast Guard icebreaker Eastwind was rammed by the Gulf Oil Corporation tanker Gulfstream in predawn fog sixty miles southeast of Barnegat, New Jersey. The tanker's bow tore into the sleeping quarters and punctured fuel tanks. Thirteen men died, and dozens of others were scalded by steam.

Captain John Glyn faced court-martial charges of neglect of duty and failure to assign an experienced and efficient watch officer. The lieutenant on watch was convicted of failure to evaluate radar information and failure to notify the captain of a radar target.

The Eastwind was cork-lined to prevent sweating for when she was on arctic duty. A short circuit caused by the collision started a fire in the cork. With no lighting, smoke cut off all visibility throughout the ship, and the entire complement of 160 officers and men, many of them naked or nearly naked, gasped for breath and scrambled to get topside. Fifty men onboard were on a cruise from the training center at Cape May, New Jersey, which had opened a year earlier.

After four hours of attempting to fight the fire (the short circuit had crippled the pumps, and hose pressure was feeble at best), the captain ordered the abandonment of the ship. The Coast Guard cutters Gentian and Sassafras arrived on scene and extinguished the blaze. Captain Glynn and the officer of the deck suffered through a court-martial, but in the end they were absolved.

∞

By now I knew the ropes of traveling on Coast Guard business, and this time I had credit cards and my ID, so I was ready for the wait-fest. It had been a year since the accident, and a number of OCS classes had entered and graduated. I stopped by the dorm. A memorial had been built in the quarterdeck of the barracks from the equipment salvaged from the bridge of the Cuyahoga. It was sitting on "the rug," so I hesitated to walk up to it.

I had a morbid curiosity about how our class statistics would be displayed in juxtaposition to all the other classes. How would they classify our "wash outs" who didn't fail but gave their lives? I went to the wailing wall and found that our class was omitted; there was 05-78 and 07-78, but no 06-78. I guessed that the memorial, rather than a statistic, was the best solution.

Walking across the base, I ran into Captain Robinson. I was shocked. He had looked so old before, far beyond his forty-something years, but now he looked younger and more fit. We exchanged pleasantries, but the whole time I was wondering why he looked so much better with all this stress on him, and I wondered how this could have happened to such a sincere and competent person. He was anything but a screw-up. It struck me right then: this could have happened to anyone.

∞

I was briefed by the administrator for the court-martial. He told me that the charges had been reduced and there were no longer any manslaughter charges, leaving one count of negligently hazarding a vessel. Hazarding a vessel can be punished with two years of hard labor. More likely, the captain would be given an dishonorable discharge, and he and his family of eight would be left with no job and no retirement benefits. In the military, it's not just the serviceman who makes sacrifices —it's his whole family.

I was one of the last to testify. Rose, Riemer, and Fairchild had testified days before me. Reading the local papers was disheartening. They reported that I gave the order but failed to pass on the contact notification from the lookouts to the captain. Flanagan was good at cross-examination.

Three days in, I finally got the chance to testify. As soon as I took the stand, the captain and I made eye contact and he gave me a reassuring nod. The prosecution was quick, but the cross-examination took hours. Every time I felt a little unsure, I looked at the captain and he nodded and smiled.

There are many versions of the truth. The charge against the captain included the phrase "inexcusable ignorance." I knew I was guilty of excusable ignorance. During the National Transportation and Safety

Board hearing, I tried to sound intelligent and perhaps overstated my competence. Realizing that I had nothing to lose, I tried to emphasize that, at that point in my career, I was ignorant and no help to the captain.

The papers said I was "precise," but that I "seemed intent [on trying to] get it over with." When asked why I didn't tell the captain of the oncoming ship, I told the court that the ship seemed so far away, and I thought it wouldn't affect us. "I had tunnel vision," I told him. I was thinking more about getting the course heading and the bearing right than thinking about piloting. I told them I hadn't had piloting or navigation training, and I had never seen a Coast Guard radarscope until that night. I went on to say I wasn't ready to contribute to the piloting of the vessel that night.

The truth is, my captors, the OCS officers, had brainwashed me into believing they were infallible. I was like a dog that has been beaten so much he stops barking and just goes along for the ride with his head out the window. I didn't recognize that the situation was much more than an inconvenience until I was fifteen feet underwater. OC Riemer was concentrating on the helm, determining how much play, if any, there was in the wheel and how best to keep a nice, steady course. He knew that qualified helmsmen would rag on "weavers," who couldn't steer a straight course. The brand new lookouts, after reporting the Santa Cruz, were focused on a ship following us that seemed to be overtaking us. The two bridge lookouts were trying to get bearings off lights for navigation; they weren't looking for contacts for piloting.

I believe my classmates and I were unknowing co-conspirators. We stressed our ignorance. In fact, one of the headlines was "Ignorance Stressed at Trial." There are two reasons we stressed our ignorance: First, we all had learned a lot since then, and we realized that we were truly ignorant; second, we were all willing to fall on our swords for the captain. That is the kind of leader he was.

The Santa Cruz was a self-loading cargo vessel with huge cranes on both sides of the ship, and during my testimony, Flanagan dwelled on the cranes. He kept asking me how many there were and how big they were. I gave an estimate, but his persistence got me irritated. I told him I was more focused on the Santa Cruz's anchor that was coming dangerously close to our bridge. But he harped on the cranes.

Flanagan's examinations up to this point had seemed tightly

planned, but his sudden fixation on the number of cranes seemed impromptu, as if a mental bulb had switched on somewhere in his brain. He finally said, "I have no further questions." I felt like the weight of the world was lifted from my chest. "But I reserve the right to call this witness back to the stand," he added.

∞

The next morning, Flanagan filed yet another motion, this time to recess the proceedings. Flanagan contended that the huge cranes on the Santa Cruz II may have hid the lights that would have indicated the ship was much larger, less maneuverable, and not going up the Potomac. This was the same argument as in the Belknap case, when the OOD couldn't make out the lights of the Kennedy because operational equipment blocked the view. The prosecution attacked his premise, claiming that he should have been able to see the light when the angle changed. But Flanagan countered: "Not if it was constant bearing, decreasing range."

According to the people in the gallery, the prosecution was incensed because this was a brand-new defense, and pure speculation at that. Flanagan was convinced his theory could be tested, but it would take an adjournment. Certainly if Robinson's freedom and the welfare of his family were at stake, the court could adjourn and conduct the test. If cranes blocked the navigation lights, then the Santa Cruz design was at fault and that illegal configuration sparked the error chain. The judge and prosecutor wanted to get the trial over with - They were tired of Flanagan's maneuvers, and after a short recess, the motion was denied. The prosecution contended that Robinson directed the course of the ship across the bow of the freighter with inexcusable ignorance, and made no attempt to take even the most basic steps in determining the position, course, and speed of the Santa Cruz.

The prosecution's best piece of evidence was the captain's standing order that required the OOD to determine a contact's position, course, and speed. Robinson said, as captain, he often took liberties on that rule if he thought that the contact wouldn't come close enough to affect the ship's course. He used his judgment, and in this case his judgment was wrong.

When the prosecution rested, Flanagan asked for a dismissal based on the fact that there were no regulations for obtaining position, course, and speed of an oncoming ship. The judge again ruled against Flanagan's motion, saying it was the common practice. All of the jurors were past skippers, and all had similar standing orders —all had done exactly what Robinson did, but none had an accident to show for it.

I was curious to see what Flanagan's defense plan would be. Although I was not allowed to observe the court-martial, through reading the papers and talking with those who were able to follow the news, I pieced it together. He was basically defending an acknowledged mistake. I was watching a litigation artist peel back the facts to reveal the truth.

One of the first to testify for the defense was Dr. David Foreman, one of the military's leading experts on pulmonary illness. In December 1978, Captain Robinson was (finally) referred to him. He revealed Captain Robinson's medical history on the stand. Since April, Captain Robinson had been treated by training center doctors and a specialist from Riverside Walter Reed Hospital in Gloucester, Virginia, for what they thought was allergic bronchitis and sinus problems. He went to sick bay or Walter Reed approximately twice a week every week for six months, including the day before the collision.

The doctors prescribed three separate drugs to help control his breathing difficulties. One of the drugs he was taking was Entex, a combination of guaifenesin and pseudoephedrine. The warning on the label read as follows: "Entex can cause side effects that may impair your thinking or reactions. Be careful if you drive or do anything that requires you to be awake and alert. This drug may make you dizzy or lightheaded; use caution engaging in activities requiring alertness, such as driving or using machinery." The Cuyahoga was one big serious piece of machinery. Flanagan told the jury, "No pilot in the Coast Guard or any other service or any commercial airline allows pilots to take these drugs and fly. There was no such rule in the Coast Guard for officers of the deck. There are no regulations or even guidelines for fitness for sea duty." In fact, there was no differentiation between the risk caused by an impaired desk jockey and a ship's captain. The risk between misspelling a word and sinking a ship was equally valued. Dr. Foreman told the court that Aspergillosis causes blockage in the lungs and fluid builds up. By the time Captain Robinson saw Dr. Foreman, he had lost nearly a third of his lung capacity and was "near death."

Because of the fluid, over the course of the past nine months, any time Robinson would lie down he would have coughing fits. According to his wife, he didn't get more than two hours of sleep at night, and they were mostly upright in a chair. Some nights his wheezing was so bad that she wasn't sure if he would make it through the night.

Over the past year, numerous people speculated that Robinson had an addiction problem. In fact, he did. He was addicted to oxygen and sleep, and he wasn't getting his usual fix.

After reading about the accident in the newspapers, and without any prompting from Flanagan or Captain Robinson, Dr. Foreman wrote a letter to Robinson's superiors stating that diminished capacity was a common symptom of Captain Robinson's illness and perhaps the catalyst of Captain Robinson's mistake. Dr. Foreman stated that sleep disturbance caused by fluid accumulation in the lungs was a serious and debilitating illness.

Witness after witness offered evidence of Captain Robison's diminished capacity. His children reported that his driving had become unsafe, and that he barely avoided two car accidents. During the six months before the collision, he had two marine accidents while at the con, and both caused material damage and resulted in letters of reprimand. Prior to that, his record was spotless.

Witnesses reported that Captain Robinson sometimes fell asleep mid-conversation. Commander Kuhnle testified that he saw Captain Robinson passing his office on the day of the accident and was alarmed by his condition. He called Robinson to ask him he was alright. Captain Robinson spent a long time thinking about his answer and finally said he was fine, just a little tired. Kuhnle reported that "he seemed like he was somewhere else." Because of the captain's gradual deterioration, his crew testified that they didn't notice the difference in his behavior until Dr. Foreman cured him. Then they could see that he had been in a fog for some time. It was like the old saying, "I didn't know he was an alcoholic until I saw him sober once." From my brief encounter, I was shocked by the difference. I remember seeing him struggling to breathe in that cold water and thinking that he might die; now I knew that he had trouble breathing before he even hit the water. At the NTSB hearings, the captain had looked older than my sixty-five-year-old father, but now he looked forty-something.

I was still wondering whether an illness could cause a bad decision. I thought about the First District commander who, while alone in his home and recuperating from an illness, gave the order to return Simas Kudirka to the Russians, triggering one of the most disgraceful incidents ever to occur on a ship flying the American flag. Like Robinson, he was sick, and he was also mission-focused, and there was no one near him to tell him that he was making a grave mistake. An expert for the defense, Dr. Lavern Johnson, stated that a person with diminished capacity "would have thought he was making the correct decision, unless someone told him he was wrong. He would not have questioned his own decision... The only people who really question their actions or question their own decisions are people who have the ability to think clearly."

Dr. Johnson went on, "The condition is characterized by reduced vigilance, visual impairment, and an inability to set priorities." He should have been piloting instead of teaching, he didn't see the Santa Cruz clearly, and the accident proves he was less than vigilant. If he had been thinking clearly, he would have avoided this collision as he had avoided every other close call over his last twenty-seven years in service, through hurricanes, gales, and fogs.

A civilian employee, Peggy Douglas, said she saw Captain Robinson two days before the accident and was "shocked by his appearance." She asked him if he was sick. "In the military you don't tell them you're sick," he replied. "They tell you."

Captain Robinson's superiors only saw him, on average, about once a month. Although they were getting daily medical reports, they really only checked for malingerers -obvious serious illness -and issues that might affect health. Certainly the system failed by not correlating the marine accidents and his medical record —"issues," indeed. This illustrates how culture affects norms, which in turn affects cultural practices. "I's tough, I is, I am, I are." At sea you have to be near death not to stand watch. In the larger world, there are not many people who puke at their desk and go right back to work, but that was pretty much general practice in the Coast Guard. A little cough, or "I didn't get a good night's sleep," was certainly no excuse for missing duty or not going out and saving someone's life. Malingering was abhorred in Coast Guard culture, and often treated with blanket parties. It meant other people had to work double shifts regardless of their physical condition. The practice is, you don't call in sick.

It's the insidious nature of a chronic illness that makes it so dangerous. It wears you down slowly until you accept the condition as your norm. Unlike an aging athlete, who has thousands of people witnessing his decreased performance, there are no statistics or objective measures that could warn a person of his deteriorating performance. The captain must have wondered, "Maybe I'm just getting old. Maybe it's time to retire." With crummy pay and six children, the Robinsons were stretched thin, and he knew he couldn't live on just 55 percent of his base salary with no housing and no health care for his family.

Besides, the Coast Guard was undermanned and truly needed experienced people like him. The Cuyahoga was critically understaffed, so how could calling in sick help the crew do their job? The Cuyahoga was an old, undependable ship that needed his constant attention, and it certainly should never have left the dock without his vast experience onboard. For the previous three years, inspection report after inspection report stated that the ship was critically undermanned: "The understaffing was affecting the maintenance of the ship and the navigational capabilities of the crew."

Moreover, in a military setting, it's hard to criticize your superior's action. Because Captain Robinson had so much experience and was conning with a relatively inexperienced team, this crew would be even more reluctant to tell him that he was starting to screw up. As complete neophytes, the thoroughly regimented OCs and the brand-new lookout were unlikely candidates to question orders, or even recognize danger. According to friends of CWO Robinson, it took Flanagan, who ultimately based much of his defense on health factors, a long time to convince Captain Robinson to consider his illness as a contributor to his mistake.

∞

Flanagan also emphasized in his defense that there was no bridge radar. Captain Robinson was the only guy conning a ship over sixty-five feet that had no radar in the wheelhouse. Any non-Coast Guard vessel stopped for inspection would have failed without wheelhouse radar installed and in operating condition. The jury heard testimony that Captain Robinson had complained about the ship's radar system and had repeatedly requested that an electrician be assigned to the Cuyahoga for repairs. Because of the overall personnel shortage in the Coast Guard, Robinson's request was denied, but the Coast Guard agreed to replace the radar system. It had failed at sea at least a dozen times during the months preceding the collision, including the cruise before ours. To get another bearing and range, the captain would have to go into another compartment, make a calculation on the radar, and come out and readjust his eyes, the whole time leaving the bridge to people who have never been out to sea.

Needless to say, Flanagan also presented evidence about the under-manning identified in three years of reports, as well as the question-able practice of using trainees to supplement the crew for piloting and navigation. While the material safety condition of the Cuyahoga was deemed "poor to unacceptable" in the captain's own self-inspection report, just one month before the sinking the commandant actually awarded the Cuyahoga a unit citation for the ship's "excellent condi-tion." The brass was always polished, the decks varnished, the rust painted over.

After sixteen days, the defense rested. The defense's closing argument centered around the fact that Captain Robinson had diminished capacity, and because of that diminished capacity, he made a mistake —a navigational mistake, not a criminal mistake.

∞

The prosecution's closing arguments centered around the Coast Guard's own medical experts, who contended that there was little likelihood that the drugs affected Robinson's visual acuity, made him drowsy, or altered his personality. The prosecution further argued that if Robinson got as little sleep as he and his wife contended, he would have been completely dysfunctional. The prosecution said the defense tried to paint Robinson as an actor stumbling onto a stage. They then took the metaphor further, claiming that he was actually the director who could yell, "Cut!" I thought that maybe the prosecutor was a frus-trated English lit major who always wanted to quote Shakespeare in his final argument, though he got the entire point of the quote wrong.

∞

Much later, I would find out about the behind-the-scenes negotiations. The prosecution presented an offer to Flanagan: The judge would instruct the jury to consider a lesser charge of dereliction of duty if all parties agreed. Normally, a jury can only consider the charges. It was high-stakes poker: if Flanagan chose to play he could hold out for complete acquittal. Supposedly, Flanagan counter-offered. If he agreed to a lesser charge, prosecution would not recommend any punishment. They settled with an oral agreement that, if Captain Robinson were found guilty, the prosecution wouldn't recommend a specific punishment. So Flanagan hedged his bet —he agreed to the deal but was still hoping for a full acquittal. A full acquittal would be a real feather in his cap and help the civil case, but his client came first. The jury went out to deliberate while everyone waited. A simple majority could convict Robinson, and all votes were conducted with secret ballots. I thought the case seemed like a slam dunk. Clearly, Captain Robinson was sick and his illness adversely affected him.

"If the jury deliberates for two hours or less they are finding for not guilty," Flanagan told the anxious press, " If it goes two to five hours, they are finding for guilty. Beyond five hours, it's anybody's guess."

On November 3rd, a year and fourteen days after the collision, after thirteen hours of deliberation, a jury of seven Coast Guard officers —two captains, a commander, and three chief warrant officers, all former skippers —found Chief Warrant Officer Donald K. Robinson guilty on a reduced charge of dereliction of duty in the collision that sank his cutter and killed eleven men. The skipper remained stone-faced. His daughter wept. There would be another hearing for sentencing. He still could face three months imprisonment and loss of benefits.

∞

Flanagan told the jury that any penalty against his pay was a penalty against his family, a Coast Guard family that earned the benefits from twenty-seven years of service to their country. Flanagan said the family had suffered and would continue to suffer from the stigma that had just been placed upon them. He again cited all the extenuating and mitigating circumstances, noting in particular that, even if the captain did make a mistake, the condition of the Cuyahoga turned his mistake from a loss of property into a loss of lives. "If anything," he said, "The only thing that should be considered is a letter of reprimand."

∞

After nineteen days of trial, the jury reached its sentencing recom-mendation. Robinson was to receive a written reprimand and lose 200 seniority places for promotion. The sentence would have no effect on his pay. It is noteworthy that this recommendation could have been achieved without a court martial.

Captain Robinson had served a tough sentence already. To have manslaughter hanging over him must have compounded his grief over the loss of his crew members, and the grief of all the people who loved him. He was reported as saying, "It was like losing eleven sons." At the end of the trial and sentencing, he shook hands with all seven members of the jury. His lawyer, Flanagan, vowed to appeal.

It was reported in the press that Captain Robinson told a friend that he couldn't have lived with a total acquittal. He told the press, "I thought the trial was fair . . . and I still love the Coast Guard."

BM1 Wild had come to the trial every day to offer his moral support. He held his own impromptu press conference and was reported as saying, "I would still work for this man at sea or on shore."

I headed back to Governors Island, disappointed not only in the outcome but in the entire process. Six weeks later, a friend faxed me an article. The Washington Post headline read, "Ruling Absolves Coast Guard on Cuyahoga." The article said: "(District Judge) C. Stanley Blair ruled yesterday that the Coast Guard is not liable for damages because the crash and sinking was caused by the negligence of Commissioned Warrant Officer Donald K. Robinson, and that his superiors were powerless to prevent it. The accident was caused by Robinson's decision to make a left turn into the freighter's path and the improper use of signals that gave Hamill (the Santa Cruz's pilot) confusing information about the cutter's intentions... The collision in question was not caused by any deficiency in equipment or manning onboard the Cuyahoga."

According to this ruling, everything was fine with the Coast Guard. There was just one lapse by one person, and the court-martial conviction served as proof of that. The conclusion was that the Coast Guard had not allowed conditions to develop on a systematic basis and thereby endangered its men or other ships.

I thought about doing as my sister suggested, writing a letter to the commandant, but I remembered that four separate senior Coast Guard officers had sent the commandant letters, and there was a letter from a physician who was an expert in respiratory illness. They still decided to blame it all on this one man.

The Error Chain

The list of contributing factors to the sinking of the Cuyahoga is ominous: a pre-existing health condition, an old ship that breeds mold that was the cause of the condition, misdiagnosis of life-threatening disease, no objective measures of fitness for sea duty, chronic under-manning in the Coast Guard in general and on the Cuyahoga in particular, an organizational culture that encouraged sick people to work, no real contact between superiors and Captain Robinson, no correlation of information between wheelhouse crew, misread lights, the captain's continuing to teach in spite of his condition and being overburdened, lack of recognition of the true situation regarding the position of the other ship, and an old ship without watertight integrity, no emergency lights, and no real safety equipment.

The age old error chain: Not learning from your mistakes.

24.

"...I went out for a ride and I never went back
Like a river that don't know where it's flowing
I took a wrong turn and I just kept going..."
-"Hungry Heart"
Bruce Springsteen

On Tuesday morning, January 29, 1980, I finished my breakfast and headed to my office in the training center. I opened my door, picked up the New York Times, and read the headline: "1 Dies in Tanker-Ship Collision; 25 Missing off Florida." The first line was, "180-foot Coast Guard Cutter collided with an oil tanker...." I put my back against the door jam and slid down until I was sitting on the hallway floor. I knew what twenty-five missing meant.

I took a couple of deep breaths and read the rest of the 462 calm, cold, clear words. The cause of the collision had not yet been determined. The cutter went down in four minutes. (There were no casualties on the tanker.) Divers were searching for air pockets.

I headed to my office hoping to hear more about the twenty-five missing. People were gathered around the coffee mess, studying their shoes and just slowly shaking their heads. Being the resident survivor, questions were promptly directed at me. "What do you think happened? How could a ship sink in four minutes? Do you think they'll find any survivors?" I didn't have any answers, nor was I going to speculate. This was just six weeks after the Coast Guard had convinced Judge Blair that the Cuyahoga collision was the act of one man; a year and three months after the Cuyahoga went down.

After twenty-eight years, this is what I have pieced together through researching written reports and articles: The U.S. Coast Guard buoy tender Blackthorn was set to return home to Galveston after a nearly four-month overhaul in Tampa, Florida, where the thirty-seven-year-old cutter had work done on her generators, hull, and sanitation system. Blackthorn's fifty crew-members, a mixture of new blood and original crew, had not been to sea in the interval.

Many of the crew members who were working on the ship maintenance and upgrade stayed at the Rodeway Inn in Tampa, and their "club" was the motel lounge, where they spent their free time listening to country western music and dancing with the ladies. There is something about men in uniform, especially sailors, that seems to get women's attention. Rumor has it the Blackthorn crew broke a lot hearts when they left for Galveston.

∞

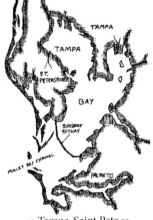

∞ Tampa-Saint Pete ∞

During the day, the ship left the pier for a brief sea trial but was forced to return immediately when the generator malfunctioned. With repairs complete, the captain, Lieutenant Commander George James Sepel Jr., decided to set out again at sunset —1804 hours —which is risky business. Traveling at night is much harder, especially during the precarious forty-two-mile transit from Tampa Bay into the Gulf of Mexico. The captain was unfamiliar with the shipping channel, but visibility was good. There was a light wind from the north, which would not affect the ship's maneuverability; the temperature was 61 degrees.

Initially, Sepel took the con to get a feel for the ship's handling ability. Then he turned control over to his executive officer and went to the engine room with the engineering officer to check a malfunctioning shaft tachometer. When Sepel returned to the bridge, the XO asked him to relieve him at the con. Instead, Sepel turned control over to the officer-of-the-deck, a young ensign, John (Randy) Ryan, who had only qualified as an OOD in September, just before the ship was dry-docked.

Because they had spent so much time ashore during the overhaul work, the crew had accumulated personal property they wanted to bring back to Galveston. Recognizing there would not be any buoy operations on the way back to Texas, Sepel allowed them to stow their new recreational baggage on the deck and in the passageways —some were tethered to hatches and doors. He didn't let the crew build drawers into the ladders, but the motorcycles and a small car were probably just as hard to climb over.

The 180-foot cutter was about to go through a narrow passage under the Sunshine Skyway Bridge, which would lead to an even narrower channel between several Keys and into the Gulf, which local mariners had nicknamed "the combat zone." This part of the passage includes an 18-to-19-degree bend in the channel, an area so treacherous that the area pilots had a gentlemen's agreement not to enter the zone if any other ship was passing through. This channel was only 500 feet wide, an extremely narrow passage considering that most ships prefer to leave at least that same distance between each other when passing in the open ocean.

If that wasn't enough, one of the channel buoys was out of position and the other channel buoy's light was out. The bend amounts to a dogleg, and the conditions made navigating it like trying to take a turn in the road without landmarks to tell you where you are.

The Blackthorn's crew apparently didn't know that the Army Corps of Engineers was in the very last stages of dredging and had widened the channel by 100 feet on the outbound side (the Blackthorn's side). Tampa Bay pilots were aware of this, and they were all moving over, effectively moving the centerline of the channel 50 feet. The local Coast Guard Aids to Navigation Team was waiting for the Army Corps of Engineers to issue the final sign-off on the widening before moving the centerline buoys and making official announcements.

Although it was getting dark, the Blackthorn's crew was navigating by seaman's eye rather than dead reckoning or plotting their position on a chart. The Blackthorn had a modified sea detail with four men ready to set anchor (to be used as an emergency brake), and a steering detail in the stern that could control the rudder in case of a steering casualty.

The anchor detail had collateral duty as bow lookouts, but none of the crewmen realized their role. The flying bridge lookout, a seaman apprentice, had no prior experience or training. This was his first time out to sea.

Just before reaching the channel bend, the Blackthorn was overtaken by a brightly lit Russian cruise ship, the Kazakhstan, traveling in excess of fourteen knots. The lights and the height of the ship made timely viewing of the buoys and oncoming traffic nearly impossible.

At the same time, a U.S.-flagged oil tanker, the 605-foot Capricorn, piloted by forty-year-old Harry Eugene Knight, was coming up the channel toward Tampa. The Capricorn had her port anchor in the ready-to-let-go position with the anchor's claws exposed, ready to imbed themselves into the harbor mud. The Capricorn was required to have six able-bodied seamen aboard; there were only two.

As the ships turned the bend, the Capricorn passed the Kazakhstan port-to-port. The pilot of the Kazakhstan apologized to the Capricorn's pilot for hogging the center of the channel. The Blackthorn and the Capricorn were both cheating in toward the middle of the narrow channel to avoid running aground. Now there were three ships in the "combat zone," two with pilots inadvertently violating their agreement and attending to the two most serious issues for a pilot —meeting and passing —with one ship piloted by an ensign who hadn't been to sea for over three months.

The XO on board the Blackthorn went into the pilothouse, checked the radar, and found another contact that had the same bearing as the Kazakhstan. He looked out but couldn't see the contact past the lights of the Kazakhstan. He asked the ensign if he could see a ship. The ensign couldn't either, so he asked the XO to make radio contact. The XO jumped on the radio and heard another ship's garbled transmission: "We're coming out of anchorage and won't be in your way." The XO replied, "Roger." The XO had heard the twenty-five-watt broadcast of the Ocean Star which was much further up the channel talking to another vessel. Most pilots use one watt of power so they are not interfering with the transmissions of other ships further away

HM3 Chamness, who was in the pilothouse, wearing the headphones, saw the lights emerging from behind the Kazakhstan and called up to the flying bridge to ask the lookout if he could see the lights. The novice seaman apprentice said he could see them. Both assumed that the ensign conning the ship saw the lights and thus there was no need to tell him. Both later testified that there was so much static on the line that no one was really sure what anyone else was saying -tin cans with string would have been better. After the sighting of the Kazakhstan, the lookout became engrossed in viewing a shrimp boat that was following them into the narrow channel. The bow watch didn't see the lights of the Capricorn until it sounded its danger single.

Ensign Ryan assumed that the XO had made contact and arranged the usual port-to-port passing. He went out on the port bridge wing to take a bearing with the gyro-repeater (compass), but he couldn't see the target because of the crane equipment installed on the ship to set buoys. Therefore, he had to go out to the starboard wing and get the bearing, losing precious time. The equipment that blocked his reading actually obstructed the view from dead on to 10 degrees on either side of the Blackthorn —quite a blind spot.

After getting his bearing, Ensign Ryan went back to the port bridge wing and detected the contact having a left bearing drift. The Capricorn was just approaching the channel dogleg and, therefore, appeared to be going to the left of the Blackthorn. However, if the Capricorn maintained that course, it would run aground. Ryan didn't realize the Capricorn would have to turn. He then turned his attention to finding a navigational buoy towards the stern, because he knew the other two buoys were not functional. While he concentrated on getting the difficult navigation bearing astern, he was distracted from the oncoming traffic. When the ensign found the bearing off the stern, he discovered he was too far to the left, so he made a slight course change to the right.

Captain Sepel stepped out onto the port bridge wing in time to see the huge Capricorn making her swing to port and bearing down on them. "WHERE THE FUCK DID THAT COME FROM!" he yelled, "RIGHT FULL RUDDER!" He put engine controls into back full engines. He also ordered the "standby for collision" be piped to the whole ship. At the same time, they heard the horns of the Capricorn signaling extremis. The ensign noted that the Capricorn's bearing drift was continuing to the right. That could only mean one thing: the Capricorn was turning hard to its left and attempting a right-to-right passing.

After passing the Kazakhstan, the Capricorn had seen the Blackthorn on the radar and made two attempts to hail it on the radio. Perhaps the Ocean Star's twenty-five-watt broadcast drowned them out, as the Blackthorn never heard them and they in turn never heard the Blackthorn's XO trying to make contact. The Capricorn had decided not to sound any horns in order to leave the option open to the more maneuverable smaller ship, which had a thirteen-foot draft as opposed to its thirty-one-foot draft.

Before the ensign on the cutter made his course change to the right, the Capricorn's pilot perceived that the Blackthorn was cutting across the channel in front of them. Recognizing the risk in that kind of maneuver, the Capricorn's master said to the pilot, "What is this guy trying to prove?"

The Capricorn was now abeam of the marker for the channel dogleg and would have to turn to port or run aground. With better maneuverability and a shallower draft, the cutter appeared to be better able to avoid going aground and avoid the Capricorn with a starboard-to-starboard passage. So the Capricorn's pilot, with the master's silent consent, decided to stay in the channel and exercise the unconventional and dangerous starboard-to-starboard passage. The Capricorn sounded two horns and proceeded to make three rudder changes to the left: 10 degrees, 20 degrees, and then full rudder as the situation became more desperate. Finally the pilot gave an order to the engine room for full reverse engines.

The Blackthorn never heard the two horns indicating starboard-to-starboard passage. Why? No rational explanation was ever given. Maybe the engines drowned out the horns or the crewmen were too focused on navigation.

With the cutter going at full right and the Capricorn at full left, the ships started to line up head-on. If the captain of the Blackthorn hadn't ordered the hard right rudder and changed course by 20 degrees very rapidly, the Capricorn would have rammed the Blackthorn's starboard beam, an exact replication of the Cuyahoga collision, a vicious push through the water by a much larger ship.

Sepel was able to get the cutter's bow head-on and slightly to the right of the Capricorn's bow, converting a bow-into-beam collision into a much less dangerous side-by-side raking collision. The bows narrowly passed each other port side, and, in a shower of sparks and screeching and groaning metal, their wider beams raked past one another in the narrow channel. It looked like a marine fender-bender not dissimilar to the USS Belknap -but with one catch.

Just before the collision, three of the four men on the anchor watch saw the gigantic Capricorn bow coming at them and made a run for it. SN Rhodes, who was wearing the headset, became entangled in the headphone wires and was frantically trying to extricate himself from the wires wrapped around his legs, just like the two OCs on the Cuyahoga: OC Robinson who had his legs torn up and OC Thomas who was nearly hung by his own headphones.

The Blackthorn listed 15 degrees to starboard from the push. When the raking ended, the ship righted itself and, disturbingly listed 10 degrees to the port. The bridge ordered damage reports, and the crew immediately scoured the ship for leakage and began securing all portholes and hatches —at least those that weren't blocked by five motorcycles, three motorbikes, a bicycle, a small car, and a refrigerator.

They sent a Mayday message to Group St. Petersburg, and Group St. Petersburg replied, "What is the nature of your distress?"

The Blackthorn bridge, gathering damage assessments, answered, "Standby."

∞

MKC Litterel and CWO2 Miller went into the forward berthing areas, checking for damage. They ran into the naked and injured MK1 LaFond. Even though he was clearly shaken up, LaFond sarcastically said, "You better get the anchor out of the shower before you wash up." Since the penetration was well above the waterline, he must have figured it posed no immediate threat, and stayed in the shower area to get dressed —his body was found there.

While the reduced-speed side-to-side collision might have caused only minor damage, the Capricorn's 13,500 pound anchor was ready for letting go and had ripped into the side of the Blackthorn, finally embedding itself in the buoy tender's port side just above the waterline —and in MK1 LaFond's shower stall. It hooked onto the joiner, and held, causing the 10 degree list.

On deck, Captain Sepel shouted, "Where's the closest shoal?" Ensign Frank Sarna, the navigator, diligently followed his last order and checked the charts. Sepel's new intent was to ground the vessel to keep it from sinking. Suddenly the ship was jerked backwards and approached a speed astern never achieved before by any Coast Guard vessel, surely a record no sane sailor would ever want to challenge.

When the Blackthorn reached the end of the Capricorn's 990-foot payout of the anchor chain, it was yanked back like an angry guard dog hitting the end of its chain. It immediately assumed the same speed and direction as the Capricorn, but in reverse —a Nantucket sleigh-ride from Hell. She wasn't being pulled by a mere whale, but a multi-thousand-ton tanker.

Before the collision, the standby for collision order had been piped through the ship and the crew was mustering on the mess deck. For five out of six new crew members who had reported straight from boot camp or via Class "A" School, these were their first hours at sea, and their last.

Given the horns, the scraping, and the sudden jerk backwards, there was confusion, and some panic. The more seasoned crew members went right to their assignments, checking for damage and injuries and securing ports and hatches for Condition Zebra (the highest level of preparedness and damage control).

The anchor watch crew, SS2 Marak and SN Ware, went back out to the forecastle and attended to their shipmate, SN Rhodes, who was slightly injured in the collision because his retreat was impeded by his headset. They accompanied him to the mess deck. FNMK Niesel, who had been in the after-berthing when the collision occurred, made it to the mess deck, securing the hatches all along the way. He looked around and suddenly feared that maybe he had left someone behind, and so he went back into the berthing area.

When the anchor embedded into the side of the Blackthorn, the Capricorn's anchor crew leaped back from the rapidly paying out anchor chain. Recognizing the danger to the Blackthorn, the moment the anchor chain reached its bitter end they desperately fell upon the chain and tried to cut it.

The reverse momentum started to slow. The Capricorn had continued its hard left and now headed for the bank of the channel, in order to ground itself and avoid going under the bridge in a damaged condition. This movement was becoming more perpendicular to the Blackthorn's direction. The chain went slack, and it slid under the keel.

On the bridge, the crew members could feel the momentum decreasing. Ensign Sarno found the shoal on the chart and uttered his last recorded words, "Due north."

Captain Sepel was moving toward the engine control to put it in full forward when, suddenly, the listed violently to port. This time the pull wasn't from the stern. Because the chain was wrapped under the hull of the Blackthorn, the continued momentum of the ships pulled it tight again. The chain was pulling from athwartships, across and underneath.

The anchor chain started to pull the boat onto her side and, when she reached the tipping point, she was flipped into a capsized position.

It was almost as if King Neptune reached up and grabbed the gunnel of the Blackthorn and pulled her under. The anchor fell to the bottom when the ship flipped, finally releasing the Blackthorn from the Capricorn's drag.

As the Blackthorn was capsizing, the extreme list immediately tripped the generators and the power shut down. Captain Sepel yelled, "Abandon ship!" but with the power out, the order couldn't be piped. No survivors reported any emergency lanterns or lighting coming on. SA William R. Flores of Fort Worth, Texas, got to the life-jacket box, struggled to open it, and finally secured it open with his own belt. He and two others started passing life jackets.

SA Gatz, who was the lookout on the flying bridge, got entangled in the headset wires and found himself being pulled under. He cut the strap with his knife, freeing himself, and made his way to the surface.

In the mess deck, everyone was thrown from the floor and fell on the overhead (ceiling) in the pitch dark with water rushing in. Instinctively going up would mean avoiding the water, but it would also mean climbing further into the interior of a sinking ship. The injured SN Rhodes, who had made it to the mess deck, went forward and, standing on the port bulkhead of the starboard vestibule, opened and held the 130-pound watertight door over his head so that his two shipmates could escape, and then he escaped as the water rushed in.

FNMK Niesel was just finishing his inspection of the after-berthing when the vessel rolled. He fought his way up the starboard ladder as the flooding water swept into the inverted mess deck, where he swam through the open starboard watertight door to the buoy deck and escaped.

SA Brewer climbed up into the engine room through the escape scuttle located just aft of the mess deck. He shined his flashlight down through the scuttle and shouted, "I found a way out! I found a way out!" His body and twelve others would be recovered from the engine room twenty days later.

Although many of the sailors in the mess deck rushed for the scuttle and to apparent safety, SA Gray, who realized that the engine room was not the way out, convinced SA Hull and another crew-member to follow him. The two crewmen tried to make their way under the water towards the starboard door and out the buoy deck. SA Gray surfaced alone and reported the situation to Captain Sepel, who was hanging on the outside of the vessel. Sepel ordered Gray not to attempt to return to the mess deck. He feared that if Gray tried to go back in he would be dragged down by the sinking vessel.

FNMK Niesel and EM3 Clutter found an unconscious CWO Roberts and brought him to the quarterdeck shack that had broken loose and was floating next to the capsized ship. Some of the sailors started climbing onto the hull of the ship, but the men in the water all shouted for them to get away from the hull. Like the Cuyahoga, the ship went rapidly down to its resting spot on the bottom of the channel.

As the Blackthorn tipped, others had jumped off, but Flores remained, throwing the life jackets to people who were escaping the vessel. He was last seen trying to help injured men. His quick thinking, securing the latch of the life-jacket box, allowed the rest of the life jackets to float to the surface when the ship sank. The survivors hung on to these jackets until they were pulled from the water.

Group St. Petersburg was anxiously awaiting further instructions from the Blackthorn. "Mayday" for the Coast Guard is equivalent to "officer down" for a police force. Group St. Petersburg repeatedly called back, asking for more information. The Bayou —the shrimp boat that was following the Blackthorn —broke in to report that the vessel had sunk and to request immediate assistance.

The Capricorn called in to say, "Send everything you've got." Group St. Pete ordered all vessels underway to the scene. They dispatched five other Coast Guard small boats, and they requested and received assistance from the Coast Guard auxiliary, Eckerd College Search and Rescue Unit, Pineallas County Sheriff's Office, St. Petersburg Police Department, Florida Marine Patrol, Florida Highway Patrol, Tampa Bay Police Department, Tampa Fire Department, Palmetto Police Department, commercial shrimp vessels, and civilian volunteers. Many of the volunteers and police officers scoured the shores for survivors.

The Bayou picked up twenty-three Coasties and provided them with clothing, food, and warmth. A Coast Guard forty-one-footer arrived on the scene within thirty minutes and picked up FNMK Niesel, EM3 Clutter, BM3 Bartell, CWO Miller, and CWO Roberts. Even though Miller didn't have a life jacket, he wouldn't leave the water until Roberts had been taken aboard. Once they had Roberts onboard, Bartell tried desperately to resuscitate him, but he was gone.

Twenty-seven crewmen were rescued, and twenty-three died. Fourteen of those who died were trapped inside the Blackthorn. The other bodies were recovered at the surface but had died as they surfaced or were dead before surfacing. No one can know for sure. The Blackthorn carried four fifteen-man life rafts. None of them inflated and made it to the surface within the first hour. Each raft had its own reason for failure: one was slashed, two didn't have canisters, one was tied down, and one wasn't properly rigged.

This was the new worst peacetime loss of life in the Coast Guard's history, breaking the Cuyahoga's tragic record in less than fifteen months. The U.S. Navy's SPRINT was called in again.

∞

Brian Flanagan, a young Coast Guard ensign, was working in the Operations Center of the U.S. Coast Guard headquarters when the Blackthorn collided with the Capricorn. He called his father, Jay, to tell him the news. Hours later, when he knew just how serious the collision was, he again called his father. This time, Jay Flanagan was not at home. He was on a plane to Tampa: Captain Sepel had already hired him.

The following day, the newspapers gave a much more detailed account. One news report said that the survivors were cold, tired, and angry. The maritime industry was getting safer but the Coast Guard was heading down another path. The Coast Guard was reeling. I knew the OOD, Ensign John Ryan, who was in the class ahead of mine. I wondered who was going to be held accountable for this shift. Naturally, another round of investigations was necessary: the NTSB, the Coast Guard, and another court-martial?

During the first four days of hearings, Lieutenant Commander Sepel sat next to his wife, turning to her when he was fighting to hold his emotions in check. He had to listen to the survivors and witnesses describe the horror of the sinking. The Capricorn's cook gave a riveting description of screams for help coming from the dark sea. It finally was just too much for him, and Sepel broke down and cried.

The Coast Guard was also being taken to task over the buoy light beacon that hadn't been replaced. The Coast Guard claimed that the missing buoy had no influence on the accident, but the harbor pilot said the missing buoy was critical to navigation, and a contributing cause to the confusion that led to the collision. Ironically, the Coast Guard had gone out to repair the light, but went to the wrong light, which was also malfunctioning by incorrectly blinking, and they assumed they had repaired the reported outage.

The marine casualty board, run by the Coast Guard, determined that the cause of the casualty was the failure of both vessels to keep well to starboard in the channel. In concurring with the marine board's determination of the cause, the commandant emphasized in his "Action" that the failure of the persons in charge of both vessels to ascertain the intentions of the other through the exchange of appropriate whistle signals was the primary contributing cause. Additionally, Admiral John Hayes pointed out that attempts to establish a passing agreement by using only radiotelephone communications was not an adequate substitute for exchanging proper whistle signals.

The Coast Guard charged the pilot, Harry Knight, with misconduct and negligence, alleging that he violated the nautical rules of the road by failing to sound a whistle signal to establish a passing agreement, failing to sound a four-blast danger signal, and failing to reduce speed or stop when he became unsure of the Blackthorn's intentions.

The National Transportation Safety Board, which drew experts from all areas of the civilian maritime industry, concluded that the collision was the Coast Guard's fault. The NTSB considered the extra hundred feet and the fifty-foot move of the centerline in their findings. The marine casualty board did not.

The marine casualty board report included a graphic to illustrate the accident, clearly showing the Capricorn on the wrong side of the channel and the Blackthorn dead on the midpoint line. The Coast Guard was in denial.

The harbor pilot's attorney submitted a letter to the Coast Guard that stated, "The Coast Guard's emotional state due to the loss of the lives of their own guardsmen [the Cuyahoga and Blackthorn] rendered the agency potentially prejudiced in finding of fault." Therefore, the marine casualty board's findings should be thrown out. The lawyers for the harbor pilot also contended that the Coast Guard did not implement many of the recommendations from the Cuyahoga and were therefore incapable of seeing their own faults and learning from them.

It's an interesting argument that a service could have a collective emotional state, but I can tell you that the news of the Blackthorn threw me and
everyone else on Governors Island into a state of grief, shock, and disbelief.

The Blackthorn sank in the main ship channel of the port of Tampa,
blocking the channel and precluding deep-draft vessels from entering or departing until the wreckage was cleared twenty-six days later.
Many ships were trapped, and their owners were angry. The power
company was running low on oil. The government dispatched forensic
teams to make sure they fully understood the remaining evidence. The
same Navy team that lifted the Cuyahoga was dispatched to raise the
Blackthorn —it was difficult process.

The Error Chain

They say that most systems are so robust that it takes at least seven
preventable errors to conspire to create a major disaster. There are
common threads in accidents at sea: in the vast majority of cases the
crew is behind schedule, in 52 percent of cases the crews have been
up more than twelve hours, and in 44 percent of the cases the crew
has not worked together recently. Minor equipment breakdown,
poor communication, and less than perfect visual conditions all
play a contributing role in major accidents. Most of these events are
not independent. One thing leads to another. An equipment failure causes a delay, which causes stress, which causes fatigue, which
causes poor communications.

Nearly everyone in the transportation business has heard of a
captain whose first officer was Jack Daniels and his navigator Jim
Beam. Because there are so many back-up systems and redundan-
cies, most drunks dodge the bullet for a lifetime. The fact is that
most major catastrophes are systemic: the odds catch up to you.
Finding a fall guy instead of taking a long hard look at your organization just keeps the system dysfunctional.

Here are the two error chains in sinister juxtaposition.

Cuyahoga	Blackthorn
Old ship that couldn't meet safety standards	Old ship that couldn't meet safety standards
Delayed start from malfunctioning equipment	Delayed start from malfunctioning equipment
Except for the captain, the team was brand new	The team was rusty and the OOD new
Captain was distracted by training	Captain was distracted by malfunction
Night piloting	Night piloting
Captain was exhausted	Crew was tired
Lookout was brand new	Lookout was brand new
Misread lights	Couldn't see light
Gave wrong whistle	Didn't hear initial whistles
Internal communication tense	Internal communication tense
Sound power phones unclear	Sound power phones unclear
No radio communication	Radio communication failed
Radar was inadequate	Radar wasn't properly used
Accident at dogleg	Accident at dogleg
Captain was confused	No local knowledge
Both vessels turned left	Capricorn turned left
Slowed down too late	Slowed down too late
Bad luck	Really bad luck
Abandon ship not piped	Abandon ship not piped
New people unfamiliar with escape routes	New people unfamiliar with escape routes
Most emergency lights didn't work	No emergency lights worked
Drawers in stairs	Recreational equipment by hatches
Head phones nearly killed people	Head phones nearly killed people
No survival swimming	No survival swimming
Rafts didn't work	Rafts didn't work
Didn't learn from mistakes	Did learn from mistakes

25.

*"Everybody knows that the boat is leaking
everybody knows the captain lied
everybody got this broken feeling
like their father or their dog just died."*
-*"Everybody Knows"*
Leonard Cohen

In the winter of 1980, the Coast Guard dropped charges against the pilot of the Santa Cruz II, John P. Hamill, essentially assuming 100 percent of the responsibility for the accident. Judge Stanley Blair had rendered an initial opinion that the accident was completely the Coast Guard's fault, but due to Section 183, the Coast Guard would have no liability. Now that the court-martial was over, the civil suit for the survivors and victims' families seemed like a long shot. Essentially, the Coast Guard was guilty but judgment-proof because of the zero value of the Cuyahoga. If the decision stood, the victims no longer had the Santa Cruz as a back door.

The journey to the truth became even more bizarre. Judge Blair, who presided over the Cuyahoga's civil trial in the U.S. District Court, died on April 20, 1980, before formally entering his decision. The Cuyahoga case was reassigned to the Honorable Roszel C. Thomsen, who reopened it. With new evidence, and with the collective emotional baggage of the Blackthorn collision still fresh for everyone, Thomsen's findings would be different.

If successful, the suit could fulfill the reason most lawsuits are brought: to provide relief and teach a lesson. Leoni Balina, a recent immigrant from the Philippines, was one of the plaintiffs. Her husband, the Cuyahoga's cook, went down with the ship. She had a day job teaching, and after his death she took on a night job cutting hair to support her nine-year-old daughter and toddler son; she could not support her family on her meager widow's benefits and Social Security. There was no real safety net for people like her, especially with her family 10,000 miles away. At one point, she found it necessary to send her children back to the Philippines to live with her family until she could catch up on her debts.

∞

Something disturbing was happening in the "New Guard," too. On January 17, three months after the Cuyahoga sank, a Coast Guard helicopter crashed, killing four. Twelve days later, another copter crashed, killing two; then another crashed in February and again in August. Four accidents in one year, ten deaths.

Helicopter accidents tend not to stick out because those contraptions have too many moving parts and so just look dangerous, but actually, the Coast Guard fatal accident rate for helicopters had averaged one in every five years since 1964. The accident rate for this year, 1979, was twenty times the norm.

Since 1942, when Igor Sikorsky, the inventor of helicopters, demonstrated the machine's lifesaving capabilities on Long Island Sound, the Coast Guard and Sikorsky Aircraft held an exclusive relationship. 1979 was a bad time to have four accidents, since a contract for a new generation of rescue helicopters was about to be awarded.

The Coast Guard awarded the program to a French helicopter manufacturer, Aerospatiale Helicopter Corporation. The Coast Guard thereby ended America's virtual monopoly on helicopter technology. While a consortium of U.S. defense contractors would be involved, the prize and much of the development money went to France along with many American jobs.

∞

There were quiet discussions in the mess hall and at the officers' club about what was wrong with the Guard, but the rest of the world was busy thinking about more important things. Three huge topics dominated 1980: inflation, the Iranian hostage crisis, and the presidential election. Inflation was nearing 15 percent and the prime rate was just under 20, the highest either had been in modern times. The budget deficit was to blame for the inflation, and the Federal Reserve was trying to squeeze out inflation by reducing the money supply. Jimmy Carter and Ronald Reagan debated who would be better at cutting the budget. Thoreau was being quoted: "The best government governs the least." The reputation of government employment went from pursuit of a low-paid but noble calling to holding an ignoble sinecure. Budgets were zero-based, and fuel for operations was rationed for each operating unit. Our morale bus was grounded by May, and we couldn't even fill the tank with our own money -it had exceeded its mileage allocation.

∞

Then tragedy again targeted Tampa Bay. On the morning of May 6, 1980, three months after the Blackthorn was dragged out to reopen the channel, this dangerous channel was blocked again. John E. Lerro was piloting the 608-foot Liberian-flagged freighter Summit Venture into the Port of Tampa when southwest winds rose to tropical-storm force, whipping the freighter with blinding rain. Then, just before the treacherous channel bend where the Blackthorn and Capricorn had collided four months prior, the Summit Venture's shipboard radar failed. Pilot Lerro judged it too risky to turn out of the shipping channel to the north, in order to anchor and ride out the storm, because stopping would risk the ship being pushed into the Sunshine Skyway bridge by the sixty-miles-per-hour winds. Turning around exposed the ship to possible collision with an outgoing tanker. At 7:33 a.m., the Summit Venture plowed into a bridge support and the roadway above gave way. Lerro frantically called the Coast Guard for help.

"Get emergency... all the emergency equipment out to the Skyway Bridge," he said. "Vessel has just hit the Skyway Bridge. The Skyway Bridge is down! Get all emergency equipment out to the Skyway Bridge. The Skyway Bridge is down. This is a Mayday. Emergency situation. Stop the traffic on that Skyway Bridge!" The warning came too late -a bus full of passengers and several cars plunged 150-feet into the water —thirty-five people died.

The skills of the Coast Guard captains were already being challenged. Now the maritime industry and the public questioned the Coast Guard's competency as managers of the U.S. shipping lanes, inspections, and licensing. Could it get any worse?

It got worse. In the spring of 1980, the government of Cuba unexpectedly announced it would permit a massive emigration through the port of Mariel. With little regard for capacity or seaworthiness, a flotilla of privately owned U.S. boats brought 125,000 refugees from Cuba to Florida between April and September 1980. The Coast Guard mobilized all its meager resources in the area to ensure the safety of the flotilla, but they were overwhelmed by the sheer numbers of boats mobilized in what would later be known as the "Mariel Boatlift."

The Coast Guard was being stretched even further. Americans got the sense that their borders were being overrun by illegal immigrants and drugs. Intense pressure was put on the Guard to plug the leaks in our porous borders.

The Coast Guard didn't have assets to keep up with the fast boats that sped past them in the Florida Keys. Gunners' mates would shoot across the bows of these craft, but they couldn't actually shoot them, so the smugglers would just flip them the bird and keep going. The Coast Guard was looking enfeebled.

In January of 1981, Ronald Reagan took the oath of office and vowed to rein in government spending. One of the items on the initial list of ways to make the government more efficient was the following: disband the Coast Guard and distribute its services to other agencies. I remember my Uncle Frank saying to me, "You've been in the Guard for two years and now they're ready to shut'er down. Good thing we don't own a family business."

One of President Reagan's first appointments was Assistant Secretary of Labor Raymond Donovan, a political contributor and an executive vice president of a New Jersey construction company. Focus on that, dear reader: a New Jersey construction company. Donovan was not fond of the Occupational Safety and Health Administration (OSHA). Even though the U.S. Postal Service was the only government organization to fall under OSHA rules, other governmental agencies looked to OSHA and the National Institute for Safety and Health (NIOSH) for best practices. No doubt, some of the OSHA regulations were too cumbersome, especially for small businesses, and certainly most managers had examples of some very poorly thought-out regulations. But few questioned the importance of occupational safety and health. Nevertheless, Secretary Donovan slashed OSHA staff, and morale plummeted. It's hard for civil servants to stand up to their political bosses when their jobs are on the line.

∞

A year after the Blackthorn tragedy in January 1981, the Coast Guard ordered a court martial for the captain of the Blackthorn, this time on the district level. Rear Admiral Paul A. Yost, commander of the Eighth Coast Guard District in New Orleans, said that the court-martial would determine responsibility for the accident.

"There is no presumption of guilt," Admiral Yost told The New York Times. "This is the opportunity for a fine officer to defend his actions." Yost said that the Blackthorn's officer of the deck, Lieutenant (jg) James R. Ryan, would face non-judicial punishment, a less serious proceeding.

The hearings were held at the Coast Guard Training Center in Yorktown. Captain Robinson appeared on a daily basis to offer support to Captain Sepel. YN1 Carter's dad, Colonel Carter, sat with the spectators in court every day. He wasn't looking for vengeance, he was just trying to make some sense of what had happened.

The charges against Captain Sepel were numerous: failure to be aware of other ships in time to prevent risk of collision, failure to sound proper sound signals, failure to keep his vessel to the right of the shipping channel, dereliction in the performance of his duty by failing to ensure a sufficient number of life rafts before leaving port, and failure to properly supervise the Blackthorn's OOD. If found guilty, Sepel faced a maximum penalty of eight years hard labor plus a dishonorable discharge.

Flanagan headed the prosecution off at the pass. He fought his battle at the Article 32 military board. When the first board didn't indict, prosecution called for another. Again, no dice. Neither would indict Captain Sepel, so a non-judicial Admiral's Mast was held, and both Sepel and Ryan had simple letters of reprimand placed in their files. These men were called up on charges for a five-second navigation error; I know most people in the Guard were thinking there but for the grace of God. . . .

∞

In the fall of 1981, my faith in government reached its low point. Congress and the president could not agree on a budget, so they announced that they would only fund the essential agencies. Evidently the Coast Guard didn't qualify as an essential agency.

We had to create a contingency plan. The special service fund would offer $50 loans for our troops to buy groceries, and we could also receive welfare and food stamps. While people in other government offices were being sent home, the Guard retained all its officers; we were willing to work even if we weren't going to get paid. People who risked their lives for meager pay, who lived paycheck-to-paycheck, were now having those meager paychecks taken away. Servicemen used to lament that at least you could count on a steady paycheck. Well, not anymore.

"We have a witty old saying in the military about pay," a chief told me. " Don't screw with my pay!" Congress did. As my mother used to sigh when my brothers or I screwed up, "It must have sounded like a good idea at the time." Maybe they didn't realize that loyalty is a two-way street. In any event, the shutdown didn't last more than half a day.

I remember someone saying, "We've done so much for so long with so little, we are now qualified to do everything with nothing."

∞

Despite financial and political issues, I liked what I was doing and really enjoyed working with the men and women in the Coast Guard. I got along really well with my supervisor, and although he did chastise me on the condition of my uniform, he liked what I was doing and how I got along with the men. Just after he submitted my second fitness report (year-end evaluation) for review, he called me in and said, "What the hell did you do to the XO?"

"Why do you ask?" I replied.

"Because the XO told me to mark down your evaluations."

I told him my story. During the two weeks my supervisor was on leave, I had sat in on the weekly officers' staff meeting held in one of our biggest classrooms. The XO was a tall, good-looking man in his mid-fifties. His voice was deep and a bit coarse from smoking cigarettes and spending a little too much time at the officers' club bar.

He was sitting at the teacher's desk, his cigarette ash dangerously drooping when he demanded, "Where the hell are the ashtrays?"

The warrant yeoman replied, "Coast Guard budget guidelines don't allow us to purchase ashtrays anymore."

"Buy them out of the special services budget," he ordered. This caught my attention because I was in charge of the special services budget.

I told the XO, "I assume that the general purchasing guidelines, or at least the spirit of them, cover all purchases using special services money, too."

He snapped back, "Don't give me that spirit crap, and assume nothing! Next week I want ashtrays on every desk in this room."

The special service budget comes from surpluses created by the PXs and the clubs. It is designed to pay for bats, balls, flowers for sick or dead Coast Guard relatives and wives with babies, and short-term loans for enlisted guys. I'd be damned if I was going to spend any of it on ashtrays for officers. Frankly, I didn't think it was moral to spend morale money on public health's number one enemy. That weekend I went to Cape Cod and gathered a peck of quahogs, shucked them, and carefully cleaned the shells. Next week there were thirty-five half-shell ashtrays —one for each desk. Not one word came from the XO, but he did glare at me. I thought the issue was dead, but apparently not.

∞

My supervisor asked me if I liked shooting myself in the foot. I told him that I actually had a thing about it, although I really didn't. He told me that if I wanted to make full lieutenant, I was pretty much disqualified now because unless I had a near-perfect fitness report each year, I would never make the cut. I had no plans to extend anyway. I also thought the Coast Guard needed to change and I wasn't particularly shy about sharing such thoughts with my fellow junior officers, which I am pretty sure was not a great career move.

∞

I remember my farewell party on my last day in the Guard. The training center was closing for the Christmas season and I had finished my three years minus accumulated leave. I was sitting with fellow officers in the officers' club near the Christmas tree, gazing out at the East River toward Brooklyn, watching a few ships, ferries, and barges go by, thinking about how I had gotten out of this alive, when I overheard a conversation at another table.

"Sorry I am late. There was a huge emergency. Mass Maritime's training ship caught fire; it's completely uncontained. They say there are still people trapped in the ship."

I whirled around. "What!?"

"I was just down at Com center," he replied, "and heard that the Bay State engine room caught fire and there are people trapped in it."

"My brother is an engineering instructor there."

"Fuck! I heard it's pretty chaotic, but the ship was on the dock, so there are land assets there, too."

My wife was in our officers' quarters apartment packing. As I was running back to her, I saw a shape jogging toward me from a distance. It was my wife. She yelled, "He's alright." Relieved, I turned around and headed back to the bar. I wasn't going miss the going-away party, or the free drinks. At least that's the way I always told the tale to my brothers and uncles.

The truth is, I ran up and hugged my wife. "Dad called," she said. "He said Donna called him and made him call everybody to tell them that Bill's OK. Why wouldn't he be OK?"

That Christmas I tried to talk to Bill about what happened, but he didn't want to discuss it. Although his wife told me a little bit, it was an event that he wanted to push into the back of his mind. Twenty-seven years later, after I finished the first draft of this book, Dad told me that I should include Bill's story. After some tenacious badgering, he reluctantly gave me his account.

In 1979, the Massachusetts Maritime Academy (MMA) was given the 533-foot, thirty-year-old troop ship USNS Geiger (originally the President Adams). She had carried countless men to their deaths in Korea and Vietnam. She was renamed Bay State, replacing the previous ship of that name, which was considered too decrepit for training by MMA and given to the New York Maritime Academy for a few more years of unsafe service.

On the first voyage of the new Bay State, she broke down twenty-three times in the course of a thirty-day journey. After six months in the yards, she was taken up from Newport News, Virginia, to her new berth on the mouth of the Cape Cod Canal in Buzzards Bay, Massachusetts. On December 23, 1981, there were approximately 150 students, instructors, and maintenance people on board the ship. At noon, classes were dismissed for Christmas vacation, and many of the maintenance workers went to lunch.

The ship was still generating its own power because the electrical connections on the dock were not in place for proper hook-up. The generators in the engine room were running at full operating capacity.

There's an old saying in the Coast Guard: "Hit to fit, bend to meet, paint to match." In the general maritime industry, the saying is: "If it don't move, get a hammer. If it still won't move, get a bigger hammer; and if it don't move after that, paint it." Following this advice, two industrious students were on the second deck of the engine room preparing to fix an oil filtration system on one of the oil-fired engines. The oil in the line was hot and under pressure. There were parallel lines that had a bifurcation valve, and the students needed to switch the valve and redirect the fluid to the alternate fuel-flow line. The valve was stuck, and one of the students decided to use additional leverage to turn the valve lever. He kicked at it with his boot, but the boot missed and knocked the top off a small petcock valve. The heavy fuel oil shot up and hit the hot pipes above and immediately burst into flames.

Along with the fuel, the many layers of paint applied to conceal the rust caught fire. When heavy fuel oil doesn't burn efficiently, it churns out thick black smoke. Everything turned black. While there was emergency lighting, the wires soon burned out along with the lanterns. Three students were on the lower deck of the engine room, and ascended the ladder through the burning second deck. In the black smoke darkness, the two upperclassmen turned right out of the engine room compartment into a compartment that was less smoky. This took them to safety. Freshman Rodney C. Morris continued up the ladder into the second floor of the engine room, which was filled with dense smoke and superheated air. He didn't make it out of the ship.

Ships have systems that automatically close all hatchways during a fire or flood. The hatchway doors were big and clumsy and stopped any flow of ventilation, so some of the doors were tied open and others had wedges that kept them from swinging shut. With the firewalls breached, the smoke immediately spread to nearly all the compartments.

Bill could see the smoke from his office. He ran to the ship. There he saw a drenched Mike Dagnello, one of the top students in the school. Mike had retreated to the chief engineer's office, climbed out the porthole, and jumped five stories into the freezing cold Cape Cod Canal. Bill said he spotted numerous other students streaming out of the ship, coughing and gasping. Teachers have a special feeling of responsibility to care for their students; even today Bill says he can still see the soot-blackened faces of his students and the terror in their eyes.

He spotted a cadet with his head sticking out of the porthole of the chief petty officers' mess. The porthole wasn't big enough to get his whole body through. The fire department extended a ladder off the dock so a fireman could get close enough to talk with him. The cadet didn't know his way out, and this was the only place he could breathe. Bill ran up to the firemen, "Why aren't you rescuing him?" he yelled.

They said they didn't know the pathway through the ship. Bill offered to lead them in, but the firemen said there were no more respirator packs and the two of them would have to go in as a team. Bill said that he would go in without an air pack as far as he could and then tell them how to navigate the rest of the way. They told him it was too risky for an unprotected person to enter the ship. Bill said they didn't have a choice. The firemen reluctantly agreed to let him go in without a respirator.

Bill entered the hatchway, battling through the thick black smoke billowing forth from it. At first he crawled on his hands and knees, and then shimmied on his belly. Growing up, my brother Bill was by far the best in our neighborhood at sneaking up on people and ambushing them. As he told me his story, I wondered if all that practice had paid off.

Bill's mind raced to his first-born, Kathryn, five days shy of her first birthday. He wondered whether she'd have a father to raise her. He also thought how wicked-mad Donna, his wife, would be if she knew he was crawling into a burning ship. He wondered how quickly he could be overcome by smoke. What was the limit?

He finally reached a point where he could successfully tell the firemen how to get the rest of the way in and make it back out. "Down this ladder," he shouted, "then the second hatchway on the right." He repeated it twice more and before starting the long crawl back out.

Coughing and choking, he made it back to the dock and tried to yell to the trapped cadet to reassure him that help was on its way. Everything seemed to take forever. There was no sign of the firemen. The boy's situation was getting desperate.

"Did I give them the right directions?" Bill wondered. "Should I have gone further?"

Then he saw a glove reach out from the porthole, cover the boy's face, and pull him in. Time found its unique way of expanding as he anxiously waited and finally saw the firemen and the cadet emerge from the ship.

Bill's wasn't the only act of heroism that day. Eight kids were trapped in a below-decks compartment when Amos Cardozza, who probably had the genes and instincts of a Portuguese sailor, was just coming off lunch. He went down shaft alley -a narrow shaft that goes down the stern into the emergency steering room at the bottom of the ship. Then he went through the pitch-black run along the keel, found the stranded cadets, and led them all to safety. He was awarded the highest citation of the U.S. Merchant Marine, the Distinguished Service Medal.

There was a delay turning on the fire-suppression system because it would have meant displacing all the oxygen with carbon dioxide. While the fire would have died, so too would the remaining humans. When they finally turned on the fire-suppression system, the flames were extinguished in a few seconds, along with any hopes of finding anyone alive.

By the grace of God, the fire didn't start until an hour after school was dismissed. One student lost his life that day, but it's impossible to say how many more kids would have died if the fire had happened an hour earlier. The smoke from the fire hung low and floated over the main street of Buzzards Bay, slowing traffic and conjuring an eerie atmosphere.

The Bay State was so badly damaged that she was eventually towed out to sea and sunk in the ocean's depths. Ironically, the investigation revealed that, a few months prior, virtually the exact same thing had happened while the craft was underway on a 300-mile trip. That fire was small and contained, but it was one of more than twenty incidents and mechanical failures in the three-day cruise that turned into a month-long ordeal, due to the endless chain of breakdowns.

Error Chain

I used to juggle, and I could handle three balls pretty well. Occasionally I would drop one. When I switched to four, I would end up dropping three —sometimes all four. I would end up looking really stupid. When you take on too much, you tend to make mistakes, even doing the things you can do perfectly. You should at least be able to hold two balls in the air, because you have two hands, but more balls substantially increases the odds against success.

26.

*"Rise again, rise again -though your heart it be broken
And life about to end.
No matter what you've lost, be it a home, a love, a friend,
Like the Mary Ellen Carter, rise again."*
-"The Mary Ellen Carter"
Stan Rodgers

As the Cuyahoga civil case dragged on I dreaded the thought of testifying again. While my active-duty obligation was fulfilled, I still had three more years left as a reservist, and I had two options: I could drill a weekend a month and train for two weeks of training a year, or I could be an individual ready reserve. The latter meant I had to maintain my readiness by either working in the industry or by taking correspondence courses, or by doing nothing —not technically, but practically. Since individual ready reservists were unpaid, the Coast Guard had no leverage on them or resources to track them. I took a job at Sikorsky Aircraft and was working in the Strategic Planning Department. Coast Guard Group New Haven wasn't far from my new home, and I wanted to see how a group command worked, so I decided to become a weekend warrior. They say a change is as a good as a rest, and I was earning some pocket money. While my main duty was administrative work, I got a chance to go on boats for real assignments.

I had taken a correspondence course on port safety, so I was practically an expert and, based on my active-duty experience, I had vowed to become the change that was needed. I would be the most fussy and non-compromising inspector in the world.

The port of New Haven, with its scrap-metal yard and huge tank farm, can easily be seen alongside Interstate-95. Even back in the early 80s, we worried that the tank farm was vulnerable to terrorists or "saboteurs," severing the East Coast's major artery. After all, the interstate system was conceived of by President Eisenhower as nothing more than an extension of the military-industrial complex.

My first real activity in New Haven was inspecting a tanker carrying styrene. I tagged along with a first-class petty officer. I'll call him Tony —if Tony wasn't his name, it should have been. He was tall, thin, with a bit of a Brooklyn accent. He was an experienced inspector. He had a droll sense of humor, and he was streetwise.

On the deck of this huge ship, we came upon a hatch on a tank. Tony said he was going to open the hatch and that he needed me to get ready to take a good strong whiff to see if there were traces of the chemical left. He unlatched it and opened it quickly. I immediately stuck my head in and took a good deep whiff. The tank was full and the fumes were intense. I pulled my head out, staggering. I had the worst headache of my life for the next hour. He told me he was just being funny and didn't think I would actually do it, or at least that I wouldn't do it with such vigor. Tony also said that he thought the tank was empty and wanted to show how me how to use a sample detector on a line. He emphasized that you use equipment, NOT your nose in unknown areas! He told me that I must never do that again. I agreed.

On another assignment, we found ourselves inspecting an old dry-bulk carrier destined for Asian shores. The dilapidated carrier was filled with scrap iron, which was spontaneously combusting. Putting water on the overheated metal didn't really solve the problem — actually it made it worse, because the problem was caused by how rapidly the steel was rusting. We walked on top of the cargo and took temperature samples to see if it was too hot.

When I asked Tony if this could be a serious problem, he said that the year before they had a cargo ship burn so hot they feared for the port of New Haven. So they towed the ship out into Long Island Sound, where fire boats drenched it and then pumped it dry, then drenched and pumped it again. Finally, they felt the temperature was low enough and sent it on its way.

"Did that fix the problem?" I asked Tony.

"I can't say for sure, but I suspect not. The ship was lost at sea. The heat probably fatigued the ship, and it broke up in heavy seas without an SOS."

The ship I was inspecting had a Polish crew who didn't speak English; they were anxious but unprepared. Theirs was a one-way passage to an Asian beach, where the ship would be destroyed. After grounding the ship, they'd get a ride to the nearest city and fly home. They were paid by the job, so they wanted to do it as fast as they could.

During the inspection, I discovered that while the waste-water valve was off, it needed to be padlocked while in the harbor. I felt good about spotting a violation. The team on the bridge found a lot more: The navigation equipment wasn't working for the most part, and the crew didn't have the proper charts for their voyage.

With so many reasons to delay the boat's passage, the message from the duty officer —"Get that ship out of here as fast as you can!" —wasn't exactly what I expected. But the Coast Guard lacked the leverage to get them fixed. We could seize a ship and fine its owners, but with the myriad international shell companies that now owned the ship, collection of the fines would be impractical. Besides, where would we put the enormous tanker? We didn't want to delay the ship and endanger the port. We helped find them a marine electronics repairman and located the charts for them. I left at five on Sunday afternoon and the real Coast Guard took over. The floating disaster waiting to happen was now someone else's problem. Experienced inspectors negotiated an agreement: The captain agreed to unload a good chunk of the scrap, and the Coast Guard escorted the ship out of the harbor. The ship and crew made it safely, but the cargo made an unfortunate landing.

Ships such as this one were not only filled with scrap metal but sold as scrap metal. They were sent to beaches in India or Bangladesh for unloading and breaking (the maritime word for scrapping), and taken apart by hand tools and torches. The pieces were put on the backs of men, women, and children wading in the water. Needless to say, the beach was littered with asbestos and other hazardous waste that had a negative value —but the scrap-metal business is all about recycling! And how bad can that be?

Imagine an eleven-year-old girl up to her neck in water, carrying on her head a hunk of jagged steel totally engulfed in asbestos insulation. When she gets to the sand, she scrapes off the asbestos and loads the steel into a truck. Certainly not globalization's finest hour.

In order to realize economies of scale, bulk carriers were being built larger and larger, and some older vessels were being cut in half and lengthened by insertion of a new midsection, like stretch limos. Bigger cargo means bigger cargo holds, which can mean more shifting of weight, which increases stresses and wear on a ship and creates listing in strong seas -just when you least want it.

More bulk cargo also means bigger hatches —up to 50 percent of the deck area above the holds. Hatches, like doors, have to be moved, so they are made lighter than anything else. If you want to break into something, the easiest way is to break in through the door. This strategy is as true on the sea as it is on land.

Huge deck hatches result in less structural integrity for the entire ship. Bigger holds also mean more cargo weight, ergo more room for spontaneous combustion of anything from grain to scrap metal. The result can be outright fire or just increased heat fatigue, often occurring in areas under stress.

While the U.S. economy represented 30 percent of the world's economy at the time, it only had 2 percent of the world's fleet, a sorry position considering our preeminence during the early nineteenth century. The remaining 98 percent of the ships in the world mainly carry Panamanian and Liberian "flags of convenience," because those countries essentially require no regulations.

∞

Most international freighter sinkings go relatively unnoticed by the general public in the U.S., unless the resulting oil slick threatens our shores. Only then the citizens of the U.S. might make a fuss. But from the late 1980s through the '90s, a period of fifteen years ,150 huge ships and 1,000 sailors were lost. A freighter sinking always entails a high mortality rate —often all souls onboard. Most of these sinkings were sudden, as Gordon Lightfoot speculated: "At 7 p.m. a main hatchway caved in . . . they might have split up or they might have capsized; They may have broke deep and took water."

Design architects speculate that extremely long ships could simply break in half, especially after being hit by a rogue wave. The rogue wave, also called a monster or killer wave, or the big kahuna, as surfers have dubbed them, is twice as large as the average of the top third highest waves measured during a given period. Such a wave is not a tsunami, which is a fast moving wave driven by earthquakes and landslides that tends to be flat in deep water. A rogue wave is an almost standing wall of water. Physicists have modeled their possibility, and there is scientific evidence from satellites using radar imaging of the ocean surfaces that leads some to conclude that these waves are in fact not so much "rogue" as commonly occurring waves in areas of funneled tides, or waves resulting from major storms. The legends of these waves precede the Bible, but most of those who experienced them never lived to tell the tale. Rogue waves of 100 feet or more play havoc with helicopter pilots, who hover at the required 50 feet above the average wave.

The maritime industry and the Coast Guard received yet another wake-up call in February 1983, when the 605-foot, World War II vintage Marine Electric, a tanker converted to a bulk carrier departing from Norfolk, Virginia, for Somerset, Massachusetts, loaded with 25,000 tons of coal, sunk off Virginia. During a record-breaking North Atlantic storm she went down, taking thirty-one sailors to their deaths. Only three survived. The investigation revealed gaping holes in the deck plating and hatch covers due to prior corrosion. The storm waters simply flooded and sank the ship. The ship, or more precisely, relic had passed numerous Coast Guard inspections, many of which were outsourced to the American Bureau of Shipping, a not-for-profit company that received most of its funding from their inspected clients —no conflict of interest there. Inspectors work for one or two key clients, and it never takes long until they start to close their eyes. In fact, many of the inspections of the Marine Electric were outright fraudulent. The ship wasn't even in port when some of the inspections were logged. The final inspection report stated, "The inexperience of the inspectors who went aboard the Marine Electric, and their failure to recognize the safety hazards raises doubt about the capabilities of the Coast Guard inspectors to enforce the laws and regulations in a satisfactory manner."

But old sailors had a lot more to worry about than rare, random accidents. In 1983, a comprehensive health study of sailors revealed that 34 percent had abnormalities in their lungs. The rate was 42 percent for sailors who worked in engine rooms. The longer the work period, the higher the correlation.

Now, this doesn't mean they would all die from lung cancer. They could die of mesothelioma, or colorectal, prostate, or gastrointestinal cancer, leukemia, or from acceleration in coronary disease. If they were smokers, they were ninety times more likely to die from cancer than a person who neither smoked nor worked with asbestos. They could also suffer pulmonary fibrosis (asbestosis) and have restricted oxygen intake. The real Popeye didn't get a barrel chest from spinach or lifting weights, but from constantly breathing hard -he got it from asbestos.

Of those thus affected, 30 percent were World War II veterans, mostly suffering from shipboard exposure. Merchant mariners, who died at higher rates than the U.S. Marines in World War II, were not eligible for VA benefits.

I remember my brother Chris telling me that aspergillosis was more prevalent among people with prior lung damage. I remember wondering if the origin of Captain Robinson's error chain was prior lung damage due to exposure to asbestos.

∞

During these years, Coast Guard aviation wasn't getting any better, either. In the course of slightly less than five years, January 29, 1977 to January 7, 1982, twenty-eight Coasties were lost in nine separate incidents. In the previous twenty-five years, the Coast Guard had only lost twenty-seven personnel in eleven helicopter crashes (non-war related). Prior to 1972, they had gone seven years without a crash.

While 1980 was void of causalities, there were three downed helicopters and nine lives lost in 1981. In 1982, the Coast Guard lost its first female aviator. For my job at Sikorsky in the strategic planning department, I often used statistical analysis to review trends. I investigated whether corporate profits were tied to corporate aircraft sales, if the price of oil was tied to offshore helicopter sales, and if copters were more risky than a longer trip by limo, or a shorter trip by plane.

Computing technology was in its infant stage, so we unraveled the data using advanced regression analysis. I'd submit our hypotheses to Data Resources, Inc. (DRI) in Stamford, Connecticut, and they would crunch the numbers on their supercomputers. We would look at the results and examine statistics: correlation and serial correlation, even multicollinearity. While this may sound really perverse, I actually enjoyed statistics and got a job teaching the subject at the University of New Haven.

I looked at all the figures and calculated whether a trend could be random or a systemic failure. The frustrating thing about statistics is that you can't prove that anything is 100 percent true -there is even a the chance that two fingerprints actually match. So statistical results must include a tolerance for error, perhaps 1-5 percent short of that 100 percent certainty. Based on my z-table score, the probability was 99.67 percent that what we were looking at was systemic failure. It wasn't random. Then there was another thing I found out: Sikorsky took accidents very seriously.

∞

Sikorsky gets a wakeup call every time one of its aircraft goes down —literally. When a helicopter goes down, everyone gets a wake-up call, from the president of the company on down. Some come straight to work and stay day and night, catnapping at the desk or sleeping on office couches. The first question asked is always: "Will this happen again, and do we ground the fleet?" The second question is: "What can we do to keep this from happening again?" As one might suspect by now, the causes are often complex, and involve a series of mistakes.

The reasons for the Coast Guard helicopter crashes all appeared to be different, but it was generally felt that the flight crews were pushing the envelope in bad weather. Each successful daring rescue brought on even more daring rescues. That was the prevailing theory; risk brings on more risk.

But Coast Guard aviation was also saving people, especially those in the most dangerous profession of all: fishing. More regulation dictated shorter seasons, and fishermen couldn't afford to let bad weather deter them in a four-week season the way they could when there had been a twelve-month season. Fishermen were also working with heavier equipment, which required heavier rigging and winches. It was dangerous —a good way to earn the nickname "Lefty."

Many vocations involve risk, but like the test pilot who is more likely to die in a car accident, it is really your free time on the sea that's most likely to kill you. The Coast Guard has to save boaters, often very stupid and reckless boaters, and that's not easy. In the late summer of 1983, my father retired and became commodore of the Woods Hole Yacht Club. Unlike the New York Yacht Club, the Woods Hole Yacht Club was a one-room half-Cape house with a long dock that moored forty small rowboats needed to service the club's fleet of twelve-foot catboats for which Woods Hole was famous. My father was paid below minimum wage, with a lump sum of $1,000 for the summer. The true value of his position was that he was allowed to dock his little aluminum, twenty-five-horsepower skiff at the floating dock, near one of the most coveted of all perks in Woods Hole, a personal parking space.

I came back to Falmouth from Governors Island at about 10 o'clock one night and found my stepmother in a state of near panic. (My father had married my aunt; no -we are not from West Virginia —she was his brother's widow.) My father had gone out to check his lobster pots and hadn't returned. The boat had never been out after sunset, and the wind was picking up dramatically, approaching a real squall, with occasional downpours. She had already called the Coast Guard, and they immediately went on a search. At about 10:30 in the evening, the Coast Guard patched through a call from one of their forty-one-footers that had spotted a swamped boat and a man standing on the windward side of Weepeckit Island. They couldn't get close due to the rocks and shoals, so they dispatched a helicopter.

Weepeckit is a series of islands, part of the Elizabeth chain, that are "wee" as the name implies. It has no buildings, no trees, and no notable bushes. Basically, it's a pile of rocks. One island is a rookery for seagulls and another is a rookery for terns. While seagulls usually spend most of their lives in their natural habitat —the dump —they come here to nest on the ground. Because they need to be away from dogs, cats, snakes, and other predators, their rookeries are on deserted islands. I don't know who was more upset, the gulls or my dad, they both squawked ceaselessly.

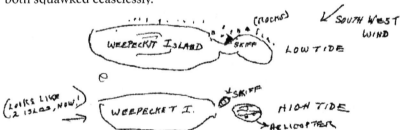

We received another call a half hour later from Group Woods Hole, and they said that the helicopter had landed but my father wouldn't come with them, ending the call with "What the Hell's wrong with him?" While totally mortified, we were incredibly thankful that the Coast Guard was able to locate him and put our worries to rest.

As first the cutter and then the helicopter approached Dad, he had waved frantically yelling, "Get the Hell away from me!" Unable to hear what he was saying, they probably thought he was enthusiastically waving for help. At about midnight, my father arrived home, furious that we had the audacity to be worried about him. He said we just cost him 7,000 bucks.

He gave us his version of the story. In the midst of pulling up the third trap, after successfully checking the first two traps, the wind suddenly picked up and a rogue wave came over his stern, killing the engine. He pulled up the motor but one wave after another sent him bouncing toward the rocks; he became beached on the windward side of the island. He was able to maneuver his skiff to the point where it was highest and driest to bail it out. Then he wedged the boat between two of the rocks, planning to wait for high tide to refloat it.

He was minding his own business when a Coast Guard cutter, fifty yards offshore, decided to blind him with a spotlight for about half an hour. Then things got worse. Overhead, a huge helicopter with green and yellow lights pointed another searchlight at him, obscuring what minimal vision he still had. The helicopter started hovering near him, blowing sand and water in his face, and finally settled down. A hatch opened and a creature jumped down to the sand. He had a huge helmet, a jumpsuit —the works. He yelled, "Come on! Jump in! We're going to Edward's Air Station."

Rubbing the sand from his eyes, cursing, my father's ungracious reply was, "Go away! I'm not abandoning my boat! I'm just waiting for the tide." The Coast Guard helicopter crew, now understanding that no good deed will ever go unpunished, left.

My dad re-launched the boat and headed back toward the Woods Hole Yacht Club, shadowed by a Coast Guard forty-one-footer. In the open sea without running lights or a compass, using only the "personal radar" he claims to have, he realized he was in violation of Coast Guard regulations. So he did two maneuvers, cutting through shallow waters to try to get the Coast Guard off his tail.

He managed to shake them, but much to his chagrin, when he arrived at the dock, headlights from a Coast Guard vehicle blinded him again, and out stepped two Coasties with big pads of paper. This wasn't going to be pretty. Like his son, Dad didn't do too well on Coast Guard inspections -this would be an expensive demerit. The Coast Guard wrote him up for what seemed to be endless violations, the fines for which totaled nearly $7,000.

"Who told them I was out of the Woods Hole Yacht Club anyway?" He stormed. "Um. All of us, we explained. That's where we told them to check first. In order for them to search for you, we had to give them your itinerary."

When he received formal notification of the Coast Guard charges, requesting he report any additional mitigating or extenuating circumstances, my father adamantly refused to even respond to them, saying, "They'll have to come and get me." He said that even if they found him guilty, he would refuse to pay, and besides, they tried to blind him.

∞

My brother decided to take action on his part and wrote the following in a letter to the Coast Guard: "He's an independent and proud old man, and he refused to be airlifted off the island. He waited until high tide, re-floated his boat, and returned to Woods Hole, where he was boarded at the dock. He had previously never used the vessel after sunset, and therefore never installed navigation lights, as it is not required for his vessel." Then my brother added, "My father realizes the danger the Coast Guardsmen place themselves in during any rescue and greatly appreciates the courage and skill of the men involved in this case. His son is a reserve Coast Guard officer who was aboard the ill-fated cutter Cuyahoga, so he has deep appreciation for the dedication of the men in this fine branch of service."

The Coast Guard reply, right at the top of the letter, was in bold and underlined: "Case Closed. No penalty." Later in the letter, it was recommended that he take a community education boating course.

∞

One of my last missions in the Coast Guard was on a Saturday morning in response to a message that a barge had hit the apron of the Interstate 95 bridge over the Naugatuck River. Bridge aprons are structures that surround the bridge pilings, so if a ship or barge comes too close, they can funnel the ship or barge through the bridge span. These aprons are made of wood, or concrete pilings and cross members. A nearby span of I-95 had collapsed earlier, killing three in the famous Minaus River Bridge collapse of June, 1983. The bridge had collapsed at 1:30 in the morning, bringing down two trucks and one car with it. If it had happened at rush hour, scores of commuters would have been killed. The drivers who saw the trucks and car disappear off the broken bridge stopped in time, and along with those on the other side of the bridge waved frantically for others to stop. They were almost 100% successful -one driver flipped the bird to the Good Samaritans and drove right past them, straight into eternity. Let's hope he didn't flip the bird to Saint Pete.

∞ Coast Guard's unique sense of irony ∞

∞ Group Long Island Sound sending a message to whoever will listen ∞

I-95, the main artery between Miami & Maine, was severed, and for six months Connecticut had the traffic jam from Hell. Between the memory of the Tampa Sunshine Skyway bridge collapse and the collapse of the Minaus River Bridge, everyone was supersensitive to vessels hitting bridges. They need not have been, however, because in the ten years preceding these accidents, on average five vessels hit bridges every week in the U.S.

∞ OC Joe Robinson multitasking ∞

Nevertheless, our crew of weekend warriors needed to inspect the I-95 Naugatuck River Bridge immediately. The weather was terrible, and every Coast Guard vessels was out, so we reverted to the index card box for plan B, which stated that what we should do next was call the local police and see if they could lend their assets. Our first call was to the Milford Police. They agreed to help us, and told us they would launch their motorboat and rendezvous in an hour. We stressed that this was a non-emergency inspection, and that the barge hit the apron of the bridge.

They offered to meet us at the landing near the I-95 bridge and ferry us out to the apron to inspect the damage. We inspected the bridge from land, and could see only minor damage to the apron.

We interviewed the tugboat captain; he thought that there would be less than $2,000 worth of damage. That left us waiting for the Milford Police boat, which was already very late. When a Milford police officer arrived with their boat, he apologized, telling us he tried to take a shortcut through the marsh and broke a sheer pin. We motored out, conducted a brief inspection, and counted four apron pilings that were tilted. As we headed back to the landing, we could hear sirens, and when we approached the landing we could saw a fleet of state police cruisers. As our small boat got further out from under the bridge we could see a half-dozen state police cars blocking all traffic from entering the bridge from either side. While it could have been an event unrelated to our inspection, I had the sneaking suspicion that communication had somehow gone awry.

As soon as we landed, we threw our life jackets into the boat, and our policeman skipper sped off quickly. That seemed a bit suspicious. We ran up to a trooper who looked like he was in charge and I said, "May I ask what's going on here?"

He said, very authoritatively, "No you can't." Then he went on talking with the other state troopers.

The lead inspector was Tony —the same guy who had me sniff styrene —and his feelings appeared to be hurt. He told the cop, "OK, just move your cruisers and we'll get out of here."

"This is an emergency and we'll move our units when we are ready," the officer snapped.

"Are you asking to be arrested for interfering with a law enforcement officer!?"

Then we got a call over the walkie-talkie from the Coast Guard station saying that they had just gotten a request from the state police to send all available assets to the I-95 bridge, and asking us what the hell was going on. Tony told them "forget about it —it was a false alarm."

"This is getting out of control," I told Tony, who was technically the only one qualified to inspect the bridge, " we have to try to identify ourselves to these jerks . . . ."

"I can't talk about the inspection until the report is approved," he interrupted me.

I overheard the police officer order everybody to clear the landing parking lot: the governor was en route by helicopter, with bridge inspectors from Hartford. At this point I broke ranks and screamed, "We're from the Coast Guard! We inspected the bridge and there is nothing wrong with it!"

I was suddenly the focus of attention. I grabbed the report with the little drawings of bent pilings from Tony. "The craft only hit the apron," I said. There were murmurs of confusion, and so I clarified, "A barge bumped the bridge's guard rail, and it didn't touch the bridge."

The trooper who had threatened to arrest us should have looked at least a little chagrined, but instead he just gave us a dirty look.

We had a lot of explaining to do when we got back to the station. It turned out that when the Milford policeman had engine trouble he called the dispatcher and told her to find a back-up boat to ferry us to the bridge. The Milford police officer said it was windy, and that he had a weak signal when he talked to the Milford dispatcher, so the message might have been garbled. She phoned around, alerting the state police, and she probably neglected to use the phrase "non-emergency." She may have said the bridge was damaged, and asked them to hurry.

While there is a lot of exaggeration in police dramas, the one thing they don't exaggerate is interagency rivalry as I learned from my previous experience with the DEA and New York police, there is no shortage of mistrust.

But that experience got me thinking: by far the biggest threat the Coast Guard faced was saboteurs sneaking in past Group New Haven with a nuclear bomb or even a huge dirty bomb in a container, fishing boat, or a pleasure craft straight into the Port of New York. Even though the odds were low, the damage could amount to billions and the loss of life enormous. I wrote to Coast Guard intelligence suggesting that they use advanced statistics to improve their data synthesis and analysis, to calculate best asset deployment. I suggested that they implement advanced data mining to find outliers and develop profiles so that their view would be more systematic in inspections for WMD, drug interdiction, and even boating safety. I suggested that they could use Bedford's law for forensics to detect fraudulent inspections: the number one shows up almost a third of the time in real life, but rarely when people fabricate numbers. People like nines, but random distributions don't.

To my surprise, I received a call from intelligence not long afterward. They said they were already using advanced statistics, but they certainly could use my help. They asked if I would consider being activated. Before the person who called me talked with his CO he wanted to make sure I could be called up for six months to a few years. He lamented that the Coast Guard had a go-ahead to beef up, and they were trying to call in reservists but many reservists were pleading financial hardship, and he suggested that I check my cash flow and see if I could afford to be called up. I did the calculations. With the lower Coast Guard pay, not working my side jobs, and not getting paid to drill, I would be bankrupt in four months.

While I was drilling, I thought I would be called up for a few weeks to storms or an oil spill, not for an entire year, or even more incredibly, two. I figured the only way they would call me to active duty was if the Soviets took the George Washington Bridge. I called him back and told him I couldn't afford to be called up. He told me I should stop drilling, because there was a waiting list of people who wanted to drill for the extra money, and many of those same people wanted to be called up for the fulltime pay -unemployment was at its highest level since World War II.

Clearly I was taking the space of a reservist who wanted to be called up, so I changed my status to individually ready, ending my physical involvement with the Coast Guard. It was kind of sad, but I was heartened to know that Coast Guard was hiring and expanding resources. Maybe the Coast Guard was regaining its bearing.

∞

In 1983, the final judgment between the Santa Cruz and the U.S. Coast Guard was announced. In the decision, Judge Roszel agreed with Judge Blair that the Coast Guard was solely responsible for the accident, but he disagreed about Captain Robinson's illness and ruled that the Coast Guard should have known about the existence of the captain's diminished capacity. Therefore, the U.S. government could not cap damages because they should have known that Captain Robinson had exhibited that diminished capacity. This meant that the Coast Guard did not exercise proper diligence prior to the Cuyahoga leaving the dock.

The U.S. government appealed the case to the United States Appeals Court before Judge Thomsen, claiming that no medical officers ruled

Captain Robinson unfit for duty; therefore, the Coast Guard chain of command would have to be "omniscient" to know that Captain Robinson was ill.

Prior to that time, Captain Robinson had never reported a maritime incident in his life. From April to October, Captain Robinson conned the ship into two accidents, both resulting in letters of reprimand that made it into his file; and Judge Thomsen noted that the frequent trips to sick bay, multiple trips to Riverside Walter Reed Hospital (one on the day before the accident), coupled with the two prior accidents, should have caught the CO, XO, or operations officers' attention. Judge Thomsen didn't think that that would have required omniscience —just common sense.

Today we have a much better understanding of how illness and fatigue can diminish capacity. Tired and overworked people make mistakes.

The final ruling for the Cuyahoga case was as follows: The collision between the Santa Cruz and the Cuyahoga was caused solely by the Cuyahoga, without fault on the part of the Santa Cruz. The collision was caused by Captain Robinson's multiple errors of judgment and perception, his absolute misapplication of the nautical rules of the road, the inexperience of his crew, and the failure of the Coast Guard to challenge his fitness for duty.

The case didn't look good for the families of the victims. The Massachusetts District Court would have to disagree with the conclusion of the Maryland District Court and with the Coast Guard's admission of full responsibility. Nevertheless, the government brought Flanagan in front of the Massachusetts Bar Association for conflict of interest in representing both Captain Robinson in the court-martial and the victims and survivors. At this time, Flanagan was without doubt the most knowledgeable person in the world regarding maritime accidents and the Coast Guard. He also may have been the only person willing to take the case on a contingency fee. He knew piloting and rules of navigation inside and out, and he knew the Coast Guard legal system and the politics behind the public facade. The victims had a right to the best possible representation —and he was it. The government tried to shoot the messenger, and they missed: the Massachusetts Bar Association did not see the conflict.

On March 21, 1986, the court ruled against the plaintiffs, stating that the Coast Guard was entirely at fault, closing the back door of liability. As my mother would always say, "You can't sue the government." At least individuals can't sue the government -the big companies can. The Argentine ship owners got $600,000. The Bilina family got nothing.

Error Chain

Pleasure boating enthusiasts have suffered about 700 fatalities a year over the past twenty years, with the trend lowering slightly over time. According to Coast Guard statistics, Florida (not surprisingly) has the highest number of deaths. North Dakota, Hawaii, and Puerto Rico didn't show any, and Vermont had one. The North Dakota and Vermont statistics are believable, but it appears Hawaii and Puerto Rico didn't bother reporting.

Water safety is pretty much the same as other forms of transport: the larger the conveyance, the safer the system. Airlines are safer per mile than cars, and cars are safer than walking. However, this statistic implies long distances. You should not use it when considering whether to drive down to your mailbox, because most accidents are due to starting and stopping or taking off and landing. Cars are safer than airlines in distances shorter than 150 miles, and walking is safer for a quarter mile or less.

Big ships are safer than little ships, which are safer than boats, and little boats are the most dangerous of all. So while registrations per accident have dropped, these statistics have not improved in the same way the land vehicle safety record has. The problem of the stubbornly high fatality rates is due to two factors: first, the growth of personal watercraft (AKA "jet ski," poor man's yacht, or mariner's motorcycle) and paddlers (canoes and especially kayaks); second, the alcohol factor. Alcohol and the sea have had a long tradition of conspiracy. About 40 percent of all fatal boating accidents involve alcohol; many are folks who just fell off a boat or dock and drowned.

27.

"Those were the days, my friend . . . .
We'd live the life we choose,
We'd fight and never lose.
For we were young and sure to have our way."
-"Those Were the Days"
Mary Hopkin

It was October 19, 2008. I was on the fourteen-hour Abu Dhabi-to-JFK flight, continuing on to LaGuardia, then Richmond, and finally driving to Yorktown. I've been making most of this round trip for twelve years, working in Abu Dhabi as an economic advisor and commuting back and forth to Connecticut. After the thirtieth Cuyahoga memorial service in Yorktown, I would be catching another jet and heading to Connecticut for the memorial service at the Officers Candidate School in New London. Commander O'Connor, the OCS commander, had invited me to speak. Knowing that I would want to attend the Yorktown memorial, he delayed the OCS program to the twenty-first.

When the OCS moved from Yorktown to New London, there was considerable debate over where the Cuyahoga Memorial should be located. Like most good decisions, there had to be a compromise. They moved the Cuyahoga's "bridge" to New London and dedicated a new stone memorial at Yorktown. On October 20 of each year, services are held at both locations. Most of the survivors and victims' relatives live in the Tidewater area, and many of the victims' families were still bitter, so the move of the Cuyahoga Memorial exacerbated those feelings. On the twentieth anniversary, Gordon Thomas obtained the Cuyahoga's holiday ensign from the OCS and presented it to Admiral Loy, asking that it be flown every year at Yorktown. Admiral Loy, by commandant's decree, mandated that the flag be flown at half-mast at the U.S. Coast Guard Training Center each October 20th, for eternity. Between services the flag rests in a shadow box displayed in the commander of Yorktown's office.

∞

For the past year, I had read every article and report I could find about Coast Guard collisions. I exchanged hundreds of emails with classmates and others affected by the Cuyahoga tragedy. As I stared out the window of the Boeing 777, I thought, "What did I learn?" For twenty-nine years, I had put the Cuyahoga way back in the corner of my mind with a "do not disturb" sign on it. I thought I understood what happened. Now, three decades after the accident, I was no longer sure. At the Yorktown memorial service, Admiral Neptun and Admiral Loy would do all the speaking. Thank God, I thought: I was sure they had a lot of practice.

I had spoken at OCS once before and advised that risk is misunderstood. Personal experience is a terrible way to measure it. If everyone in the Coast Guard took a chance with odds at 1 in 30,000 the result would be an accident every day. I also told them that risk was a dependent event; if a junior officer compromised on safety, then all the men would probably follow down that same slippery slope, and their elaborate safety net would fray. I made them pledge that, in the memory of the Cuyahoga, they would not tolerate safety violations.

But there had to be more than my dire warnings, and a simple pledge; more in fact than each and every one of them taking that pledge seriously.

What would I say to the OCs at the service? The most cynical quote ever written occurred to me, lines from Macbeth: "Life's but a walking shadow, a poor player,/ That struts and frets his hour upon the stage,/ And then is heard no more. It is a tale/ Told by an idiot, full of sound and fury,/ Signifying nothing."

Contrary to what the prosecutor in the Cuyahoga court-martial who misconstrued Shakespeare's meaning argued, "We can just say 'cut' and change the scene or the script," our fate lies in both the stars and the decisions of our superiors. The reason that fault lies not in the stars but in ourselves is because we are underlings, in one way or another.

I wasn't able to let my shipmates' lives signify nothing. The OCs spend a few moments everyday standing at attention and staring at the memorial, but what were they wondering? What they scored on their last exam? Perhaps they'd be more like me and wonder about the day's lunch menu." I knew I had to make them feel before I could make them think.

∞

There were no good pictures of our fallen classmates who were unable to attend the portrait sittings prior to graduation. I commissioned a former art professor and Rhode Island School of Design grad to sketch each one of them from copies of the pictures in our OC yearbook. The yearbook pictures were amateur snapshots taken during liberty, or drilling, so the faces were small. Heistend's picture was of him with Big Mutha. It still brought a smile to my face. Clark's picture showed him in the back of our class marching in formation — I wish I could have found that film canister. In mounted frames, these portraits would be my gift to the OCS. I wanted the memorial service to be about people, not bells and ships' wheels.

I arrived at JFK only to find that my luggage decided it wanted to spend an extra day in Abu Dhabi. I went to Yorktown without a change of clothes. Normally I would have carried an extra change of clothes in my carry-on, but this trip I brought ten copies of my manuscript to distribute to my classmates - I do have priorities.

I arrived in Yorktown, late afternoon to see the end of the reenactment of Surrender Day at the Yorktown Battlefield. I heard the British tribute, "The World Turned Upside Down," and the American response, "Yankee Doodle." Irony lives on.

I then spent the night at the majestic Yorktown Motor Inn at an off season rate of $49.95 in unfulfilling jet-lagged sleep. Mostly, I lay awake wondering if someone would approach me and say, "Who gave you the right to force us to think about this again.

∞

Every year, anyone associated with the Cuyahoga receives an invitation to the memorial service from the USCG Training Center in Yorktown. I asked the officer in charge if I could have the mailing list but was denied because of privacy restrictions.

I followed up with another letter asking if they would distribute a letter from me to their mailing list. I received a brief email explaining this would not happen either. That seemed unreasonable. I called Lieutenant Darkeim Brown, Deputy Op-Intel School Chief. He told me that some people didn't want to be on the list and had asked to be removed and a few were downright angry about getting the invitation. They just wanted to forget about the sinking of the Cuyahoga and never be reminded again.

I was really surprised, but I guess I shouldn't have been. I hadn't walked a mile in their shoes. I thanked Mr. Brown for his frankness, and told him that he had provided me with a very important piece of information.

I hadn't gone to the fifth, tenth, twentieth or twenty-fifth memorial services. To be honest, I had never gone to a single memorial service. I guess I too was angry, and still felt guilty. I tried to forget about the sinking, but couldn't.

∞

I first thought seriously about writing this book when at the Marine Ball in Abu Dhabi. Because U.S. Marines guard every embassy, there is a Marine Ball on November 10 in nearly every country in the world. The ball I attended was held shortly after the second Gulf War started.

There was a tribute to Chesty Puller, the most-decorated marine of all time: five Navy Crosses, and a Distinguished Service Award. When he was in the Marines, he seemed to always be wherever there was trouble in the world. Before World War II, he was fighting rebels in Haiti and Nicaragua, and the Japanese in China. He went on to fight in World War II and Korea.

If you close your eyes and imagine what a Marine should look like, you will conjure an image of Chesty. He had a barrel chest, towering forehead, a chiseled face with a square jaw, and he looked like he never cracked a smile. Some Marines end their day with the declaration, "Good night, Chesty Puller, wherever you are!"

At the Marine Ball, one table is set with a single place setting and a vase with a rose. This, we were told, was for the fallen Marine. As they poured the wine in the lost Marine's glass at that first Marine Ball I attended, I imagined my lost shipmates sitting at the table instead of imagining a fallen Marine. I decided then and there that I would try to write about my heroes. They might not have a rose in a vase, but they would have a book dedicated to their memory.

∞

With these thoughts weighing on my mind, I headed over to the pre-memorial "no-host breakfast" (Coast Guard speak for Dutch treat). I was the first to arrive. Dan Neptun arrived early and I talked with him about the manuscript project and the concept of Bearing Drift. Then Rick arrived and was quick to note that I needed a haircut —and I had I just gotten a haircut! —and that I looked like shit. "Were you up all night?" he asked. I certainly was in no condition to con a ship. I was the only one without a suit; I flunked another Coast Guard inspection.

The service commenced with group colors on the parade ground where thirty years earlier OC Heistend flipped his M1 in the direction of Lieutenant Emory. The Cuyahoga's holiday ensign was hauled to the top of the mast and then down to half-mast. The students stood in formation; the old guys, classmates, friends, and relatives sat in a special section reserved for them. Admiral Neptun recalled the old days, and then he made reference to the fact that the Coast Guard had gone through a bad time and drifted off course, but the memory of the Cuyahoga put us back on course. Family and friends proceeded to the chapel, where the Cuyahoga's bell tolled eleven times and retired Admiral Loy gave a short address. After the Lord's Prayer, the service was over -or at least I thought it was over.

∞

I was introduced to Lieutenant Colonel William Carter, father of YNI Carter, the comedy play writer who was doing extra duty on the Cuyahoga to get into OCS. Lieutenant Colonel was the Cuyahoga's historian. He had compiled a scrapbook of articles on the Cuyahoga and had presented a copy to the Yorktown commander, which is displayed in the main office. He, along with his wife and daughter Kate, had attended nearly every service for the past thirty years. That day, his steel-magnolia wife was too sick to attend.

Kate Carter Lemon later told me that the incredible bond between her parents was what kept her parents going through all these years, propping each other up when the other was down. Growing up and living in the Tidewater area, she had occasionally run into people involved in the Cuyahoga tragedy. She attended college with Captain Robinson's son, and tried to strike up a conversation with him, but both were uncomfortable. She bore no ill will toward Captain Robinson. "He was a good, decent man. He just shouldn't have gone out that night." I caught a glimpse of true grace and forgiveness. Today, she keeps her brother's memory alive by telling her children stories about him, but she says it gets harder every year.

It was spontaneously decided that all the classmates and families would have a morning cap at the York Officers' Club. Coffee flowed freely. I was the only non-lifer in the group. I heard incredible stories of lives dedicated to service to their country. I was again in awe of my classmates. Bittersweet stories were served along with the coffee. Bruce Wood's daughter, who was two in 1978, attended the twentieth reunion searching for the father she never knew. My classmates stayed in touch for a while, but like everything else, time took its toll, and contact faded.

The stories went back to the old Coast Guard ,and the clip-on lights on the life jackets that hadn't worked for years. Rick Riemer's son, BM1 Robert Riemer, interjected that something like that could never happen now. That made me feel good.

I was the first to leave; I got up and crushed my paper cup. I had to catch a flight to Connecticut. All my classmates thanked me for attempting to write a book about the tragedy. They didn't realize that I was really trying to write a book about courage.

I recalled what Chuck Margiotta's brother said about courage, reflecting on what could have made him run into a burning tower to his death. According to a guy named Webster, "bravery" is a combination of confidence and firm resolution in the presence of danger. "Courageous," however, is more than brave: it adds a moral element. The courageous man "steadily encounters perils to which he may be keenly sensitive," but he follows his call of duty, regardless. At no time do either of these definitions mention being fearless: fearless is just the inability to recognize danger.

∞

I met my luggage and the portrait sketches in my Connecticut home. The portraits reflected youthful optimism, and invoked an innocent patriotism that we all once shared. I tried to sleep. I still wondered what I was going to say.

I arrived at the Coast Guard Academy chapel, which is sits atop a hill, overlooking the beautiful academy campus, an hour before the memorial service. I handed over the portraits and they were placed on the altar. I went outside to look at the grave of Hopley Yeaton.

Approximately seventy OCs and perhaps another thirty people from the base, including Rear Admiral Scott Burhoe, the superintendent of the Academy, were in attendance. The OCs had practiced the night before, and the service was carried out with utmost precision.

After a few prayers and some tolling of bells, it was my turn to say something. I walked to the altar and checked my watch; it was 0910. "It's been thirty years, twelve hours, and nine minutes since I walked onto the bridge of the Cuyahoga." I spent the next twenty minutes describing my eight minutes on the bridge, and my time on the hull. I spoke somberly but used simple humor to describe my naivety. It worked: they laughed. At first the laughter was nervous, like, "Am I supposed to be laughing at a memorial service?" But the laughter of the others told them it was OK. Soon, to my delight, there were even some whole-body laughs.

After fifteen minutes, I posed Gordon Lightfoot's question: "Does anyone know where the love of God goes, when the waves turn the minutes to hours?" I ended my speech with the request made by my shipmates to the crew on the lifeboat that was trying to pull us out of the water: Keep searching.

I keep searching. . . .

It was one year ago that I decided to write a book to memorialize the friends we lost because I wondered if anyone still cared. In December I walked into Chase Hall and the first thing I saw was the bridge of the Cuyahoga. I went right up to it and an OC greeted me with "Good Afternoon, Sir," and he turned toward the memorial and stood for a brief moment at attention and I was awestruck. You haven't forgotten. Thank you.

I went down the hall and met with Commander O'Connor and he said to me, "If we forget the Cuyahoga, they will have died in vain."

But what are we to remember?

I think they would want us to remember why accidents happen and how we can prevent them, because maybe we will be able to learn more from our mistakes than our triumphs. I think they would want us to remember all the great things the Coast Guard has done and the dedication of all those before us.

∞

Right after the accident I was angry and I was ready to quit. I had lost my bearings. I went to the bulletin board and I saw the letter —it was to us and I mean to all of us here today. I have to hand the letter to someone else to read because I can't do it. I will let OC William Fediw have the last word."

I had asked Commander O'Connor to find an OC to read Wood's parents' letter. I had heard that Admiral Neptun had read it at a previous memorial service and it was a real struggle to get through it. Even though OC William Fediw had practiced reading it, he too had trouble getting through it.

To all officers, crewmen, and especially the survivors of the Cuyahoga tragedy,

I have put off writing until now, hoping I could find the words, the unemotional moment, the wisdom, necessary to handle the task at hand. Time hasn't been any help. The heart hasn't healed, and the shock and loss is permanent. However, I must not think of my feelings and loss, rather the men who were there through God's grace were selected to carry on what our son died for.

It would be easier for me to write to you if I could remember one instance of displeasure with Bruce, some conflict of opinions and even the heartaches that some parents have —we were spared because Bruce was kind and sensitive to the needs of others and had a deep love for us. Therefore, I must tell you how sorry we are that your class had to have such a tragic interruption and a dark shadow cast on your dreams. I can't let you feel sorry for yourselves or for us and let this interfere with your aims and goals —I must ask each and every one from the bottom of my heart to continue with your ambitions for me with added strength and resolution. This was Bruce's dream, this is what he would want of his buddies and I would be so happy and so proud to know you carried his dreams to success. If yours was but a desire in the past, it should now be a dedication.

Look to Lt. Roger Emory and your superiors for guidance, and trust in their ability to help you through your trials —as we, parents of Bruce, have had to do recently. I will be in contact with Lt. Emory and will follow your progress and share all your setbacks, trials, and hopefully success.

If there is a need for a letter from home, a word of encouragement, or just a friend, we have a vacancy.

With much love,
*   Ray and Laura Wood*

Standing next to OC Fediw, I noticed that there wasn't a dry eye in the room. I wish I could write like that, and I am sure if you made this far in the book, you probably do too (thanks, Dad, for that addition).

After the speech, I went over to the framed portraits and introduced my fallen classmates one by one, telling the OCs a little something about each. All fell in love with Heistend.

I sat down. People clapped. Then they stood up and clapped. People aren't supposed to laugh or clap at a memorial, I thought.

I stood up and turned around to acknowledge them until I realized they were all looking at the sketches. The clapping really wasn't for me. I went over to the portraits, turned to them, and I clapped, too. The applause doubled. It was amazing; we were giving a standing ovation to our fallen shipmates thirty years after they gave their lives to their country. I knew there were eleven souls in heaven, looking down, smiling, as they finally received the standing ovation they deserved. The End

Epilogue

"I'm suggesting that neither of those events should have occurred; both could have been prevented. And therefore, in each instance, there should have been punishment associated with the incidents. I was not satisfied that the punishment was adequate, considering the loss of life and the circumstances in each instance."
— The Reminiscences of Admiral John Briggs Hayes,
USCG (Ret.) Commandant, United States Coast Guard.

Captain Robinson died before I began writing the manuscript, and despite emails and phone messages, I was unable to make contact with his family. The acting XO, Roger Wild, was ill for the thirtieth memorial service and I wasn't able to talk to him either. It took many months to get the feedback from classmates and incorporate their contributions into the book. But I was getting there by the next memorial service.

At the thirty-first memorial service, the keynote speaker, Rear Admiral , William Lee, read a letter from Marcelo Abelardo Albornoz, the son of the captain of the Santa Cruz II. "I can only say that it has not been easy for my father either, Captain Abelardo Albornoz. He passed away on July 13, 2005, a victim of a cruel and devastating illness, including indefinite depression which he was never able to recover from, thinking that those young Cadets were the same age as his own sons at the time of the collision. Humbly, I feel the pain of the fathers and mothers of these sailors and of the U.S. Coast Guard. I can't say anything else, but I say a prayer, from the bottom of my heart: May these sailors rest in peace for all eternity."

I was astonished. He had a pilot on board. How could the captain ever blame himself? What his son admitted to us said so much about that captain's sense of humanity, and how the effect on people involved in a tragedy are truly immeasurable.

Admiral Lee recounted Thomas's escape from the bridge, and I noticed that Mrs. Balina's son, Ronnie, was crying. When the service was over, I walked over to Ronnie and he told me that he and his sister Irene had gone to every memorial service, and that each year he finds out a little something he can hang on to, something more about the father he never had the chance to know.

Someone once told him that his father was a great cook; his uncle told him that his dad was a motor-head and liked Road Runners. He told me why he started to cried when he heard the story of Gordon's escape: he had never really held an idea of what it was like for his father in his last moments. He felt so sorry for his dad. He was quick to add that his older sister, Irene, was like another mother to him, trying to fill the hole left by his dad's death.

I later got a chance to meet Roger Wild. He was big, even in a wheel chair. He had long unkempt hair, an eye patch, and he talked slowly. I introduced myself to him and his wife. He said, "Oh... you're one of the students."

It had been a long time since I had been called a student, but I had certainly been called worse. It actually made me feel good.

They say opposites attract. His wife, Lil, was short, fit, had neat, short-cropped hair, and talked with authority. She struck me as the kind of person who could run a small country.

"Roger had a serious motorcycle accident and he forgets a lot," Lil said. "But we would love to talk about the Cuyahoga. The sinking had a big effect on Roger. Roger had a bout with alcoholism. I once got a call and was told that Roger was stuck at an intersection. When I got there, he was crying and said he couldn't cross because he kept seeing a freighter coming. We moved to Block Island but his alcoholism got worse."

"What do you expect," Roger jumped in. For nine months a year, there are, like, fifty people there, and three bars. The entertainment is drinking."

"More like 300 people, Roger," Lil corrected him. She went on to say that more than a few times she got a call from fellow islanders asking her to go get her husband. She often found him passed out on the side of road.

"Roger entered the Coast Guard substance-abuse program and stayed for three weeks. He hasn't had a drink since."

Roger turned his life around. He made chief, and he and Lil raised seven children, five of their own and two adopted. The two they adopted were foster children Lil had taken in. She also took care of a number of other foster children who were troubled. Roger is a member of the Christian Motorcycle Association and counsels people with substance-abuse problems. Roger told me that although he is confined to a wheelchair, he still rides. I saw Lil roll her eyes. "Maybe we'll make it stable with a sidecar, and you can ride it then."

I asked Roger about the captain. "I had only been on the ship since June, but after the accident the captain and I became close friends," he told me. " The captain stayed in the Guard for a few years after the court-martial and then he worked at a car-rental agency until he died." He relayed that the captain suffered from chronic depression and lung disease.

"Did the captain have a drinking problem?"

He looked startled by the question. "The captain didn't drink: everybody who knew him knew that. Is that what people thought?" I guess only people who didn't know him said that.

∞

On the internet, I found a copy of an invitation to Captain Robinson's funeral. Obviously, this was written by someone who knew him: "On May 6, 1999, CWO Don Robinson died after a long illness. Don was a great friend and teacher. He will be greatly missed by all who ever knew him... Don, may God grant you the comfort and peace promised in His word. Those left behind will miss you. Fair winds, my friend." My research also uncovered a quote by Captain Robinson: "The Lord has given me strength to realize that some good will come from this, somehow —some day."

∞

Among the people I talked with about the Coast Guard and the concept of Bearing Drift there was general disbelief that anything had ever been wrong with the Coast Guard. From a distance, most people view the Coast Guard as one of the best-run services in our government, and at this point in time, I couldn't agree more. There is no doubt that the Coast Guard performed brilliantly during Hurricane Katrina.

When I started my research, I first looked, predictably, at current statistics. Since the Blackthorn, the Coast Guard has not suffered a cutter collision that resulted in a loss of life. Coast Guard helicopter usage has grown dramatically, but over the last twenty-five-year period, the average fatal accident rate dropped back to one in every five years. There were only seventeen helicopter fatalities, twelve fewer than the twenty-nine during that five-year period covered in Bearing Drift. A sad footnote to that is the rise in fatalities of Coast Guard Auxiliary pilots. During that same period, fourteen died while flying their own planes on volunteer search-and-rescue missions. It is a tribute to the American sense of volunteerism that these people risked their lives, often in bad conditions, as unpaid volunteers, trying to rescue people.

∞

In 2007, the Bureau of Labor Statistics reported a total of eighteen deaths in the U.S. maritime industry: three from assault and violence (blanket parties gone awry), three from equipment malfunctions, six from chemicals, and six from the actual transportation part mishaps. More merchant mariners probably died falling off their barstools than at sea.

Following the Yorktown visit, I went to speak again at the OCS service in New London, Connecticut. Commander Flynn, the new OCS commander, invited me to come early to watch the survival swimming. After the service, I had a tour of the simulation center and was shown a simulated mission to rescue a ship. On the way to the rescue site, the OCs had to navigate through a regatta.

Unlike the merchant-marine training simulator that just has navigation and piloting, the Coast Guard's simulations include mission scenarios with decision points and coordination with other assets in the area. The mission is always planned ahead, and there are three designations —green, amber, and red —calculated through a worksheet that determines whether or not they call the mission a go.

In one scenario given to the OCs, the correct decision is not to go out. I asked what happened to the motto under which I served: "You have to go out, but you don't have to come back." My tour guides looked at each other and bristled.

"While we recognize that as part of our heritage, today we strongly encourage our people to come back with all their assets. Recklessness is unacceptable. Of course, when lives are on the line, the decision criteria does change. For example, in the scenario where 'they shouldn't go out,' it's after a hurricane and we got to reposition a buoy -no lives were in imminent danger. As guardians, our jobs are to save lives, not create more victims."

"I noticed the word is now 'Guardian,' not Coastie."

"We guard more than the Coast," he replied.

While the book Guardians of the Sea by Robert Erwin Johnson has been around since 1987, it wasn't until the Kevin Costner movie about the Coast Guard rescue swimmers, The Guardian, that the name started to take. My Catholic background immediately brings to mind a guardian angel image. The new Coast Guard understands that budgets can fluctuate, and that citizens and businesses require value for their tax dollars. Talk softly and carry a big stick doesn't work anymore. Now, it seems "carry as big a stick as Congress will allocate funds for and walk around with a megaphone telling everybody what a good job you're doing" is how things work.

During the eighties, letters to the editor and editorials across the U.S. lambasted Congress for under-funding the Guard while expanding its scope of work. Congress increased funding for awhile. Even President Reagan came around. On his last day in office, he signed a bill that allowed merchant mariners the right to be declared veterans, and thus receive VA benefits. This was especially important to those battling cancer.

In August 4, 2008 —its 218th anniversary —the Coast Guard announced its one millionth rescue. The Coast Guard Public Affairs office is worked overtime to promote the Guard, and they invite cities and towns to become official Coast Guard cities. Today, there are nine congressional districts designated "Coast Guard Cities."

I also discovered that, as Matthew Mitchell's book suggests, this is "Not Your Father's Coast Guard." Under Admiral Yost, the "Yost Guard" created a special forces unit that went deep into jungles, catching drug runners at their source.

But the Coast Guard's path has been circuitous. When the jungle forays were cited as a duplication of effort —read "turf violation" —by other agencies, the Coast Guard curtailed these activities. Under Commandant Admiral Loy, the Coast Guard began competing with the Navy, going into deep water. Then 9/11 happened and the Coast Guard was sent off in a new direction: homeland security. Today nearly a third of all Coast Guard assets are dedicated to that role, because unlike the military, the Coast Guard can shoot U.S. civilians (hopefully terrorists) without a declaration of martial law. Deliberately, the Coast Guard changed course and made many sea changes. But theirs was a quiet revolution. "Gung ho-ism" was replaced by professionalism. It has been reported that COs now refuse orders to go underway until the ships meet safety standards. Safety has become more than something you do, but something you live by. "Mission first, safety always" is now the new paradigm.

As a result of the Cuyahoga and Blackthorn investigations, the Coast Guard's safety procedures, policies, and training were revised. New schools for sea duty were created, including refresher courses after long port calls, training on how to transit at night, and training to increase minimum swimming capability from 50 to 100 yards.

Admiral Neptun showed me a commandant's notice that required familiarization courses and specifically referenced the Cuyahoga and Blackthorn and an email from CWO4 "Mo" Etiemble, the CO of USCGC Frank Drew out of Portsmouth, Virginia, who stated that on October 20 of every year he runs a safety course. On all relevant charts, the Cuyahoga collision site is penciled in; while in Tampa Bay, all Coast Guard charts have the site of the Blackthorn sinking penciled in. The Captain of Eagle told me that on their last cadet cruise they anchored at the sight.

John O'Connor explained the safety measures. "Most importantly, the Coast Guard now emphasizes improved communication to break the error chains. All crew-members are encouraged to speak up when risk is perceived, and their input is treated with dignity and respect. The Coast Guard, more than any other service, recognizes that they have access to the input of the best specialists of their craft."

Protocols were established to provide Rules-of-the-Road testing for all underway duty officers, annual physicals for COs, and blindfolded-egress training for newly reporting personnel within their first forty-eight hours aboard (cheaper than emergency lights, I guess).

Still, the Coast Guard isn't without its problems. It is under-funded, and homeland defense has become its primary focus to the point where recent congressional hearings have chastised the Coast Guard for not attending to what the Coast Guard coined its "legacy missions" —marine and commercial vessel safety. Some of our legislators have even suggested that the legacy missions be reassigned away from the Coast Guard, due to inattention.

Admiral Neptun and I went to the mess deck and walked through a dinner room where they were just about to start the all-day chief-initiation ceremony. As we walked through, I heard one of the chiefs mutter few comments, like "Get those birds out of here," and "The guy with the suit, too. These guys don't work for a living." It was comforting to see the dynamic between chief petty officers and officers was back in full force.

According to David Helvarg, author of Rescue Warriors, the Coast Guard's biggest asset remains its empowered enlisted ranks: NCOs who can act independently. No admiral in Washington told Ida how and when to save all those twenty-three sailors. Whether it's protecting a port, rescuing a boater, or guarding against border intrusions, smart empowered Guardians can do it best.

When we sat down for coffee, I asked Admiral Neptun what he would say to those who claim that we can't guard our ports if we only inspect 5 percent or less of incoming cargo. The Admiral told me that we can profile. If it's a cargo container from Sony that has been weighed and inspected, we would know if one remote was missing in any one of the TV boxes. On the other hand, he told me, if a one-time cash transaction from Abdullah's Jihad Fertilizer Plant in Yemen came through, it would be searched before arrival. "We look for outliers and rely on intelligence to focus our time on the most likely scenarios. If we had to search every ship, it would cost billions, and the economy would be slowed. Much of the production in the U.S. is 'just in time,' and we don't want to hold that up." I thought of the version of Murphy's law "It works, until doesn't.

At the luncheon, Admiral Neptun was much more of a hit than I was. He was in charge of personnel, and everyone wanted to know what was in store. Admiral Neptun said that due to the huge government deficit, the Coast Guard was probably looking to reduce manpower and its budget.

It's always about the money.

To quote Senator Ted Kennedy: "The Coast Guard has been shortchanged. What others are doing to secure the air space over the United States, our Coast Guard is doing every single day in ports all over this nation. While their personnel strength is not greatly higher than what it was in the early 1960s, the demands placed on them have increased dramatically. Unfortunately, their resources have not kept pace. The Coast Guard is essential to our homeland security. . . . The Coast Guard has been stretched too far and for too long a time, and I think they need the support and resources they require to do their job."

∞

I am concerned that history may be repeating itself. Today we are engaged in another very expensive and unpopular war. I hope that despite the cost, my government provides the best possible safety training and equipment for our volunteer servicemen and women, whether they are in Baghdad or Woods Hole. When they come home, I hope the government will provide for our veterans and their families for all their illnesses, mental and emotional.

That day, I had a burning question on my mind: Had there ever been an OC class that made it through without a single washout? While the records were not completely accessible, as far as I was able to determine, it seemed that not a single class went through without at least one dropout. Except for one class. We were that perfect class. We had no dropouts. We had done it.

Error Chain

We all want to blame someone when something bad happens. When I started writing this book, I wanted to become another muckraker, like Upton Sinclair. I had spent countless days raking actual muck, clamming, on the Cape as a kid. But, the only thing I found in my muckraking was a clam that had made the benign mistake of planting itself in front of my rake.

Here's the problem: this is not fiction, and war isn't just hell. I'm not John Grisham, so I can't create and reveal evil people. This is non-fiction, and the tale that is the truth doesn't come together nicely. Instead, the truth, even when it involves the deaths of good men, is just a bunch of happy and sad stories about people making benign mistakes.

When I was young, I demanded justice; now that I'm old, I hope for mercy.

P.S. -I never found the socket set.

Where They Are Now

―――――∞―――――

Roger Emory

Lieutenant Emory received a medical discharge from the Coast Guard and worked for Ford Motor Company for twenty years as a labor relations manager. He now has a real estate development company in Virginia.

Arne Denny

As reported by Arne Denny: "I was emotionally bent at the CG during my first tour in Seattle as a Junior Officer (JO) in the small boat inspection team. The Cuyahoga problem stayed with me for years. I couldn't ride a ferry without anxiety for at least three years." Arne decided to torture himself by working fulltime during the day, with weekend duty, and also going to law school fulltime. He finished in three and a half years. He essentially worked from 6 a.m. to midnight for four years. He traded his last two years' tuition payment for a two-year extension in the Coast Guard legal offices in Juneau and Kodiak. Arne said, "I think the focus saved my life. . . . Being a CG lawyer turned out to be fun. Being a county deputy prosecutor is even more fun. I haven't looked back."

Jim Loy

Jim Loy was promoted to Captain Loy, then Admiral Loy, then Commandant of the Coast Guard Loy. Later, Congress confirmed him as the Under Secretary of Transportation for Security, and his penultimate position in the government was deputy secretary of the Department of Homeland Security (though rumor has it that he later turned down a cabinet position). He now works as a senior counselor for the Cohen Group (as in Secretary of Defense William Cohen), a Washington-based strategic consulting firm.

Jerome Flanagan

Jerome V. Flanagan continued practicing maritime law in Boston and was a professor at both Suffolk University and the Coast Guard Academy. In a speech to Coast Guard cadets, he said the most important lesson learned from the Cuyahoga and Belknap tragedies was that OODs, when in doubt, should slow down and communicate, not guess. He died in 1995 at age sixty-four.

James Sepel Jr.

Lieutenant Commander George James Sepel Jr. left the Coast Guard after twenty-one years. He is a marine surveyor in Alaska, inspecting boats for seaworthiness and compliance with safety regulations. He has become, in his own words, an enthusiastic nitpicker on behalf of safety. He has been quoted as saying, "I'm just trying to do the right thing in my life. I can't tell you the hundreds of nights of sleep I have lost. Hardly a day passes without the Blackthorn coming to mind in some way. I couldn't deal with it if I didn't have the loving support of my family and friends."

William Flores

On September 16, 2000, a posthumous ceremony was held for Seaman Apprentice William R. Flores in Fort Worth to award the Coast Guard's highest service medal. The Coast Guard's recognition of Flores's heroism came twenty years after the sinking. His surviving shipmates realized that he had not been recognized for his heroism, for going down with the Blackthorn while handing out life jackets and saving lives. They brought it to the attention of the Coast Guard and he was finally awarded the recognition so deserved. I wonder what would have happened if I had been able to get the life-jacket box open on the Cuyahoga. Somebody else might have survived, and somebody else might have had to write this book.

Bill Eident

My brother Bill, who was "Employee of the Year" at Massachusetts Maritime in 2006, still teaches young merchant marine engineers their trade. He is also considered "a pain in the ass" to all those who stand in the way of his pursuit of increased safety standards and better equipment for cadets. His family fleet of three cars all burn recycled vegetable oils that he gathers from our cousin's restaurant, Art's Place, in Falmouth.

Bethanie Eident Wilkinson

My sister Bethanie works as a clinical scientist for Pfizer, and is testing a new drug that suppresses the autoimmune system to provide relief for diseases like rheumatoid arthritis and lupus. Initial results are promising, and it looks like this could be Pfizer's new blockbuster drug. Her work now is not a long way from those early studies with horseshoe crab blood.

Chris Eident

My brother Chris is a founder and chief expert for Mystic Air Quality Consultants. Mystic is where they are located, not their methodology. He has already converted six vehicles of his fleet to hybrids.

Paul Eident Jr.

My brother Paul got as far away from the ocean as possible and is now working for the University of Chicago at Argonne National Laboratories. Lord knows what he does.

John and Jim Godlewski

John died when an engine fell on him while he was in the U.S. Air Force. Jim is a charter captain somewhere in the Caribbean (a true pirate).

The Captain Kidd Gang

The Captain Kidd is still alive and kicking and trying not to serve minors. Steve Dodigan owns the Conference Table bar on Worcester Court in Falmouth Heights. Bill Wixon runs a health club in Falmouth and coaches at Mass Maritime Academy.

Paul Eident Sr.

My dad worked for the Woods Hole Yacht Club for just one year, and then he teamed up with Dick Issack and Johnny Macedo, captain of the Ananta, and fished four-to-seven days a week, five months a year, until he was eighty-two. They once went 180 times in a row without getting skunked. Thanks to the Coast Guard and other conservation efforts, the stripers made a big comeback. Then, in order to better take care of my stepmother, Dad moved permanently out to Alhambra, California, where "there's no darn ice to slip on!" He now lives with his grandson, Greg Eident, an actor who can be seen as an extra in CSI and Greek (waiting for his big break).

Acknowledgments
—∞—

"It's those changes in latitudes, changes in attitudes
Nothing remains quite the same.
With all of my running and all of my cunning,
If I couldn't laugh, I would just go insane."
-"Changes in Latitudes, Changes in Attitudes"
Jimmy Buffett

∞ **My offset classmates:**

Captain John C. O'Connor III, EdD, for his advice, and for helping me understand what the Cuyahoga means to the Coast Guard today. Captain O'Connor is now Dean of student at the Academy.

Captain William Uberti USCG (ret.), who was one of the first people I called and the first to review my hundred page manuscript. Bill now lives in sunny San Diego.

LCdr Dave Conklin USCG (ret.), who did a tremendous job editing and fact checking one of my first drafts. Dave spent 20 years in marine inspection in the Guard and for the past 16 years has worked in the private sector in Houston and runs marathons around the country.

Cdr. Gordon Thomas, USCG (ret.), whose story of his escape from the radar room still send shivers down my spine. Special thanks for retrieving the Cuyahoga's Holiday Ensign.

RAdm. Dan Neptun, for edits, comments and support. Dan is the First District Commander and he oversees all Coast Guard missions across eight states in the Northeast and 2,000 miles of coastline from the U.S.-Canadian border to northern New Jersey.

Rick Riemer, for his stories, advice and his editing. Rick made LCdr but left Guard before retirement.

Fred Fairchild, for his support and stories. He was one of guys that kept me moving ahead when writer's block would kick in.

∞ **My friends and professional advisors:**

Mary Walker, for taking time off from writing the great American expatriate novel, while battling cancer, to help me write my story. She is to blame for all the multi-syllabic words and much of the intelligent humor. Good luck with *The Only American Woman*, soon on sale everywhere!

Michael McIrvin, author of *The Blue Man Dreams the End of Time* and other works, for his invaluable literary insight, suggestions, and professional touch.

Dan and Dee Dee O'Connell, for many hours of careful editing and their insightful comments.

Dennis Rodgers and Kevin Payne for their comments and suggestions and for assisting me thirty-eight years ago in getting off a burning island and not getting arrested.

Austin Boyd, for his comments and his guidance and for captaining our summer sailing trips to the Vineyard. I'm sure that after reading this book he won't be spending too much time below decks with me at the helm.

Brian Flanagan, for his great edits, research and advice. If you're looking for a great maritime lawyer, I heard the apple doesn't fall far from the tree.

Robert McKenna of Flat Hammock Press, for his suggestions, reviews and moral support.

∞ **My family:**

My entire nuclear family: **Jenny, Kelly, Drew and my wife Sue**, who had to listen to me read the entire first draft of this book while trapped in a car and driving through the desert. They had no route of escape. Their laughter and suggestions, and sometimes groans, gave me the direction and enthusiasm to redouble my efforts and turn the manuscript into something I could call a book...

Special thanks to **Sue** for her editing, support and patience during this whole process, **Jen** for creating the website and **Drew**, the real writer in the family, for spending a summer improving the manuscript.

Elizbeth Eident, for her drawings, typesetting and graphic design.

Kathryn Eident, a journalism graduate of Boston University, for her field research. Kathryn is working on the WHOI ships to pay back her student loan.

Bill Eident, for his art work. Bill, like his father, is a graduate of Mass Maritime Academy and is a marine engineer sailing whenever he runs out of money.

My father-in-law, **Ray D. Leoni**, who recently wrote Black Hawk: *The Story of a World Class Helicopter*, for guidance and support.

My mother-in-law, **Patricia Morrow Leoni**, for inspiring me with her love of books and family history, and with her stories about summers in Chautauqua.

My brothers **Paul Eident, Christopher Eident, Bill Eident, and sister Beth Wilkinson,** for sharing their stories with me around the kitchen table and allowing me to use them for my own personal gain and evil intent.

My mother, **Thelma Robichaud,** for teaching me how to tell a story, and to her brother, **Captain Arthur Robichaud,** for keeping me out of jail.

My deceased uncle, **Frank Eident,** for his incredible sense of humor.

And most importantly, to my dad, **Paul Eident,** who read four books a week for eighty years, and who has always said, "Pete, you oughta write a book." OK, it's done. Can you get off my back now? And for the record, I didn't lose the socket set!

WEISENT

Index

———∞———

About the Author
—∞—

PETER SLOAN EIDENT

Peter Sloan Eident was on board the U.S. Coast Guard cutter Cuyahoga on the fateful evening of October 20, 1978. Upon completion of Officer Candidate School, he served in the active reserves for three years on Governor's Island and then drilled for several years at Group Long Island Sound. Eident is a graduate of Brown University and holds a doctorate in business administration. He has worked in the Middle East for the past twenty years as an offset specialist. This is his first book.

More Praise for Bearing Drift
───────────────∞───────────────

"*I greatly enjoyed your book… I also loved your stories of growing up in New England. This will be a great book. Am looking forward to seeing it on the shelf at Barnes and Noble.*"
   —**Dave Conklin**, Houston TX, Marine Inspection Expert

"*Congratulations on a fine piece of writing. I was very impressed with the detail that you included that makes the story come to life. I also enjoyed the humor as well as the sad episodes of your story; you certainly stimulated the full range of human emotions.*"
   —**Ray Leoni**, Woodbridge CT, Author of Blackhawk

"*The book is tremendous! Is it one of those books that's hard to put down? Absolutely! I read it in 3 shifts.*"
   —**Kevin Payne**, San Francisco CA, Electrician

"*I read your manuscript and enjoyed it… I'm ready to hoist a few at the Captain Kidd when you are. Did the error chain on why I ended up here -it wasn't pretty!*"
   —**Jim Corcoran**, Stratford CT, International Executive

"*I love the humor in it and amazed by how well researched. I look forward to reading the book and the NY times review. Nice job describing the Horseshoe crab technology!*"
   —**Bethanie Wilkinson PhD**, Clinton CT, Molecular Biologist

"*Your book is very interesting and humorous! I think that it will be a hit for many readers, particularly Cape Codders!*"
   —**Robert Merchellano**, West Falmouth, Retired NOAA Scientist

"A salty "Wonder Years" with a little history and science mixed in with bar fights... and two shipwrecks that rock the Guard to its core... I thought the style was very reminiscent of the witty travel writer, Bill Bryson... I enjoyed it immensely. I read it with my wife and her whole family on a ski vacation. We all found it to be gripping. In general it was very funny, and yes at times it was irreverent..."
—**Dan O'Connell**, Sun Valley ID, Retired Engineer

"You made me laugh so the time was well spent. This is excellent writing. I'll admit to taking the morning away from the puissant litigation to read it."
—**Arne Denny**, Skagit County WA, County Deputy Prosecutor

"I really enjoyed reading Bearing Drift. I found all of the stories from your childhood and young adulthood interesting and fun to read and they really developed your character for the reader. The story flows nicely and keeps your attention building up to the collision. I like your sense of humor and I think a lot of my female friends would, too. Maybe it's because most of us have sons so we can relate a little to what you were feeling/thinking. The letter written by Ray and Laura Wood is heartbreaking! Still brings tears to my eyes."
—**Greta Jones**, Mystic CT, Literary Editor

"I love your writing style... with your ability to include humor to what was a very serious situation. Good luck with the final version... can't wait to read it!"
—**Carolee Fairchild**, Clearwater FL, Wife of a Survivor

"I'm very excited about seeing this book in print... you nailed it."
—**Rick Riemer**, Richmond VA, Technical Writer